THE COLLECTED POEMS
OF
WALTER DE LA MARE

by Walter de la Mare

THE COMPLETE POEMS
COLLECTED RHYMES AND VERSES
SELECTED POEMS
PEACOCK PIE
COLLECTED STORIES FOR CHILDREN
SOME STORIES
THE THREE ROYAL MONKEYS
ANIMAL STORIES
TALES TOLD AGAIN
STORIES FROM THE BIBLE
THE STORY OF JOSEPH

The Collected Poems

of

WALTER DE LA MARE

FABER AND FABER

London   Boston

First published in 1979
by Faber and Faber Limited
3 Queen Square London WC1N 3AU
Printed and bound in Great Britain by
Redwood Burn Limited
Trowbridge & Esher
All rights reserved

British Library Cataloguing in Publication Data

De la Mare, Walter
  The collected poems of Walter de la Mare
  I. Title
  821'.9'12   PR6007.E34A17

ISBN 0-571-11381-8
ISBN 0-571-11382-6   Pbk

CONTENTS

EDITORIAL NOTE

The publication of *The Complete Poems of Walter de la Mare* made it possible to produce definitive versions of his two separate collections for adults and children, *Collected Poems* (first published in 1942) and *Collected Rhymes and Verses* (1944). The revised *Collected Rhymes and Verses* appeared in 1970, and that is now followed by the new version of *Collected Poems*.

It differs from the original in two important respects. First, it is very much longer because de la Mare produced no less than five volumes of poetry between 1942 and his death in 1956; so that, whereas the 1942 version had 342 poems, this has 598, including his two long poems, *The Traveller* and *Winged Chariot*, which were published separately in 1945 and 1951. Second, it is arranged chronologically by collections and not by themes. The three late collections were *The Burning-Glass* (1945), *Inward Companion* (1950) and *O Lovely England* (1953). The general principle of the new *Collected Poems* is exactly the same. It contains no poems that were not included by de la Mare himself in his main collections, the uncollected and unpublished poems and poems from prose and other miscellaneous works in *The Complete Poems* being omitted. What is more, all the poems in those collections have been put in, among them sixteen from *Poems* (1906), three from *The Listeners* (1912), two from *Motley* (1918), one from *The Fleeting* (1933) and eight from *Poems 1919-1934* (1935) that were left out of the original volume. The text is based on that of *The Complete Poems* throughout, and, with a few minor exceptions, uses the latest printed versions.

Poems (1906)

FALSTAFF

'Twas in a tavern that with old age stooped
And leaned rheumatic rafters o'er his head —
A blowzed, prodigious man, which talked, and stared,
And rolled, as if with purpose, a small eye
Like a sweet Cupid in a cask of wine.
I could not view his fatness for his soul,
Which peeped like harmless lightnings and was. gone;
As haps to voyagers of the summer air.
And when he laughed, Time trickled down those beams,
As in a glass; and when in self-defence
He puffed that paunch, and wagged that huge, Greek head,
Nosed like a Punchinello, then it seemed
A hundred widows wept in his small voice,.
Now tenor, and now bass of drummy war.
He smiled, compact of loam, this orchard man;
Mused like a midnight, webbed with moonbeam snares
Of flitting Love; woke — and a King he stood,
Whom all the world hath in sheer jest refused
For helpless laughter's sake. And then, forfend!
Bacchus and Jove reared vast Olympus there;
And Pan leaned leering from Promethean eyes.
'Lord!' sighed his aspect, weeping o'er the jest,
'What simple mouse brought such a mountain forth?'

MACBETH

Rose, like dim battlements, the hills and reared
Steep crags into the fading primrose sky;
But in the desolate valleys fell small rain,
Mingled with drifting cloud. I saw one come,
Like the fierce passion of that vacant place,
His face turned glittering to the evening sky;
His eyes, like grey despair, fixed satelessly
On the still, rainy turrets of the storm;
And all his armour in a haze of blue.
He held no sword, bare was his hand and clenched,

[11]

As if to hide the inextinguishable blood
Murder had painted there. And his wild mouth
Seemed spouting echoes of deluded thoughts.
Around his head, like vipers all distort,
His locks shook, heavy-laden, at each stride.
If fire may burn invisible to the eye;
O, if despair strive everlastingly;
Then haunted here the creature of despair,
Fanning and fanning flame to lick upon
A soul still childish in a blackened hell.

BANQUO

What dost thou here far from thy native place?
What piercing influences of heaven have stirred
Thy heart's last mansion all-corruptible to wake,
To move, and in the sweets of wine and fire
Sit tempting madness with unholy eyes?
Begone, thou shuddering, pale anomaly!
The dark presses without on yew and thorn;
Stoops now the owl upon her lonely quest;
The pomp runs high here, and our beauteous women
Seek no cold witness — O, let murder cry,
Too shrill for human ear, only to God.
Come not in power to wreak so wild a vengeance!
Thou knowest not now the limit of man's heart;
He is beyond thy knowledge. Gaze not then,
Horror enthroned lit with insanest light!

MERCUTIO

Along an avenue of almond-trees
Came three girls chattering of their sweethearts three
And lo! Mercutio, with Byronic ease,
Out of his philosophic eye cast all
A mere flowered twig of thought, whereat —
Three hearts fell still as when an air dies out
And Venus falters lonely o'er the sea.
But when within the furthest mist of bloom
His step and form were hid, the smooth child Ann
Said, 'La, and what eyes he had!' and Lucy said,
'How sad a gentleman!' and Katherine,
'I wonder, now, what mischief he was at.'
And these three also April hid away,
Leaving the Spring faint with Mercutio.

JULIET

Sparrow and nightingale — did ever such
Strange birds consort in one untravelled heart?
And yet what signs of summer, and what signs
Of the keen snows humanity hath passed
To come to this wild apple-day! To think
So young a throat might rave so old a tune!
Youth's amber eyes reflect such ardent stars,
And capture heav'n with glancing! Was she not
Learn'd by some angel from her mother's womb
At last to be Love's mistress? doth not he
Rest all his arrows now and mutely adream
Seek his own peace in her Italian locks?
Cometh not Romeo singing in the night?—
Singing of youth — whose clust'ring locks do nod
And weave confusing shadows o'er his brow.
Sing on bright tongue and quench these fears of silence! —
But at the end waits Death to pluck his bloom,
Which is of yew the everlasting star.

JULIET'S NURSE

In old-world nursery vacant now of children,
With posied walls, familiar, fair, demure,
And facing southward o'er romantic streets,
Sits yet and gossips winter's dusk away
One gloomy, vast, glossy, and wise, and sly:
And at her side a cherried country cousin.
Her tongue claps ever like a ram's sweet bell;
There's not a name but calls a tale to mind —
Some marrowy patty of farce or melodram;
There's not a soldier but hath babes in view;
There's not on earth what minds not of the midwife:
'O, widowhood that left me still espoused!'
Beauty she sighs o'er, and she sighs o'er gold;
Gold will buy all things, even a sweet husband.
Else only Heaven is left and — farewell youth!
Yet, strangely, in that money-haunted head,
The sad, gemmed crucifix and incense blue
Is childhood come again. Her memory
Is like an ant-hill which a twig disturbs,
But twig stilled never. And to see her face,
Broad with sleek homely beams; her babied hands,

Ever like 'lighting doves, and her small eyes —
Blue wells a-twinkle, arch and lewd and pious —
To darken all sudden into Stygian gloom,
And paint disaster with uplifted whites,
Is life's epitome. She prates and prates —
A waterbrook of words o'er twelve small pebbles.
And when she dies — some grey, long, summer evening,
When the bird shouts of childhood through the dusk,
'Neath night's faint tapers — then her body shall
Lie stiff with silks of sixty thrifty years.

DESDEMONA

A stony tomb guards one who simply dreams
Of peace that shines, tho' love went down in storm—
Dreams ever a dark visage stoopeth o'er,
Whose darkness is not hatred but a mask
Love took for tend'rer loving. And when night
Steals thro' the sky to mock Othello, then
Rises she, counting at the windows high
Star after star till all her prayer be told,
And dawn repeat the glory of her end.
But on one day, in affluence of June,
At topmost flood of noon a shadow falls
Sweet at her side, chill head to snowy foot;
And then it seems the cypresses obscure
Whisper, 'O willow!'; and a shrill bird swoops,
As if the Moor had flown a silver soul
To take her captive at the key of Heaven!

IAGO

A dark lean face, a narrow, slanting eye,
Whose deeps of blackness one pale taper's beam
Haunts with a flitting madness of desire;
A heart whose cinder at the breath of passion
Glows to a momentary core of heat
Almost beyond indifference to endure:
So parched Iago frets his life away.
His scorn works ever in a brain whose wit
This world hath fools too many and gross to seek.

Ever to live incredibly alone,
Masked, shivering, deadly, with a simple Moor
Of idiot gravity, and one pale flower
Whose chill would quench in everlasting peace
His soul's unmeasured flame — O paradox!
Might he but learn the trick! — to wear her heart
One fragile hour of heedless innocence,
And then, farewell, and the incessant grave.
'O fool! O villain!'—'tis the shuttlecock
Wit never leaves at rest. It is his fate
To be a needle in a world of hay,
Where honour is the flattery of the fool;
Sin, a tame bauble; lies, a tiresome jest;
Virtue, a silly, whitewashed block of wood
For words to fell. Ah! but the secret lacking,
The secret of the child, the bird, the night,
Faded, flouted, bespattered, in days so far
Hate cannot bitter them, nor wrath deny;
Else were this Desdemona. . . . Why!
Woman a harlot is, and life a nest
Fouled by long ages of forked fools. And God —
Iago deals not with a tale so dull:
To have made the world! Fie on thee, Artisan!

CASCA

Butchers are honest though their agile knives
They wield with an engrossed dexterity.
To smile with natural hatred like a dog,
Dull, fretful, thirsty; — this is to be he
Who may unheated lave in burning blood
Hands white and large with idleness and sleep.
He is earth's hero — this plain, bloated Casca.
He glides like a great woman; while a hare
Squats in his shaggy breast, and stares, and trembles
If peeps the lightning in. So, let him pass;
His bloody hands his chosen orators.
There is much pig's flesh in a world of swine,
White as the lily.

Poems (1906)

IMOGEN

Even she too dead! all languor on her brow,
All mute humanity's last simpleness, —
And yet the roses in her cheeks unfallen!
Can death haunt silence with a silver sound?
Can death, that hushes all music to a close,
Pluck one sweet wire scarce-audible that trembles
As if a little child, called Purity,
Sang heedlessly on of his dear Imogen?
Surely if some young flowers of Spring were put
Into the tender hollow of her heart,
'Twould faintly answer, trembling in their petals.
Poise but a wild bird's feather, it will stir
On lips that even in silence wear the badge
Only of truth. Let but a cricket wake,
And sing of home, and bid her lids unseal
The unspeakable hospitality of her eyes.
O childless soul — call once her husband's name!
And even if indeed from these green hills
Of England, far, her spirit flits forlorn,
Back to its youthful mansion it will turn,
Back to the floods of sorrow these sweet locks
Yet heavy bear in drops; and Night shall see,
Unwearying as her stars, still Imogen,
Pausing 'twixt death and life on one hushed word.

POLONIUS

There haunts in Time's bare house an active ghost,
Enamoured of his name, Polonius.
He moves small fingers much, and all his speech
Is like a sampler of precisest words,
Set in the pattern of a simpleton.
His mirth floats eerily down chill corridors;
His sigh — it is a sound that loves a keyhole;
His tenderness a faint court-tarnished thing;
His wisdom prates as from a wicker cage;
His very belly is a pompous nought;
His eye a page that hath forgot his errand.
Yet in his bran — his spiritual bran —
Lies hid a child's demure, small, silver whistle
Which, to his horror, God blows, unawares.

[16]

And sets men staring. It is sad to think,
Might he but don indeed thin flesh and blood,
And pace important to Law's inmost room,
He would see, much marvelling, one immensely wise,
Named Bacon, who, at sound of his youth's step,
Would turn and call him Cousin — for the likeness.

OPHELIA

There runs a crisscross pattern of small leaves
Espalier, in a fading summer air,
And there Ophelia walks, an azure flower,
Whom wind, and snowflakes, and the sudden rain
Of love's wild skies have purified to heaven.
There is a beauty past all weeping now
In that sweet, crooked mouth, that vacant smile;
Only a lonely grey in those mad eyes,
Which never on earth shall learn their loneliness.
And when amid startled birds she sings lament,
Mocking in hope the long voice of the stream,
It seems her heart's lute hath a broken string.
Ivy she hath, that to old ruin clings;
And rosemary, that sees remembrance fade;
And pansies, deeper than the gloom of dreams;
But ah! if utterable, would this earth
Remain the base, unreal thing it is?
Better be out of sight of peering eyes;
Out — out of hearing of all-useless words,
Spoken of tedious tongues in heedless ears.
And lest, at last, the world should learn heart-secrets;
Lest that sweet wolf from some dim thicket steal;
Better the glassy horror of the stream.

HAMLET

Umbrageous cedars murmuring symphonies
Stooped in late twilight o'er dark Denmark's Prince:
He sat, his eyes companioned with dream —
Lustrous large eyes that held the world in view
As some entrancèd child's a puppet show.
Darkness gave birth to the all-trembling stars,
And a far roar of long-drawn cataracts,
Flooding immeasurable night with sound.

[17]

He sat so still, his very thoughts took wing,
And, lightest Ariels, the stillness haunted
With midge-like measures; but, at last, even they
Sank 'neath the influences of his night.
The sweet dust shed faint perfume in the gloom;
Through all wild space the stars' bright arrows fell
On the lone Prince — the troubled son of man —
On Time's dark waters in unearthly trouble:
Then, as the roar increased, and one fair tower
Of cloud took sky and stars with majesty,
He rose, his face a parchment of old age,
Sorrow hath scribbled o'er, and o'er, and o'er.

COME!

From an island of the sea
Sounds a voice that summons me, —
'Turn thy prow, sailor, come
    With the wind home!'

Sweet o'er the rainbow foam,
Sweet in the treetops, 'Come,
Coral, cliff, and watery sand,
    Sea-wave to land!

'Droop not thy lids at night,
Furl not thy sails from flight! . . .'
Cease, cease, above the wave,
    Deep as the grave!

O, what voice of the salt sea
Calls me so insistently?
Echoes, echoes, night and day, —
    'Come, come away!'

THE WINTER-BOY

I saw Jack Frost come louping o'er
    A hill of blinding snow;
And hooked upon his arm he bore
    A basket all aglow.

Cherries and damsons, peach and pear,
    The faint and moonlike quince;
Never before were fruits as rare,
    And never have been since.

[18]

'Come, will ye buy, ma'am?' says he sweet;
   And lo! began to fly
Flakes of bright, arrowy, frozen sleet
   From out the rosy sky.

'Silver nor pence, ma'am, ask I; but
   One kiss my cheek to warm, —
One with your scarlet lips tight shut
   Can do you, ma'am, no harm.'

O, and I stooped in that still place
   And pressed my lips to his;
And his cold locks about my face
   Shut darkness in my eyes.

Never, now never shall I be
   Lonely where snow is laid;
Sweet with his fruits comes louping he,
   And says the words he said.

His shrill voice echoes, slily creep
   His fingers cold and lean,
And lull my dazzled eyes asleep
   His icy locks between,

THEY TOLD ME

They told me Pan was dead, but I
   Oft marvelled who it was that sang
Down the green valleys languidly
   Where the grey elder-thickets hang.

Sometimes I thought it was a bird
   My soul had charged with sorcery;
Sometimes it seemed my own heart heard
   Inland the sorrow of the sea.

But even where the primrose sets
   The seal of her pale loveliness,
I found amid the violets
   Tears of an antique bitterness.

SORCERY

'What voice is that I hear
  Crying across the pool?'
'It is the voice of Pan you hear,
Crying his sorceries shrill and clear,
  In the twilight dim and cool.'

'What song is it he sings,
  Echoing from afar;
While the sweet swallow bends her wings,
Filling the air with twitterings,
  Beneath the brightening star?'

The woodman answered me,
  His faggot on his back: —
'Seek not the face of Pan to see;
Flee from his clear note summoning thee
  To darkness deep and black!

'He dwells in the thickest shade,
  Piping his notes forlorn
Of sorrow never to be allayed;
Turn from his coverts sad
  Of twilight unto morn!'

The woodman passed away
  Along the forest path;
His axe shone keen and grey
In the last beams of day:
  And all was still as death: —

Only Pan singing sweet
  Out of Earth's fragrant shade;
I dreamed his eyes to meet,
And found but shadow laid
  Before my tired feet.

Comes no more dawn to me,
  Nor bird of open skies.
Only his woods' deep gloom I see
  Till, at the end of all, shall rise,
Afar and tranquilly,
  Death's stretching sea.

[20]

THE CHILDREN OF STARE

Winter is fallen early
On the house of Stare;
Birds in reverberating flocks
Haunt its ancestral box;
Bright are the plenteous berries
In clusters in the air.

Still is the fountain's music,
The dark pool icy still,
Whereupon a small and sanguine sun
Floats in a mirror on,
Into a West of crimson,
From a South of daffodil.

'Tis strange to see young children
In such a wintry house;
Like rabbits' on the frozen snow
Their tell-tale footprints go;
Their laughter rings like timbrels
'Neath evening ominous:

Their small and heightened faces
Like wine-red winter buds;
Their frolic bodies gentle as
Flakes in the air that pass,
Frail as the twirling petal
From the briar of the woods.

Above them silence lours,
Still as an arctic sea;
Light fails; night falls; the wintry moon
Glitters; the crocus soon
Will open grey and distracted
On earth's austerity:

Thick mystery, wild peril,
Law like an iron rod: —
Yet sport they on in Spring's attire,
Each with his tiny fire
Blown to a core of ardour
By the awful breath of God.

AGE

This ugly old crone —
Every beauty she had
When a maid, when a maid.
Her beautiful eyes,
Too youthful, too wise
Seemed ever to come
To so lightless a home,
Cold and dull as a stone.
And her cheeks — who would guess
Cheeks cadaverous as this
Once with colours were gay
As the flower on its spray?
And who would believe
Life could bring one to grieve
So much as to make
Lips bent for love's sake
So thin and so grey?

O Youth, come away!
All she asks is her lone,
This old, desolate crone.
She needs us no more;
She is too old to care
For the charms that of yore
Made her body so fair.
Past repining, past care,
She lives but to bear
One or two fleeting years
Earth's indifference. Her tears
Have lost now their heat.
Her hands and her feet
Now shake but to be
Shed as leaves from a tree,
And her poor heart beats on
Like a sea — the storm gone.

THE GLIMPSE

Art thou asleep? or have thy wings
Wearied of my unchanging skies?
Or, haply, is it fading dreams
 Are in my eyes?

Not even an echo in my heart
Tells me the courts thy feet trod last,
Bare as a leafless wood it is,
 The summer past.

My inmost mind is like a book
The reader dulls with lassitude,
Wherein the same old lovely words
 Sound poor and rude.

Yet through this vapid surface, I
Seem to see old-time deeps; I see,
Past the dark painting of the hour,
 Life's ecstasy.

Only a moment; as when day
Is set, and in the shade of night,
Through all the clouds that compassed her,
 Stoops into sight.

Pale, changeless, everlasting Dian,
Gleams on the prone Endymion,
Troubles the dulness of his dreams:
 And then is gone.

REMEMBRANCE

The sky was like a waterdrop
 In shadow of a thorn,
Clear, tranquil, beautiful,
 Dark, forlorn.

Lightning along its margin ran;
 A rumour of the sea
Rose in profundity and sank
 Into infinity.

[23]

Lofty and few the elms, the stars
    In the vast boughs most bright;
I stood a dreamer in a dream
    In the unstirring night.

Not wonder, worship, not even peace
    Seemed in my heart to be:
Only the memory of one,
    Of all most dead to me.

SHADOW

Even the beauty of the rose doth cast,
When its bright, fervid noon is past,
A still and lengthening shadow in the dust
    Till darkness come
    And take its strange dream home.

The transient bubbles of the water paint
'Neath their frail arch a shadow faint;
The golden nimbus of the windowed saint,
    Till shine the stars,
    Casts pale and trembling bars.

The loveliest thing earth hath, a shadow hath,
A dark and livelong hint of death,
Haunting it ever till its last faint breath . . .
    Who, then, may tell
The beauty of heaven's shadowless asphodel?

UNREGARDING

Put by thy days like withered flowers
    In twilight hidden away:
Memory shall up-build thee bowers
    Sweeter than they.

Hoard not from swiftness of thy stream
    The shallowest cruse of tears:
Pools still as heaven shall lovelier dream
    In future years.

Squander thy love as she that flings
    Her soul away on night;
Lovely are love's far echoings,
    Height unto height.

O, make no compact with the sun,
    No compact with the moon!
Night falls full-cloaked, and light is gone
    Sudden and soon.

TREACHERY

She had amid her ringlets bound
Green leaves to rival their dark hue;
How could such locks with beauty bound
    Dry up their dew,
    Wither them through and through?

She had within her dark eyes lit
Sweet fires to burn all doubt away;
Yet did those fires, in darkness lit,
    Burn but a day,
    Not even till twilight stay.

She had within a dusk of words
A vow in simple splendour set;
How, in the memory of such words,
    Could she forget
    That vow — the soul of it?

IN VAIN

I knocked upon thy door ajar,
While yet the woods with buds were grey;
Nought but a little child I heard
    Warbling at break of day.

I knocked when June had lured her rose
To mask the sharpness of its thorn;
Knocked yet again, heard only yet
    Thee singing of the morn.

The frail convolvulus had wreathed
Its cup, but the faint flush of eve
Lingered upon thy Western wall;
    Thou hadst no word to give.

Once yet I came; the winter stars
Above thy house wheeled wildly bright;
Footsore I stood before thy door —
    Wide open into night.

THE MIRACLE

Who beckons the green ivy up
    Its solitary tower of stone?
What spirit lures the bindweed's cup
        Unfaltering on;
Calls even the starry lichen to climb
By agelong inches endless Time?

Who bids the hollyhock uplift
    Her rod of fast-sealed buds on high;
Fling wide her petals — silent, swift,
        Lovely to the sky?
Since as she kindled, so she will fade,
Flower above flower in squalor laid.

Ever the heavy billow rears
    All its sea-length in green, hushed wall;
But totters as the shore it nears,
        Foams to its fall;
Where was its mark? on what vain quest
Rose that great water from its rest? . . .

So creeps ambition on; so climb
    Man's vaunting thoughts. He, set on high,
Forgets his birth, small space, brief time,
        That he shall die;
Dreams blindly in his stagnant air;
Consumes his strength; strips himself bare;

Rejects delight, ease, pleasure, hope;
    Seeking in vain, but seeking yet,
Past earthly promise, earthly scope,
        On one aim set:
As if, like Chaucer's child, he thought
All but '*O Alma!*' nought.

EVEN ROSEMARY

I have seen a grave this day,
Yet no worm did therein lie; —
Only sweet Faith laid away,
　　Lonely to die,
Lonely as he lived, to die.

There's no buds. Ev'n rosemary
Hath sad dreams for smell withal;
Ev'n Hope's rose's leaf would be
　　Restless to fall;
To have done, and fade, and fall.

I will never walk again
Where such brittle dust doth lie;
Where to weep were quite in vain;
　　Vain too to sigh,
Only vain to weep and sigh.

Flee afar, then, heart, lest thou,
Quick with brooding on that spot,
Feign to see a dead face now,
　　Features forgot,
Eyes ev'n Heaven shall open not!

KEEP INNOCENCY

Like an old battle, youth is wild
With bugle and spear, and counter cry,
Fanfare and drummery, yet a child
Dreaming of that sweet chivalry,
The piercing terror cannot see.

He, with a mild and serious eye,
Along the azure of the years,
Sees the sweet pomp sweep hurtling by;
But he sees not death's blood and tears,
Sees not the plunging of the spears.

[27]

And all the strident horror of
Horse and rider, in red defeat,
Is only music fine enough
To lull him into slumber sweet
In fields where ewe and lambkin bleat.

O, if with such simplicity
Himself take arms and suffer war;
With beams his targe shall gilded be,
Though in the thickening gloom be far
The steadfast light of any star!

Though hoarse War's eagle on him perch,
Quickened with guilty lightnings — there
It shall in vain for terror search,
Where a child's eyes 'neath bloody hair
Gaze purely through the dingy air.

And when the wheeling rout is spent,
Though in the heaps of slain he lie;
Or lonely in his last content;
Quenchless shall burn in secrecy
The flame Death knows his victors by.

THE PHANTOM

Wilt thou never come again,
  Beauteous one?
Yet the woods are green and dim,
Yet the birds' deluding cry
Echoes in the hollow sky,
Yet the falling waters brim
The clear pool which thou wast fain
To paint thy lovely cheek upon,
  Beauteous one!

I may see the thorny rose
  Stir and wake
The dark dewdrop on her gold;
But thy secret will she keep
Half divulged — yet all untold,
Since a child's heart woke from sleep.

The faltering sunbeam fades and goes;
The night-bird whistles in the brake;
　　The willows quake;
Utter quiet falls; the wind
　　　Sighs no more.
Yet it seems the silence yearns
But to catch thy fleeting foot;
Yet the wandering glow-worm burns
Lest her lamp should light thee not —
Thee whom I shall never find;
Though thy shadow lean before,
Thou thyself return'st no more —
　　　Never more.

All the world's woods, tree o'er tree,
　　Come to nought.
Birds, flowers, beasts, how transient they,
Angels of a flying day.
Love is quenched; dreams drown in sleep;
Ruin nods along the deep:
Only thou immortally
　　　Hauntest on
This poor earth in Time's flux caught;
Hauntest on, pursued, unwon,
Phantom child of memory,
　　　Beauteous one!

VOICES

Who is it calling by the darkened river
　　Where the moss lies smooth and deep,
And the dark trees lean unmoving arms,
　　Silent and vague in sleep,
And the bright-heeled constellations pass
　　In splendour through the gloom;
Who is it calling o'er the darkened river
　　In music, 'Come!'?

Who is it wandering in the summer meadows
  Where the children stoop and play
In the green faint-scented flowers, spinning
  The guileless hours away?
Who touches their bright hair? who puts
  A wind-shell to each cheek,
Whispering betwixt its breathing silences,
    'Seek! seek!'?

Who is it watching in the gathering twilight
  When the curfew bird hath flown
On eager wings, from song to silence,
  To its darkened nest alone?
Who takes for brightening eyes the stars,
  For locks the still moonbeam,
Sighs through the dews of evening peacefully
    Falling, 'Dream!'?

THULE

If thou art sweet as they are sad
  Who on the shores of Time's salt sea
Watch on the dim horizon fade
  Ships bearing love to night and thee;

If past all beacons Hope hath lit
  In the dark wanderings of the deep
They who unwilling traverse it
  Dream not till dawn unseal their sleep;

Ah, cease not in thy winds to mock
  Us, who yet wake, but cannot see
Thy distant shores; who at each shock
  Of the waves onset faint for thee!

THE BIRTHNIGHT: TO F.

Dearest, it was a night
That in its darkness rocked Orion's stars;
A sighing wind ran faintly white
Along the willows, and the cedar boughs
Laid their wide hands in stealthy peace across
The starry silence of their antique moss:
No sound save rushing air
Cold, yet all sweet with Spring,
And in thy mother's arms, couched weeping there,
    Thou, lovely thing.

THE DEATH-DREAM

Who, now, put dreams into thy slumbering mind?
Who, with bright Fear's lean taper, crossed a hand
Athwart its beam, and stooping, truth maligned,
Spake so thy spirit speech should understand,
And with a dread 'He's dead!' awaked a peal
Of frenzied bells along the vacant ways
Of thy poor earthly heart; waked thee to steal,
Like dawn distraught upon unhappy days,
To prove nought, nothing? Was it Time's large voice
Out of the inscrutable future whispered so?
Or but the horror of a little noise
Earth wakes at dead of night? Or does Love know
When his sweet wings weary and droop, and even
In sleep cries audibly a shrill remorse?
Or, haply, was it I who out of dream
Stole but a little way where shadows course,
Called back to thee across the eternal stream?

'WHERE IS THY VICTORY?'

None, none can tell where I shall be
When the unclean earth covers me;
Only in surety if thou cry
Where my perplexèd ashes lie,
Know, 'tis but death's necessity
That keeps my tongue from answering thee.

Even if no more my shadow may
Lean for a moment in thy day;
No more the whole earth lighten, as if,
Thou near, it had nought else to give:
Surely 'tis but Heaven's strategy
To prove death immortality.

Yet should I sleep — and no more dream,
Sad would the last awakening seem,
If my cold heart, with love once hot,
Had thee in sleep remembered not:
How could I wake to find that I
Had slept alone, yet easefully?

Or should in sleep glad visions come:
Sick, in an alien land, for home
Would be my eyes in their bright beam;
Awake, we know 'tis not a dream;
Asleep, some devil in the mind
Might truest thoughts with false enwind.

Life is a mockery if death
Have the least power men say it hath.
As to a hound that mewing waits,
Death opens, and shuts to, his gates;
Else even dry bones might rise and say, —
"'Tis *ye* are dead and laid away.'

Innocent children out of nought
Build up a universe of thought,
And out of silence fashion Heaven:
So, dear, is this poor dying even,
Seeing thou shalt be touched, heard, seen,
Better than when dust stood between.

FOREBODING

Thou canst not see him standing by —
   Time — with a poppied hand
Stealing thy youth's simplicity,
Even as falls unceasingly
   His waning sand.

He'll pluck thy childish roses, as
  Summer from her bush
Strips all the loveliness that was;
Even to the silence evening has
  Thy laughter hush.

Thy locks too faint for earthly gold,
  The meekness of thine eyes,
He will darken and dim, and to his fold
Drive, 'gainst the night, thy stainless, old
  Innocencies;

Thy simple words confuse and mar,
  Thy tenderest thoughts delude,
Draw a long cloud athwart thy star,
Still with loud timbrels heaven's far
  Faint interlude.

Thou canst not see; I see, dearest;
  O, then, yet patient be,
Though love refuse thy heart all rest,
Though even love wax angry, lest
  Love should lose *thee*!

THE HAPPY ENCOUNTER

I saw sweet Poetry turn troubled eyes
  On shaggy Science nosing on the grass,
  For by that way poor Poetry must pass
On her long pilgrimage to Paradise.
He snuffled, grunted, squealed; perplexed by flies,
  Parched, weatherworn, and near of sight, alas,
  From peering close where very little was
In dens secluded from the open skies.

But Poetry in bravery went down,
  And called his name, soft, clear, and fearlessly;
Stooped low, and stroked his muzzle overgrown;
  Refreshed his drought with dew; wiped pure and free
  His eyes: and lo! laughed loud for joy to see
In those grey deeps the azure of her own.

COUP DE GRÂCE

So Malice sharp'd his pen, and nibbled it,
  And leered 'neath faltering eyelids at the flame
  Of his calm candle till a notion came,
Coarse, acrid, with a distant hint of wit.
Once more he simmered, and once more he writ,
  Till not a dash was dull, a comma lame;
  Then exquisitely failed to sign his name,
Leaving the world to trace a slug by its spit.

Such was the barb, O Keats, (vain tongues would have),
  Troubled in its calm flight thy lovely art;
Cankered thy youth, thy faith; abashed the brave,
  Untarnishable sweetness of thy heart:
  How should these dullards dream *they* winged the dart
That pierced thee, silent, in th'unanswering grave!

APRIL

Come, then, with showers; I love thy cloudy face
  Gilded with splendour of the sunbeams thro'
  The heedless glory of thy locks. I know
The arch, sweet languour of thy fleeting grace,
The windy lovebeams of thy dwelling-place,
  Thy dim dells wherein azure bluebells blow,
  The brimming rivers where thy lightnings go
Harmless and full and swift from race to race.

Thou takest all young hearts captive with thine eyes;
  At rumour of thee the tongues of children ring
Louder than bees; the golden poplars rise
  Like trumps of peace; and birds, on homeward wing,
Fly mocking echoes shrill along the skies,
  Above the waves' grave diapasoning.

SEA-MAGIC
To R.I.

My heart faints in me for the distant sea.
  The roar of London is the roar of ire
  The lion utters in his old desire
For Libya out of dim captivity.

[34]

The long bright silver of Cheapside I see,
    Her gilded weathercocks on roof and spire
    Exulting eastward in the western fire;
All things recall one heart-sick memory:—

Ever the rustle of the advancing foam,
    The surges' desolate thunder, and the cry
    As of some lone babe in the whispering sky;
Ever I peer into the restless gloom
    To where a ship clad dim and loftily
Looms steadfast in the wonder of her home.

MESSENGERS

A few all-faithful words, a glance from eyes
    That in their deeps hide hosts they cannot see —
    Phantoms of loveliest simplicity;
A transient touch — some bird's that twittering flies
Into the primrose of the deepening skies;
    A child's pure cheek pressed cold and tranquilly
    Upon a brow ashamed, in misery;
A voice that sings easefully echo-wise:

Whence are they in a world so alien?
    Are they the waterdrops of that vast flood
Death shall unloose? Shall all they hint, again
    In fulness be retold? Shall this wild blood
That rocks to them, lull down to stillness when
    These light-wing messengers flit back to God?

IRREVOCABLE

I sometimes wonder what my life doth mean
    Now you are gone; the long, bright days, the nights
    Of silence, the vicissitudes, the sights,
The intrusive sounds, the dull, continuous scene —
It only minds me of the might-have-been,
    And in itself a taper is that lights
    Its own dark solitude: my spirit fights
In vain to pierce the veil and look within.

[35]

The fountain of my tears is sealed and dry;
  I do not grieve; my laughter is a jest;
My prayers an arid bitterness; each sigh
  The heedless habit of a tired breast.
My heart is dead; and when I come to die,
  Only to think of you no more were best.

WINTER COMING

O, thou art like an autumn to my days,
  Shining in still, sweet light on lonelier hours
  Of yellowing leaves, and well-nigh faded flowers;
In thy dear sight the birds renew their lays,
But with how faint a cheer! how meek their praise
  Rememb'ring April gone! — his crystal showers,
  His heav'n-surmounting wind-engirdled towers,
And all the graveness of his childlike ways.

The hours press closer on to winter now;
  In misty solitudes brief suns arise;
  And all the wonder now hath left my eyes,
And all my heart sinks to remember how
  Once, once we loved, we who are grown so wise —
Youth vanished, winter coming — I and thou!

THE MARKET-PLACE

My mind is like a clamorous market-place.
  All day in wind, rain, sun, its babel wells;
  Voice answering to voice in tumult swells.
Chaffering and laughing, pushing for a place,
My thoughts haste on, gay, strange, poor, simple, base;
  This one buys dust, and that a bauble sells:
  But none to any scrutiny hints or tells
The haunting secrets hidden in each sad face.

The clamour quietens when the dark draws near;
  Strange looms the earth in twilight of the West,
Lonely with one sweet star serene and clear,
  Dwelling, when all this place is hushed to rest,
  On vacant stall, gold, refuse, worst and best,
Abandoned utterly in haste and fear.

ANATOMY

By chance my fingers, resting on my face,
  Stayed suddenly where in its orbit shone
  The lamp of all things beautiful; then on,
Following more heedfully, did softly trace
Each arch and prominence and hollow place
  That shall revealed be when all else is gone —
  Warmth, colour, roundness — to oblivion,
And nothing left but darkness and disgrace.

Life like a moment passed seemed then to be;
  A transient dream this raiment that it wore;
While spelled my hand out its mortality,
  Made certain all that had seemed doubt before:
Proved — O how vaguely, yet how lucidly! —
  How much death does: and yet can do no more.

EVEN IN THE GRAVE

I laid my inventory at the hand
  Of Death, who in his gloomy arbour sate;
  And while he conned it, sweet and desolate
I heard Love singing in that quiet land.
He read the record even to the end —
  The heedless, livelong injuries of Fate,
  The burden of foe, the burden of love and hate;
The wounds of foe, the bitter wounds of friend:

All, all, he read, ay, even the indifference,
  The vain talk, vainer silence, hope and dream.
He questioned me: 'What seek'st thou then instead?'
  I bowed my face in the pale evening gleam.
Then gazed he on me with strange innocence:
  'Even in the grave thou wilt have thyself,' he said.

[37]

OMNISCIENCE

Why look'd'st thou on the beauties of the earth
So gravely in thy deep omniscience;
Turn'd'st from the dews of their unclouded birth
In woods where children call, and innocence
Broods like a dream within a lovely face,
To one wan hint, one backward glance on grief,
On darken'd eyes beyond Time's fleeting grace —
Death heavy and endless of a life too brief?

O love immeasurably meek that scanned,
Past all earth's fickle hopes, past beauty, lust,
The tottering palaces of wind and sand,
Pride and vain pomp, tears, ashes, rapture, dust,
The unearthly tomb whose fading stone shall keep
Man, till his Saviour come, at peace asleep!

BRIGHT LIFE

'Come now,' I said, 'put off these webs of death,
  Distract this leaden yearning of thine eyes
  From lichened banks of peace, sad mysteries
Of dust fallen-in where passed the flitting breath:
Turn thy sick thoughts from him that slumbereth
  In mouldered linen to the living skies,
  The sun's bright-clouded principalities,
The salt deliciousness the sea-breeze hath!

'Lay thy warm hand on earth's cold clods and think
  What exquisite greenness sprouts from these to grace
The moving fields of summer; on the brink
  Of archèd waves the sea-horizon trace,
Whence wheels night's galaxy; and in silence sink
  Thy pride in rapture of life's dwelling-place!'

HUMANITY

'Ever exulting in thyself; on fire
  To flaunt the purple of the Universe,
  To strut and strut, and thy great part rehearse;
Ever the slave of every proud desire;
Come now a little down where sports thy sire;
  Choose thy small better from thy abounding worse;
  Prove thou thy lordship who hadst dust for nurse,
And for thy swaddling the primeval mire!'

Then stooped our Manhood nearer, deep and still,
  As from earth's mountains an unvoyaged sea;
Hushed my faint voice in its great peace until
  It seemed but a bird's cry in eternity;
And in its future loomed the undreamable,
  And in its past slept simple men like me.

GLORIA MUNDI

Upon a bank, easeless with knobs of gold,
  Beneath a canopy of noonday smoke,
I saw a measureless Beast, morose and bold,
  With eyes like one from filthy dreams awoke,
Who stares upon the daylight in despair
For very terror of the nothing there.

This beast in one flat hand clutched vulture-wise
  A glittering image of itself in jet,
And with the other groped about its eyes
  To drive away the dreams that pestered it;
And never ceased its coils to toss and beat
The mire encumbering its feeble feet.

Sharp was its hunger, though continually
  It seemed a cud of stones to ruminate,
And often like a dog let glittering lie
  This meatless fare, its foolish gaze to sate;
Once more convulsively to stoop its jaw,
Or seize the morsel with an envious paw.

Indeed, it seemed a hidden enemy
  Must lurk within the clouds above that bank,

[39]

It strained so wildly its pale, stubborn eye,
  To pierce its own foul vapours dim and dank;
Till, wearied out, it raved in wrath and foam,
Daring that Nought Invisible to come.

Ay, and it seemed some strange delight to find
  In this unmeaning din, till, suddenly,
As if it heard a rumour on the wind,
  Or far away its freër children cry,
Lifting its face made-quiet, there it stayed,
Till died the echo its own rage had made.

That place alone was barren where it lay;
  Flowers bloomed beyond, utterly sweet and fair;
And even its own dull heart might think to stay
  In livelong thirst of a clear river there,
Flowing from unseen hills to unheard seas,
Through a still vale of yew and almond trees.

And then I spied in the lush green below
  Its tortured belly, One, like silver, pale,
With fingers closed upon a rope of straw,
  That bound the Beast, squat neck to hoary tail;
Lonely in all that verdure faint and deep,
He watched the monster as a shepherd sheep.

I marvelled at the power, strength, and rage
  Of this poor creature in such slavery bound;
Fettered with worms of fear; forlorn with age;
  Its blue wing-stumps stretched helpless on the ground;
While twilight faded into darkness deep,
And he who watched it piped its pangs asleep.

IDLENESS

I saw old Idleness, fat, with great cheeks
Puffed to the huge circumference of a sigh,
But past all tinge of apples long ago.
His boyish fingers twiddled up and down
The filthy remnant of a cup of physic
That thicked in odour all the while he stayed.

His eyes were sad as fishes that swim up
And stare upon an element not theirs
Through a thin skin of shrewish water, then
Turn on a languid fin, and dip down, down,
Into unplumbed, vast, oozy deeps of dream.
His stomach was his master, and proclaimed it;
And never were such meagre puppets made
The slaves of such a tyrant, as his thoughts
Of that obese epitome of ills.

Trussed up he sat, the mockery of himself;
And when upon the wan green of his eye
I marked the gathering lustre of a tear,
Thought I myself must weep, until I caught
A grey, smug smile of satisfaction smirch
His pallid features at his misery.
And laugh did I, to see the little snares
He had set for pests to vex him: his great feet
Prisoned in greater boots; so narrow a stool
To seat such elephantine parts as his;
Ay, and the book he read, a Hebrew Bible;
And, to incite a gross and backward wit,
An old, crabbed, wormed, Greek dictionary; and
A foxy Ovid bound in dappled calf.

GOLIATH

Still as a mountain with dark pines and sun
He stood between the armies, and his shout
Rolled from the empyrean above the host:
'Bid any little flea ye have come forth,
And wince at death upon my finger-nail!'
He turned his large-boned face; and all his steel
Tossed into beams the lustre of the noon;
And all the shaggy horror of his locks
Rustled like locusts in a field of corn.
The meagre pupil of his shameless eye
Moved like a cormorant over a glassy sea.
He stretched his limbs, and laughed into the air,

[41]

To feel the groaning sinews of his breast,
And the long gush of his swol'n arteries pause:
And, nodding, wheeled, towering in all his height.
Then, like a wind that hushes, he gazed and saw
Down, down, far down upon the untroubled green,
A shepherd-boy that swung a little sling.

Goliath shut his lids to drive that mote
Which vexed the eastern azure of his eye,
Out of his vision; and stared down again.
Yet stood the youth there, ruddy in the flare
Of his vast shield, nor spake, nor quailed, gazed up,
As one might scan a mountain to be scaled.
Then, as it were, a voice unearthly still
Cried in the cavern of his bristling ear,
'His name is Death!' . . . And, like the flush
That dyes Sahara to its lifeless verge,
His brows' bright brass flamed into sudden crimson;
And his great spear leapt upward, lightning-like,
Shaking a dreadful thunder in the air;
Span betwixt earth and sky, bright as a berg
That hoards the sunlight in a myriad spires,
Crashed: and struck echo through an army's heart.

Then paused Goliath, and stared down again.
And fleet-foot Fear from rolling orbs perceived
Steadfast, unharmed, a stooping shepherd-boy
Frowning upon the target of his face.
And wrath tossed suddenly up once more his hand;
And a deep groan grieved all his strength in him.
He breathed; and, lost in dazzling darkness, prayed —
Besought his reins, his gloating gods, his youth:
And turned to smite what he no more could see.

Then sped the singing pebble-messenger,
The chosen of the Lord from Israel's brooks,
Fleet to its mark, and hollowed a light path
Down to the appalling Babel of his brain.
And, like the smoke of dreaming Soufrière,
Dust rose in cloud, spread wide, slow silted down
Softly all softly on his armour's blaze.

YOUTH

With splendour shod sweeps Sirius through the night,
But Youth yet brightlier runs his course than he.
Youth hath the raiment of his childhood doffed
At morning-prime by life's resounding sea,
And lonely in beauty stands confronting Heaven.
He strides lithe-limbed, magnificently armed;
His young head helmeted with high desire;
His heart a haven of braveries fleet and eager;
His eyes like heroes never to be subdued,
And all man's passionate history in his blood.
Youth is Adonis, panting for the chase,
Scorning all languor, blandishment, all ease,
Scorning to dally while the noon slips by,
While rings the horn, fleets golden and sweet the hour,
And bursts untamed Ambition through the glades.
Oh, in what wrath he sees still Evening pour
Her crystal vial from the darkening West!
Now is an end to day's bright prowess come;
The flaming sunbeams multitudinous
Fade, as they kindled, on the unfolded rose.
He loves not Night's pale solitary brows,
Nor silver Hesper in the shadowy steep,
But like a panther fretteth in his lair,
Turning to slumb'r as to his strength's disgrace;
To sigh in dream 'neath moonlight's arrowy showers,
Marv'ling what makes Apollo's lute so still.
But dawn ascends. The night-watch'd stars shall not
Cry from heav'n's battlements in vain of day.
Earth wakens, cold with flowers, and the mists,
Smitten of light, fly, fall in radiant dew.
Birds mounting to the dayspring pour their throats;
And in like music she beguileth him: —
'Thou babe, here is my breast! Thou foolish one,
Strip off dull sleep; thy mother — here am I!'
And frowning up he leaps to her smooth arms,
As mounts the fledgling eagle tow'rd the sun . . .
How hasten his echoing feet when sweet tongues call,
And Love's unerring archery sings nigh!
Dim then with incense burns his heart of flame;
His thoughts are aisles where ever voices quire:
And silence is divine with folded wings.
He voyages at a hazard Arctic seas;
Scales, as for pastime, ice-encinctured Alps;
No torrent daunts him; no abyss appals;

Wind ne'er so faintly the far horn of danger,
Its echo tingles on a listening ear;
Whithersoever summon it he'll follow,
And vain were every bounty earth can squander
To salve the sorrow for a deed undared.
He pines to set desire beyond his scope,
And beauteous childhood wells into his soul
In covet of the fruits that droop and burn
Where rise th' unchanging terraces of death.
What worth renown when all that dawn conceived
Fades to a phantom in the chimes of night?
What worth the flattery of a myriad tongues
If mute be the proud umpire of his heart?
He'll strive him for an amaranthine crown
Outlasting laurel and the world's applause.
Earth but a shadow is of beauty cast
In trembling beams upon the stream of Time:
He'll set his heart no more on shadows now;
But brood in envy of those high summits Man
Hath left to sparkle in midmost heav'n alone;
Strive with smooth lead to plumb the unanswering deeps,
Where Wisdom heark'ns the music of her wells.
He'll walk in sure confederacy with truth.
Betwixt him and the Hills Celestial falls
Only a blinding avalanche of sun . . .
Flow'rs, birds, the river rushing in its strength,
The pine upon the mountains, the broad wind
Burdened with snowy coldness, the salt sea,
The shalms of morning — Youth's wild heart holds all; —
All glory, all wonder, purity, beauty, grace,
All things conceived of man, except defeat.
So spurns he hope: his hope is certainty.
And faith — while every act is faith transfigured,
How should through mournful shadows glance such eyes?
God walketh in His brightness on the hills,
And sitteth in the wonder of the bow,
And calleth o'er the waters of delight: —
What were all Time to prove all gratitude?
What life's brief dust to Heav'n's unfading rose? . . .
How fleet a foot then Youth's for long pursuit!
How high a courage to search wisdom out,
While he unwitting of't burns folly away!
Is aught too bold, too infinite, to dream
Fate's arm may guard for babes to spring from him,
Who flings his life down, drenched with rapture through,
To buy unchallenged honour for his bones?

THE VOICE OF MELANCHOLY

'Return from out thy stillness, though the dust
Lie thick upon thy earthly beauty, though
The ever-wandering shapes of Night creep through
Youth's fallen tabernacle! Now in long
Surge of recurrent light the days swing by,
Soundless above thine ears once musical,
Unnumbered by a heart expert in love,
Unmarked by those fall'n princes once thine eyes.—
Oh, what defeat, bright warrior, what disgrace,
To fret entwinèd in the bindweed's root,
And rot like manna, lovelier than the rose!
Once thou would'st turn thy face enriched with smiles,
Thy lips a thought asunder, and thy hair
Shining within the sun's magnificent ray;
Stand would'st thou like a beacon by deep seas: —
All light, all excellence, all joy, gone now;
Even the classic beauty of thy face
Melted like snow; dark as a moon eclipsed;
Never to bright'n again 'neath endless night . . .'
So did I brood, unanswered and alone,
Crying, 'Return, return!'
                                O simple fool!
What would'st thou out of the deep grave should rise?
What, from amid death's cypresses, awake;
Heave up the sod; press back the fruited boughs;
And lift his eyes across the tombs on thee?
Would love burn there, or measureless reproach?
Would Life's bright mantle, stiff with idiot pomp,
Lie easy on shoulders whence a shroud had fall'n?
Would Morn's shrill nightingale above his brows
Ring sweet on ears long-sealed in echoless peace?
Would those grey hands caress earth's tarnish'd orb,
And those still feet be amorous of spurs?
And that unutterably agèd head,
Darken'd with pansies fadeless, changeless, still,
How would it don again youth's triple crown,
Piercing the keenlier as its roses die?
Nay, but the very wind that stirred his hair
Would seem a tempest to sleep deep as his;
And the perplexèd galaxy of the stars
Intolerable cressets to his eyes,
Accustomed to a night as dark as his;
And the pale dew of daisied turf at dawn
The wine of madness to lips dry as his.

[45]

Oh, with what shuddering would those atoms meet!
With what a burning sluggardry that blood
Creep thro' its long disusèd channels from
The roaring chaos of his heart! What grief
Would wildly ring in the first words he said!
What sad astonishment besteep that brain,
And tears more pitiable than infancy's
Blur the estrangèd beauty of the dawn! ...
Leave thou his memory, as his dust, at rest;
Nor burden peace with lamentable cries!
There lurks no shadow in the crypt of death;
Nor any shadow in the height of heaven:
Beyond the survey of the dark earth gone
He bides encloistered ev'n from love's surmise.
Cry then no more, 'Return, return!' — no more!
Thy thoughts are shallow, thy experience brief;
Whence learnedst *thou* of the riches of the grave?

'PORTRAIT OF A BOY'

Velazquez

At evens with the copious April clouds;
With meek, wild face he stands; and in his eye
Deeps where the empyrean ever broods,
And in his mouth some femininity.—
Ah! for we know his secret, hath not life
So strangely shod his feet lest, suddenly,
He should remember him — the babbling strife
Of Venus' sparrows — lest he stoop and fly,
Chafing at earth, into that April sky?

UNPAUSING

O sweetest, stay!
One moment in thy lonely play
Turn, child, and look
Ev'n but a little on that great-leaf book,
Whose livelong record when thine eyes are old
Will seem, how lovely a tale, how briefly told!

[46]

VAIN FINDING

Ever before my face there went
  Betwixt earth's buds and me
A beauty beyond earth's content,
  A hope — half memory:
Till in the woods one evening —
  Ah! eyes as dark as they,
Fastened on mine unwontedly,
  Grey, and dear heart, how grey!

VIRTUE

Her breast is cold; her hands how faint and wan!
  And the deep wonder of her starry eyes
  Seemingly lost in cloudless Paradise,
And all earth's sorrows out of memory gone.
Yet sings her clear voice unrelenting on
  Of loveliest impossibilities;
  Though echo only answer her with sighs
Of effort wasted and delights forgone.

Spent, baffled, 'wildered, hated and despised,
  Her straggling warriors hasten to defeat;
By wounds distracted, and by night surprised,
  Fall where death's darkness and oblivion meet:
Yet, yet: O breast how cold! O hope how far!
Grant my son's ashes lie where these men are!

NAPOLEON

'What is the world, O soldiers?
    It is I:
I, this incessant snow,
    This northern sky;
Soldiers, this solitude
    Through which we go
      Is I.'

[47]

ENGLAND

No lovelier hills than thine have laid
  My tired thoughts to rest:
No peace of lovelier valleys made
  Like peace within my breast.

Thine are the woods whereto my soul,
  Out of the noontide beam,
Flees for a refuge green and cool
  And tranquil as a dream.

Thy breaking seas like trumpets peal;
  Thy clouds — how oft have I
Watched their bright towers of silence steal
  Into infinity!

My heart within me faints to roam
  In thought even far from thee:
Thine be the grave whereto I come,
  And thine my darkness be.

THE SEAS OF ENGLAND

The seas of England are our old delight;
  Let the loud billow of the shingly shore
  Sing freedom on her breezes evermore
To all earth's ships that sailing heave in sight!

The gaunt sea-nettle be our fortitude,
  Sturdily blowing where the clear wave sips;
  O, be the glory of our men and ships
Rapturous, woe-unheeding hardihood!

There is great courage in a land that hath
  Liberty guarded by the unearthly seas;
  And ev'n to find peace at the last in these
How many a sailor hath sailed down to death!

Their names are like a splendour in old song;
  Their record shines like bays along the years;
  Their jubilation is the cry man hears
Sailing sun-fronted the vast deeps among.

The seas of England are our old delight;
  Let the loud billow of the shingly shore
  Sing freedom on her breezes evermore
To all earth's ships that sailing heave in sight!

[48]

TRUCE

Far inland here Death's pinions mocked the roar
        Of English seas;
We sleep to wake no more,
        Hushed, and at ease;
Till sound a trump, shore on to echoing shore,
Rouse from a peace, unwonted then to war,
        Us and our enemies.

EVENING

When twilight darkens, and one by one,
The sweet birds to their nests have gone;
When to green banks the glow-worms bring
Pale lamps to lighten evening;
Then stirs in his thick sleep the owl,
Through the dewy air to prowl.

Hawking the meadows, swiftly he flits,
While the small mouse a-trembling sits
With tiny eye of fear upcast
Until his brooding shape be past,
Hiding her where the moonbeams beat,
Casting black shadows in the wheat.

Now all is still: the field-man is
Lapped deep in slumbering silentness.
Not a leaf stirs, but clouds on high
Pass in dim flocks across the sky,
Puffed by a breeze too light to move
Aught but these wakeful sheep above.

O, what an arch of light now spans
These fields by night no longer Man's!
Their ancient Master is abroad,
Walking beneath the moonlight cold:
His presence is the stillness, He
Fills earth with wonder and mystery.

[49]

NIGHT

All from the light of the sweet moon
    Tired men now lie abed;
Actionless, full of visions, soon
    Vanishing, soon sped.

The starry night aflock with beams
    Of crystal light scarce stirs:
Only its birds — the cocks, the streams,
    Call 'neath heaven's wanderers.

All's silent; all hearts still;
    Love, cunning, fire, fallen low:
When faint morn straying on the hill
    Sighs, and his soft airs flow.

THE UNIVERSE

I heard a little child beneath the stars
    Talk as he ran along
To some sweet riddle in his mind that seemed
    A-tiptoe into song.

In his dark eyes lay a wild universe, —
    Wild forests, peaks, and crests;
Angels and fairies, giants, wolves and he
    Were that world's only guests.

Elsewhere was home and mother, his warm bed: —
    Now, only God alone
Could, armed with all His power and wisdom, make
    Earths richer than his own.

O Man! — thy dreams, thy passions, hopes, desires! —
    He in his pity keep
A homely bed where love may lull a child's
    Fond Universe asleep!

REVERIE

Bring not bright candles, for his eyes
　　In twilight have sweet company;
Bring not bright candles, else they fly —
　　His phantoms fly —
Gazing aggrieved on thee!

Bring not bright candles, startle not
　　The phantoms of a vacant room,
Flocking above a child that dreams —
　　Deep, deep in dreams, —
Hid, in the gathering gloom!

Bring not bright candles to those eyes
　　That between earth and stars descry,
Lovelier for the shadows there,
　　Children of air,
Palaces in the sky!

THE MASSACRE

The shadow of a poplar tree
　　Lay in that lake of sun,
As I with my little sword went in —
　　Against a thousand, one.

Haughty, and infinitely armed,
　　Insolent in their wrath,
Plumed high with purple plumes they held
　　The narrow meadow path.

The air was sultry; all was still;
　　The sun like flashing glass;
And snip-snap my light-whispering steel
　　In arcs of light did pass.

[51]

Lightly and dull fell each proud head,
   Spiked keen without avail,
Till swam my uncontented blade
   With ichor green and pale.

And silence fell: the rushing sun
   Stood still in paths of heat,
Gazing in waves of horror on
   The dead about my feet.

Never a whir of wing, no bee
   Stirred o'er the shameful slain;
Nought but a thirsty wasp crept in
   Stooped, and came out again.

The very air trembled in fear;
   Eclipsing shadow seemed
Rising in crimson waves of gloom —
   On one who dreamed.

ECHO

'Who called?' I said, and the words
   Through the whispering glades,
Hither, thither, baffled the birds —
   'Who called? Who called?'

The leafy boughs on high
   Hissed in the sun;
The dark air carried my cry
   Faintingly on:

Eyes in the green, in the shade,
   In the motionless brake,
Voices that said what I said,
   For mockery's sake:

'Who cares?' I bawled through my tears;
   The wind fell low:
In the silence, 'Who cares? Who cares?'
   Wailed to and fro.

FEAR

I know where lurk
The eyes of Fear;
I, I alone,
Where shadowy-clear,
Watching for me,
Lurks Fear.

'Tis ever still
And dark, despite
All singing and
All candlelight,
'Tis ever cold,
And night.

He touches me;
Says quietly,
'Stir not, nor whisper,
I am nigh;
Walk noiseless on,
I am by!'

He drives me
As a dog a sheep;
Like a cold stone
I cannot weep.
He lifts me,
Hot from sleep,

In marble hands
To where on high
The jewelled horror
Of his eye
Dares me to struggle
Or cry.

No breast wherein
To chase away
That watchful shape!
Vain, vain to say,
'Haunt not with night
The day!'

[53]

THE MERMAIDS

Sand, sand; hills of sand;
   And the wind where nothing is
Green and sweet of the land;
   No grass, no trees,
   No bird, no butterfly,
But hills, hills of sand,
   And a burning sky.

Sea, sea; mounds of the sea,
   Hollow, and dark, and blue,
Flashing incessantly
   The whole sea through;
   No flower, no jutting root,
Only the floor of the sea,
   With foam afloat.

Blow, blow, winding shells;
   And the watery fish,
Deaf to the hidden bells,
   In the waters plash;
   No streaming gold, no eyes,
   Watching along the waves,
But far-blown shells, faint bells,
   From the darkling caves.

MYSELF

There is a garden, grey
   With mists of autumntide;
Under the giant boughs,
   Stretched green on every side,

Along the lonely paths,
   A little child like me,
With face, with hands, like mine,
   Plays ever silently;

On, on, quite silently,
   When I am there alone,
Turns not his head; lifts not his eyes;
   Heeds not as he plays on.

[54]

After the birds are flown
  From singing in the trees,
When all is grey, all silent,
  Voices, and winds, and bees;

And I am there alone:
  Forlornly, silently,
Plays in the evening garden
  Myself with me.

AUTUMN

There is a wind where the rose was;
Cold rain where sweet grass was;
  And clouds like sheep
  Stream o'er the steep
Grey skies where the lark was.

Nought gold where your hair was;
Nought warm where your hand was;
  But phantom, forlorn,
  Beneath the thorn,
Your ghost where your face was.

Sad winds where your voice was;
Tears, tears where my heart was;
  And ever with me,
  Child, ever with me,
Silence where hope was.

WINTER

Green Mistletoe!
Oh, I remember now
A dell of snow,
Frost on the bough;
None there but I:
Snow, snow, and a wintry sky.

[55]

None there but I,
And footprints one by one,
Zigzaggedly,
Where I had run;
Where shrill and powdery
A robin sat in the tree.

And he whistled sweet;
And I in the crusted snow
With snow-clubbed feet
Jigged to and fro,
Till, from the day,
The rose-light ebbed away.

And the robin flew
Into the air, the air,
The white mist through;
And small and rare
The night-frost fell
Into the calm and misty dell.

And the dusk gathered low,
And the silver moon and stars
On the frozen snow
Drew taper bars,
Kindled winking fires
In the hooded briers.

And the sprawling Bear
Growled deep in the sky;
And Orion's hair
Streamed sparkling by:
But the North sighed low:
'*Snow, snow, more snow!*'

TO MY MOTHER

Thine is my all, how little when 'tis told
    Beside thy gold!
Thine the first peace, and mine the livelong strife;
Thine the clear dawn, and mine the night of life;
    Thine the unstained belief,
    Darkened in grief.

Scarce even a flower but thine its beauty and name,
    Dimmed, yet the same;
Never in twilight comes the moon to me,
Stealing thro' those far woods, but tells of thee,
    Falls, dear, on my wild heart,
    And takes thy part.

Thou art the child, and I — how steeped in age!
    A blotted page
From that clear, little book life's taken away:
How could I read it, dear, so dark the day?
    Be it all memory
    'Twixt thee and me!

The Listeners and Other Poems (1912)

THE THREE CHERRY TREES

There were three cherry trees once,
Grew in a garden all shady;
And there for delight of so gladsome a sight,
Walked a most beautiful lady,
Dreamed a most beautiful lady.

Birds in those branches did sing,
Blackbird and throstle and linnet,
But she walking there was by far the most fair —
Lovelier than all else within it,
Blackbird and throstle and linnet.

But blossoms to berries do come,
All hanging on stalks light and slender,
And one long summer's day charmed that lady away,
With vows sweet and merry and tender;
A lover with voice low and tender.

Moss and lichen the green branches deck;
Weeds nod in its paths green and shady:
Yet a light footstep seems there to wander in dreams,
The ghost of that beautiful lady,
That happy and beautiful lady.

OLD SUSAN

When Susan's work was done, she'd sit,
With one fat guttering candle lit,
And window opened wide to win
The sweet night air to enter in.
There, with a thumb to keep her place,
She'd read, with stern and wrinkled face,
Her mild eyes gliding very slow
Across the letters to and fro,
While wagged the guttering candle flame
In the wind that through the window came.

And sometimes in the silence she
Would mumble a sentence audibly,
Or shake her head as if to say,
'You silly souls, to act this way!'
And never a sound from night I'd hear,
Unless some far-off cock crowed clear;
Or her old shuffling thumb should turn
Another page; and rapt and stern,
Through her great glasses bent on me,
She'd glance into reality;
And shake her round old silvery head,
With —'You! — I thought you was in bed!'—
Only to tilt her book again,
And rooted in Romance remain.

OLD BEN

Sad is old Ben Thistlethwaite,
    Now his day is done,
And all his children
    Far away are gone.

He sits beneath his jasmined porch,
    His stick between his knees,
His eyes fixed, vacant,
    On his moss-grown trees.

Grass springs in the green path,
    His flowers are lean and dry,
His thatch hangs in wisps against
    The evening sky.

He has no heart to care now,
    Though the winds will blow
Whistling in his casement,
    And the rain drip through.

He thinks of his old Bettie,
    How she would shake her head and say,
'You'll live to wish my sharp old tongue
    Could scold — some day.'

But as in pale high autumn skies
  The swallows float and play,
His restless thoughts pass to and fro,
  But nowhere stay.

Soft, on the morrow, they are gone;
  His garden then will be
Denser and shadier and greener,
  Greener the moss-grown tree.

MISS LOO

When thin-strewn memory I look through,
I see most clearly poor Miss Loo;
Her tabby cat, her cage of birds,
Her nose, her hair, her muffled words,
And how she'd open her green eyes,
As if in some immense surprise,
Whenever as we sat at tea
She made some small remark to me.
It's always drowsy summer when
From out the past she comes again;
The westering sunshine in a pool
Floats in her parlour still and cool;
While the slim bird its lean wires shakes,
As into piercing song it breaks;

Till Peter's pale-green eyes ajar
Dream, wake; wake, dream, in one brief bar.
And I am sitting, dull and shy,
And she with gaze of vacancy,
And large hands folded on the tray,
Musing the afternoon away;
Her satin bosom heaving slow
With sighs that softly ebb and flow,
And her plain face in such dismay,
It seems unkind to look her way:
Until all cheerful back will come
Her gentle gleaming spirit home:
And one would think that poor Miss Loo
Asked nothing else, if she had you.

THE TAILOR

Few footsteps stray when dusk droops o'er
The tailor's old stone-lintelled door.
There sits he, stitching, half asleep,
Beside his smoky tallow dip.
'*Click, click,*' his needle hastes, and shrill
Cries back the cricket beneath the sill.
Sometimes he stays, and over his thread
Leans sidelong his old tousled head;
Or stoops to peer with half-shut eye
When some strange footfall echoes by;
Till clearer gleams his candle's spark
Into the dusty summer dark.
Then from his cross legs he gets down,
To find how dark the evening's grown;
And hunched up in his door he'll hear
The cricket whistling crisp and clear;
And so beneath the starry grey
He'll mutter half a seam away.

MARTHA

'Once ... once upon a time ...'
  Over and over again,
Martha would tell us her stories,
  In the hazel glen.

Hers were those clear grey eyes
  You watch, and the story seems
Told by their beautifulness
  Tranquil as dreams.

She'd sit with her two slim hands
  Clasped round her bended knees;
While we on our elbows lolled,
  And stared at ease.

Her voice and her narrow chin,
  Her grave small lovely head,
Seemed half the meaning
  Of the words she said.

'Once . . . once upon a time . . .'
  Like a dream you dream in the night,
Fairies and gnomes stole out
  In the leaf-green light.

And her beauty far away
  Would fade, as her voice ran on,
Till hazel and summer sun
  And all were gone:

All fordone and forgot;
  And like clouds in the height of the sky,
Our hearts stood still in the hush
  Of an age gone by.

THE SLEEPER

As Ann came in one summer's day,
  She felt that she must creep,
So silent was the clear cool house,
  It seemed a house of sleep.
And sure, when she pushed open the door,
  Rapt in the stillness there,
Her mother sat, with stooping head,
  Asleep upon a chair;
Fast — fast asleep; her two hands laid
  Loose-folded on her knee,
So that her small unconscious face
  Looked half unreal to be:
So calmly lit with sleep's pale light
  Each feature was; so fair
Her forehead — every trouble was
  Smoothed out beneath her hair.
But though her mind in dream now moved,
  Still seemed her gaze to rest —
From out beneath her fast-sealed lids,
  Above her moving breast —
On Ann; as quite, quite still she stood;
  Yet slumber lay so deep
Even her hands upon her lap
  Seemed saturate with sleep.
And as Ann peeped, a cloudlike dread
  Stole over her, and then,
On stealthy, mouselike feet she trod,
  And tiptoed out again.

THE KEYS OF MORNING

While at her bedroom window once,
  Learning her task for school,
Little Louisa lonely sat
  In the morning clear and cool,
She slanted her small bead-brown eyes
  Across the empty street,
And saw Death softly watching her
  In the sunshine pale and sweet.

His was a long lean sallow face;
  He sat with half-shut eyes,
Like an old sailor in a ship
  Becalmed 'neath tropic skies.
Beside him in the dust he had set
  His staff and shady hat;
These, peeping small, Louisa saw
  Quite clearly where she sat —
The thinness of his coal-black locks,
  His hands so long and lean
They scarcely seemed to grasp at all
  The keys that hung between:
Both were of gold, but one was small,
  And with this last did he
Wag in the air, as if to say,
  'Come hither, child, to me!'

Louisa laid her lesson book
  On the cold window-sill;
And in the sleepy sunshine house
  Went softly down, until
She stood in the half-opened door,
  And peeped. But strange to say,
Where Death just now had sunning sat
  Only a shadow lay:
Just the tall chimney's round-topped cowl,
  And the small sun behind,
Had with its shadow in the dust
  Called sleepy Death to mind.
But most she thought how strange it was
  Two keys that he should bear,
And that, when beckoning, he should wag
  The littlest in the air.

RACHEL

Rachel sings sweet —
  Oh, yes, at night,
Her pale face bent
  In the candle-light,
Her slim hands touch
  The answering keys,
And she sings of hope
  And of memories:
Sings to the little
  Boy that stands
Watching those slim,
  Light, heedful hands.
He looks in her face;
  Her dark eyes seem
Dark with a beautiful
  Distant dream;
And still she plays,
  Sings tenderly
To him of hope,
  And of memory.

ALONE

A very old woman
Lives in yon house.
The squeak of the cricket,
The stir of the mouse,
Are all she knows
Of the earth and us.

Once she was young,
Would dance and play,
Like many another
Young popinjay;
And run to her mother
At dusk of day.

And colours bright
She delighted in;
The fiddle to hear,
And to lift her chin,
And sing as small
As a twittering wren.

But age apace
Comes at last to all;
And a lone house filled
With the cricket's call;
And the scampering mouse
In the hollow wall.

THE BELLS

Shadow and light both strove to be
The eight bell-ringers' company,
As with his gliding rope in hand,
Counting his changes, each did stand;
While rang and trembled every stone,
To music by the bell-mouths blown:
Till the bright clouds that towered on high
Seemed to re-echo cry with cry.
Still swang the clappers to and fro,
When, in the far-spread fields below,
I saw a ploughman with his team
Lift to the bells and fix on them
His distant eyes, as if he would
Drink in the utmost sound he could;
While near him sat his children three,
And in the green grass placidly
Played undistracted on: as if
What music earthly bells might give
Could only faintly stir their dream,
And stillness make more lovely seem.
Soon night hid horses, children, all,
In sleep deep and ambrosial.
Yet, yet, it seemed, from star to star,
Welling now near, now faint and far,
Those echoing bells rang on in dream,
And stillness made even lovelier seem.

THE SCARECROW

All winter through I bow my head
  Beneath the driving rain;
The North Wind powders me with snow
  And blows me black again;
At midnight in a maze of stars
  I flame with glittering rime,

And stand, above the stubble, stiff
    As mail at morning-prime.
But when that child, called Spring, and all
    His host of children, come,
Scattering their buds and dew upon
    These acres of my home,
Some rapture in my rags awakes;
    I lift void eyes and scan
The skies for crows, those ravening foes,
    Of my strange master, Man.
I watch him striding lank behind
    His clashing team, and know
Soon will the wheat swish body high
    Where once lay sterile snow;
Soon shall I gaze across a sea
    Of sun-begotten grain,
Which my unflinching watch hath sealed
    For harvest once again.

NOD

Softly along the road of evening,
    In a twilight dim with rose,
Wrinkled with age, and drenched with dew,
    Old Nod, the shepherd, goes.

His drowsy flock streams on before him,
    Their fleeces charged with gold,
To where the sun's last beam leans low
    On Nod the shepherd's fold.

The hedge is quick and green with brier,
    From their sand the conies creep;
And all the birds that fly in heaven
    Flock singing home to sleep.

His lambs outnumber a noon's roses,
    Yet, when night's shadows fall,
His blind old sheep-dog, Slumber-soon,
    Misses not one of all.

His are the quiet steeps of dreamland,
    The waters of no-more-pain,
His ram's bell rings 'neath an arch of stars,
    'Rest, rest and rest again.'

THE BINDWEED

The bindweed roots pierce down
  Deeper than men do lie,
Laid in their dark-shut graves
  Their slumbering kinsmen by.

Yet what frail thin-spun flowers
  She casts into the air,
To breathe the sunshine, and
  To leave her fragrance there.

But when the sweet moon comes,
  Showering her silver down,
Half-wreathèd in faint sleep,
  They droop where they have blown.

So all the grass is set,
  Beneath her trembling ray,
With buds that have been flowers,
  Brimmed with reflected day.

WINTER

Clouded with snow
  The bleak winds blow,
And shrill on leafless bough
The robin with its burning breast
  Alone sings now.

The rayless sun,
  Day's journey done,
Sheds its last ebbing light
On fields in leagues of beauty spread
  Unearthly white.

Thick draws the dark,
  And spark by spark,
The frost-fires kindle, and soon
Over that sea of frozen foam
  Floats the white moon.

[68]

THERE BLOOMS NO BUD IN MAY

There blooms no bud in May
    Can for its white compare
With snow at break of day,
    On fields forlorn and bare.

For shadow it hath rose,
    Azure, and amethyst;
And every air that blows
    Dies out in beauteous mist.

It hangs the frozen bough
    With flowers on which the night
Wheeling her darkness through
    Scatters a starry light.

Fearful of its pale glare
    In flocks the starlings rise;
Slide through the frosty air,
    And perch with plaintive cries.

Only the inky rook,
    Hunched cold in ruffled wings,
Its snowy nest forsook,
    Caws of unnumbered Springs.

NOON AND NIGHT FLOWER

Not any flower that blows
But shining watch doth keep;
Every swift changing chequered hour it knows
Now to break forth in beauty; now to sleep.

This for the roving bee
Keeps open house, and this
Stainless and clear is, that in darkness she
May lure the moth to where her nectar is.

[69]

Lovely beyond the rest
Are these of all delight: —
The tiny pimpernel that noon loves best,
The primrose palely burning through the night.

One 'neath day's burning sky
With ruby decks her place,
The other when eve's chariot glideth by
Lifts her dim torch to light that dreaming face.

ESTRANGED

No one was with me there —
Happy I was — alone;
Yet from the sunshine suddenly
  A joy was gone.

A bird in an empty house
Sad echoes makes to ring,
Flitting from room to room
  On restless wing:

Till from its shades he flies,
And leaves forlorn and dim
The narrow solitudes
  So strange to him.

So, when with fickle heart
I joyed in the passing day,
A presence my mood estranged
  Went grieved away.

THE TIRED CUPID

The thin moonlight with trickling ray,
Thridding the boughs of silver may,
Trembles in beauty, pale and cool,
On folded flower, and mantled pool.
All in a haze the rushes lean —
And he — he sits, with chin between
His two cold hands; his bare feet set
Deep in the grasses, green and wet.

About his head a hundred rings
Of gold loop down to meet his wings,
Whose feathers, arched their stillness through,
Gleam with slow-gathering drops of dew.
The mouse-bat peers; the stealthy vole
Creeps from the covert of its hole;
A shimmering moth its pinions furls,
Grey in the moonshine of his curls;
'Neath the faint stars the night-airs stray,
Scattering the fragrance of the may;
And with each stirring of the bough
Shadow beclouds his childlike brow.

DREAMS

Be gentle, O hands of a child;
Be true: like a shadowy sea
In the starry darkness of night
      Are your eyes to me.

But words are shallow, and soon
Dreams fade that the heart once knew;
And youth fades out in the mind,
      In the dark eyes too.

What can a tired heart say,
Which the wise of the world have made dumb?
Save to the lonely dreams of a child,
      'Return again, come!'

FAITHLESS

The words you said grow faint;
   The lamp you lit burns dim;
Yet, still be near your faithless friend
   To urge and counsel him.

Still with returning feet
   To where life's shadows brood,
With steadfast eyes made clear in death
   Haunt his vague solitude.

So he, beguiled with earth,
   Yet with its vain things vexed,
Keep even to his own heart unknown
   Your memory unperplexed.

[71]

THE SHADE

Darker than night; and, oh, much darker, she
Whose eyes in deep night darkness gaze on me.
No stars surround her; yet the moon seems hid
Afar somewhere, beneath that narrow lid.
She darkens against the darkness; and her face
Only by adding thought to thought I trace,
Limmed shadowily: O dream, return once more
To gloomy Hades and the whispering shore!

BE ANGRY NOW NO MORE!

Be angry now no more!
    If I have grieved thee — if
Thy kindness, mine before,
No hope may now restore:
    Only forgive, forgive!

If still resentment burns
    In thy cold breast, oh, if
No more to pity turns,
No more, once tender, yearns
    Thy love; oh, yet forgive!...

Ask of the winter rain
June's withered rose again:
Ask grace of the salt sea:
She will not answer thee.
God would ten times have shriven
A heart so riven;
In her cold care thou wouldst be
Still unforgiven.

SPRING

Once when my life was young,
I, too, with Spring's bright face
By mine, walked softly along,
    Pace to his pace.

Then burned his crimson may,
Like a clear flame outspread,
Arching our happy way:
    Then would he shed

Strangely from his wild face
Wonderful light on me —
Like hounds that keen in chase
  Their quarry see.

Oh, sorrow now to know
What shafts, what keenness cold
His are to pierce me through,
  Now that I'm old.

EXILE

. Had the gods loved me I had lain
    Where darnel is, and thorn,
And the wild night-bird's nightlong strain
    Trembles in boughs forlorn.

Nay, but they loved me not; and I
    Must needs a stranger be,
Whose every exiled day gone by
    Aches with their memory.

WHERE?

  Where is my love —
In silence and shadow she lies,
Under the April-grey calm waste of the skies;
    And a bird above,
  In the darkness tender and clear,
Keeps saying over and over, Love lies here!

  Not that she's dead;
  Only her soul is flown
Out of its last pure earthly mansion;
    And cries instead
  In the darkness, tender and clear,
Like the voice of a bird in the leaves, Love —
    Love lies here.

[73]

MUSIC UNHEARD

Sweet sounds, begone —
　　Whose music on my ear
Stirs foolish discontent
　　Of lingering here;
When, if I crossed
　　The crystal verge of death,
Him I should see
　　Who these sounds murmureth.

Sweet sounds, begone —
　　Ask not my heart to break
Its bond of bravery for
　　Sweet quiet's sake;
Lure not my feet
　　To leave the path they must
Tread on, unfaltering,
　　Till I sleep in dust.

Sweet sounds, begone!
　　Though silence brings apace
Deadly disquiet
　　Of this homeless place;
And all I love
　　In beauty cries to me,
'We but vain shadows
　　And reflections be.'

ALL THAT'S PAST

Very old are the woods;
　　And the buds that break
Out of the brier's boughs,
　　When March winds wake,
So old with their beauty are —
　　Oh, no man knows
Through what wild centuries
　　Roves back the rose.

Very old are the brooks;
    And the rills that rise
Where snow sleeps cold beneath
    The azure skies
Sing such a history
    Of come and gone,
Their every drop is as wise
    As Solomon.

Very old are we men;
    Our dreams are tales
Told in dim Eden
    By Eve's nightingales;
We wake and whisper awhile,
    But, the day gone by,
Silence and sleep like fields
    Of amaranth lie.

WHEN THE ROSE IS FADED

When the rose is faded,
    Memory may still dwell on
Her beauty shadowed,
    And the sweet smell gone.

That vanishing loveliness,
    That burdening breath
No bond of life hath then
    Nor grief of death.

'Tis the immortal thought
    Whose passion still
Makes of the changing
    The unchangeable.

Oh, thus thy beauty,
    Loveliest on earth to me,
Dark with no sorrow, shines
    And burns, with Thee.

SLEEP

Men all, and birds, and creeping beasts,
  When the dark of night is deep,
From the moving wonder of their lives
  Commit themselves to sleep.

Without a thought, or fear, they shut
  The narrow gates of sense;
Heedless and quiet, in slumber turn
  Their strength to impotence.

The transient strangeness of the earth
  Their spirits no more see:
Within a silent gloom withdrawn,
  They slumber in secrecy.

Two worlds they have — a globe forgot,
  Wheeling from dark to light;
And all the enchanted realm of dream
  That burgeons out of night.

THE STRANGER

Half-hidden in a graveyard,
  In the blackness of a yew,
Where never living creature stirs,
  Nor sunbeam pierces through,

Is a tomb-stone, green and crooked —
  Its faded legend gone —
With one rain-worn cherub's head
  To sing of the unknown.

There, when the dusk is falling,
  Silence broods so deep
It seems that every air that breathes
  Sighs from the fields of sleep.

Day breaks in heedless beauty,
  Kindling each drop of dew,
But unforsaking shadow dwells
  Beneath this lonely yew.

[76]

And, all else lost and faded,
  Only this listening head
Keeps with a strange unanswering smile
  Its secret with the dead.

NEVER MORE, SAILOR

Never more, Sailor,
Shalt thou be
Tossed on the wind-ridden,
Restless sea.
Its tides may labour;
All the world
Shake 'neath that weight
Of waters hurled:
But its whole shock
Can only stir
Thy dust to a quiet
Even quieter.
Thou mock'st at land
Who now art come
To such a small
And shallow home;
Yet bore the sea
Full many a care
For bones that once
A sailor's were.
And though the grave's
Deep soundlessness
Thy once sea-deafened
Ear distress,
No robin ever
On the deep
Hopped with his song
To haunt thy sleep.

THE WITCH

Weary went the old Witch,
Weary of her pack,
She sat her down by the churchyard wall,
And jerked it off her back.

The cord brake, yes, the cord brake,
Just where the dead did lie,
And Charms and Spells and Sorceries
Spilled out beneath the sky.

Weary was the old Witch;
She rested her old eyes
From the lantern-fruited yew trees,
And the scarlet of the skies;

And out the dead came stumbling,
From every rift and crack,
Silent as moss, and plundered
The gaping pack.

They wish them, three times over,
Away they skip full soon:
Bat and Mole and Leveret,
Under the rising moon;

Owl and Newt and Nightjar:
They take their shapes and creep
Silent as churchyard lichen,
While she squats asleep.

All of these dead were stirring:
Each unto each did call,
'A Witch, a Witch is sleeping
Under the churchyard wall;

'A Witch, a Witch is sleeping . . .'
The shrillness ebbed away;
And up the way-worn moon clomb bright,
Hard on the track of day.

She shone, high, wan, and silvery;
Day's colours paled and died:
And, save the mute and creeping worm,
Nought else was there beside.

Names may be writ; and mounds rise;
Purporting, Here be bones:
But empty is that churchyard
Of all save stones.

Owl and Newt and Nightjar,
Leveret, Bat, and Mole
Haunt and call in the twilight
Where she slept, poor soul.

ARABIA

Far are the shades of Arabia,
    Where the Princes ride at noon,
'Mid the verdurous vales and thickets,
    Under the ghost of the moon;
And so dark is that vaulted purple
    Flowers in the forest rise
And toss into blossom 'gainst the phantom stars
    Pale in the noonday skies.

Sweet is the music of Arabia
    In my heart, when out of dreams
I still in the thin clear mirk of dawn
    Descry her gliding streams;
Hear her strange lutes on the green banks
    Ring loud with the grief and delight
Of the dim-silked, dark-haired Musicians
    In the brooding silence of night.

They haunt me — her lutes and her forests;
    No beauty on earth I see
But shadowed with that dream recalls
    Her loveliness to me:
Still eyes look coldly upon me,
    Cold voices whisper and say —
'He is crazed with the spell of far Arabia,
    They have stolen his wits away.'

[79]

THE MOUNTAINS

Still and blanched and cold and lone
    The icy hills far off from me
With frosty ulys overgrown
    Stand in their sculptured secrecy.

No path of theirs the chamois fleet
    Treads, with a nostril to the wind;
O'er their ice-marbled glaciers beat
    No wings of eagles in my mind —

Yea, in my mind these mountains rise,
    Their perils dyed with evening's rose;
And still my ghost sits at my eyes
    And thirsts for their untroubled snows.

QUEEN DJENIRA

When Queen Djenira slumbers through
    The sultry noon's repose,
From out her dreams, as soft she lies,
    A faint thin music flows.

Her lovely hands lie narrow and pale
    With gilded nails, her head
Couched in its banded nets of gold
    Lies pillowed on her bed.

The little Nubian boys who fan
    Her cheeks and tresses clear,
Wonderful, wonderful, wonderful voices
    Seem afar to hear.

They slide their eyes, and nodding, say,
    'Queen Djenira walks to-day
The courts of the lord Pthamasar
    Where the sweet birds of Psuthys are.'

And those of earth about her porch
    Of shadow cool and grey
Their sidelong beaks in silence lean,
    And silent flit away.

[80]

NEVER-TO-BE

Down by the waters of the sea
Reigns the King of Never-to-be.
His palace walls are black with night;
His torches star and moon's light,
And for his timepiece deep and grave
Beats on the green unhastening wave.

Windswept are his high corridors;
His pleasance the sea-mantled shores;
For sentinel a shadow stands
With hair in heaven, and cloudy hands;
And round his bed, king's guards to be,
Watch pines in iron solemnity.

His hound is mute; his steed at will
Roams pastures deep with asphodel;
His queen is to her slumber gone;
His courtiers mute lie, hewn in stone;
He hath forgot where he did hide
His sceptre in the mountain-side.

Grey-capped and muttering, mad is he —
The childless King of Never-to-be;
For all his people in the deep
Keep, everlasting, fast asleep;
And all his realm is foam and rain,
Whispering of what comes not again.

THE DARK CHÂTEAU

In dreams a dark château
    Stands ever open to me,
In far ravines dream-waters flow,
    Descending soundlessly;
Above its peaks the eagle floats,
    Lone in a sunless sky;
Mute are the golden woodland throats
    Of the birds flitting by.

[81]

No voice is audible. The wind
    Sleeps in its peace.
No flower of the light can find
    Refuge beneath its trees;
Only the darkening ivy climbs
    Mingled with wilding rose,
And cypress, morn and evening, time's
    Black shadow throws.

All vacant, and unknown;
    Only the dreamer steps
From stone to hollow stone,
    Where the green moss sleeps,
Peers at the river in its deeps,
    The eagle lone in the sky,
While the dew of evening drips,
    Coldly and silently.

Would that I could steal in! —
    Into each secret room;
Would that my sleep-bright eyes could win
    To the inner gloom;
Gaze from its high windows,
    Far down its mouldering walls,
Where amber-clear still Lethe flows,
    And foaming falls.

But ever as I gaze,
    From slumber soft doth come
Some touch my stagnant sense to raise
    To its old earthly home;
Fades then that sky serene;
    And peak of ageless snow;
Fades to a paling dawn-lit green,
    My dark château.

THE DWELLING-PLACE

Deep in a forest where the kestrel screamed,
    Beside a lake of water, clear as glass,
The time-worn windows of a stone house gleamed
    Named only 'Alas'.

Yet happy as the wild birds in the glades
    Of that green forest, thridding the still air
With low continued heedless serenades,
      Its heedless people were.

The throbbing chords of violin and lute,
    The lustre of lean tapers in dark eyes,
Fair colours, beauteous flowers, faint-bloomed fruit
      Made earth seem Paradise

To them that dwelt within this lonely house:
    Like children of the gods in lasting peace,
They ate, sang, danced, as if each day's carouse
      Need never pause, nor cease.

Some to the hunt would wend, with hound and horn,
    And clash of silver, beauty, bravery, pride,
Heeding not one who on white horse upborne
      With soundless hoofs did ride.

Dreamers there were who watched the hours away
    Beside a fountain's foam. And in the sweet
Of phantom evening, 'neath the night-bird's lay,
      Did loved with loved-one meet.

All, all were children, for, the long day done,
    They barred the heavy door against lightfoot fear;
And few words spake though one known face was gone,
      Yet still seemed hovering near.

They heaped the bright fire higher; poured dark wine;
    And in long revelry dazed the questioning eye;
Curtained three-fold the heart-dismaying shine
      Of midnight streaming by.

They shut the dark out from the painted wall,
    With candles dared the shadow at the door,
Sang down the faint reiterated call
      Of those who came no more.

Yet clear above that portal plain was writ,
    Confronting each at length alone to pass
Out of its beauty into night star-lit,
      That worn 'Alas!'

[83]

THE LISTENERS

'Is there anybody there?' said the Traveller,
   Knocking on the moonlit door;
And his horse in the silence champed the grasses
   Of the forest's ferny floor:
And a bird flew up out of the turret,
   Above the Traveller's head:
And he smote upon the door again a second time;
   'Is there anybody there?' he said.
But no one descended to the Traveller;
   No head from the leaf-fringed sill
Leaned over and looked into his grey eyes,
   Where he stood perplexed and still.
But only a host of phantom listeners
   That dwelt in the lone house then
Stood listening in the quiet of the moonlight
   To that voice from the world of men:
Stood thronging the faint moonbeams on the dark stair,
   That goes down to the empty hall,
Hearkening in an air stirred and shaken
   By the lonely Traveller's call.
And he felt in his heart their strangeness,
   Their stillness answering his cry,
While his horse moved, cropping the dark turf,
   'Neath the starred and leafy sky;
For he suddenly smote on the door, even
   Louder, and lifted his head: —
'Tell them I came, and no one answered,
   That I kept my word,' he said.
Never the least stir made the listeners,
   Though every word he spake
Fell echoing through the shadowiness of the still house
   From the one man left awake:
Ay, they heard his foot upon the stirrup,
   And the sound of iron on stone,
And how the silence surged softly backward,
   When the plunging hoofs were gone.

TIME PASSES

There was nought in the Valley
But a Tower of Ivory,
Its base enwreathed with red
Flowers that at evening
Caught the sun's crimson
As to Ocean low he sped.

Lucent and lovely
It stood in the morning
Under a trackless hill;
With snows eternal
Muffling its summit,
And silence ineffable.

Sighing of solitude
Winds from the cold heights
Haunted its yellowing stone;
At noon its shadow
Stretched athwart cedars
Whence every bird was flown.

Its stair was broken,
Its starlit walls were
Fretted; its flowers shone
Wide at the portal,
Full-blown and fading,
Their last faint fragrance gone.

And on high in its lantern
A shape of the living
Watched o'er a shoreless sea,
From a Tower rotting
With age and weakness,
Once lovely as ivory.

BEWARE!

An ominous bird sang from its branch,
'Beware, O Wanderer!
Night 'mid her flowers of glamourie spilled
Draws swiftly near:

'Night with her darkened caravans,
    Piled deep with silver and myrrh,
Draws from the portals of the East,
    O Wanderer, near.

'Night who walks plumèd through the fields
    Of stars that strangely stir —
Smitten to fire by the sandals of him
    Who walks with her.'

THE JOURNEY

Heart-sick of his journey was the Wanderer;
    Footsore and parched was he;
And a Witch who long had lurked by the wayside,
    Looked out of sorcery.

'Lift up your eyes, you lonely Wanderer,'
    She peeped from her casement small;
'Here's shelter and quiet to give you rest, young man,
    And apples for thirst withal.'

And he looked up out of his sad reverie,
    And saw all the woods in green,
With birds that flitted feathered in the dappling,
    The jewel-bright leaves between.

And he lifted up his face towards her lattice,
    And there, alluring-wise,
Slanting through the silence of the long past,
    Dwelt the still green Witch's eyes.

And vaguely from the hiding-place of memory
    Voices seemed to cry:
'What is the darkness of one brief life-time
    To the deaths thou hast made us die?

'Heed not the words of the Enchantress
    Who would us still betray!'
And sad with the echo of their reproaches,
    Doubting, he turned away.

'I may not shelter beneath your roof, lady,
　　Nor in this wood's green shadow seek repose,
Nor will your apples quench the thirst
　　A homesick wanderer knows.'

'"Homesick" forsooth!' she softly mocked him:
　　And the beauty in her face
Made in the sunshine pale and trembling
　　A stillness in that place.

And he sighed, as if in fear, that young Wanderer,
　　Looking to left and to right,
Where the endless narrow road swept onward,
　　Till in distance lost to sight.

And there fell upon his sense the brier,
　　Haunting the air with its breath,
And the faint shrill sweetness of the birds' throats,
　　Their tent of leaves beneath.

And there was the Witch, in no wise heeding;
　　Her arbour, and fruit-filled dish,
Her pitcher of well-water, and clear damask —
　　All that the weary wish.

And the last gold beam across the green world
　　Faltered and failed, as he
Remembered his solitude and the dark night's
　　Inhospitality.

And he looked upon the Witch with eyes of sorrow
　　In the darkening of the day;
And turned him aside into oblivion;
　　And the voices died away. . . .

And the Witch stepped down from her casement:
　　In the hush of night he heard
The calling and wailing in dewy thicket
　　Of bird to hidden bird.

And gloom stole all her burning crimson,
　　Remote and faint in space
As stars in gathering shadow of the evening
　　Seemed now her phantom face.

And one night's rest shall be a myriad,
  Mid dreams that come and go;
Till heedless fate, unmoved by weakness, bring him
  This same strange by-way through:

To the beauty of earth that fades in ashes,
  The lips of welcome, and the eyes
More beauteous than the feeble shine of Hesper
  Lone in the lightening skies:

Till once again the Witch's guile entreat him;
  But, worn with wisdom, he
Steadfast and cold shall choose the dark night's
  Inhospitality.

HAUNTED

The rabbit in his burrow keeps
No guarded watch, in peace he sleeps;
The wolf that howls in challenging night
Cowers to her lair at morning light;
The simplest bird entwines a nest
Where she may lean her lovely breast,
Couched in the silence of the bough: —
But thou, O man, what rest hast thou?

Thy emptiest solitude can bring
Only a subtler questioning
In thy divided heart. Thy bed
Recalls at dawn what midnight said.
Seek how thou wilt to feign content,
Thy flaming ardour's quickly spent;
Soon thy last company is gone,
And leaves thee — with thyself — alone.

Pomp and great friends may hem thee round,
A thousand busy tasks be found;
Earth's thronging beauties may beguile
Thy longing lovesick heart awhile;
And pride, like clouds of sunset, spread
A changing glory round thy head;
But fade with all; and thou must come,
Hating thy journey, homeless, home.

Rave how thou wilt; unmoved, remote,
That inward presence slumbers not,
Frets out each secret from thy breast,
Gives thee no rally, pause, nor rest,
Scans close thy very thoughts, lest they
Should sap his patient power away;
Answers thy wrath with peace, thy cry
With tenderest taciturnity.

SILENCE

With changeful sound life beats upon the ear;
    Yet, striving for release,
    The most seductive string's
        Sweet jargonings,
        The happiest throat's
    Most easeful, lovely notes
Fall back into a veiling silentness.

Ev'n 'mid the rumour of a moving host,
    Blackening the clear green earth,
    Vainly 'gainst that thin wall
        The trumpets call,
        Or with loud hum
    The smoke-bemuffled drum:
From that high quietness no reply comes forth.

When, all at peace, two friends at ease alone
    Talk out their hearts — yet still,
    Between the grace-notes of
        The voice of love
        From each to each
    Trembles a rarer speech,
And with its presence every pause doth fill.

Unmoved it broods, this all-encompassing hush
    Of one who stooping near,
    No smallest stir will make
        Our fear to wake;
        But yet intent
    Upon some mystery bent
Hearkens the lightest word we say, or hear.

WINTER DUSK

Dark frost was in the air without,
  The dusk was still with cold and gloom,
When less than even a shadow came
  And stood within the room.

But of the three around the fire,
  None turned a questioning head to look,
Still read a clear voice, on and on,
  Still stooped they o'er their book.

The children watched their mother's eyes
  Moving on softly line to line;
It seemed to listen too — that shade,
  Yet made no outward sign.

The fire-flames crooned a tiny song,
  No cold wind stirred the wintry tree;
The children both in Faërie dreamed
  Beside their mother's knee.

And nearer yet that spirit drew
  Above that heedless one, intent
Only on what the simple words
  Of her small story meant.

No voiceless sorrow grieved her mind,
  No memory her bosom stirred,
Nor dreamed she, as she read to two,
  'Twas surely three who heard.

Yet when, the story done, she smiled
  From face to face, serene and clear,
A love, half dread, sprang up, as she
  Leaned close and drew them near.

AGES AGO

Launcelot loved Guinevere,
  Ages and ages ago,
Beautiful as a bird was she,
Preening its wings in a cypress tree,
Happy in sadness, she and he,
  They loved each other so.

Helen of Troy was beautiful
  As tender flower in May,
Her loveliness from the towers looked down,
With the sweet moon for silver crown,
Over the walls of Troy Town,
  Hundreds of years away.

Cleopatra, Egypt's Queen,
  Was wondrous kind to ken,
As when the stars in the dark sky
Like buds on thorny branches lie,
So seemed she too to Antony,
  That age-gone prince of men.

The Pyramids are old stones,
  Scarred is that grey face,
That by the greenness of Old Nile
Gazes with an unchanging smile,
Man with all mystery to beguile
  And give his thinking grace.

HOME

Rest, rest — there is no rest,
Until the quiet grave
Comes with its narrow arch
  The heart to save
From life's long cankering rust,
From torpor, cold and still —
The loveless, saddened dust,
  The jaded will.

And yet, be far the hour
Whose haven calls me home;
Long be the arduous day
  Till evening come;

[91]

What sureness now remains
But that through livelong strife
Only the loser gains
    An end to life?

Then in the soundless deep
Of even the shallowest grave
Childhood and love he'll keep,
    And his soul save;
All vext desire, all vain
Cries of a conflict done
Fallen to rest again;
    Death's refuge won.

THE GHOST

Peace in thy hands,
Peace in thine eyes,
Peace on thy brow;
Flower of a moment in the eternal hour,
Peace with me now.

Not a wave breaks,
Not a bird calls,
My heart, like a sea,
Silent after a storm that hath died,
Sleeps within me.

All the night's dews,
All the world's leaves,
All winter's snow
Seem with their quiet to have stilled in life's dream
All sorrowing now.

AN EPITAPH

Here lies a most beautiful lady,
Light of step and heart was she;
I think she was the most beautiful lady
That ever was in the West Country.

But beauty vanishes; beauty passes;
However rare — rare it be;
And when I crumble, who will remember
This lady of the West Country?

'THE HAWTHORN HATH A DEATHLY SMELL'

The flowers of the field
　　Have a sweet smell;
Meadowsweet, tansy, thyme,
　　And faint-heart pimpernel;
But sweeter even than these,
　　The silver of the may
Wreathed is with incense for
　　The Judgment Day.

An apple, a child, dust,
　　When falls the evening rain,
Wild brier's spicèd leaves,
　　Breathe memories again;
With further memory fraught,
　　The silver of the may
Wreathed is with incense for
　　The Judgment Day.

Eyes of all loveliness —
　　Shadow of strange delight,
Even as a flower fades
　　Must thou from sight;
But, oh, o'er thy grave's mound,
　　Till come the Judgment Day,
Wreathed shall with incense be
　　Thy sharp-thorned may.

Motley and Other Poems (1918)

THE LITTLE SALAMANDER

To Margot

When I go free,
I think 'twill be
A night of stars and snow,
And the wild fires of frost shall light
My footsteps as I go;
Nobody — nobody will be there
With groping touch, or sight,
To see me in my bush of hair
Dance burning through the night.

THE LINNET

Upon this leafy bush
    With thorns and roses in it,
Flutters a thing of light,
    A twittering linnet,
And all the throbbing world
    Of dew and sun and air
By this small parcel of life
    Is made more fair:
As if each bramble-spray
    And mounded gold-wreathed furze,
Harebell and little thyme,
    Were only hers;
As if this beauty and grace
    Did to one bird belong,
And, at a flutter of wing,
    Might vanish in song.

THE SUNKEN GARDEN

Speak not — whisper not;
Here bloweth thyme and bergamot;
Softly on the evening hour,
Secret herbs their spices shower.
Dark-spiked rosemary and myrrh,
Lean-stalked purple lavender;

Hides within her bosom, too,
All her sorrows, bitter rue.

Breathe not — trespass not;
Of this green and darkling spot,
Latticed from the moon's beams,
Perchance a distant dreamer dreams;
Perchance upon its darkening air,
The unseen ghosts of children fare,
Faintly swinging, sway and sweep,
Like lovely sea-flowers in the deep;
While, unmoved, to watch and ward,
Amid its gloomed and daisied sward,
Stands with bowed and dewy head
That one little leaden Lad.

THE RIDDLERS

'Thou solitary!' the Blackbird cried,
'I, from the happy Wren,
Linnet and Blackcap, Woodlark, Thrush,
Perched all upon a sweetbrier bush,
Have come at cold of midnight-tide
To ask thee, Why and when
Grief smote thy heart so thou dost sing
In solemn hush of evening,
So sorrowfully, lovelorn Thing —
Nay, nay, not sing, but rave, but wail,
Most melancholy Nightingale?
Do not the dews of darkness steep
All pinings of the day in sleep?
Why, then, when rocked in starry nest
We mutely couch, secure, at rest,
Doth thy lone heart delight to make
Music for sorrow's sake?'

A Moon was there. So still her beam,
It seemed the whole world lay in dream,
Lulled by the watery sea.
And from her leafy night-hung nook
Upon this stranger soft did look
The Nightingale: sighed he: —

''Tis strange, my friend; the Kingfisher
But yestermorn conjured me here
Out of his green and blue to say
Why thou, in splendour of the day,
Wearest, of colour, but bill gold-gay,
And else dost thee array
In a most sombre suit of black?
"Surely," he sighed, "some load of grief,
Past all our thinking — and belief —
Must weigh upon his back!"
Do, then, in turn, tell me, If joy
Thy heart as well as voice employ,
Why dost thou now, most Sable, shine
In plumage woefuller far than mine?
Thy silence is a sadder thing
Than any dirge I sing!'

Thus, then, these two small birds, perched there,
Breathed a strange riddle both did share
Yet neither could expound.
And we — who sing but as we can,
In the small knowledge of a man —
Have we an answer found?
Nay, some are happy whose delight
Is hid even in themselves from sight;
And some win peace who spend
The skill of words to sweeten despair
Of finding consolation where
Life has but one dark end;
Who, in rapt solitude, tell o'er
A tale as lovely as forelore,
Into the midnight air.

MOONLIGHT

The far moon maketh lovers wise
  In her pale beauty trembling down,
Lending curved cheeks, dark lips, dark eyes,
  A strangeness not her own.
And, though they shut their lids to kiss,
  In starless darkness peace to win,
Even on that secret world from this
  Her twilight enters in.

[97]

THE BLIND BOY

'I have no master,' said the Blind Boy,
  'My mother, "Dame Venus" they do call;
Cowled in this hood she sent me begging
  For whate'er in pity may befall.

'Hard was her visage, me adjuring, —
  "Have no fond mercy on the kind!
Here be sharp arrows, bunched in quiver,
  Draw close ere striking — thou art blind."

'So stand I here, my woes entreating,
  In this dark alley, lest the Moon
Point with her sparkling my barbed armoury,
  Shine on my silver-lacèd shoon.

'Oh, sir, unkind this Dame to me-ward;
  Of the salt billow was her birth. . . .
In your sweet charity draw nearer
  The saddest rogue on Earth!'

THE QUARRY

You hunted me with all the pack,
  Too blind, too blind, to see
By no wild hope of force or greed
  Could you make sure of me.

And like a phantom through the glades,
  With tender breast aglow,
The goddess in me laughed to hear
  Your horns a-roving go.

She laughed to think no mortal ever
  By dint of mortal flesh
The very Cause that was the Hunt
  One moment could enmesh:

That though with captive limbs I lay,
  Stilled breath and vanquished eyes,
He that hunts Love with horse and hound
  Hunts out his heart and eyes.

MRS. GRUNDY

'Step very softly, sweet Quiet-foot,
Stumble not, whisper not, smile not:
By this dark ivy stoop cheek and brow.
Still even thy heart! What seest thou? . . .'

'High-coifed, broad-browed, aged, suave yet grim,
A large flat face, eyes keenly dim,
Staring at nothing — that's me! — and yet,
With a hate one could never, no, never forget . . .'

'This is my world, my garden, my home,
Hither my father bade mother to come
And bear me out of the dark into light,
And happy I was in her tender sight.

'And then, thou frail flower, she died and went,
Forgetting my pitiless banishment,
And that Old Woman — an Aunt — she said,
Came hither, lodged, fattened, and made her bed.

'Oh, yes, thou most blessed, from Monday to Sunday,
Has lived on me, preyed on me, Mrs. Grundy:
Called me, "dear Nephew"; on each of those chairs
Has gloated in righteousness, heard my prayers.

'Why didst thou dare the thorns of the grove,
Timidest trespasser, huntress of love?
Now thou hast peeped, and now dost know
What kind of creature is thine for foe.

'Not that she'll tear out thy innocent eyes,
Poison thy mouth with deviltries.
Watch thou, wait thou: soon will begin
The guile of a voice: hark! . . .' 'Come in. Come in!'

THE TRYST

Flee into some forgotten night and be
Of all dark long my moon-bright company:
Beyond the rumour even of Paradise come,
There, out of all remembrance, make our home:

Seek we some close hid shadow for our lair,
Hollowed by Noah's mouse beneath the chair
Wherein the Omnipotent, in slumber bound,
Nods till the piteous Trump of Judgment sound.
Perchance Leviathan of the deep sea
Would lease a lost mermaiden's grot to me,
There of your beauty we would joyance make —
A music wistful for the sea-nymph's sake:
Haply Elijah, o'er his spokes of fire,
Cresting steep Leo, or the heavenly Lyre,
Spied, tranced in azure of inanest space,
Some eyrie hostel, meet for human grace,
Where two might happy be — just you and I —
Lost in the uttermost of Eternity.
Think! In Time's smallest clock's minutest beat
Might there not rest be found for wandering feet?
Or, 'twixt the sleep and wake of Helen's dream,
Silence wherein to sing love's requiem?

No, no. Nor earth, nor air, nor fire, nor deep
Could lull poor mortal longingness asleep.
Somewhere there Nothing is; and there lost Man
Shall win what changeless vague of peace he can.

ALONE

The abode of the nightingale is bare,
Flowered frost congeals in the gelid air,
The fox howls from his frozen lair:
  Alas, my loved one is gone,
  I am alone;
  It is winter.

Once the pink cast a winy smell,
The wild bee hung in the hyacinth bell,
Light in effulgence of beauty fell:
  Alas, my loved one is gone,
  I am alone;
  It is winter.

My candle a silent fire doth shed,
Starry Orion hunts o'erhead;
Come moth, come shadow, the world is dead:
  Alas, my loved one is gone,
  I am alone;
  It is winter.

THE EMPTY HOUSE

See this house, how dark it is
Beneath its vast-boughed trees!
Not one trembling leaflet cries
To that Watcher in the skies —
'Remove, remove thy searching gaze,
Innocent of heaven's ways,
Brood not, Moon, so wildly bright,
On secrets hidden from sight.'

'Secrets,' sighs the night-wind,
'Vacancy is all I find;
Every keyhole I have made
Wails a summons, faint and sad,
No voice ever answers me,
      Only vacancy.'
'Once, once . . .' the cricket shrills,
And far and near the quiet fills
With its tiny voice, and then
      Hush falls again.

Mute shadows creeping slow
Mark how the hours go.
Every stone is mouldering slow.
And the least winds that blow
Some minutest atom shake,
Some fretting ruin make
In roof and walls. How black it is
Beneath these thick-boughed trees!

MISTRESS FELL

'Whom seek you here, sweet Mistress Fell?'
'One who loved me passing well.
Dark his eye, wild his face —
Stranger, if in this lonely place
Bide such an one, then, prythee, say
I am come here to-day.'

[101]

'Many his like, Mistress Fell?'
'I did not look, so cannot tell.
Only this I surely know,
When his voice called me, I must go;
Touched me his fingers, and my heart
Leapt at the sweet pain's smart.'

'Why did he leave you, Mistress Fell?'
'Magic laid its dreary spell —
Stranger, he was fast asleep;
Into his dream I tried to creep;
Called his name, soft was my cry;
He answered — not one sigh.

'The flower and the thorn are here;
Falleth the night-dew, cold and clear;
Out of her bower the bird replies,
Mocking the dark with ecstasies,
See how the earth's green grass doth grow,
Praising what sleeps below!

'Thus have they told me. And I come,
As flies the wounded wild-bird home.
Not tears I give; but all that he
Clasped in his arms, sweet charity;
All that he loved — to him I bring
For a close whispering.'

THE GHOST

'Who knocks?' 'I, who was beautiful,
    Beyond all dreams to restore,
I, from the roots of the dark thorn am hither.
    And knock on the door.'

'Who speaks?' 'I — once was my speech
    Sweet as the bird's on the air,
When echo lurks by the waters to heed;
    'Tis I speak thee fair.'

'Dark is the hour!' 'Ay, and cold.'
  'Lone is my house.' 'Ah, but mine?'
'Sight, touch, lips, eyes yearned in vain.'
  'Long dead these to thine . . .'

Silence. Still faint on the porch
  Brake the flames of the stars.
In gloom groped a hope-wearied hand
  Over keys, bolts, and bars.

A face peered. All the grey night
  In chaos of vacancy shone;
Nought but vast sorrow was there —
  The sweet cheat gone.

THE STRANGER

In the woods as I did walk,
  Dappled with the moon's beam,
I did with a Stranger talk,
  And his name was Dream.

Spurred his heel, dark his cloak,
  Shady-wide his bonnet's brim;
His horse beneath a silvery oak
  Grazed as I talked with him.

Softly his breast-brooch burned and shone;
  Hill and deep were in his eyes;
One of his hands held mine, and one
  The fruit that makes men wise.

Wondrously strange was earth to see,
  Flowers white as milk did gleam;
Spread to Heaven the Assyrian Tree,
  Over my head with Dream.

Dews were still betwixt us twain;
  Stars a trembling beauty shed;
Yet, not a whisper comes again
  Of the words he said.

[103]

BETRAYAL

She will not die, they say,
She will but put her beauty by
    And hie away.

Oh, but her beauty gone, how lonely
Then will seem all reverie,
    How black to me!

All things will sad be made
And every hope a memory,
    All gladness dead.

Ghosts of the past will know
My weakest hour, and whisper to me,
    And coldly go.

And hers in deep of sleep,
Clothed in its mortal beauty I shall see,
    And, waking, weep.

Naught will my mind then find
In man's false Heaven my peace to be:
    All blind, and blind.

THE CAGE

Why did you flutter in vain hope, poor bird,
    Hard-pressed in your small cage of clay?
'Twas but a sweet, false echo that you heard,
    Caught only a feint of day.

Still is the night all dark, a homeless dark.
    Burn yet the unanswering stars. And silence brings
The same sea's desolate surge — sans bound or mark —
    Of all your wanderings.

Fret now no more; be still. Those steadfast eyes,
    Those folded hands, they cannot set you free;
Only with beauty wake wild memories —
    Sorrow for where you are, for where you would be.

THE REVENANT

O all ye fair ladies with your colours and your graces,
  And your eyes clear in flame of candle and hearth,
Toward the dark of this old window lift not up your smiling faces,
  Where a Shade stands forlorn from the cold of the earth.

God knows I could not rest for one I still was thinking of;
  Like a rose sheathed in beauty her spirit was to me;
Now out of unforgottenness a bitter draught I'm drinking of,
  'Tis sad of such beauty unremembered to be.

Men all are shades, O Women. Winds wist not of the way they
    blow.
  Apart from your kindness, life's at best but a snare.
Though a tongue, now past praise, this bitter thing doth say, I
    know
  What solitude means, and how, homeless, I fare.

Strange, strange, are ye all — except in beauty shared with her —
  Since I seek one I loved, yet was faithless to in death.
Not life enough I heaped, so thus my heart must fare with her,
  Now wrapt in the gross clay, bereft of life's breath.

MUSIC

When music sounds, gone is the earth I know,
And all her lovely things even lovelier grow;
Her flowers in vision flame, her forest trees
Lift burdened branches, stilled with ecstasies.

When music sounds, out of the water rise
Naiads whose beauty dims my waking eyes,
Rapt in strange dreams burns each enchanted face,
With solemn echoing stirs their dwelling-place.

When music sounds, all that I was I am
Ere to this haunt of brooding dust I came;
While from Time's woods break into distant song
The swift-winged hours, as I hasten along.

THE REMONSTRANCE

I was at peace until you came
And set a careless mind aflame.
I lived in quiet; cold, content;
All longing in safe banishment,
Until your ghostly lips and eyes
      Made wisdom unwise.

Naught was in me to tempt your feet
To seek a lodging. Quite forgot
Lay the sweet solitude we two
In childhood used to wander through;
Time's cold had closed my heart about;
      And shut you out.

Well, and what then? . . . O vision grave,
Take all the little all I have!
Strip me of what in voiceless thought
Life's kept of life, unhoped, unsought! —
Reverie and dream that memory must
      Hide deep in dust!

This only I say: — Though cold and bare
The haunted house you have chosen to share,
Still 'neath its walls the moonbeam goes
And trembles on the untended rose;
Still o'er its broken roof-tree rise
The starry arches of the skies;
And in your lightest word shall be
The thunder of an ebbing sea.

NOCTURNE

'Tis not my voice now speaks; but as a bird
In darkling forest hollows a sweet throat —
Pleads on till distant echo too hath heard
      And doubles every note:
So love that shrouded dwells in mystery
      Would cry and waken thee.

Thou Solitary, stir in thy still sleep!
All the night waits thee, must thou still dream on?
Furtive the shadows that about thee creep,
And cheat the shining footsteps of the moon:
Unseal thine eyes, it is my heart that sings,
  And beats in vain its wings.

Lost in heaven's vague, the stars burn softly through
The world's dark latticings, we prisoned stray
Within its lovely labyrinth, and know
  Mute seraphs guard the way
Even from silence unto speech, from love
To that self's self it still is dreaming of.

THE EXILE

I am that Adam who, with Snake for guest,
Hid anguished eyes upon Eve's piteous breast.
I am that Adam who, with broken wings,
Fled from the Seraph's brazen trumpetings.
Betrayed and fugitive, I still must roam
A world where sin, and beauty, whisper of Home.

Oh, from wide circuit, shall at length I see
Pure daybreak lighten again on Eden's tree?
Loosed from remorse and hope and love's distress,
Enrobe me again in my lost nakedness?
No more with worldless grief a loved one grieve,
But to Heaven's nothingness re-welcome Eve?

THE UNCHANGING

After the songless rose of evening,
  Night quiet, dark, still,
In nodding cavalcade advancing
  Starred the deep hill:
You, in the valley standing,
  In your quiet wonder took

All that glamour, peace, and mystery
    In one grave look.
Beauty hid your naked body,
    Time dreamed in your bright hair,
In your eyes the constellations
    Burned far and fair.

NIGHTFALL

The last light fails — that shallow pool of day!
The coursers of the dark stamp down to drink,
Arch their wild necks, lift their wild heads and neigh;
Their drivers, gathering at the water-brink,
With eyes ashine from out their clustering hair,
Utter their hollow speech, or gaze afar,
Rapt in irradiant reverie, to where
Languishes, lost in light, the evening star.
Come the wood-nymphs to dance within the glooms,
Calling these charioteers with timbrels' din;
Ashen with twilight the dark forest looms
O'er the nocturnal beasts that prowl within.
'O glory of beauty which the world makes fair!'
Pant they their serenading on the air.

Sound the loud hooves, and all abroad the sky
The lusty charioteers their stations take;
Planet to planet do the sweet Loves fly,
And in the zenith silver music wake.
Cities of men, in blindness hidden low,
Fume their faint flames to that arched firmament,
But all the dwellers in the lonely know
The unearthly are abroad, and weary and spent,
With rush extinguished, to their dreaming go.
And world and night and star-enclustered space
The glory of beauty are in one enravished face.

INVOCATION

The burning fire shakes in the night,
    On high her silver candles gleam,
With far-flung arms enflamed with light,
    The trees are lost in dream.

Come in thy beauty! 'tis my love,
    Lost in far-wandering desire,
Hath in the darkling deep above
    Set stars and kindled fire.

EYES

O strange devices that alone divide
The seër from the seen —
The very highway of earth's pomp and pride
That lies between
The traveller and the cheating, sweet delight
Of where he longs to be,
But which, bound hand and foot, he, close on night,
Can only see.

LIFE

Hearken, O dear, now strikes the hour we die;
We, who in one strange kiss
Have proved a dream the world's realities,
Turned each from other's darkness with a sigh,
Need heed no more of life, waste no more breath
On any other journey, but of death.

And yet: Oh, know we well
How each of us must prove Love's infidel;
Still out of ecstasy turn trembling back
To earth's same empty track
Of leaden day by day, and hour by hour, and be
Of all things lovely the cold mortuary.

THE DISGUISE

Why in my heart, O Grief,
Dost thou in beauty hide?
Dead is my well-content,
And buried deep my pride.
Cold are their stones, beloved,
To hand and side.

The shadows of evening are gone,
Shut are the day's clear flowers,
Now have her birds left mute
Their singing bowers,
Lone shall we be, we twain,
In the night hours.

Thou with thy cheek on mine,
And dark hair loosed, shalt see
Take the far stars for fruit
The cypress tree,
And in the yew's black
Shall the moon be.

We will tell no old tales,
Nor heed if in wandering air
Die a lost song of love
Or the once fair;
Still as well-water be
The thoughts we share!

And, while the ghosts keep
Tryst from chill sepulchres,
Dreamless our gaze shall sleep,
And sealed our ears;
Heart unto heart will speak,
Without tears.

O, thy veiled, lovely face —
Joy's strange disguise —
Shall be the last to fade
From these rapt eyes,
Ere the first dart of daybreak
Pierce the skies.

VAIN QUESTIONING

What needest thou? — a few brief hours of rest
Wherein to seek thyself in thine own breast;
A transient silence wherein truth could say
Such was thy constant hope, and this thy way? —
    O burden of life that is
    A livelong tangle of perplexities!

What seekest thou? — a truce from that thou art;
Some steadfast refuge from a fickle heart;
Still to be thou, and yet no thing of scorn,
To find no stay here, and yet not forlorn? —
    O riddle of life that is
    An endless war 'twixt contrarieties.

Leave this vain questioning. Is not sweet the rose?
Sings not the wild bird ere to rest he goes?
Hath not in miracle brave June returned?
Burns not her beauty as of old it burned?
    O foolish one to roam
    So far in thine own mind away from home!

Where blooms the flower when her petals fade,
Where sleepeth echo by earth's music made,
Where all things transient to the changeless win,
There waits the peace thy spirit dwelleth in.

VIGIL

Dark is the night,
   The fire burns faint and low,
Hours — days — years,
   Into grey ashes go;
I strive to read,
   But sombre is the glow.

Thumbed are the pages,
   And the print is small;
Mocking the winds
   That from the darkness call;
Feeble the fire that lends
   Its light withal.

O ghost, draw nearer;
   Let thy shadowy hair
Blot out the pages
   That we cannot share;
Be ours the one last leaf
   By Fate left bare!

Let's Finis scrawl,
   And then Life's book put by;
Turn each to each
   In all simplicity:
Ere the last flame is gone
   To warm us by.

THE OLD MEN

Old and alone, sit we,
  Caged, riddle-rid men;
Lost to Earth's 'Listen!' and 'See!'
  Thought's 'Wherefore?' and 'When?'

Only far memories stray
  Of a past once lovely, but now
Wasted and faded away,
  Like green leaves from the bough.

Vast broods the silence of night,
  The ruinous moon
Lifts on our faces her light,
  Whence all dreaming is gone.

We speak not; trembles each head;
  In their sockets our eyes are still;
Desire as cold as the dead;
  Without wonder or will.

And One, with a lanthorn, draws near,
  At clash with the moon in our eyes:
'Where art thou?' he asks: 'I am here,'
  One by one we arise.

And none lifts a hand to withhold
  A friend from the touch of that foe:
Heart cries unto heart, 'Thou art old!'
  Yet, reluctant, we go.

THE DREAMER

O thou who giving helm and sword,
  Gav'st too the rusting rain,
And starry dark's all tender dews
  To blunt and stain:

Out of the battle I am sped,
  Unharmed, yet stricken sore;
A living shape amid whispering shades
  On Lethe's shore.

No trophy in my hands I bring,
    To this sad, sighing stream,
The neighings and the trumps and cries
    Were but a dream.

Traitor to life, of life betrayed
    O, of thy mercy deep,
A dream my all, the all I ask
    Is sleep.

HAPPY ENGLAND

Now each man's mind all Europe is:
    Boding and fear in dread array
Daze every heart: O grave and wise,
    Abide in hope the judgment day.

This war of millions in arms
    In myriad replica we wage;
Unmoved, then, Soul, by earth's alarms
    The dangers of the dark engage.

Remember happy England: keep
    For her bright cause thy latest breath;
Her peace that long hath lulled to sleep,
    May now exact the sleep of death.

Her woods and wilds, her loveliness,
    With harvest now are richly at rest;
Safe in her isled securities,
    Thy children's heaven is her breast.

O what a deep contented night
    The sun from out her Eastern seas
Would bring the dust which in her sight
    Had given its all for these!

MOTLEY

Come, Death, I'd have a word with thee;
And thou, poor Innocency;
And Love — a Lad with broken wing;
And Pity, too:
The Fool shall sing to you,
As Fools will sing.

Ay, music hath small sense,
And a tune's soon told,
And Earth is old,
And my poor wits are dense;
Yet have I secrets, — dark, my dear,
To breathe you all. Come near.
And lest some hideous listener tells,
I'll ring my bells.

They are all at war! —
Yes, yes, their bodies go
'Neath burning sun and icy star
To chaunted songs of woe,
Dragging cold cannon through a mire
Of rain and blood and spouting fire,
The new moon glinting hard on eyes
Wide with insanities!

Ssh! . . . I use words
I hardly know the meaning of;
And the mute birds
Are glancing at Love
From out their shade of leaf and flower,
Trembling at treacheries
Which even in noonday cower.
Heed, heed not what I said
Of frenzied hosts of men,
More fools than I,
On envy, hatred fed,
Who kill, and die —
Spake I not plainly, then?
Yet Pity whispered, 'Why?'

And Death — no ears hath. He hath supped where
    creep

Eyeless worms in hush of sleep;
Yet, when he smiles, the hand he draws
Athwart his grinning jaws —
Faintly the thin bones rattle, and — there, there!
Hearken how my bells in the air
Drive away care! . . .

Nay, but a dream I had
Of a world all mad.
Not simple happy mad like me,
Who am mad like an empty scene
Of water and willow tree,
Where the wind hath been;
But that foul Satan-mad,
Who rots in his own head,
And counts the dead,
Not honest one — and two —
But for the ghosts they were,
Brave, faithful, true,
When, head in air,
In Earth's clear green and blue
Heaven they did share
With beauty who bade them there. . . .

There, now! Death goes —
Mayhap I've wearied him.
Ay, and the light doth dim;
And asleep's the rose;
And tired Innocence
In dreams is hence. . . .
Come, Love, my lad,
Nodding that drowsy head,
'Tis time thy prayers were said!

THE MARIONETTES

Let the foul Scene proceed:
    There's laughter in the wings;
'Tis sawdust that they bleed,
    Only a box Death brings.

[115]

How rare a skill is theirs —
 These extreme pangs to show,
How real a frenzy wears
 Each feigner of woe!

Gigantic dins uprise!
 Even the gods must feel
A smarting of the eyes
 As these fumes upsweel.

Strange, such a Piece is free,
 While we Spectators sit,
Aghast at its agony,
 Yet absorbed in it!

Dark is the outer air,
 Coldly the night draughts blow,
Mutely we stare, and stare
 At the frenzied Show.

Yet heaven hath its quiet shroud
 Of deep, immutable blue —
We cry 'An end!' We are bowed
 By the dread, 'It's true!'

While the Shape who hoofs applause
 Behind our deafened ear,
Hoots — angel-wise — 'the Cause!'
 And affrights even fear.

TO E.T.: 1917

You sleep too well — too far away,
 For sorrowing word to soothe or wound;
Your very quiet seems to say
 How longed-for a peace you have found.

Else, had not death so lured you on,
 You would have grieved — 'twixt joy and fear —
To know how my small loving son
 Had wept for you, my dear.

APRIL MOON

Roses are sweet to smell and see,
   And lilies on the stem;
But rarer, stranger buds there be,
   And she was like to them.

The little moon that April brings,
   More lovely shade than light,
That, setting, silvers lonely hills
   Upon the verge of night —

Close to the world of my poor heart
   So stole she, still and clear;
Now that she's gone, O dark, and dark,
   The solitude, the fear.

THE FOOL'S SONG

Never, no never, listen too long,
To the chattering wind in the willows, the night bird's song.

   'Tis sad in sooth to lie under the grass,
But none too gladsome to wake and grow cold where life's
     shadows pass.

   Dumb the old Toll-Woman squats,
And, for every green copper battered and worn, doles out
     Nevers and Nots.

   I know a Blind Man, too,
Who with a sharp ear listens and listens the whole world
     through.

   Oh, sit we snug to our feast,
With platter and finger and spoon — and good victuals
     at least.

CLEAR EYES

Clear eyes do dim at last,
   And cheeks outlive their rose.
Time, heedless of the past,
   No loving-kindness knows;
Chill unto mortal lip
   Still Lethe flows.

Griefs, too, but brief while stay,
   And sorrow, being o'er,
Its salt tears shed away,
   Woundeth the heart no more.
Stealthily lave those waters
   That solemn shore.

Ah, then, sweet face, burn on,
   While yet quick memory lives!
And Sorrow, ere thou art gone,
   Know that my heart forgives —
Ere yet, grown cold in peace,
   It loves not, nor grieves.

DUST TO DUST

Heavenly Archer, bend thy bow;
Now the flame of life burns low,
Youth is gone; I, too, would go.

Ever Fortune leads to this:
Harsh or kind, at last she is
Murderess of all ecstasies.

Yet the spirit, dark, alone,
Bound in sense, still hearkens on
For tidings of a bliss foregone.

Sleep is well for dreamless head,
At no breath astonishèd,
From the Gardens of the Dead.

I the immortal harps hear ring,
By Babylon's river languishing.
Heavenly Archer, loose thy string.

THE THREE STRANGERS

Far are those tranquil hills,
    Dyed with fair evening's rose;
On urgent, secret errand bent,
    A traveller goes.

Approach him strangers three,
    Barefooted, cowled; their eyes
Scan the lone, hastening solitary
    With dumb surmise.

One instant in close speech
    With them he doth confer:
God-sped, he hasteneth on,
    That anxious traveller . . .

I was that man — in a dream:
    And each world's night in vain
I patient wait on sleep to unveil
    Those vivid hills again.

Would that they three could know
    How yet burns on in me
Love — from one lost in Paradise —
    For their grave courtesy.

ALEXANDER

It was the Great Alexander,
    Capped with a golden helm,
Sate in the ages, in his floating ship,
    In a dead calm.

Voices of sea-maids singing
    Wandered across the deep:
The sailors labouring on their oars
    Rowed, as in sleep.

All the high pomp of Asia,
    Charmed by that siren lay,
Out of their weary and dreaming minds,
    Faded away.

[119]

Like a bold boy sate their Captain,
　His glamour withered and gone,
In the souls of his brooding mariners,
　While the song pined on.

Time, like a falling dew,
　Life, like the scene of a dream,
Laid between slumber and slumber,
　Only did seem. . . .

O Alexander, then,
　In all us mortals too,
Wax thou not bold — too bold
　On the wave dark-blue!

Come the calm, infinite night,
　Who then will hear
Aught save the singing
　Of the sea-maids clear?

THE REAWAKENING

Green in light are the hills, and a calm wind flowing
　Filleth the void with a flood of the fragrance of Spring;
Wings in this mansion of life are coming and going,
　Voices of unseen loveliness carol and sing.

Coloured with buds of delight the boughs are swaying,
　Beauty walks in the woods, and wherever she rove
Flowers from wintry sleep, her enchantment obeying,
　Stir in the deep of her dream, reawaken to love.

Oh, now begone, sullen care — this light is my seeing;
　I am the palace, and mine are its windows and walls;
Daybreak is come, and life from the darkness of being
　Springs, like a child from the womb, when the lonely one calls.

THE VACANT DAY

As I walked out in meadows green
   I heard the summer noon resound
With call of myriad things unseen
   That leapt and crept upon the ground.

High overhead the windless air
   Throbbed with the homesick coursing cry
Of swifts that ranging everywhere
   Woke echo in the sky.

Beside me, too, clear waters coursed
   Which willow branches, lapsing low,
Breaking their crystal gliding forced
   To sing as they did flow.

I listened; and my heart was dumb
   With praise no language could express;
Longing in vain for him to come
   Who had breathed such blessedness

On this fair world, wherein we pass
   So chequered and so brief a stay;
And yearned in spirit to learn, alas,
   What kept him still away.

THE FLIGHT

How do the days press on, and lay
   Their fallen locks at evening down,
While the clear stars in darkness play
   And moonbeams weave a crown —

A crown of flower-like light in heaven,
   Where in the hollow arch of space
Morn's mistress dreams, and the Pleiads seven
   Stand watch about her place.

Stand watch — O days, no number keep
   Of hours when this dark clay is blind.
When the world's clocks are dumb in sleep
   'Tis then I seek my kind.

THE TWO HOUSES[1]

In the strange city of Life
Two houses I know well:
One wherein Silence a garden hath,
And one where Dark doth dwell.

Roof unto roof they stand,
Shadowing the dizzied street,
Where Vanity flaunts her gilded booths
In the noontide glare and heat.

Green-graped upon their walls
An ancient, hoary vine
Hath clustered their carven, lichenous stones
With tendril serpentine.

And ever and anon,
Dazed in that clamorous throng,
I thirst for the soundless fount that stills
Those orchards mute of song.

Knock, knock, nor knock in vain:
Heart all thy secrets tell
Where Silence a fast-sealed garden hath,
Where Dark doth dwell.

FOR ALL THE GRIEF

For all the grief I have given with words
     May now a few clear flowers blow,
In the dust, and the heat, and the silence of birds,
     Where the friendless go.

For the thing unsaid that heart asked of me
     Be a dark, cool water calling — calling
To the footsore, benighted, solitary,
     When the shadows are falling.

[1] A later version on p. 289 has the title 'Nostalgia'.

O, be beauty for all my blindness,
    A moon in the air where the weary wend,
And dews burdened with loving-kindness
    In the dark of the end.

THE SCRIBE

What lovely things
    Thy hand hath made:
The smooth-plumed bird
    In its emerald shade,
The seed of the grass,
    The speck of stone
Which the wayfaring ant
    Stirs — and hastes on!

Though I should sit
    By some tarn in thy hills,
Using its ink
    As the spirit wills
To write of Earth's wonders,
    Its live, willed things,
Flit would the ages
    On soundless wings
Ere unto Z
    My pen drew nigh;
Leviathan told,
    And the honey-fly:
And still would remain
    My wit to try —
My worn reeds broken,
    The dark tarn dry,
All words forgotten —
    Thou, Lord, and I.

FARE WELL

When I lie where shades of darkness
Shall no more assail mine eyes,
Nor the rain make lamentation
    When the wind sighs;
How will fare the world whose wonder
Was the very proof of me?
Memory fades, must the remembered
    Perishing be?

Oh, when this my dust surrenders
Hand, foot, lip, to dust again,
May these loved and loving faces
    Please other men!
May the rusting harvest hedgerow
Still the Traveller's Joy entwine,
And as happy children gather
    Posies once mine.

Look thy last on all things lovely,
Every hour. Let no night
Seal thy sense in deathly slumber
    Till to delight
Thou have paid thy utmost blessing;
Since that all things thou wouldst praise
Beauty took from those who loved them
    In other days.

The Veil and Other Poems (1921)

THE IMP WITHIN

'Rouse now, my dullard, and thy wits awake;
'Tis first of the morning. And I bid thee make —
No, not a vow; we have munched our fill of these
From crock of bone-dry crusts and mouse-gnawn cheese —
Nay, just one whisper in that long, long ear —
Awake; rejoice. Another Day is here! —

'A virgin wilderness, which, hour by hour,
Mere happy idleness shall bring to flower.
Barren and arid though its sands now seem,
Wherein oasis becks not, shines no stream,
Yet wake — and lo, 'tis lovelier than a dream!

'Plunge on, thy every footprint shall make fair
Its thirsty waste; and thy forecome despair
Undarken into sweet birds in the air,
Whose coursing wings and love-crazed summoning cries
Into infinity shall attract thine eyes.

'No . . .? Well, lest promise in performance faint,
A less inviting prospect will I paint.
I bid thee adjure thy Yesterday, and say:
"As *thou* wast, Enemy, so be To-day! —
Immure me in the same close narrow room;
Be hated toil the lamp to light its gloom;
Make stubborn my pen; sift dust into my ink;
Forbid mine eyes to see, my brain to think.
Scare off the words whereon the mind is set.
Make memory the power to forget.
Constrain imagination; bind its wing;
Forbid the unseen Enchantresses to sing.
Ay, do thy worst!"
                              'Vexed Spectre, prythee smile.
Even though that yesterday was bleak and sour,
Art thou a slave beneath its thong to cower?
Thou hast survived! And hither am I — again,
Kindling with mockery thy o'erlaboured brain.

[125]

Though scant the moments be wherein we meet,
Think what dark months would even one make sweet!

'Thy pen? Thy paper? Ah, my dear, be true.
Come quick To-morrow. Until then, Adieu.'

THE OLD ANGLER

Twilight leaned mirrored in a pool
  Where willow boughs swept green and hoar,
Silk-clear the water, calm and cool,
  Silent the weedy shore:

There in abstracted, brooding mood
  One fishing sate. His painted float
Motionless as a planet stood;
  Motionless his boat.

A melancholy soul was this,
  With lantern jaw, gnarled hand, vague eye;
Huddled in pensive solitariness
  He had fished existence by.

Empty his creel; stolen his bait —
  Impassively he angled on,
Though mist now showed the evening late
  And daylight wellnigh gone.

Suddenly, like a tongueless bell,
  Downward his gaudy cork did glide;
A deep, low-gathering, gentle swell
  Spread slowly far and wide.

Wheeped out his tackle from noiseless winch,
  And furtive as a thief, his thumb,
With nerve intense, wound inch by inch
  A line no longer numb.

What fabulous spoil could thus unplayed
  Gape upward to a mortal air? —
He stoops engrossed; his tanned cheek greyed;
  His heart stood still: for there,

[126]

Wondrously fairing, beneath the skin
   Of secretly bubbling water seen,
Swims, not the silver of scale and fin —
   But gold inmixt with green.

Deeply astir in oozy bed,
   The darkening mirror ripples and rocks:
And lo — a wan-pale, lovely head,
   Hook tangled in its locks!

Cold from her haunt — a Naiad slim.
   Shoulder and cheek gleamed ivory white;
Though now faint stars stood over him,
   The hour hard on night.

Her green eyes gazed like one half-blind
   In sudden radiance; her breast
Breathed the sweet air, while gently twined,
   'Gainst the cold water pressed,

Her lean webbed hands. She floated there,
   Light as a scentless petalled flower,
Water-drops dewing from her hair
   In tinkling beadlike shower.

So circling sidelong, her tender throat
   Uttered a grieving, desolate wail;
Shrill o'er the dark pool lapsed its note,
   Piteous as nightingale.

Ceased Echo. And he? — a life's remorse
   Welled to a tongue unapt to charm,
But never a word broke harsh and hoarse
   To quiet her alarm.

With infinite stealth his twitching thumb
   Tugged softly at the tautened gut,
Bubble-light, fair, her lips now dumb,
   She moved, and struggled not;

But with set, wild, unearthly eyes
   Pale-gleaming, fixed as if in fear,
She couched in the water, with quickening sighs
   And floated near.

[127]

In hollow heaven the stars were at play;
  Wan glow-worms greened the pool-side grass;
Dipped the wide-bellied boat. His prey
  Gazed on; nor breathed. Alas! —

Long sterile years had come and gone;
  Youth, like a distant dream, was sped;
Heart, hope, and eyes had hungered on. . . .
  He turned a shaking head,

And clumsily groped amid the gold,
  Sleek with night dews, of that tangling hair,
Till pricked his finger keen and cold
  The barb imbedded there.

Teeth clenched, he drew his knife —'Snip, snip,'—
  Groaned, and sate shivering back; and she,
Treading the water with birdlike dip,
  Shook her sweet shoulders free:

Drew backward, smiling, infatuate fair,
  His life's disasters in her eyes,
All longing and folly, grief, despair,
  Daydreams and mysteries.

She stooped her brow; laid low her cheek,
  And, steering on that silk-tressed craft,
Out from the listening, leaf-hung creek,
  Tossed up her chin, and laughed —

A mocking, icy, inhuman note.
  One instant flashed that crystal breast,
Leaned, and was gone. Dead-still the boat:
  And the deep dark at rest.

Flits moth to flower. A water-rat
  Noses the placid ripple. And lo!
Streams a lost meteor. Night is late,
  And daybreak zephyrs flow. . . .

And he — the cheated? Dusk till morn,
  Insensate, even of hope forsook,
He muttering squats, aloof, forlorn,
  Dangling a baitless hook.

THE WILLOW

Leans now the fair willow, dreaming
Amid her locks of green.
In the driving snow she was parched and cold,
And in midnight hath been
Swept by blasts of the void night,
Lashed by the rains.
Now of that wintry dark and bleak
No memory remains.

In mute desire she sways softly;
Thrilling sap up-flows;
She praises God in her beauty and grace,
Whispers delight. And there flows
A delicate wind from the Southern seas,
Kissing her leaves. She sighs.
While the birds in her tresses make merry;
Burns the Sun in the skies.

TITMOUSE

If you would happy company win,
Dangle a palm-nut from a tree,
Idly in green to sway and spin,
Its snow-pulped kernel for bait; and see
    A nimble titmouse enter in.

Out of earth's vast unknown of air,
Out of all summer, from wave to wave,
He'll perch, and prank his feathers fair,
Jangle a glass-clear wildering stave,
    And take his commons there —

This tiny son of life; this spright,
By momentary Human sought,
Plume will his wing in the dappling light,
Clash timbrel shrill and gay —
And into Time's enormous Nought,
    Sweet-fed, will flit away.

THE VEIL

I think and think; yet still I fail —
Why does this lady wear a veil?
Why thus elect to mask her face
Beneath that dainty web of lace?
The tip of a small nose I see,
And two red lips, set curiously
Like twin-born cherries on one stem,
And yet she has netted even them.
Her eyes, it's plain, survey with ease
All that to glance upon they please.
Yet, whether hazel, grey, or blue,
Or that even lovelier lilac hue,
I cannot guess: why — why deny
Such beauty to the passer-by?
Out of a bush a nightingale
May expound his song; beneath that veil
A happy mouth no doubt can make
English sound sweeter for its sake.
But then, why muffle in, like this,
What every blossomy wind would kiss?
Why in that little night disguise
A daylight face, those starry eyes?

THE FAIRY IN WINTER

There was a Fairy — flake of winter —
Who, when the snow came, whispering, Silence,
Sister crystal to crystal sighing,
Making of meadow argent palace,
    Night a star-sown solitude,
Cried 'neath her frozen eaves, 'I burn here!'

Wings diaphanous, beating bee-like,
Wand within fingers, locks enspangled,
Icicle foot, lip sharp as scarlet,
She lifted her eyes in her pitch-black hollow —
Green as stalks of weeds in water —
Breathed: stirred.

Rilled from her heart the ichor, coursing,
Flamed and awoke her slumbering magic.
Softlier than moth's her pinions trembled;
Out into blackness, light-like, she flittered,
Leaving her hollow cold, forsaken.

In air, o'er crystal, rang twangling night-wind.
Bare, rimed pine-woods murmured lament.

THE FLOWER

Horizon to horizon, lies outspread
The tenting firmament of day and night;
Wherein are winds at play; and planets shed
Amid the stars their gentle gliding light.

The huge world's sun flames on the snow-capped hills;
Cindrous his heat burns in the sandy plain;
With myriad spume-bows roaring ocean swills
The cold profuse abundance of the rain.

And man — a transient object in this vast,
Sighs o'er a universe transcending thought,
Afflicted by vague bodings of the past,
Driven toward a future, unforeseen, unsought.

Yet, see him, stooping low to naked weed
That meeks its blossom in his anxious eye,
Mark how he grieves, as if his heart did bleed,
And wheels his wondrous features to the sky;
As if, transfigured by so small a grace,
He sought Companion in earth's dwelling-place.

BEFORE DAWN

Dim-berried is the mistletoe
With globes of sheenless grey,
The holly mid ten thousand thorns
Smoulders its fires away;
And in the manger Jesu sleeps
This Christmas Day.

Bull unto bull with hollow throat
Makes echo every hill,
Cold sheep in pastures thick with snow
The air with bleatings fill;
While of his mother's heart this Babe
Takes His sweet will.

All flowers and butterflies lie hid,
The blackbird and the thrush
Pipe but a little as they flit
Restless from bush to bush;
Even to the robin Gabriel hath
Cried softly, 'Hush!'

Now night's astir with burning stars
In darkness of the snow;
Burdened with frankincense and myrrh
And gold the Strangers go
Into a dusk where one dim lamp
Burns faintly, Lo!

No snowdrop yet its small head nods,
In winds of winter drear;
No lark at casement in the sky
Sings matins shrill and clear;
Yet in this frozen mirk the Dawn
Breathes, Spring is here!

THE SPECTRE

In cloudy quiet of the day,
While thrush and robin perched mute on spray,
A spectre by the window sat,
Brooding thereat.

He marked the greenness of the Spring,
Daffodil blowing, bird a-wing —
Yet dark the house the years had made
Within that Shade.

Blinded the rooms wherein no foot falls.
Faded the portraits on the walls.
Reverberating, shakes the air
A river there.

Coursing in flood, its infinite roars;
From pit to pit its water pours;
And he, with countenance unmoved,
Hears cry: —'Beloved,

'Oh, ere the day be utterly spent,
Return, return, from banishment.
The night thick-gathers. Weep a prayer
For the true and fair!'

THE VOICE

'We are not often alone, we two,'
Mused a secret voice in my ear,
As the dying hues of afternoon
Lapsed into evening drear.

A withered leaf, wafted on in the street,
Like a wayless spectre, sighed;
Aslant on the roof-tops a sickly moon
Did mutely abide.

Yet waste though the shallowing day might seem,
And fainter than hope its rose,
Strangely that speech in my thoughts welled on;
As water in-flows:

Like remembered words once heard in a room
Wherein death kept far-away tryst;
'Not often alone, we two; but thou,
How sorely missed!'

THE HOUR-GLASS

Thou who know'st all the sorrows of this earth —
I pray Thee, ponder, ere again Thou turn
Thine hour-glass o'er again, since one sole birth,
To poor clay-cold humanity, makes yearn
A heart at passion with life's endless coil.
Thou givest thyself too strait a room therein.
For so divine a tree too poor a soil.
For so great agony what small peace to win.

[133]

Cast from that Ark of Heaven which is Thy home
The raven of hell may wander without fear;
But sadly wings the dove o'er floods to roam,
Nought but one tender sprig his eyes to cheer.
Nay, Lord, I speak in parables. But see!
'Tis stricken Man in Men that pleads with Thee.

IN THE DOCK

Pallid, mis-shapen he stands. The World's grimed thumb,
Now hooked securely in his matted hair,
Has haled him struggling from his poisonous slum
And flung him, mute as fish, close-netted there.

His bloodless hands entalon that iron rail.
He gloats in beastlike trance. His settling eyes
From staring face to face rove on — and quail.
Justice for carrion pants; and these the flies.

Voice after voice in smooth impartial drone
Erects horrific in his darkening brain
A timber framework, where agape, alone,
Bright life will kiss good-bye the cheek of Cain.

Sudden like wolf he cries; and sweats to see
When howls man's soul, it howls inaudibly.

THE WRECK

Storm and unconscionable winds once cast
On grinding shingle, masking gap-toothed rock,
This ancient hulk. Rent hull, and broken mast,
She sprawls sand-mounded, of sea birds the mock.
Her sailors, drowned, forgotten, rot in mould,
Or hang in stagnant quiet of the deep —
The brave, the afraid into one silence sold;
Their end a memory fainter than of sleep.
She held good merchandise. She paced in pride
The uncharted paths men trace in ocean's foam.
Now laps the ripple in her broken side,
And zephyr in tamarisk softly whispers, Home.

The dreamer scans her in the sea-blue air,
And, sipping of contrast, finds the day more fair.

THE SUICIDE

Did these night-hung houses,
Of quiet, starlit stone,
Breathe not a whisper — 'Stay,
Thou unhappy one;
Whither so secret away?'

Sighed not the unfriending wind,
Chill with nocturnal dew,
'Pause, pause, in thy haste,
O thou distraught! I too
Tryst with the Atlantic waste.'

Steep fell the drowsy street;
In slumber the world was blind:
Breathed not one midnight flower
Peace in thy broken mind? —
'Brief, yet sweet, is life's hour.'

Syllabled thy last tide —
By as dark moon stirred,
And doomed to forlorn unrest —
Not one compassionate word? . . .
'Cold is this breast.'

DRUGGED

Inert in his chair,
In a candle's guttering glow;
His bottle empty,
His fire sunk low;
With drug-sealed lids shut fast,
Unsated mouth ajar,
This darkened phantasm walks
Where nightmares are:

In a frenzy of life and light,
Crisscross — a menacing throng —
They gibe, they squeal at the stranger,
Jostling along,
Their faces cadaverous grey:
While on high from an attic stare
Horrors, in beauty apparelled,
Down the dark air.

A stream gurgles over its stones,
The chambers within are a-fire.
Stumble his shadowy feet
Through shine, through mire;
And the flames leap higher.
In vain yelps the wainscot mouse;
In vain beats the hour;
Vacant, his body must drowse
Until daybreak flower —

Staining these walls with its rose,
And the draughts of the morning shall stir
Cold on cold brow, cold hands.
And the wanderer
Back to flesh house must return.
Lone soul — in horror to see,
Than dream more meagre and awful,
Reality.

WHO'S THAT?

Who's that? Who's that? . . .
Oh, only a leaf on the stone;
And the sigh of the air in the fire.
    Yet it seemed, as I sat,
Came company — not my own;
Stood there, with ardent gaze over dark, bowed shoulder
        thrown,
    Till the dwindling flames leaped higher,
    And showed fantasy flown.

Yet, though the cheat is clear —
From transient illusion grown;
In the vague of my mind those eyes
    Still haunt me. One stands so near
I could take his hand, and be gone: —
No more in this house of dreams to sojourn aloof, alone:
    Could sigh, with full heart, and arise,
    And choke, 'Lead on!'

HOSPITAL

Welcome! Enter! This is the Inn at the Cross Roads,
Sign of the *Rising Sun*, of the *World's End*:
Ay, O Wanderer, footsore, weary, forsaken,
    Knock, and we will open unto thee — Friend.

Gloomy our stairs of stone, obscure the portal;
Burdened the air with a breath from the further shore;
Yet in our courtyard plays an invisible fountain,
    Ever flowers unfading nod at the door.

Ours is much company, and yet none is lonely;
Some with a smile may pay and some with a sigh;
So all be healed, restored, contented — it is no matter;
    So all be happy at heart to bid good-bye.

But know, our clocks are the world's; Night's wings are leaden;
Pain languidly sports with the hours: have courage, sir!
We wake but to bring thee slumber, our drowsy syrups
    Sleep beyond dreams on the weary will confer.

Ghosts may be ours; but gaze thou not too closely
If haply in chill of the dark thou rouse to see
One silent of foot, hooded, and hollow of visage,
    Pause, with secret eyes, to peer out at thee.

He is the Ancient Tapster of this Hostel,
To him at length even we all keys must resign;
And if he beckon, Stranger, thou too must follow —
    Love and all peace be thine.

A SIGN

How shall I know when the end of things is coming?
The dark swifts flitting, the drone-bees humming;
The fly on the window-pane bedazedly strumming;
Ice on the waterbrooks their clear chimes dumbing —
How shall I know that the end of things is coming?

The stars in their stations will shine glamorous in the black:
Emptiness, as ever, haunt the great Star Sack;
And Venus, proud and beautiful, go down to meet the day,
Pale in phosphorescence of the green sea spray —
How shall I know that the end of things is coming?

Head asleep on pillow; the peewits at their crying;
A strange face in dreams to my rapt phantasma sighing;
Silence beyond words of anguished passion;
Or stammering an answer in the tongue's cold fashion —
How shall I know that the end of things is coming?

Haply on strange roads I shall be, the moorland's peace around me;
Or counting up a fortune to which Destiny hath bound me;
Or — Vanity of Vanities — the honey of the Fair;
Or a greybeard, lost to memory, on the cobbles in my chair —
How shall I know that the end of things is coming?

The drummers will be drumming; the fiddlers at their thrumming;
Nuns at their beads; the mummers at their mumming;
Heaven's solemn Seraph stoopt weary o'er his summing;
The palsied fingers plucking, the way-worn feet numbing —
    And the end of things coming.

GOOD-BYE

The last of last words spoken is, Good-bye —
The last dismantled flower in the weed-grown hedge,
The last thin rumour of a feeble bell far ringing,
The last blind rat to spurn the mildewed rye.

A hardening darkness glasses the haunted eye,
Shines into nothing the watcher's burnt-out candle,
Wreathes into scentless nothing the wasting incense,
Faints in the outer silence the hunting-cry.

Love of its muted music breathes no sigh,
Thought in her ivory tower gropes in her spinning,
Toss on in vain the whispering trees of Eden,
Last of all last words spoken is, Good-bye.

THE MONOLOGUE

Alas, O Lovely One,
    Imprisoned here,
I tap; thou answerest not,
    I doubt, and fear.
Yet transparent as glass these walls,
    If thou lean near.

Last dusk, at those high bars
    There came, scarce-heard,
Claws, fluttering feathers,
    Of deluded bird —
With one shrill, scared, faint note
    The silence stirred.

Rests in that corner,
    In puff of dust, a straw —
Vision of harvest-fields
    I never saw,
Of strange green streams and hills,
    Forbidden by law.

These things I whisper,
    For I see — in mind —
Thy caged cheek whiten
    At the wail of wind,
That thin breast wasting; unto
    Woe resigned.

Take comfort, listen!
    Once we twain were free;
There was a Country —
    Lost the memory . . .
Lay thy cold brow on hand,
    And dream with me.

Awaits me torture;
    I have smelt their rack;
From spectral groaning wheel
    Have turned me back;
Thumbscrew and boot, and then —
    The yawning sack.

Lean closer, then!
    Lay palm on stony wall.

Let but thy ghost beneath
    Thine eyelids call:
'Courage, my brother!' Nought
    Can then appal.

Yet coward, coward am I,
    And drink I must
When clanks the pannikin
    With the longed-for crust;
Though heart within is sour
    With disgust.

Long hours there are,
    When mutely tapping — well,
Is it to Vacancy
    I these tidings tell?
Knock these numb fingers against
    An empty cell?

Nay, answer not.
    Let still mere longing make
Thy presence sure to me,
    While in doubt I shake:
Be but my Faith in thee,
    For sanity's sake.

AWAKE!

Why hath the rose faded and fallen, yet these eyes have not seen?
Why hath the bird sung shrill in the tree — and this mind deaf
    and cold?
Why have the rains of summer veiled her flowers with their sheen
    And this black heart untold?

Here is calm Autumn now, the woodlands quake,
And, where this splendour of death lies under the tread,
The spectre of frost will stalk, and a silence make,
    And snow's white shroud be spread.

O self! O self! Wake from thy common sleep!
Fling off the destroyer's net. He hath blinded and bound thee.
In nakedness sit; pierce thy stagnation, and weep;
    Or corrupt in thy grave — all Heaven around thee.

NOT THAT WAY

No, no. Guard thee. Get thee gone.
  Not that way.
See; the louring clouds glide on,
Skirting West to South; and see,
The green light under that sycamore tree —
  Not that way.

There the leaden trumpets blow,
  Solemn and slow.
There the everlasting walls
Frown above the waterfalls
  Silver and cold;
  Timelessly old:
  Not that way.

Not toward Death, who, stranger, fairer,
Than any siren turns his head —
Than sea-couched siren, arched with rainbows,
Where knell the waves of her ocean bed.
Alas, that beauty hangs her flowers
For lure of his demoniac powers:
Alas, that from these eyes should dart
Such piercing summons to thy heart;
That mine in frenzy of longing beats,
Still lusting for these gross deceits.
  Not that way!

FOG

Stagnant this wintry gloom. Afar
The farm-cock bugles his 'Qui vive?'
The towering elms are lost in mist;
Birds in the thorn-trees huddle a-whist;
 The mill-race waters grieve.
  Our shrouded day
  Dwindles away
 To final black of eve.

Beyond these shades in space of air
Ride exterrestrial beings by?
Their colours burning rich and fair,

Where noon's sunned valleys lie?
With inaudible music are they sweet —
Bell, hoof, soft lapsing cry?

Turn marvellous faces, each to each? —
Lips innocent of sigh,
Or groan or fear, sorrow and grief,
Clear brow and falcon eye;
Bare foot, bare shoulder in the heat,
And hair like flax? Do their horses beat
Their way through wildernesses infinite
Of starry-crested trees, blue sward,
And gold-chasm'd mountain, steeply shored
O'er lakes of sapphire dye?

Mingled with lisping speech, faint laughter,
Echoes the Phoenix' scream of joyance
        Mounting on high? —
Light-bathed vistas and divine sweet mirth,
Beyond dream of spirits penned to earth,
Condemned to pine and die? . . .
Hath serving Nature, bidden of the gods,
Thick-screened Man's narrow sky,
And hung these Stygian veils of fog
        To hide his dingied sty? —
The gods who yet, at mortal birth,
        Bequeathed him Fantasy?

SOTTO VOCE

To Edward Thomas

The haze of noon wanned silver-grey
The soundless mansion of the sun:
The air made visible in his ray,
Like molten glass from furnace run,
Quivered o'er heat-baked turf and stone
And the flower of the gorse burned on —
Burned softly as gold of a child's fair hair
Along each spiky spray, and shed
Almond-like incense in the air
Whereon our senses fed.

[142]

At foot — a few sparse harebells: blue
And still as were the friend's dark eyes
That dwelt on mine, transfixèd through
With sudden ecstatic surmise.

'Hst!' he cried softly, smiling, and lo,
Stealing amidst that maze gold-green,
I heard a whispering music flow
From guileful throat of bird, unseen: —
So delicate the straining ear
Scarce carried its faint syllabling
Into a heart caught up to hear
That inmost pondering
Of bird-like self with self. We stood,
In happy trance-like solitude,
Hearkening a lullay grieved and sweet —
As when on isle uncharted beat
'Gainst coral at the palm-tree's root,
With brine-clear, snow-white foam afloat,
The wailing, not of water or wind —
A husht, far, wild, divine lament,
When Prospero his wizardry bent
Winged Ariel to bind. . . .

Then silence, and o'er-flooding noon.
I raised my head; smiled too. And he —
Moved his great hand, the magic gone —
Gently amused to see
My ignorant wonderment. He sighed.
'It was a nightingale,' he said,
'That *sotto voce* cons the song
He'll sing when dark is spread;
And Night's vague hours are sweet and long,
And we are laid abed.'

THE IMAGINATION'S PRIDE

Be not too wildly amorous of the far,
  Nor lure thy fantasy to its utmost scope.
Read by a taper when the needling star
  Burns red with menace in heaven's midnight cope.
Friendly thy body: guard its solitude.
  Sure shelter is thy heart. It once had rest
Where founts miraculous thy lips endewed,
  Yet nought loomed further than thy mother's breast.

O brave adventure! Ay, at danger slake
  Thy thirst, lest life in thee should, sickening, quail;
But not toward nightmare goad a mind awake,
  Nor to forbidden horizons bend thy sail —
Seductive outskirts whence in trance prolonged
  Thy gaze, at stretch of what is sane-secure,
Dreams out on steeps by shapes demoniac thronged
  And vales wherein alone the dead endure.

Nectarous those flowers, yet with venom sweet.
  Thick-juiced with poison hang those fruits that shine
Where sick phantasmal moonbeams brood and beat,
  And dark imaginations ripe the vine.
Bethink thee: every enticing league thou wend
  Beyond the mark where life its bound hath set
Will lead thee at length where human pathways end
  And the dark enemy spreads his maddening net.

Comfort thee, comfort thee. Thy Father knows
  How wild man's ardent spirit, fainting, yearns
For mortal glimpse of death's immortal rose,
  The garden where the invisible blossom burns.
Humble thy trembling knees; confess thy pride;
  Be weary. Oh, whithersoever thy vaunting rove,
His deepest wisdom harbours in thy side,
  In thine own bosom hides His utmost love.

THE WANDERERS

Within my mind two spirits strayed
From out their still and purer air,
And there a moment's sojourn made;
As lovers will in woodlands bare.
Nought heeded they where now they stood,
Since theirs its alien solitude
Beyond imagination fair.

The light an earthly candle gives,
When it is quenched leaves only dark;
Theirs yet in clear remembrance lives
And, still within, I whispered, 'Hark';
As one who faintly on high has heard
The call note of a hidden bird
Even sweeter than the lark.

[144]

Yet 'twas their silence breathed only this —
'I love you.' As if flowers might say,
'Such is our natural fragrantness';
Or dewdrop at the break of day
Cry, 'Thus I beam.' Each turned a head,
But each its own clear radiance shed
With joy and peace at play.

So in a gloomy London street
Princes from Eastern realms might pause
In secret converse, then retreat.
Yet without haste passed these from sight;
As if a human mind were not
Wholly a dark and dismal spot —
At least in their own light.

THE CORNER STONE

Sterile these stones
By time in ruin laid.
Yet many a creeping thing
Its haven has made
In these least crannies, where falls
Dark's dew, and noonday shade.

The claw of the tender bird
Finds lodgement here;
Dye-winged butterflies poise;
Emmet and beetle steer
Their busy course; the bee
Drones, laden, near.

Their myriad-mirrored eyes
Great day reflect.
By their exquisite farings
Is this granite specked;
Is trodden to infinite dust;
By gnawing lichens decked.

Toward what eventual dream
Sleeps its cold on,
When into ultimate dark
These lives shall be gone,
And even of man not a shadow remain
Of all he has done?

THE SPIRIT OF AIR

Coral and clear emerald,
And amber from the sea,
Lilac-coloured amethyst,
Chalcedony;
The lovely Spirit of Air
Floats on a cloud and doth ride,
Clad in the beauties of earth
Like a bride.

So doth she haunt me; and words
Tell but a tithe of the tale.
Sings all the sweetness of Spring
Even in the nightingale?
Nay, but with echoes she cries
Of the valley of love;
Dews on the thorns at her feet,
And darkness above.

THE UNFINISHED DREAM

Rare-sweet the air in that unimagined country —
    My spirit had wandered far
From its weary body close-enwrapt in slumber
    Where its home and earth-friends are;

A milk-like air — and of light all abundance;
    And there a river clear
Painting the scene like a picture on its bosom,
    Green foliage drifting near.

No sign of life I saw, as I pressed onward,
    Fish, nor beast, nor bird,
Till I came to a hill clothed in flowers to its summit,
    Then shrill small voices I heard.

And I saw from concealment a company of elf-folk
    With faces strangely fair,
Talking their unearthly scattered talk together,
    A bind of green-grasses in their hair,

Marvellously gentle, feater far than children,
    In gesture, mien and speech,
Hastening onward in translucent shafts of sunshine
    And gossiping each with each.

Straw-light their locks, on neck and shoulder falling,
    Faint of almond the silks they wore,
Spun not of worm, but as if inwoven of moonbeams
    And foam on rock-bound shore;

Like lank-legged grasshoppers in June-tide meadows,
    Amalillios of the day,
Hungrily gazed upon by me — a stranger,
    In unknown regions astray.

Yet, happy beyond words, I marked their sunlit faces,
    Stealing soft enchantment from their eyes,
Tears in my own confusing their small image,
    Hearkening their bead-like cries.

They passed me, unseeing, a waft of flocking linnets;
    Sadly I fared on my way;
And came in my dream to a dreamlike habitation,
    Close-shut, festooned, and grey.

Pausing, I gazed at the porch dust-still, vine-wreathèd,
    Worn on the stone steps thereto,
Mute hung its bell, whence a stony head looked downward,
    Grey 'gainst the sky's pale-blue —

Strange to me: strange. . . .

MUSIC

O restless fingers — not that music make!
Bidding old griefs from out the past awake,
And pine for memory's sake.

Those strings thou callest from quiet to yearn,
Of other hearts did hapless secrets learn,
And thy strange skill will turn

To uses that thy bosom dreams not of:
Ay, summon from their dark and dreadful grove
The chaunting, pale-cheeked votaries of love.

Stay now, and hearken! From that far-away
Cymbal on cymbal beats, the fierce horns bray,
Stars in their sapphire fade, 'tis break of day.

[147]

Green are those meads, foam-white the billow's crest,
And Night, withdrawing in the cavernous West,
Flings back her shadow on the salt sea's breast.

Snake-haired, snow-shouldered, pure as flame and dew,
Her strange gaze burning slumbrous eyelids through,
Rises the Goddess from the waves dark blue.

THE SON OF MELANCHOLY

Unto blest Melancholy's house one happy day
    I took my way:
Into a chamber was shown, whence could be seen
Her flowerless garden, dyed with sunlit green
    Of myrtle, box, and bay.

Cool were its walls, shade-mottled, green and gold.
    In heavy fold
Hung antique tapestries, from whose fruit and flower
Light had the bright hues stolen, hour by hour,
    And time worn thin and old.

Silence, as of a virginal laid aside,
    Did there abide.
But not for voice or music was I fain,
Only to see a long-loved face again —
    For her sole company sighed.

And while I waited, giving memory praise,
    My musing gaze
Lit on the one sole picture in the room,
Which hung, as if in hiding, in the gloom
    From evening's stealing rays.

Framed in fast-fading gilt, a child gazed there,
    Lovely and fair;
A face whose happiness was like sunlight spent
On some poor desolate soul in banishment,
    Mutely his grief to share.

Long, long I stood in trance of that glad face,
    Striving to trace
The semblance that, disquieting, it bore
To one whom memory could not restore,
    Nor fix in time and space.

[148]

Sunk deep in brooding thus, a voice I heard
    Whisper its word:
I turned — and, stooping in the threshold, stood
She — the dark mistress of my solitude,
    Who smiled, nor stirred.

Her ghost gazed darkly from her pondering eyes
    Charged with surmise;
Challenging mine, between mockery and fear,
She breathed her greeting, '*Thou*, my only dear!
    Wherefore such heavy sighs?'

'But this?' One instant lids her scrutiny veiled;
    Her wan cheek paled.
'This child?' I asked. 'Its picture brings to mind
Remembrance faint and far, past thought to find,
    And yet by time unstaled.'

Smiling, aloof, she turned her narrow head,
'Make thou my face thy glass,' she cried and said.
'What wouldst thou see therein — thine own, or mine?
O foolish one, what wonder thou didst pine?

'Long thou hast loved me; yet hast absent been.
See now: Dark night hath pressed an entrance in.
Jealous! thou dear? Nay, come; by taper's beam
Share thou this pictured Joy with me, though only a dream.'

THE QUIET ENEMY

Hearken! — now the hermit bee
Drones a quiet threnody;
Greening on the stagnant pool
The criss-cross light slants silken-cool;
In the venomed yew tree wings
Preen and flit. The linnet sings.

Gradually the brave sun
Droops to a day's journey done;
In the marshy flats abide
Mists to muffle midnight-tide.
Puffed within the belfry tower
Hungry owls drowse out their hour. . . .

Walk in beauty. Vaunt thy rose.
Flaunt thy transient loveliness.
Pace for pace with thee there goes
A shape that hath not come to bless.
I thine enemy? . . . Nay, nay.
I can only watch and wait
Patient treacherous time away,
Hold ajar the wicket gate.

THE FAMILIAR

'Are you far away?'
'Yea, I am far — far;
Where the green wave shelves to the sand,
And the rainbows are;
And an ageless sun beats fierce
From an empty sky:
There, O thou Shadow forlorn,
Is the wraith of thee, I.'

'Are you happy, most Lone?'
'Happy, forsooth!
Who am eyes of the air; the voice of the foam;
Ah, happy in truth.
My hair is astream, this cheek
Glistens like silver, and see,
As the gold to the dross, the ghost in the mirk,
I am calling to thee.'

'Nay, I am bound.
And your cry faints out in your mind.
Peace not on earth have I found,
Yet to earth am resigned.
Cease thy shrill mockery, Voice,
Nor answer again.'
'O Master, thick cloud shuts thee out
And cold tempests of rain.'

MAERCHEN

Soundless the moth-flit, crisp the death-watch tick;
Crazed in her shaken arbour bird did sing;
Slow wreathed the grease adown from soot-clogged wick:
   The Cat looked long and softly at the King.

Mouse frisked and scampered, leapt, gnawed, squeaked;
Small at the window looped cowled bat a-wing;
The dim-lit rafters with the night-mist reeked:
   The Cat looked long and softly at the King.

O wondrous robe enstarred, in night dyed deep:
O air scarce-stirred with the Court's far junketing:
O stagnant Royalty — A-swoon? Asleep?
   The Cat looked long and softly at the King.

GOLD

Sighed the wind to the wheat: —
'The Queen who is slumbering there,
Once bewildered the rose;
Scorned, "Thou un-fair!"
Once, from that bird-whirring court,
Ascended the ruinous stair.
Aloft, on that weed-hung turret, suns
Smote on her hair —
Of a gold by Archiac sought,
Of a gold sea-hid,
Of a gold that from core of quartz
No flame shall bid
Pour into light of the air
For God's Jews to see.'

Mocked the wheat to the wind: —
'Kiss me! Kiss me!'

THE GALLIASS

'Tell me, tell me,
   Unknown stranger,
When shall I sight me
   That tall ship
On whose flower-wreathed counter is gilded, *Sleep*?'

'Landsman, landsman,
Lynx nor kestrel
Ne'er shall descry from
Ocean steep
That midnight-stealing, high-pooped galliass, *Sleep*.'

'Promise me, Stranger,
Though I mark not
When cold night-tide's
Shadows creep
Thou wilt keep unwavering watch for *Sleep*.'

'Myriad the lights are,
Wayworn landsman,
Rocking the dark through
On the deep:
She alone burns none to prove her *Sleep*.

THE DECOY

'Tell us, O pilgrim, what strange She
Lures and decoys your wanderings on?
Cheek, eye, brow, lip, you scan each face,
Smile, ponder — and are gone.

'Are we not flesh and blood? Mark well,
We touch you with our hands. We speak
A tongue that may earth's secrets tell:
Why further will you seek?'

'Far have I come, and far must fare.
Noon and night and morning-prime,
I search the long road, bleak and bare,
That fades away in Time.

'On the world's brink its wild weeds shake,
And there my own dust, dark with dew,
Burns with a rose that, sleep or wake,
Beacons me —"Follow true!"'

'Her name, crazed soul? And her degree?
What peace, prize, profit in her breast?'
'A thousand cheating names hath she;
And none fore-tokens rest.'

[152]

SUNK LYONESSE

In sea-cold Lyonesse,
When the Sabbath eve shafts down
On the roofs, walls, belfries
Of the foundered town,
The Nereids pluck their lyres
Where the green translucency beats,
And with motionless eyes at gaze
Make minstrelsy in the streets.

And the ocean water stirs
In salt-worn casemate and porch.
Plies the blunt-snouted fish
With fire in his skull for torch.
And the ringing wires resound;
And the unearthly lovely weep,
In lament of the music they make
In the sullen courts of sleep:
Whose marble flowers bloom for aye:
And — lapped by the moon-guiled tide —
Mock their carver with heart of stone,
Caged in his stone-ribbed side.

THE CATECHISM

'Hast thou then nought wiser to bring
Than worn-out songs of moon and of rose?'
'Cracked my voice, and broken my wing,
       God knows.'

'Tell'st thou no truth of the life that *is*;
Seek'st thou from heaven no pitying sign?'
'Ask thine own heart these mysteries,
       Not mine.'

'Where then the faith thou hast brought to seed?
Where the sure hope thy soul would feign?'
'Never ebbed sweetness — even out of a weed —
       In vain.'

'Fool. The night comes. . . . 'Tis late. Arise.
Cold lap the waters of Jordan stream.'
'Deep be their flood, and tranquil thine eyes
       With a dream.'

[153]

FUTILITY

Sink, thou strange heart, unto thy rest.
Pine now no more, to pine in vain.
Doth not the moon on heaven's breast
Call the floods home again?

Doth not the summer faint at last?
Do not her restless rivers flow
When that her transient day is past
To hide them in ice and snow?

All this — thy world — an end shall make,
Planet to sun return again;
The universe, to sleep from wake,
In a last peace remain.

Alas, the futility of care
That, spinning thought to thought, doth weave
An idle argument on the air
We love not, nor believe.

WHO?

1st Stranger: Who walks with us on the hills?
2nd Stranger: I cannot see for the mist.
3rd Stranger: Running water I hear,
Keeping lugubrious tryst
With its cresses and grasses and weeds,
In the white obscure light from the sky.
2nd Stranger: Who walks with us on the hills?
Wild Bird: Ay! . . . Aye! . . . *Ay! . . .*

A RIDDLE

The mild noon air of Spring again
Lapped shimmering in that sea-lulled lane.
Hazel was budding; wan as snow
The leafless blackthorn was a-blow.

A chaffinch clankt, a robin woke
An eerie stave in the leafless oak.
Green mocked at green; lichen and moss
The rain-worn slate did softly emboss.

From out her winter lair, at sigh
Of the warm South wind, a butterfly
Stepped, quaffed her honey; on painted fan
Her labyrinthine flight began.

Wondrously solemn, golden and fair,
The high sun's rays beat everywhere;
Yea, touched my cheek and mouth, as if,
Equal with stone, to me 'twould give

Its light and life.
                    O restless thought,
Contented not! With 'Why' distraught.
Whom asked you then your riddle small? —
'If hither came no man at all

'Through this grey-green, sea-haunted lane,
Would it mere blackened naught remain?
Strives it this beauty and life to express
Only in human consciousness?

'Or, rather, idly breaks he in
To an Eden innocent of sin;
And, prouder than to be afraid,
Forgets his Maker in the made?'

THE OWL

What if to edge of dream,
When the spirit is come,
Shriek the hunting owl,
And summon it home —
To the fear-stirred heart
And the ancient dread
Of man, when cold root or stone
Pillowed roofless head?

Clangs not at last the hour
When roof shelters not;
And the ears are deaf,
And all fears forgot:
Since the spirit too far has fared
For summoning scream
Of any strange fowl on earth
To shatter its dream?

THE LAST COACHLOAD

To Colin

Crashed through the woods that lumbering Coach. The dust
Of flinted roads bepowdering felloe and hood.
Its gay paint cracked, its axles red with rust,
It lunged, lurched, toppled through a solitude

Of whispering boughs, and feathery, nid-nod grass.
Plodded the fetlocked horses. Glum and mum,
Its ancient Coachman recked not where he was,
Nor into what strange haunt his wheels were come.

Crumbling the leather of his dangling reins;
Worn to a cow's tuft his stumped, idle whip;
Sharp eyes of beast and bird in the trees' green lanes
Gleamed out like stars above a derelict ship.

'Old Father Time — Time — Time!' jeered twittering throat.
A squirrel capered on the leader's rump,
Slithered a weasel, peered a thief-like stoat,
In sandy warren beat on the coney's thump.

Mute as a mammet in his saddle sate
The hunched Postilion, clad in magpie trim;
The bright flies buzzed around his hairless pate;
Yaffle and jay squawked mockery at him.

Yet marvellous peace and amity breathed there.
Tranquil the labyrinths of this sundown wood.
Musking its chaces, bloomed the brier-rose fair;
Spellbound as if in trance the pine-trees stood.

Through moss and pebbled rut the wheels rasped on;
That Ancient drowsing on his box. And still
The bracken track with glazing sunbeams shone;
Laboured the horses, straining at the hill. . . .

But now — a verdurous height with eve-shade sweet;
Far, far to West the Delectable Mountains glowed.
Above, Night's canopy; at the horses' feet
A sea-like honied waste of flowers flowed.

There fell a pause of utter quiet. And —
Out from one murky window glanced an eye,
Stole from the other a lean, groping hand,
The padded door swung open with a sigh.

And — *Exeunt Omnes!* None to ask the fare —
A myriad human Odds in a last release
Leap out incontinent, snuff the incensed air;
A myriad parched-up voices whisper, 'Peace.'

On, on, and on — a stream, a flood, they flow.
O wondrous vale of jocund buds and bells!
Like vanishing smoke the rainbow legions glow,
Yet still the enravished concourse sweeps and swells.

All journeying done. Rest now from lash and spur —
Laughing and weeping, shoulder and elbow — 'twould seem
That Coach capacious all Infinity were,
And these the fabulous figments of a dream.

Mad for escape; frenzied each breathless mote,
Lest rouse the Old Enemy from his death-still swoon,
Lest crack that whip again — they fly, they float,
Scamper, breathe — 'Paradise!' abscond, are gone. . . .

AN EPITAPH

Last, Stone, a little yet;
And then this dust forget.
But thou, fair Rose, bloom on.
For she who is gone
Was lovely too; nor would she grieve to be
Sharing in solitude her dreams with thee.

BITTER WATERS

In a dense wood, a drear wood,
    Dark water is flowing;
Deep, deep, beyond sounding,
    A flood ever flowing.

There harbours no wild bird,
    No wanderer stays there;
Wreathed in mist, sheds pale Ishtar
    Her sorrowful rays there.

Take thy net; cast thy line;
    Manna sweet be thy baiting;
Time's desolate ages
    Shall still find thee waiting

For quick fish to rise there,
    Or butterfly wooing,
Or flower's honeyed beauty,
    Or wood-pigeon cooing.

Inland wellsprings are sweet;
    But to lips, parched and dry,
Salt, salt is the savour
    Of these; faint their sigh.

Bitter Babylon's waters.
    Zion, distant and fair.
We hanged up our harps
    On the trees that are there.

[158]

THE MOTH

Isled in the midnight air,
Musked with the dark's faint bloom,
Out into glooming and secret haunts
    The flame cries, 'Come!'

Lovely in dye and fan,
A-tremble in shimmering grace,
A moth from her winter swoon
    Uplifts her face:

Stares from her glamorous eyes;
Wafts her on plumes like mist;
In ecstasy swirls and sways
    To her strange tryst.

THE FLOWER

Listen, I who love thee well
Have travelled far, and secrets tell;
Cold the moon that gleams thine eyes,
Yet beneath her further skies
Rests, for thee, a paradise.

I have plucked a flower in proof,
Frail, in earthly light, forsooth:
See, invisible it lies
In this palm: now veil thine eyes:
Quaff its fragrancies!

Would indeed my throat had skill
To breathe thee music, faint and still—
Music learned in dreaming deep
In those lands, from Echo's lip. . . .
'Twould lull thy soul to sleep.

FORGIVENESS

'O thy flamed cheek,
Those locks with weeping wet,
Eyes that, forlorn and meek,
On mine are set.

'Poor hands, poor feeble wings,
Folded, a-droop, O sad!
See, 'tis my heart that sings
To make thee glad.

'My mouth breathes love, thou dear.
All that I am and know
Is thine. My breast — draw near:
Be grieved not so!'

MIRAGE

. . . And burned the topless towers of Ilium

Strange fabled face! From sterile shore to shore
O'er plunging seas, thick-sprent with glistening brine,
The voyagers of the world with sail and heavy oar
    Have sought thy shrine.
    Beauty inexorable hath lured them on:
Remote unnamèd stars enclustering gleam —
Burn in thy flowered locks, though creeping daylight wan
    Prove thee but dream.

Noonday to night the enigma of thine eyes
Frets with desire their travel-wearied brain,
Till in the vast of dark the ice-cold moon arise
    And pour them peace again:
    And with malign mirage uprears an isle
Of fountain and palm, and courts of jasmine and rose,
Whence far decoy of siren throats their souls beguile,
    And maddening fragrance flows.

Lo, in the milken light, in tissue of gold
Thine apparition gathers in the air —
Nay, but the seas are deep, and the round world old,
    And thou art named, Despair.

FLOTSAM

Screamed the far sea-mew. On the mirroring sands
Bell-shrill the oyster-catchers. Burned the sky.
Couching my cheeks upon my sun-scorched hands,
Down from bare rock I gazed. The sea swung by

Dazzling dark blue and verdurous, quiet with snow,
Empty with loveliness, with music a-roar,
Her billowing summits heaving noon-aglow —
Crashed the Atlantic on the cliff-ringed shore.

Drowsed by the tumult of that moving deep,
Sense into outer silence fainted, fled;
And rising softly, from the fields of sleep,
Stole to my eyes a lover from the dead;

Crying an incantation — learned, Where? When? . . .
White swirled the foam, a fount, a blinding gleam
Of ice-cold breast, cruel eyes, wild mouth — and then
A still dirge echoing on from dream to dream.

CRAZED

I know a pool where nightshade preens
Her poisonous fruitage in the moon;
Where the frail aspen her shadow leans
In midnight cold a-swoon.

I know a meadow flat with gold —
A million million burning flowers
In moon-sun's thirst their buds unfold
Beneath his blazing showers.

I saw a crazèd face, did I,
Stare from the lattice of a mill,
While the lank sails clacked idly by
High on the windy hill.

[161]

MOURN'ST THOU NOW?

Long ago from radiant palace,
Dream-bemused, in flood of moon,
Stole the princess Seraphita
Into forest gloom.

Wail of hemlock; cold the dewdrops;
Danced the Dryads in the chace;
Heavy hung ambrosial fragrance;
Moonbeams blanched her ravished face.

Frail and clear the notes delusive;
Mocking phantoms in a rout
Thridded the night-cloistered thickets,
Wove their sorceries in and out. . . .

Mourn'st thou not? Or do thine eyelids
Frame a vision dark, divine,
O'er this imp of star and wild-flower —
Of a god once thine?

The Fleeting and Other Poems (1933)

IN THE GARDEN

A mild parochial talk was ours;
The air of afternoon was sweet
With burthen of the sun-parched flowers;
His fiery beams in fury beat
From out the O of space, and made,
Wherever leaves his glare let through,
Circlets of brilliance in the shade
Of his unfathomable blue.

Old Dr. Salmon sat pensive and grey,
And Archie's tongue was never still,
While dear Miss Arbuthnot fanned away
The stress of walking up the hill.
And little Bertha? — how bony a cheek!
How ghast an eye! Poor mite. . . . That pause —
When not even tactful tongues could speak! . . .
The drowsy Cat pushed out her claws.

A bland, unvexing talk was ours —
Sharing that gentle gilded cage —
Manners and morals its two brief hours
Proffered alike to youth and age.
Why break so pleasing a truce? — forfend!
Why on such sweetness and light intrude?
Why bid the child, 'Cough, "*Ah!*" ' — and end
Our complaisance; her solitude?

PEEPING TOM

I was there — by the curtains
When some men brought a box:
And one at the house of
    Miss Emily knocks:

[163]

A low *rat-tat-tat*.
The door opened — and then,
Slowly mounting the steps, stooped
In the strange men.

Then the door darkly shut,
And I saw their legs pass,
Like an insect's, Miss Emily's
Window-glass —

Though why all her blinds
Have been hanging so low
These dumb foggy days,
I don't know.

Yes, only last week
I watched her for hours,
Potting out for the winter her
Balcony flowers.

And this very Sunday
She mused there a space,
Gazing into the street, with
The vacantest face:

Then turned her long nose
And looked up at the skies —
One you would not have thought
Weather-wise!

Yet . . . well, out stepped the men —
One ferrety-fair —
With gentlemen's hats, and
Whiskers and hair;

And paused in the porch.
Then smooth, solemn, grey,
They climbed to their places,
And all drove away

In their square varnished carriage,
The horse full of pride,
With a tail like a charger's:
They all sate outside.

Then the road became quiet:
Her house stiff and staid —
Like a Stage — while you wait
  For the Harlequinade . . .

But what can Miss Emily
Want with a box
So long, narrow, shallow,
  And without any locks?

EPISODES

'Oh! Raining! Look!' she whispered —
        Gazing out
On wheat-fields parched with drought,
And trees that yet in prime
Even of summertime
Showed yellow in their green;
But now, as with delight,
Showered down their withered leaves
Among the untimely sheaves
Of harvest, poor and lean:
      'And I, alas!'
      She sighed,
'This day to be a bride!'

Fair shone the sick man's moon
        Upon his bed,
And her cold silver shed.
Glazed eyes, in wasted face,
He marked her solemn pace,
As on, from height to height,
She to her zenith won,
And the wide fields below
Made lovely — as with snow —
Transfiguring the night.
      'Thou courtesan!'
      Mocked he,
'Would'st thou, then, lie with *me*!'

Loud sounded out the Trump:
        In vestry chill.
Its every stone a thrill,
The parson leaned an ear,
With pouted lip, to hear.

But now a silence wells,
As of a sea at rest,
Stilling the honeyed air —
With fruit and flowers made fair —
As mute as his own bells.
   He frowned. He sighed.
    'To come
Just now! — at Harvest Home!'

ON THE ESPLANADE

The autumnal gales had wreaked their will;
Now lipped the wave its idle stones;
And winter light lay grey and chill;
Snow-capped the town's one distant hill,
Snow-cloaked its churchyard bones.

Sole farers on the esplanade,
A mother with her daughter walked.
Across a sea of pallid jade
The air thin fretful music made
And whimpered while they talked: —

'It's not the *present* that I dread,
No vulgar talk of chances lost.
Your heart seems stranger to your head,
And time wears on,' the elder said;
'My only fear, the cost.

'Sheer habit numbs the mind, my dear;
And lips by lover never kissed
Taste only at last the bitter cheer
Repining memory brings near
Of sweetness they have missed.

'You frown. Ah, yes! But why forget
I too was once in youth astray?
If ghosts at noonday could be met
And suns have heat that long have set —
Well, well, I have had my day.

[166]

'And now for you alone I live.
Think not I speak to pry, or vex;
Mere cold advice not mine to give;
Be truth and love between us, if
We share one heart, one sex!'

Awhile these two in silence paced,
Vacant the windows shoreward set.
Thin-screened with cloud the West they faced,
No glint of sun their shadows traced
On the flat flags; and yet

A burning, proud, defiant flare
Gleamed in the younger's eyes, as she
'Neath louring brows, as cold as fair,
Gazed straightly through the wintry air
Over the restless sea.

'Yes, Mother, all you say is true.'
She shrugged her slender shoulders. 'I —
Well, nothing I can say, or do
Has any meaning through and through;
What use to question, why?

'Infatuated bees may spend
Their silly lives of droning trance
In gathering nectar without end,
For other busy bees to blend,
And die in like mischance —

'The old, old tale. You say we share
One sex. It's that has gone askew.
The butterflies still dance on air
Without an instant's thought or care
And "sip the morning dew";

'As for the rest, they ape the Man,
And sacrifice their shapes and skin;
In freedom's blaze their faces tan;
Utopian revolutions plan;
Bemoan the Might-have-been.

'Not I. I loathe them both. I know
My very instincts are at war —
Another kind of neuter. So,
Whatever now may come or go,
There's nothing I deplore.

'Pity I laugh at. Flatterer
Flatters not twice the self-same way!
And when at last I come to where
Mere growing old brings solace — there!
I shall have had my day.

'A day as deadly black as night
For fatuous dream of a strange fate —
That long, long since has taken flight —
A lover not of sense or sight:
For him I used to wait.

'I ask you, Mother, how could a mind
Farced up with all I have learned and read —
The lies that curious fools have spread —
A vestige of him hope to find?
Enough of that!' she said.

Turned then the twain about to see
An East as rayless, grey, and bland,
Stretching into infinity,
And vacant windows glassily
Edging the pebbled strand;

While, poised in air, a bird of snow
Faltered on lifted wing — to glide
And glance at this strange to-and-fro,
That greying hair, that cheek's young glow —
And shrill, sad challenge cried.

THE FAT WOMAN

Massed in her creaseless black,
She sits; vast and serene;
Light — on glossed hair, large knees,
Huge bust — a-sheen.

A smile lurks deep in her eyes,
Thick-lidded, motionless, pale,
Taunting a world grown old,
Faded, and stale.

Enormous those childless breasts:
God in His pity knows
Why, in her bodice stuck,
Reeks a mock rose.

THE FECKLESS DINNER-PARTY

'Who are we waiting for?' '*Soup* burnt?' '... Eight —'
'Only the tiniest party.— Us!'
'Darling! Divine!' 'Ten minutes late —'
'And my digest —' 'I'm *rav*enous!'
' "Toomes"?' — 'Oh, he's new.' 'Looks crazed, I guess.'
' "Married" — *Again*!' 'Well; more or less!'

'Dinner is *served*!' ' "Dinner is served"!'
'Is served?' 'Is served.' 'Ah, yes.'

'Dear Mr. Prout, will you take down
The Lilith in leaf-green by the fire?
Blanche Ogleton? ...' 'How coy a frown! —
Hasn't she borrowed *Eve's* attire?'
'Morose Old Adam!' 'Charmed — I vow.'
'Come then, and meet her now.'

'Now, Dr. Mallus — would you please? —
Our daring poetess, Delia Seek?'
'The lady with the bony knees?'
'And — *entre nous* — less song than beak.'
'Sharing her past with Simple Si —'
'*Bare* facts! He'll blush!' 'Oh, fie!'

'And *you*, Sir Nathan — false but fair! —
That fountain of wit, Aurora Pert.'
'More wit than It, poor dear! But there ...'
'Pitiless Pacha! *And* such a flirt!'
' "Flirt"! *Me?*' 'Who else?' 'You here.... Who can ...?'
'Incorrigible man!'

'And now, Mr. Simon — little me! —
Last and —' 'By no means least!' 'Oh, come!
What naughty, naughty flattery!

Honey! — I *hear* the creature hum!'
'Sweets for the sweet, *I* always say!'
  ' "Always"? . . . We're last.' '*This* way?' . . .

'No, sir; straight on, please.' 'I'd have vowed! —
I came the other . . .' 'It's queer; I'm sure . . .'
'What frightful pictures!' 'Fiends!' 'The *crowd!*'
'Such nudes!' 'I can't endure . . .'

'Yes, *there* they go.' 'Heavens! *Are* we right?'
'Follow up closer!' ' "Prout"? — sand-blind!'
'This endless . . .' 'Who's turned down the light?'
'Keep calm! They're close behind.'

'Oh! Dr. Mallus; what dismal stairs!'
'I hate these old Victor . . .' 'Dry rot!'
'Darker and darker!' 'Fog!' 'The air's . . .'
'Scarce breathable!' 'Hell!' '*What?*'

'The banister's gone!' 'It's deep; keep close!'
'We're going down and down!' 'What fun!'
'Damp! Why, my shoes . . .' 'It's slimy . . . Not *moss!*'
'I'm freezing cold!' 'Let's run.'

'. . . Behind us. I'm giddy. . . .' 'The catacombs . . .'
'That shout!' 'Who's there?' 'I'm *alone!*' 'Stand back!'
'She said, Lead . . .' 'Oh!' 'Where's Toomes?' '*Toomes!*'
        'Toomes!'
'Stifling!' 'My skull will crack!'

'Sir Nathan! *Ai!*' 'I *say! Toomes!* Prout!'
'Where? Where?' ' "Our silks and fine array" . . .'
'She's mad.' 'I'm dying!' 'Oh, Let me *out!*'
'My God! We've lost our way!' . . .

And now how sad-serene the abandoned house,
Whereon at dawn the spring-tide sunbeams beat;
And time's slow pace alone is ominous,
And naught but shadows of noonday therein meet;
Domestic microcosm, only a Trump could rouse:
And, pondering darkly, in the silent rooms,
He who misled them all — the butler, Toomes.

COMFORT

As I mused by the hearthside,
　　Puss said to me:
'There burns the Fire, man,
　　And here sit we.

'Four Walls around us
　　Against the cold air;
And the latchet drawn close
　　To the draughty Stair.

'A Roof o'er our heads
　　Star-proof, moon immune,
And a wind in the chimney
　　To wail us a tune.

'What Felicity!' miaowed he,
　　'Where none may intrude;
Just Man and Beast — met
　　In this Solitude!

'Dear God, what security,
　　Comfort and bliss!
And to think, too, what ages
　　Have brought us to this!

'You in your sheep's-wool coat,
　　Buttons of bone,
And me in my fur-about
　　On the warm hearthstone.'

THE SLUM CHILD

No flower grew where I was bred,
No leafy tree
Its canopy of greenness spread
Over my youthful head.

My woodland walk was gutter stone.
Nowhere for me
Was given a place where I alone
Could to myself be gone.

[171]

In leafless Summer's stench and noise
I'd sit and play
With other as lean-faced girls and boys,
And sticks and stones for toys —

Homeless, till evening dark came down;
And street lamp's ray
On weary skulking beggary thrown
Flared in the night-hung town.

Then up the noisome stairs I'd creep
For food and rest,
Or, empty-bellied, lie, and weep
My wordless woes to sleep:

And wept in silence — shaken with fear —
But cautious lest
Those on the mattress huddled near
Should, cursing, wake and hear. . . .

O wondrous Life! though plainly I see,
Thus looking back,
What evil, and filth, and poverty,
In childhood harboured me,

And marvel that merciless man could so
The innocent rack;
Yet, in bare truth, I also know
A well-spring of peace did flow,

Secretly blossomed, along that street;
And — foul-mouthed waif —
Though I in no wise heeded it
In the refuse at my feet,

Yet, caged within those spectral bones,
Aloof and safe,
Some hidden one made mock of groans,
Found living bread in stones.

O mystery of mysteries!
Between my hands I take that face,
Bloodless and bleak, unchildlike wise —
Epitome of man's disgrace —

I search its restless eyes,
And, from those woe-flecked depths, at me
Looks back through all its misery
A self beyond surmise.

NEWS

'Hearken! 'Tis news I cry!'
The shades drift by . . .
'Strange and ominous things:
A four-foot Beast upon Wings,
Thieves in a burning Mill,
An empty Cross on a Hill,
Ravin of swine in Beauty's places,
And a Woman with two Faces!
News! — News! I call. . . .'

But a wind from the cold unknown
Scatters the words as they fall —
Into naught they are blown.
What do these Walkers seek,
Pranked up in silk and in flax,
With a changeless rose on the cheek,
And Hell's hump on their backs?
These of the mincing gait,
And an ape in each sidelong leer;
These for the Way that is strait
To the pomp-hung bier;
These of the wasted dream,
Of the loveless silver and gold,
And the worm of disgust in them
That shall never grow old?

'Not unto such I cry,
But to thee, O Solitary! . . .
The world founders in air,
Plague-stricken Vanity Fair
Dyed hath its booths with blood;
Quenched are its stars in mud;
Come now the Mourners to chaunt
End and lament.'

[173]

There is a stream I know,
Sullen in flood its waters flow,
Heavy with secrets, slow,
Leaden and lightless, deep
With slumber and sleep.
Shall not even Innocence find
Peace of body and mind?

'Ay, but thou also art old,
And there's news to be told.
News, strange to hearing and sight . . .
It is Winter. And Night.
An icy and pitiless moon
Witched hath our sea-tides. And soon
The Nymph in her grottoes will hear
The loud trumpet of fear!
She weepeth cold tears in the sea! . . .
You shall *buy* not such tidings of me:
Stoop an ear, bow a desolate head:
It is breathed, "Love is dead".'

I SIT ALONE

I sit alone,
And clear thoughts move in me,
Pictures, now near, now far,
Of transient fantasy.
Happy I am, at peace
In my own company.

Yet life is a dread thing, too,
Dark with horror and fear.
Beauty's fingers grow cold,
Sad cries I hear,
Death with a stony gaze
Is ever near.

Lost in myself I hide
From the cold unknown:
Lost, like a world cast forth
Into space star-sown:
And the songs of the morning are stilled,
And delight in them flown.

So even the tender and dear
Like phantoms through memory stray —
Creations of sweet desire,
That faith can alone bid stay:
They cast off the cloak of the real
And vanish away.

Only love can redeem
This truth, that delight;
Bring morning to blossom again
Out of plague-ridden night;
Restore to the lost the found,
To the blinded, sight.

FORESTS

Turn, now, tired mind, unto your rest,
Within your secret chamber lie,
Doors shut, and windows curtained, lest
Footfall or moonbeam, stealing by,
Wake you, or night-wind sigh.

Now, Self, we are at peace — we twain;
The house is silent, except that — hark!
Against its walls wells out again
That rapture in the empty dark;
Where, softly beaming, spark by spark,

The glow-worms stud the leaves with light;
And unseen flowers, refreshed with dew —
Jasmine, convolvulus, glimmering white,
The air with their still life endue,
And sweeten night for me and you.

Be mute all speech; and not of love
Talk we, nor call on hope, but be —
Calm as the constant stars above —
The friends of fragile memory,
Shared only now by you and me.

Thus hidden, thus silent, while the hours
From gloom to gloom their wings beat on,
Shall not a moment's peace be ours,
Till, faint with day, the East is wan,
And terrors of the dark are gone?

Nay — in the forest of the mind
Lurk beasts as fierce as those that tread
Earth's rock-strown wilds, to night resigned,
There stars of heaven no radiance shed —
Bleak-eyed Remorse, Despair becowled in lead.

With dawn these ravening shapes will go —
Though One at watch will still remain:
Till knell the sunset hour, and lo!
The listening soul once more will know
Death and his pack are hot afield again.

THE BOTTLE

Of green and hexagonal glass,
    With sharp, fluted sides —
Vaguely transparent these walls,
    Wherein motionless hides
A simple so potent it can
    To oblivion lull
The weary, the racked, the bereaved,
    The miserable.

Flowers in silent desire
    Their life-breath exhale —
Self-heal, hellebore, aconite,
    Chamomile, dwale:
Sharing the same gentle heavens,
    The sun's heat and light,
And, in the dust at their roots,
    The same shallow night.

Each its own livelihood hath,
    Shape, pattern, hue;
Age on to age unto these
    Keeping steadfastly true;

[176]

And, musing amid them, there moves
   A stranger, named Man,
Who of their ichor distils
   What virtue he can;

Plucks them ere seed-time to blazon
His house with their radiant dyes;
Prisons their attar in wax;
Candies their petals; denies
Them freedom to breed in their wont;
Buds, fecundates, grafts them at will;
And with cunningest leechcraft compels
   Their good to his ill.

Intrigue fantastic as this
   Where shall we find?
Mute in their beauty they serve him,
   Body and mind.
And one — but a weed in his wheat —
Is the poppy — frail, pallid, whose juice
With its saplike and opiate fume
   Strange dreams will induce

Of wonder and horror. And none
   Can silence the soul,
Wearied of self and of life,
   Earth's darkness and dole,
More secretly, deeply . . . But finally? —
   Waste not thy breath;
The words that are scrawled on this phial
   Have for synonym, *death* —

Wicket out into the dark
   That swings but one way;
Infinite hush in an ocean of silence
   Aeons away —
Thou forsaken! — even thou! —
   The dread good-bye;
The abandoned, the thronged, the watched,
   the unshared —
   Awaiting me — I!

WHAT?

What dost thou surely know?
What will the truth remain,
When from the world of men thou go
To the unknown again?

What science — of what hope?
What heart-loved certitude won
From thought shall then for scope
Be thine — thy thinking done?

'Tis said, that even the wise,
When plucking at the sheet,
Have smiled with swift-darkening eyes,
As if in vision fleet

Of some mere flower, or bird,
Seen in dream, or in childhood's play;
And then, without sign or word,
Have turned from the world away.

RECONCILIATION

Leave April now, and autumn having,
Leave hope to fade, and darkness braving,
    Take thine own soul
    Companion,
    And journey on.

The cresset fire of noon is waning,
Shadow the lonelier hills is staining;
    Watch thou the West
    Whence pale shall shine
    Hesper divine!

Beauty, what is it but love's vision?
Earth's fame, the soul's supreme derision?
    O ardent dust,
    Turn to thy grave,
    And quiet have!

THE HOUSE

'Mother, it's such a lonely house,'
The child cried; and the wind sighed.
'A narrow but a lovely house,'
The mother replied.

'Child, it is such a narrow house,'
The ghost cried; and the wind sighed.
'A narrow and a lonely house,'
The withering grass replied.

THE TACITURN

Countless these crosses and these ruinous stones,
Which taunt the living with but sighs and groans!
Thou canst not in this quiet a moment stray
      But dust cries, *Vanity!* and, *Welladay!*
Not mine such tedious tidings, Stranger. Yet,
Think not because I am silent, I forget.

THE THORN

O thou who pausest here,
With naught but some thorned wilding near
To tell of beauty; be not sad.
For he who in this grave is laid
Would give the all on earth he had
One moment but by thee to stand
And with warm hand touch hand.

ARIEL

This lad, when but a child of six,
Had learned how earth and heaven may mix —
At this so innocent an age
He, as light Ariel, trod the stage;
So nimble-tongued, and silver-fleet,
Air, fire, did in one body meet.
Ay; had he hied to where the bones
Of Shakespeare lie 'neath Stratford's stones,
And whispered: 'Master, hearken!'— so:
One might have answered — Prospero!

BENEATH A MOTIONLESS YEW

Beneath a motionless yew, and tower,
Hoary with age, whose clock's one bell
Of Sexton Time had hour by hour
As yet in vain rung out the knell,

A worn old woman, in her black,
Knelt in the green churchyard alone;
And, self-forgotten, crook'd arm, bent back,
Scrubbed at her husband's burial stone.

Here lies J—— H——: Aged 34:
'He giveth his beloved sleep':
Fainter the letters than of yore —
Where lichens had begun to creep —

Showed 'neath the pale-blue vacant sky,
Under that dust-dry shadowiness;
She stayed to read — with a long sigh,
Less of regret than weariness.

Evening's last gleam now tinged the yew;
The gilded hand jerked on; a bird
Made stony rattle; and anew
She scanned the tombstone's every word.

For forty years she had kept her tryst,
And grief long since had ceased to upbraid
Him whose young love she had sorely missed,
And at whose side she would soon be laid.

Tired out, and old; past hope or thought,
She pined no more to meet some day
Her dead; and yet, still faithfully sought
To wash the stains of Time away.

GOOD COMPANY

The stranger from the noisy inn
Strode out into the quiet night,
Tired of the slow sea-faring men.

The wind blew fitfully in his face;
He smelt the salt, and tasted it,
In that sea-haunted, sandy place.

Dim ran the road down to the sea
Bowered in with trees, and solitary;
Ever the painted sign swang slow —
An Admiral staring moodily.

The stranger heard its silly groan;
The beer-mugs rattling to and fro;
The drawling gossip: and the glow
Streamed thro' the door on weed and stone.

Better this star-sown solitude,
The empty night-road to the sea,
Than company so dull and rude.

He smelt the nettles sour and lush,
About him went the bat's shrill cry,
Pale loomed the fragrant hawthorn-bush.

And all along the sunken road —
Green with its weeds, though sandy dry —
Bugloss, hemlock and succory —
The night-breeze wavered from the sea.
And soon upon the beach he stood.

A myriad pebbles in the faint
Horned radiance of a sinking moon
Shone like the rosary of a saint —
A myriad pebbles which, through time,
The bitter tides had visited,
Flood and ebb, by a far moon led,
Noon and night and morning-prime.

He stood and eyed the leaping sea,
The long grey billows surging on,
Baying in sullen unison
Their dirge of agelong mystery.

And, still morose, he went his way,
Over the mounded shingle strode,
And reached a shimmering sand that lay
Where transient bubbles of the froth
Like eyes upon the moonshine glowed,
Faint-coloured as the evening moth.

But not on these the stranger stared,
Nor on the stars that spanned the deep,
But on a body, flung at ease,
As if upon the shore asleep,
Hushed by the rocking seas.

Of a sudden the air was wild with cries —
Shrill and high and violent,
Fled fast a soot-black cormorant,
'Twixt ocean and the skies.

It seemed the sea was like a heart
That stormily a secret keeps
Of what it dare to none impart.
And all its waves rose, heaped and high —
And communed with the moon-grey sky.

The stranger eyed the sailor there,
Mute, and stark, and sinister —
His stiffening sea-clothes grey with salt;
His matted hair, his eyes ajar,
And glazed after the three-fold fear.

And ever the billows cried again
Over the rounded pebble stones,
Baying that heedless sailor-man.

He frowned and glanced up into the air —
Where star with star all faintly shone,
Cancer and the Scorpion,
In ancient symbol circling there:

Gazed inland over the vacant moor;
But ancient silence, and a wind
That whirls upon a sandy floor,
Were now its sole inhabitants.

Forthwith, he wheeled about — away
From the deep night's sad radiance;
The yells of gulls and cormorants
Rang shrilly in his mind.

Pursued by one who noiseless trod,
Whose sharp scythe whistled as he went,
O'er sand and shingle, tuft and sod,
Like hunted hare he coursing ran,
Nor stayed until he came again
Back to the old convivial inn —
The mugs, the smoke, the muffled din —
Packed with its slow-tongued sailor-men.

THE RAILWAY JUNCTION

From here through tunnelled gloom the track
Forks into two; and one of these
Wheels onward into darkening hills,
And one toward distant seas.

How still it is; the signal light
At set of sun shines palely green;
A thrush sings; other sound there's none,
Nor traveller to be seen —

Where late there was a throng. And now,
In peace awhile, I sit alone;
Though soon, at the appointed hour,
I shall myself be gone.

But not their way: the bow-legged groom,
The parson in black, the widow and son,
The sailor with his cage, the gaunt
Gamekeeper with his gun,

That fair one, too, discreetly veiled —
All, who so mutely came, and went,
Will reach those far nocturnal hills,
Or shores, ere night is spent.

I nothing know why thus we met —
Their thoughts, their longings, hopes, their fate:
And what shall I remember, except —
The evening growing late —

That here through tunnelled gloom the track
Forks into two; of these
One into darkening hills leads on,
And one toward distant seas?

REFLECTIONS

Three Sisters — and the youngest
   Was yet lovelier to see
Than wild flower palely blooming
   Under Ygdrasil Tree,

Than this well at the woodside
   Whose waters silver show,
Though in womb of the blind earth
   Ink-like, ebon, they flow.

Creeps on the belled bindweed;
   The bee, in hoverings nigh,
Sucks his riches of nectar;
   Clouds float in the sky;

And she, O pure vanity,
   Newly-wakened, at that brink,
Crouches close, smiling dreamlike,
   To gaze, not to drink.

She sees not earth's morning
   Darkly framed in that cold deep:
Naught, naught but her beauty
   Made yet fairer by sleep.

And though glassed in that still flood
   She peer long, and long,
As faithful stays that image,
   As echo is to song . . .

Anon — in high noontide
   Comes her sister, wan with fear,
Lest the love in her bosom
   Even the bright birds should hear

[184]

Wail divine grieved enchantment.
  She kneels; and, musing, sighs;
Unendurable strangenesses
  Darken the eyes

That meet her swift searchings.
  From her breast there falls a flower.
Down, down — as she ponders —
  The fair petals shower,

Hiding brow, mouth, cheek — all
  That reflected there is seen.
And she gone, that Mirror
  As of old rests serene. . . .

Comes moth-light, faint dusk-shine,
  The green woods still and whist;
And their sister, the eldest
  To keep her late tryst.

Long thought and lone broodings
  Have wanned, have withered, lined
A face, without beauty,
  Which no dream hath resigned

To love's impassioned grieving.
  She stands. The louring air
Breathes cold on her cheekbone,
  Stirs thief-like her hair;

And a still quiet challenge
  Fills her dark, her flint-grey eyes,
As she lifts her bowed head
  To survey the cold skies.

Wherein stars, hard and restless,
  Burn in station fore-ordained,
As if mocking for ever
  A courage disdained.

And she stoops wearied shoulders,
  Void of scorn, of fear, or ruth,
To confront in that well-spring
  The dark gaze of Truth.

SELF TO SELF

Wouldst thou then happy be
On earth, where woes are many?
Where naught can make agree
Men paid for wage a penny?
Wherein ambition hath
Set up proud gate to Death;
And fame with trump and drum
Cannot undeaf the dumb
Who unto dust are come?
Wouldst thou then happy be? —
Impossibility?

Maybe, when reasons rule
Dunces kept in at school;
Or while mere Logic peers
Sand-blind at her bright shears
Snip-snapping this, and this,
Ay, on my soul, it is —
Till, looking up, thou see
Noonday's immensity,
And, turning back, see too
That in a bead of dew.

Heart-near or fancy-far,
All's thine to make or mar.
Thine its sole consciousness,
Whether thou ban or bless.
Loving delight forgot,
Life's very roots must rot.
Be it for better or worse,
Thou art thy universe.
If then at length thou must
Render them both to dust,
Go with their best in trust.
If thou wake never — well:
But if perchance thou find
Light, that brief gloom behind,
Thou'lt have wherewith to tell
If thou'rt in heaven or hell.

THE SLEEPER

The Lovely, sleeping, lay in bed,
  Her limbs, from quiet foot to chin,
Still as the dust of one that's dead
  Whose spirit waits the entering-in.

Yet her young cheek with life's faint dye
  Was mantled o'er; her gentle breast
Like sea at peace with starry sky,
  Moved with a heart at rest.

Fair country of a thousand springs,
  Calm hill and vale! Those hidden eyes
And tongue that daylong talks and sings,
  Wait only for the sun to rise.

Let but a bird call in that ear,
  Let beam of day that window wan,
This hidden one will, wakening, hear,
  And deathlike slumber-swoon be gone:

Her ardent eyes once more will shine,
  She will uplift her hair-crowned head;
At lip, miraculous, life's wine,
  At hand, its wondrous bread.

THE HUNTER

'Why wilt thou take my heart? It fawnlike flies,
'Frighted at clarion of thy hunting cries,
And shrinks benumbed beneath thy jealous eyes.

'Shun those green solitudes, these paths and vales
Where winds the grasses tell their faint-sung tales
Of distant Ocean's secret nightingales;

'Of frail foam-bubbles, spun of light and air,
From glass wherein sirens braid their sun-gilt hair,
Watching their round mouths chaunt a dying air. . . .

'O arrows, pierce me not! O horns, be still!
Sweet God, divine compassion have: or kill!'

[187]

THE VISIONARY

There is a pool whose waters clear
Reflect not what is standing near;
The silver-banded birch, the grass
Find not therein a looking-glass;
Nor doth Orion, pacing night,
Scatter thereon his wintry light.
Nor ever to its darnelled brink
Comes down the hare or deer to drink;
Sombre and secret it doth keep
Stilled in unshaken, crystal sleep.

But once, a Wanderer, parched, forlorn,
Worn with night-wayfaring, came at morn,
By pathless thickets grey with dew;
And stooping at its margent blue
To lave his wearied eyes, discerned
Somewhat that in the water burned —
A face like amber, pale and still,
With eyes of light, unchangeable,
Whose grave and steadfast scrutiny
Pierced through all earthly memory.
Voiceless and windless the green wood,
Above its shadowy quietude,
Sighed faintly through its unfading leaves;
And still he stooped; and still he yearned
To kiss the lips that therein burned;
To close those eyes that from the deep
Gazed on him, wearied out for sleep.

He drank; he slumbered; and he went
Back into life's wild banishment,
Like one whose every thought doth seem
The wreckage of a wasting dream;
All savour gone from life, delight
Charged with foreboding dark as night;
Love but the memory of what
Woke once, but reawakens not.

THE CAPTIVE

I twined a net; I drove a stake; I laid a glittering bait.
With still of dewfall stepped my prey; cried — and cried too late.
I clutched him by his golden curls: I penned his flutterings.
Secure within a golden cage he beats in vain his wings.

> But why is now their beauty gone
> From woods where once it happy shone?
> Why is my bosom desolate,
> When entering in at fall of eve,
> I listen at the wicket gate,
> And hear my captive grieve?

THUS HER TALE

Spake the fire-tinged bramble, bossed with gleaming fruit and
   blossoming,
   Gently serpentining in the air a blunted tongue: —
'Far too long these bones I hide have blackened in my covert here,
   Too long their noxious odour to my sweetness now hath clung.
Would they were gross clay, and their evil spell removed from me;
   How much lovelier I, if my roots not thence had sprung.'

Breathed the wind of sundown, 'Ay, this haunt is long years sour to
   me;
   But naught on earth that's human can my fancy free beguile.
Wings are mine far fleeter than the birds' that clip these branches;
   Arabian rich the burden which for honeyed mile on mile
Is wafted on my bosom, hill to ocean, wood to valeland.
   Anathema on relics that my fragrances defile!'

Stirred a thousand frondlets and the willow tree replied to it: —
   'Sty and mixen, foetid pool, and carrion-shed — whose these?
Yet earth makes sweet the foulest; naught — naught stays long
   unclean to her;
   Thou, too, howe'er reluctant, art her servant, gliding Breeze.
Restrain thy fretting pudency; in pity sigh for one I knew —
   The woman whose unburied bones in thornbrake take their
   ease.'

[189]

'*Urkkh:* when dark hath thicked to night,' croaked vermin toad that
    crouched near-by,
  'And the stars that mock in heaven unto midnight's cope have
    clomb,
When the shades of all the humans that in life were brutal foes to me
    Lift thready lamentation from the churchyard's rancid loam —
Return doth she in mortal guise 'gainst whom I bear no enmity,
    Foredoomed by fate this treacherous field for aye to haunt and
    roam.'

'Pictured once her image I,' sang sliding brook its rushes from,
  'That sallow face, and eyes that seemed to stare as if in dream,
Narrow shoulders, long lean hands, and hair like withered grass in
    hue,
    Pale lips drawn thwart with grieving in stars' silver mocking beam.
Once, too, I heard her story, but little I remember now,
    Though the blood that gave her power to suffer them imbrued my
    stream.'

Stony rock groaned forth its voice, 'No mirror featly shattered I,
  Blind I am by nature, but, I boast, not deaf or dumb,
Small truck I pay to Time's decay, nor mark what wounds black
    winter makes.
    Not mine to know what depths of snow have thawed and left
    me numb —
Since an eve when flowers had cast their seed, and evening cooled my
    brow again.
    And I echoed to a voice that whispered, "Loved one, I have
    come."'

Wafting through the woodland swept an owl from out the silentness,
  '*Too wittoo woo*,' she hooted. 'A human comes this way,
Gliding as on feathered heel, so tenuous that the thorns she skirts
    To eyes bright-glassed for glooms like mine show black beyond
    her grey.
A tryst she keeps. Beware, good friends, not mine day's mortal
    company,
    Hungry my brood for juicier fare,' she squawked, and plumed
    away.

Lone, in a shoal of milk-white cloud, bathed now the punctual
    fickle moon
  That nook of brook and willow, long unpolled, with silvery
    glare: —
'Unstilled yet tranquil Phantom, see, thou canst not hide thy form
    from me:

When last thy anguished body trod these meadows fresh and fair,
I, the ringing sand-dunes of the vast Sahara hoared with light:
What secret calls thee from the shades; why hither dost thou
    fare?' . . .

Small beauty graced the spectre pondering mute beneath the
    willow-boughs
O'er relics long grown noisome to the bramble and the breeze;
A hand upon her narrow breast, her head bent low in shadowiness;
    'I've come,' sighed voice like muted bell of nightbird in the trees,
'To tell again for all to hear, the wild remorse that suffers me,
    No single thought of rest or hope whereon to muse at ease.

'Self-slaughtered I, for one I loved, who could not give me love
    again,
Uncounted now the Autumns since that twilight hour malign
When, insensate for escape from a hunger naught could satisfy,
    I vowed to God no more would I in torment live and pine.
Alas! He turned His face away, and woeful penance laid on me —
    That every night make tryst must I till life my love resign.'

Furtive fell the anxious glance she cast that dreadful hiding-place;
    Strangely still and muted ceased the tones in which she spake.
Shadow filled her vacant place. The moon withdrew in cloud again.
    Hushed the ripples grieving to the pebbles in their wake.
'Thus her *tale*!' quoth sod to sod. 'Not ours, good friends, to
    challenge it;
Though her blood still cries for vengeance on her murderer from
    this brake!'

ADIEU

Had these eyes never seen you,
This heart kept its paces,
If this mind — flooded river —
Had glassed not your graces;
Though lone my cold pillow,
In peace I had slumbered,
Whose hours now of waking
By moments are numbered.

You came; ice-still, asp-like;
You glanced 'neath your lashes;
You smiled — and you sighed out
Life's flame into ashes.

No compassion you showed me,
Void breast, cheating laughter:
Now I swing to my tryst
From this night-clotted rafter.

Peep out with your eyes.
Pout your mouth. Tilt your nose.
'Gainst the stench and the flies
Cull a balm-sprig, a rose.
This tongue that is stilled —
Not a tremor! Oh, else,
The whole roof of heaven
  Would cry, False!

THE OUTSKIRTS

The night was cloyed with flowers
In the darkness deep and sweet,
When, at the window of the World,
I heard the dancing feet;
And viol and tambour
Made musical the air,
While yet a voice within me cried,
  Beware!

My eyes upon the glow were set
From out that thorny grot:
I hungered for the lips and eyes
And hearts remembering not;
And still the thrill and thud beat on
With sorcery in the air;
And, luring, leaping, called to me,
  Beware!

O all you hapless souls, like birds
Within night's branching may,
Hearken the words of him who speaks,
And fly from hence — away.
These dancers with their wiles and gauds,
That music on the air —
'Tis the swart Fowler with his nets
To play you false, though fair;
Hearken — an outcast I — I cry,
  Beware!

ROSE

Three centuries now are gone
Since Thomas Campion
Left men his airs, his verse, his heedful prose.
Few other memories
Have we of him, or his,
And, of his sister, none, but that her name was Rose.

Woodruff, far moschatel
May the more fragrant smell
When into brittle dust their blossoming goes.
His, too, a garden sweet,
Where rarest beauties meet,
And, as a child, he shared them with this Rose.

Faded, past changing, now,
Cheek, mouth, and childish brow.
Where, too, her phantom wanders no man knows.
Yet, when in undertone
That eager lute pines on,
Pleading of things he loved, it sings of Rose.

LUCY

Strange — as I sat brooding here,
While memory plied her quiet thread,
Your once-loved face came back, my dear,
    Amid the distant dead.

That pleasant cheek, hair smooth and brown,
Clear brows, and wistful eyes — yet gay:
You stand, in your alpaca gown,
    And ghost my heart away.

I was a child then; nine years old —
And you a woman. Well, stoop close,
To heed a passion never told
    Under how faded a rose!

Do you remember? Few my pence:
I hoarded them with a miser's care,
And bought you, in passionate innocence,
    A birthday maidenhair.

[193]

I see its fronds. Again I sit,
Hunched up in bed, in the dark, alone,
Crazed with those eyes that, memory-lit,
    Now ponder on my own.

You gave me not a thought, 'tis true —
Precocious, silly child; and yet,
Perhaps of all you have loved — loved you,
    I may the last forget.

And though no single word of this
You heed — a lifetime gone — at rest;
I would that all remembrances
    As gently pierced my breast!

A YOUNG GIRL

I search in vain your childlike face to see
The thoughts that hide behind the words you say;
I hear them singing, but close-shut from me
Dream the enchanted woods through which they stray.
Cheek, lip, and brow — I glance from each to each,
And watch that light-winged Mercury, your hand;
And sometimes when brief silence falls on speech
I seem your hidden self to understand.

Mine a dark fate. Behind his iron bars
The captive broods, with ear and heart a-strain
For jangle of key, for glimpse of moon or stars,
Grey shaft of daylight, sighing of the rain.
Life built these walls. Past all my dull surmise
Must burn the inward innocence of your eyes.

TWILIGHT

When to the inward darkness of my mind
I bid your face come, not one hue replies
Of that curved cheek, no, nor the faint-tinged rose
Of lips, nor smile between the mouth and eyes:
Only the eyes themselves, past telling, seem
To break in beauty in the twilight there,
And out of solitude your very ghost
Steals through the scarce-seen shadow of your hair.

THE TRYST

Faint now the colours in the West;
    And, stilled with lapse of day,
All life within it laid to rest,
    The wintry wood grows grey.

Frost enlines the withered flower,
    Its hips and haws now blackening are,
The slender naked tree-tops cower
    Beneath the evening-star.

Pace we then softly, you and I,
    Nor stir one England-wintering bird —
Start not! — 'twas but some wild thing's cry,
    No wailing ghost you heard.

Yet ghosts there are, remote and chill,
    Waiting the moon's phantasmal fire,
But not for us to heed, until
    We too doff Earth's attire.

Oh, far from home we both shall be,
    When we, with them, shall coldly brood
On lovers twain, like you and me,
    Trespassing in this wood.

THE ENCOUNTER

'Twixt dream and wake we wandered on,
Thinking of naught but you and me;
And lo, when day was nearly gone,
   A wondrous sight did see.

There, in a bed of rushes, lay
A child all naked, golden and fair —
Young Eros dreaming time away,
   With roses in his hair.

Tender sleep had o'ertaken him,
Quenched his bright arrows, loosed his bow,
And in divine oblivion dim
   Had stilled him through and through.

Never have I such beauty seen
As burned in his young dreaming face,
Cheek, hair, and lip laid drowsily
   In slumber's faint embrace.

Oh, how he started, how his eyes
Caught back their sudden shiningness
To see you stooping, loving-wise,
   Him, slumbering, to caress!

How flamed his brow, what childish joy
Leapt in his heart at sight of thee,
When, 'Mother, mother!' cried the boy:
   And — frowning — turned on me!

FULL CIRCLE

When thou art as little as I am, Mother,
And I as old as thou,
I'll feed thee on wild-bee honeycomb,
And milk from my cow.
I'll make thee a swan's-down bed, Mother;
Watch over thee then will I.
And if in a far-away dream you start
I'll sing thee lullaby.
It's many — Oh, ages and ages, Mother,
We've shared, we two. Soon, now:
Thou shalt be happy, grown again young,
And I as old as thou.

THE GLANCE

Dearest one, daughter! at glance of your brow-shaded eye,
Fixed gravely in all its young scrutiny dark on my own,
Lone seemed my soul as this earth was itself 'neath the sky,
When at word of creation the trumps of the angels were blown.

They rang to the verge of the universe, solemn and deep,
Clanging untellable joy to the heavens above,
And, at core of that clangour, in silence profounder than sleep,
Adam and Eve lay adream in their Eden of love.

But you, in your bird-eyed wonder, gazed steadily on,
Knowing naught of the tempest so stirred. I stooped down my
    head,
And, shutting my eyes to a prayer whereof words there are none,
Could but clasp your cold hand in my own and was dumb as the
    dead.

HOW BLIND!

How blind 'twas to be harsh, I know —
    And to be harsh to *thee*;
To let one hour in anger go,
    And unforgiven be!

And now — O idiot tongue to dart
    That venomed fang, nor heed
Not thine but mine the stricken heart
    Shall never cease to bleed.

MAKING A FIRE

Scatter a few cold cinders into the empty grate;
    On these lay paper puffed into airy balloon,
Then wood — parched dry by the suns of Summer drowsy and
    sweet;
A flash, a flare, a flame; and a fire will be burning soon —

    Fernlike, fleet, and impetuous. But unless you give heed,
        It will faint, fade, fall, lose fervour, ash away out.
So it is with anger in heart and in brain; the insensate seed
Of dangerous fiery enkindling leaps into horror and rout;

[197]

But remaining untended, it dies. And the soul within
Is refreshed by the dews of sweet amity, pity's cool rain.
Not so with the flames Hell has kindled for unassoiled sin,
As soon as God's mercy would quench them, Love, weeping,
    lights them again.

THE ROUND

I watched, upon a vase's rim,
An earwig — strayed from honeyed cell —
Circling a track once strange to him,
    But now known far too well.

With vexed antennae, searching space,
And giddy grope to left and right,
On — and still on — he pressed apace,
    Out of, and into, sight.

In circumambulation drear,
He neither wavered, paused nor stayed;
But now kind Providence drew near —
    A slip of wood I laid

Across his track. He scaled its edge:
And soon was safely restored to where
A sappy, dew-bright, flowering hedge
    Of dahlias greened the air.

Ay, and as apt may be my fate! . . .
Smiling, I turned to work again:
But shivered, where in shade I sate,
    And idle did remain.

THE OMEN

Far overhead — the glass set fair —
I heard a raven in the air;
'Twixt roof and stars it fanning went,
And croaked in sudden dreariment.

Over the pages of my book
I, listening, cast a sidelong look.
Curtained the window; shut the door;
I turned me to my book once more;
But in that quiet strove in vain
To win its pleasure back again.

WHICH WAY?

Wander, spirit? — *I!*
Who do not even know
Which way I'd go:
Yet sigh:

Who cannot even, first,
What far-off living well
I pine for, tell:
Yet thirst!

Unfailing joys I share;
No hour, however fleet,
But brings its sweet
And fair:

And yet — scoff not! — day gone,
Some silly ghost creeps back,
'What do you lack?'
To groan.

MIST

Sometimes in moods of gloom — like mist
    Enswathing hill and wood —
A miracle of sunshine breaks
    Into my solitude.

In scattered splendour burns the dew;
    Still as in dream, the trees
Their vaulted branches echo make
    To the birds' ecstasies.

What secret influence was this
    Made all dark brooding vain?
Has then the mind no inward sun? —
    The mists cloud down again:

Stealthily drape the distant heights
    Blot out the songless tree:
Into cold silence flit the thoughts
    That sang to me.

THE ARGUMENT

Why, then, if love is all there is need to give,
　　All love be thine.
Thine the bright wonder of this life I live,
　　Its doubt's dark broodings mine.

Serene that marvellous waste of crystal sky,
　　And that gaunt crook-backed tree!
Hush! breathes the wind invisibly rippling by,
　　Hush! to the wild bird's cry . . .

Yet even as mind vowed no more to grieve,
　　Heart answered with a sigh.

DAWN

Near, far, unearthly, break the birds
From spectral bush and tree,
Into a strange and drowsy praise,
The flush of dawn to see.

Old ashen rooks, on ragged wing,
And heads with sidling eye,
Sweep in the silvery heights of daybreak,
Silent through the sky.

The restless robin — like a brook
Tinkling in frozen snow —
Shakes his clear, sudden, piercing bells,
Flits elf-like to and fro.

Cock to cock yells, the enormous earth
Lies like a dream outspread
Under the canopy of space,
Stretched infinite overhead.

[200]

Light on the wool-fleeced ewes pours in;
Meek-faced, they snuff the air;
The glint-horned oxen sit agaze;
The east burns orient-fair.

The milk-white mists of night wreathe up
From meadows greenly grey —
Their every blade of grass ablaze
With dewdrops drenched in day.

THE SPARK

Calm was the evening, as if asleep,
But sickled on high with brooding storm,
Couched in invisible space. And, lo!
I saw in utter silence sweep
Out of that darkening starless vault
A gliding spark, as blanched as snow,
That burned into dust, and vanished in
A hay-cropped meadow, brightly green.

A meteor from the cold of space,
Lost in Earth's wilderness of air? —
Presage of lightnings soon to shine
In splendour on this lonely place? —
I cannot tell; but only how fair
It glowed within the crystalline
Pure heavens, and of its strangeness lit
My mind to joy at sight of it.

Yet what is common as lovely may be:
The petalled daisy, a honey bell,
A pebble, a branch of moss, a gem
Of dew, or fallen rain — if we
A moment in their beauty dwell;
Entranced, alone, see only them.
How blind to wait, till, merely unique,
Some omen thus the all bespeak!

JENNY WREN

Of all the birds that rove and sing,
  Near dwellings made for men,
None is so nimble, feat, and trim
  As Jenny Wren.

With pin-point bill, and tail a-cock,
  So wildly shrill she cries,
The echoes on their roof-tree knock
  And fill the skies.

Never was sweeter seraph hid
  Within so small a house —
A tiny, inch-long, eager, ardent,
  Feathered mouse.

THE SNAIL

All day shut fast in whorled retreat
You slumber where — no wild bird knows;
While on your rounded roof-tree beat
The petals of the rose.
The grasses sigh above your house;
Through drifts of darkest azure sweep
The sun-motes where the mosses drowse
That soothe your noonday sleep.

But when to ashes in the west
Those sun-fires die; and, silver, slim,
Eve, with the moon upon her breast,
Smiles on the uplands dim;
Then, all your wreathèd house astir,
Horns reared, grim mouth, deliberate pace,
You glide in silken silence where
The feast awaits your grace.

Strange partners, Snail! Then I, abed,
Consign the thick-darked vault to you,
Nor heed what sweetness night may shed
Nor moonshine's slumbrous dew.

SPEECH

The robin's whistled stave
Is tart as half-ripened fruit;
Wood-sooth from bower of leaves
The blackbird's flute;
Shrill-small the ardent wren's;
And the thrush, and the long-tailed tit —
Each hath its own apt tongue,
   Shrill, harsh, or sweet.

The meanings they may bear
Is long past ours to guess —
What sighs the wind, of the past,
In the wilderness?
Man also in ancient words
His thoughts may pack,
But if he not sing them too,
   Music they lack.

Oh, never on earth was bird,
Though perched on Arabian tree,
Nor instrument echoing heaven
Made melody strange as he;
Since even his happiest speech
Cries of his whither and whence,
And in mere sound secretes
   His inmost sense.

TOM'S ANGEL

No one was in the fields
But me and Polly Flint,
When, like a giant across the grass,
The flaming angel went.

It was budding time in May,
And green as green could be,
And all in his height he went along
Past Polly Flint and me.

We'd been playing in the woods,
And Polly up, and ran,
And hid her face, and said,
'Tom! Tom! The Man! The Man!'

And I up-turned; and there.
Like flames across the sky,
With wings all bristling, came
The Angel striding by.

And a chaffinch overhead
Kept whistling in the tree
While the Angel, blue as fire, came on
Past Polly Flint and me.

And I saw his hair, and all
The ruffling of his hem,
As over the clovers his bare feet
Trod without stirring them.

Polly — she cried; and, oh!
We ran, until the lane
Turned by the miller's roaring wheel,
And we were safe again.

ENGLISH DOWNS

Here, long ere kings to battle rode
    In thunder of the drum,
And trumps fee-faughed defiance,
    And taut bow-strings whistled, 'Come!' —

This air breathed milky sweet
    With nodding columbine,
Dangled upon the age-gnarled thorn
    The clematis twine;

Meek harebell hung her head
    Over the green-turfed chalk,
And the lambs with their dams forgathered
    Where the shepherds talk.

'HOW SLEEP THE BRAVE'

Bitterly, England must thou grieve —
    Though none of these poor men who died
But did within his soul believe
    That death for thee was glorified.

Ever they watched it hovering near —
    A mystery beyond thought to plumb —
And often, in loathing and in fear,
    They heard cold danger whisper, Come! —

Heard, and obeyed. Oh, if thou weep
    Such courage and honour, woe, despair;
Remember too that those who sleep
    No more remorse can share.

THE IMAGE

Faint sighings sounded, not of wind, amid
That chasmed waste of boulder and cactus flower,
Primeval sand its sterile coverlid,
Unclocked eternity its passing hour.

Naught breathed or stirred beneath its void of blue,
Save when in far faint dying whisper strained
Down the sheer steep, where not even lichen grew,
Eroded dust, and, where it fell, remained.

Hewn in that virgin rock, nude 'gainst the skies,
Loomed mighty Shape — of granite brow and breast,
Its huge hands folded on its sightless eyes,
Its lips and feet immovably at rest.

Where now the wanderers who this image scored
For age-long idol here? — Death? Destiny? Fame? —
Mute, secret, dreadful, and by man adored;
Yet not a mark in the dust to tell its name?

A ROBIN

Ghost-grey the fall of night,
    Ice-bound the lane,
Lone in the dying light
    Flits he again;
Lurking where shadows steal,
Perched in his coat of blood,
Man's homestead at his heel,
    Death-still the wood.

[205]

Odd restless child; it's dark;
    All wings are flown
But this one wizard's — hark!
    Stone clapped on stone!
Changeling and solitary,
Secret and sharp and small,
Flits he from tree to tree,
    Calling on all.

SNOWING

Snowing; snowing;
Oh, between earth and sky
A wintry wind is blowing,
Scattering with its sigh
Petals from trees of silver that shine
Like invisible glass, when the moon
In the void of night on high
Paces her orchards divine.

Snowing; snowing;
Ah me, how still, and how fair
The air with flakes interflowing,
The fields crystal and bare,
When the brawling brooks are dumb
And the parched trees matted with frost,
And the birds in this wilderness stare
    Dazzled and numb!

Snowing . . . snowing . . . snowing:
Moments of time through space
Into hours, centuries growing,
Till the world's marred lovely face,
Wearied of change and chance,
Radiant in innocence dream —
Lulled by an infinite grace
To rest in eternal trance.

MEMORY

When summer heat has drowsed the day
With blaze of noontide overhead,
And hidden greenfinch can but say
What but a moment since it said;

[206]

When harvest fields stand thick with wheat,
And wasp and bee slave — dawn till dark —
Nor home, till evening moonbeams beat,
Silvering the nightjar's oaken bark:
How strangely then the mind may build
A magic world of wintry cold,
Its meadows with frail frost-flowers filled —
Bright-ribbed with ice, a frozen wold! ...

When dusk shuts in the shortest day,
And huge Orion spans the night;
Where antlered fireflames leap and play
Chequering the walls with fitful light —
Even sweeter in mind the summer's rose
May bloom again; her drifting swan
Resume her beauty; while rapture flows
Of birds long since to silence gone:
Beyond the Nowel, sharp and shrill,
Of Waits from out the snowbound street,
Drums to their fiddle beneath the hill
June's mill wheel where the waters meet ...

O angel Memory that can
Double the joys of faithless Man!

A BALLAD OF CHRISTMAS

It was about the deep of night,
   And still was earth and sky,
When in the moonlight, dazzling bright,
   Three ghosts came riding by.

Beyond the sea — beyond the sea,
   Lie kingdoms for them all:
I wot their steeds trod wearily —
   The journey is not small.

By rock and desert, sand and stream,
   They footsore late did go:
Now, like a sweet and blessed dream,
   Their path was deep with snow.

[207]

Shining like hoarfrost, rode they on,
  Three ghosts in earth's array:
It was about the hour when wan
  Night turns at hint of day.

Oh, but their hearts with woe distraught
  Hailed not the wane of night,
Only for Jesu still they sought
  To wash them clean and white.

For bloody was each hand, and dark
  With death each orbless eye; —
It was three Traitors mute and stark
  Came riding silent by.

Silver their raiment and their spurs,
  And silver-shod their feet,
And silver-pale each face that stared
  Into the moonlight sweet.

And he upon the left that rode
  Was Pilate, Prince of Rome,
Whose journey once lay far abroad,
  And now was nearing home.

And he upon the right that rode,
  Herod of Salem sate,
Whose mantle dipped in children's blood
  Shone clear as Heaven's gate.

And he, these twain betwixt, that rode
  Was clad as white as wool,
Dyed in the Mercy of his God,
  White was he crown to sole.

Throned mid a myriad Saints in bliss
  Rise shall the Babe of Heaven
To shine on these three ghosts, i-wis,
  Smit through with sorrows seven;

Babe of the Blessed Trinity
  Shall smile their steeds to see:
Herod and Pilate riding by,
  And Judas, one of three.

THE SNOWDROP

Now — now, as low I stooped, thought I,
I will see what this snowdrop *is*;
So shall I put much argument by,
    And solve a lifetime's mysteries.

A northern wind had frozen the grass;
Its blades were hoar with crystal rime,
Aglint like light-dissecting glass
    At beam of morning-prime.

From hidden bulb the flower reared up
Its angled, slender, cold, dark stem,
Whence dangled an inverted cup
    For tri-leaved diadem.

Beneath these ice-pure sepals lay
A triplet of green-pencilled snow,
Which in the chill-aired gloom of day
    Stirred softly to and fro.

Mind fixed, but else made vacant, I,
Lost to my body, called my soul
To don that frail solemnity,
    Its inmost self my goal.

And though in vain — no mortal mind
Across that threshold yet hath fared! —
In this collusion I divined
    Some consciousness we shared.

Strange roads — while suns, a myriad, set —
Had led us through infinity;
And where they crossed, there then had met
    Not two of us, but three.

THE FLEETING

The late wind failed; high on the hill
The pine's resounding boughs were still:
Those wondrous airs that space had lent
To wail earth's night-long banishment
From heat and light and song of day
In a last sighing died away.

Alone in the muteness, lost and small,
I watched from far-off Leo fall
An ebbing trail of silvery dust,
And fade to naught; while, near and far,
Glittered in quiet star to star;
And dreamed, in midnight's dim immense,
Heaven's universal innocence.

O transient heart that yet can raise
To the unseen its pang of praise,
And from the founts in play above
Be freshed with that sweet love!

HERESY

*Enter on to a prodigious headland, a little before noon, two men in alien
dress, and between them a third, younger than they, blindfold, and in the
raiment of a prince. They remove the bandage from his eyes, and seat
themselves on the turf. His hands bound behind his back, the Prince stands
between them, looking out to sea. Dazed for a moment by the sudden glare,
he stays silent.*

Prince. What place is this?
                              All's strange to me, and I
Had fallen at last accustomed to the dark.
Why, then, to this vast radiance bring me blindfold?
   Hangman. Why, Prince, a happy surprise!
      First coach-room; then,
A steady creeping upward; and now — this.
Once died — and lived — a corse named Lazarus:
Remember, then, to all men else than they
Who will not blab, you have been three days dead —
And, that far gone, even princes are soon forgot.
Lo, then, your resurrection! — take your fill.
Nor need we three have joy in it alone.
Legions of listeners surround us here,

Alert, though out of hearing and of sight.
    Prince. Like many journeys, this is best being done.
My lungs ache with the ascent and the thin air.
After your souring 'coach-room' it smells sweet.

                                      (He turns away.)

How wondrous a scene of universal calm,
These last days' troubles and distractions done!
Look, how that pretty harebell nods her head,
Whispering, *ay*, *ay*. How fresh the scent of thyme!
The knife-winged birds that haunt this sea-blue vault
Even in their droppings mock the eye with flowers
Whiter than snow.
    Hangman. Yes, and as bleached have picked
This coney's bones that dared their empire here.
    Prince. How dark a shadow in so little a head
Peers from its thin-walled skull.
    Hangman.   By Gis,
Not thyme but stark Eternity domes this perch;
And who needs hempseed when his ghost's gone home?
    Courtier. When yours goes home, the bitterest weed earth fats
Would taste more savoury to the hawks of hell.
    Hangman. Meanwhile, a civil tongue hang in your head!
You've bribed your coming hither; let it rest.
    Prince. I pray you cut these ropes from off my wrists.
Here's neither need nor hour to challenge why
And by whose tyranny I have endured
Monstrous humiliations. That may wait.
But I am faint, and have no hope in flight.
In quiet we'll sit, and you shall then rehearse
What wrongs are yours a little thought may right.
We all are human, and the heavens be judge.
    Hangman (as he picks up the skull of the rabbit from the turf).
'We all are human, and the heavens be judge'! —
A dainty saying, Prince, in either part;
Come noon, and ample proof is yours of both!
I've heard of hermits drowned so deep in silence
Their hairy ears dreamed voices in their brains.
I'd be a hermit too, if in my cell
A homelier music than this bleaching wind's
In these sharp-bladed grasses lulled me asleep.
It seemed an instant gone a halting voice
Sighed, *flight* — as if in envy of these mews
That scream defiance o'er our innocent heads.
Alackaday, the dirge they seem to sing!
    Courtier. This is sole solitude. It utterly dwarfs
Not merely man's corporeal girth and stature,

But melts to naught the imaginings of his soul.
    Hangman (*mocking him*). So empty this wide salt-tang'd vast of air
'Twould gobble up the cries of all the dying
As artlessly as God Man's sabbath prayers!
Raved here some fell she-Roc a shrill lament
Over her brood struck cold by heedless thunder,
The nearest listener would softly smile
Dreaming him lulled by sigh of passing zephyr!
(*To the Prince.*) So, sir, our talk has edged again to'rd you.
    Prince. Ay, has it so? What would you?
    Hangman.   Our sole selves,
And a something motionless in a huddle of clothes,
Which soon air's birds, earth's ants will disinfect,
Leaving it naught more talkative than bones.
    Prince. Murder is in your thoughts?
    Hangman.   Ah, sir, a boy
That lugs poor Puss close-bagged and stone-companioned
Off to her first — and only — watery bath
May have misgivings; but not so grown men.
Murder's no worse a thing when it's called Justice.
We promise you your remorse shall vex no ear
Unwonted to reproaches. Scan this height!
    Courtier (*sotto voce*). It is a table open to the eye of heav'n:
And lo, beyond that girdle of huge egg-boulders,
Sun-shivering waters to the horizon's verge —
The Ocean Sea — self-lulled, like full-fed babe
That mumbles its mother's nipple in its dreams.
    Hangman. You see, sir, though Fate may on Kings cry, 'Check!',
Princes she merely pushes off the board.
Ay, and one broken down there, upon those stones,
Frenzied with thirst and pain, need not despair!
The lapping comfort of the inning tide,
Though of a languid pace as tardy as time's,
Will, at its leisure, muffle all lamentings.
And what care lobsters if their supper talk?
    Prince. You speak as if some devil in your brains
Had stolen their sanity.
    Hangman (*smiling closely into his face*). There runs a silly saying in
        my mind,
Moaned by poor lovers cheated of desire,
Two's company; three's none!
    Prince (*ironically*).   So be it, my friend.
Adieu. I will turn back without delay!
Doubtless the paths by which you have led me blindfold
Some instinct of direction will recall.
    Hangman. I'm told that cats have such a sense of home

[212]

They'll dog their would-be murderers twenty miles,
To miaow defiance.
　Prince (facing him, eye to eye). Yes. And so would I!
Wait but till I am free from fleshly bonds!
　Hangman (laughing hollowly). An assignation past the post of
　　death!
So be it! tho' night grows cold to'rd crow of cock!
　Courtier (to the Hangman). Hold now your festering tongue awhile,
　　and wait;
A few more minutes, and it's final noon.
　　　(*He cuts the ropes that bind the Prince's wrists. The Prince seats*
　　　　himself on the turf. The Courtier paces the edge of the cliff,
　　　　pausing at times to peer into the abyss.)
　Courtier. This three days gone — and now no hope can help me —
A last brief message from the King's been mine
To bring you, Prince. In vain, in vain I stayed,
Pining in misery it might harmless prove,
Since Fate the while held all things in the balance.
The waiting's over; and the balance down.
The wild resolve I neither loved nor shared
Has fallen to worse than nothing; and the foes
That hated you can now feed full on scorn.
　Prince. Cut to the bone, friend; I am sick of snippets.
　Hangman. Well said, cut softly to the very bone.
The minutes dwindle, and the tide has turned.
　Courtier. I'll keep my Master's pace. . . . There was a realm,
A state, a hive, a human emmet heap,
Ruled over by a king whose sceptre of iron
He wielded wisely, and bade kiss or crush,
According to his kingdom's need and crisis.
Merciful he when mercy he knew well
Could virtue serve, his People, justice, peace;
But swift and pitiless when his anxious gaze
Pierced to the cancer of that People's ill.
Such rulers win more confidence than love.
None ever assailed his lealty to the good
That in his inmost soul he deemed the best —
Best for the most, less, least — since best for all.
　Hangman. A pleasing purge — and kingly common sense.
Think now, had this bold rabbit, gone to dust,
Ruled o'er his warren — why, this bright green turf
Were now a rodents' Golgotha of bones.
He who brews poison should be first to taste it.
　Prince. Of your twin voices one is wolfish bass,
But keeps the nearer to the tune they share.

Courtier. But little more of *that*, God knows — then none.
    (*He continues almost as if he were talking to himself.*)
In hives of Bees, whose summer is all spent
Toiling and moiling against wintry want,
It's not the worker, or the fatted drone,
May breed disaster, but some royal she
Fed only on nectar in her nymphal cell,
And yet uniquely sensed, who issues out
Into the whispering business of the hive,
Intent on some pre-natal paradise,
To find it but a maze of servile instinct.
What wonder if in heat of youth she rove,
Plagued and impatient at a fate so pinched,
Lusting to free her kind, to entice them on —
On to some dreamed chimera of workless bliss!
Treason! she trumps to her contented kin.
'Awake! Arouse! Fools, fools, your Queen is mad!'
But skeps of straw are not of the weaving of heaven,
And Nature's neutral tyranny is such
She'll sate with sunshine, and then starve in ice.
This jade I tell of, ardent, selfless, rash,
May of truth's essence have sucked, but what of that?
One born too wise within a polity
As ancient as the Bee's is curse more dire
Than countless generations of the dull.
    Hangman. All that this prating means is, Look at me! —
Crafty enough to feign I have few wits,
But yet can do with skill the things I'm bid.
And after, bloody-fingered, fist my wages.
    Prince. So plain the gallows shows upon your face
You need no hangman tongue to draw the trap.
(*To the other.*) Of you I ask only a moment's peace
To be alone in commune with myself.
I weary of your parables and am dumb.
Were I led hither again, again, again,
And at this bleak abyss which now I face
My bowels in a frenzy of fear should melt —
Again, again; I would no word recant,
No act recall, nor one ideal betray
Which these last few vain hours have brought to naught.
Oh, I am weary, give me leave to die.
Words may worse torture wreak than screw or rack.
    Hangman. And that's why we have given you words in plenty.
    Courtier (*still ignoring him*). One other grief — to share; and *I* have done.
This She I spoke of was, in fact, a prince;
The hive, his father's realm: a prince held dear

Beyond idolatry; the wonder and hope
Of this wise monarch's soul. No Absalom —
Since thrones in time began — was more endued
With beauty, genius, grace, fame, fortune, zeal.
He'd but to turn his head to be beloved.
The dumb-tongued stones that paved his palace court
Echoed of glory when he trod; no bliss
Was past his full achievement. Yes, my lord,
Our royal master grudged you nothing; and
He bade me breathe you peace on this account;
Avow again — though you are past his pity —
That not one blotch of envy in his blood
Did ever incite him to a thought's revenge.
He loved you . . . So, 'tis done. And I am here
To bring his blessing ere your feet go on
Into the dark unknown. There this world's kings
May find them less in rank than scullions
In service of the gods; who yet decreed
That they reign faithfully and reign unmoved
By any hope too high for human practice.
To call men equal is a heresy;
And worse — denial of the divine. Think you,
Doth jealousy green the hyssop in the wall
That with the cedar shares her mote of sunlight?
Is pain the blesseder for being shared?
Is aught in life worth having but what the mind
Hath sealed its own within its secret silence?
What is heart's ease — ambition, or the peace
That only comes of loving its poor best? . . .
When death is in the pulpit — thus he speaks!
And I, alas, his deputy. But now
I cease. No more the mouthpiece of my Master,
I stay to keep you company to the end.

> (*With a gesture the Hangman bids the Prince stand. He leads
> him to the brink of the abyss.*)

    Prince. So wild a light, and then the little dark.
This is the end, then. And, to you, farewell.
What was between my father and his son
I gave you never warranty to share.
What was between my inmost self and me
Yours never the faintest insight to descry.
He gave me life — scant born in world half-dead.
And now he craves it of me, since his seed
Has fruited past his liking. Tell him this —
When you from your day's pleasuring have gone back:
I died remorseless, yet in shame — for one

So rich in magnanimity who yet
Refused his realm the very elixir of life;
And sick with terror of what the truth might tell,
Uncharged, untried, has chos'n me *this* for end.
I am gone forth on my high errand; he
Breathes on in infamy.
    Hangman. Ha, ha, *ha, ha!* The pity that a roost
So fecund as this gives the young cock no hens!
    Courtier. Great deeds great crimes may be; and so
Of their extravagance win doom at last,
Commensurate in scope, in kind, in awe,
With him whose blinded wisdom brought them forth.
Hence this immensity on which we stand.
Such was his edict.
    Prince.   And is *this* the sot
He of his own sole choice bade bring me here?
We two — though at this pass — are of a kin;
I loved you; love you yet, but —
    Courtier. I know not, sir. The King's mouth now says nothing.
I came at no man's orders; only lest
This hangman here . . .
        (*A triple fanfare of trumpets is heard echoing up from where beyond
        view of the headland the three legions of soldiery have been
        awaiting noon.*)
                      But hark, we're for a journey
Beyond the talisman of our wits to scan.
    Hangman (*spitting upon the ground in contempt of both of them*).
    'Ware, then! Lift princely eyes into the void
And watch as 'twere your soul's winged silver slide
Into the empyrean. Get you gone!
    Prince (*leaping out into space*). Away!
    Courtier. And I! . . . Away! . . .
    (*A triple roll of drums reverberates in the parched air of noonday
    from out of the valley, ascends into the heavens, ceases.*)

BREAK OF MORNING

Sound the invisible trumps. In circuit vast
    The passive earth, like scene in dream, is set.
The small birds flit and sing, their dark hours past,
    And their green sojournings with dewdrops wet.

With giant boughs outspread, the oaks on high
    Brood on in slumbrous quiet in the air.
Sole in remote inane of vacant sky
    Paling Arcturus sparkles wildly fair.

Sound the invisible trumps. The waters weep.
  A stealing wind breathes in the meads, is gone.
Into their earthen burrows the wild things creep;
  Cockcrow to thinning cockcrow echoes on.

Avert thine eyes, sleep-ridden face! Nor scan
  Those seraph hosts that in divine array
Girdle the mortal-masked empyrean:
  Their sovereign beauty is this break of day.

Theirs is the music men call silence here;
  What wonder grief distorts thy burning eyes?
Turn to thy pillow again — in love and fear;
  Not thine to see the Son of Morning rise.

THE OWL

'Well, God 'ild you! They say the owle was a baker's daughter'. Hamlet, **IV, v**

The door-bell jangled in evening's peace,
Its clapper dulled with verdigris.
Lit by the hanging lamp's still flame
Into the shop a beggar came,
Glanced gravely around him — counter, stool,
Ticking clock and heaped-up tray
Of bakers' dainties, put to cool;
And quietly turned his eyes away.

Stepped out the goodwife from within —
Her blandest smile from brow to chin
Fading at once to blank chagrin
As she paused to peer, with keen blue eyes
Sharpened to find a stranger there,
And one, she knew, no customer.
'We never give . . .' she said, and stayed;
Mute and intent, as if dismayed
At so profoundly still a face.
'What do you want?' She came a pace
Nearer, and scanned him, head to foot.
He looked at her, but answered not.

The tabby-cat that, fathom deep,
On the scoured counter lay asleep,
Reared up its head to yawn, and then,
Composing itself to sleep again,
With eyes by night made black as jet,
Gazed on the stranger. 'A crust,' he said.
    'A crust of bread.'
Disquiet in the woman stirred —
No plea, or plaint, or hinted threat —
So low his voice she had scarcely heard.
She shook her head; he turned to go.
'We've nothing here for beggars. And so . . .
If we gave food to all who come
They'd eat us out of house and home —
Where charity begins, they say;
And ends, as like as not — or may.'

Still listening, he answered not,
His eyes upon the speaker set,
Eyes that she tried in vain to evade
    But had not met.
She frowned. 'Well, that's my husband's rule;
But stay a moment. There's a stool —
Sit down and wait. Stale bread we've none.
And else . . .' she shrugged. 'Still, rest awhile,'
Her smooth face conjured up a smile,
'And I'll go see what can be done.'

He did as he was bidden. And she
Went briskly in, and shut the door;
To pause, in brief uncertainty,
Searching for what she failed to find.
Then tiptoed back to peer once more
In through the ribboned muslin blind,
And eyed him secretly, askance,
With a prolonged, keen, searching glance;
As if mere listening might divine
Some centuries-silent countersign . . .
Scores of lean hungry folk she had turned
Even hungrier from her door, though less
From stint and scorn than heedlessness.
Why then should she a scruple spare
For one who, in a like distress,
Had spoken as if in heart he yearned
Far more for peace than bread? But now

No mark of gloom obscured his brow,
No shadow of darkness or despair.
Still as an image of age-worn stone
That from a pinnacle looks down
Over the seas of time, he sat;
His stooping face illumined by
The burnished scales that hung awry
Beside the crusted loaves of bread.
Never it seemed shone lamp so still
   On one so sore bestead.
'Poor wretch,' she muttered, 'he minds me of . . .'
A footfall sounded from above;
And, hand on mouth, immovable,
She watched and pondered there until,
Stepping alertly down the stair,
Her daughter — young as she was fair —
Came within earshot.
         'H'st,' she cried.
'A stranger here! And Lord betide,
He may have been watching till we're alone,
Biding his time, your father gone.
Come, now; come quietly and peep! —
Rags! — he would make a Christian weep!
I've promised nothing; but, good lack!
What shall I say when I go back?'

Her daughter softly stepped to peep.
'Pah! begging,' she whispered; 'I know that tale.
Money is all he wants — for ale!'
Through the cold glass there stole a beam
Of lamplight on her standing there,
Stilling her beauty as in a dream.
It smote to gold her wing-soft hair,
It scarleted her bird-bright cheek,
With shadow tinged her childlike neck,
Dreamed on her rounded bosom, and lay —
Like a sapphire pool at break of day,
Where martin and wagtail preen and play —
In the shallow shining of her eye.

'T't, mother,' she scoffed, with a scornful sigh,
And peeped again, and sneered — her lip
Drawn back from her small even teeth,
Showing the bright-red gums beneath.
'Look, now! The wretch has fallen asleep —

Stark at the counter, there; still as death.
As I sat alone at my looking-glass,
I heard a footstep — watched him pass,
Turn, and limp thief-like back again.
Out went my candle. I listened; and then
Those two faint *dings*. Aha! thought I,
Honest he may be, though old and blind,
But *that's* no customer come to buy.
So down I came — too late! I knew
He'd get less comfort from me than you!
I warrant, a pretty tale he told!
"Alone"! Lord love us! Leave him to me.
I'll teach him manners. Wait and see.'
She nodded her small snake-like head,
Sleeked with its strands of palest gold,
'Waste not, want not, say I,' she said.

Her mother faltered. Their glances met —
Furtive and questioning; hard and cold —
In mute communion mind with mind,
Though little to share could either find.
'Save us!' she answered, 'sharp eyes you have,
If in the dark you can see the blind!
He was as tongueless as the grave.
"Tale"! Not a sigh. Not one word said.
    Except that he asked for bread.'

Uneasy in her thoughts, she yet
Knew, howsoever late the hour,
And none in call, small risk they ran
From any homeless beggar-man.
While as for this — worn, wasted, wan —
    A nod, and he'd be gone.
Waste not, want not, forsooth! The chit —
To think that she should so dictate!

' "Asleep" you say? Well, what of that?
What mortal harm can come of it?
A look he gave me; and his eyes . . .
Leave him to me, Miss Worldly-wise!
Trouble him not. Stay here, while I
See how much broken meat's put by.
God knows the wretch may have his fill.
And you — keep watch upon the till!'

She hastened in, with muffled tread.
Meanwhile her daughter, left alone,
Waited, watching, till she was gone;
Then softly drew open the door, to stare
More nearly through the sombre air
At the still face, dark matted hair,
Scarred hand, shut eyes, and silent mouth,
Parched with the long day's bitter drouth;
Now aureoled in the lustre shed
From the murky lamp above his head.
Her tense young features distorted, she
Gazed on, in sharpening enmity,
Her eager lips tight shut, as if
The very air she breathed might be
Poisoned by this foul company.
That such should be allowed to live!
Yet, as she watched him, needle-clear,
   Beneath her contempt stirred fear.
Fear, not of body's harm, or aught
Instinct or cunning may have taught
Wits edged by watchful vanity:
It seemed her inmost soul made cry —
Wild thing, bewildered, the huntsmen nigh —
Of hidden ambush, and a flood
Of vague forebodings chilled her blood.
Kestrel keen, her eyes' bright blue
Narrowed, as she stole softly through.

'H'st, you!' she whispered him. 'Waken! Hear!
I come to warn you. Danger's near!'
Cat-like she scanned him, drew-to the door,
'She is calling for help. No time to wait! —
Before the neighbours come — before
They hoick their dogs on, and it's too late!'
The stranger listened; turned; and smiled:
'But whither shall I go, my child?
All ways are treacherous to those
Who, seeking friends, find only foes.'

My child! — the words like poison ran
Through her quick mind. 'What!' she began,
In fuming rage; then stayed; for, lo,
This visage, for all its starven woe,
That now met calmly her scrutiny,
Of time's corruption was wholly free.

[221]

The eyes beneath the level brows,
Though weary for want of sleep, yet shone
With strange directness, gazing on.
In her brief life she had never seen
A face so eager yet serene,
And, in its deathless courage, none
To bear with it comparison.

'I will begone,' at length he said.
  'All that I asked was bread.'

Her anger died away; she sighed;
Pouted; then laughed. 'So Mother tried
To scare me? Told me I must stop
In there — some wretch was in the shop
Who'd come to rob and . . . Well, thought I,
Seeing's believing; I could but try
To keep *her* safe. What else to do —
Till help might come?' She paused, and drew
A straying lock of yellow hair
Back from her cheek — as palely fair —
In heedless indolence; as when
A wood-dove idly spreads her wing
Sunwards, and folds it in again.
Aimless, with fingers slender and cold,
She fondled the tress more stealthily
  Than miser with his gold.
And still her wonder grew: to see
A man of this rare courtesy
So sunken in want and poverty.
What was his actual errand here?
And whereto was he journeying?
A silence had fallen between them. Save
The weight-clock's ticking, slow and grave,
No whisper, in or out, she heard;
The cat slept on; and nothing stirred.
'Is it only hungry?' she cajoled,
In this strange quiet made more bold.
'Far worse than hunger seems to me
The cankering fear of growing old.
That is a kind of hunger too —
Which even *I* can share with you.
And, heaven help me, always alone!
Mother cares nothing for that. But wait;
See now how dark it is, and late;
Nor any roof for shelter. But soon

Night will be lovely — with the moon.
When all is quiet, and she abed,
Do you come back, and click the latch;
And I'll sit up above, and watch.
A supper then I'll bring,' she said,
'Sweeter by far than mouldy bread!'

Like water chiming in a well
Which uncropped weeds more sombre make,
The low seductive syllables fell
⠀⠀⠀⠀Of every word she spake —
Music lulling the listening ear,
Note as of nightbird, low and clear,
⠀⠀⠀⠀⠀That yet keeps grief awake.
But still he made no sign. And she,
Now, fearing his silence, scoffed mockingly,
'God knows I'm not the one to give
For the mere asking. As I live
I loathe the cringing skulking scum,
Day in, day out, that begging come;
Sots, tramps, who pester, whine, and shirk —
They'd rather starve to death than work.
And lie!'— She aped, ' "God help me, m'm;
'Tisn't myself but them at home!
Crying for food they are. Yes, seven! —
And their poor mother safe in heaven!" '
Glib as a prating parrot she
Mimicked the words with sidling head,
Bright-red tongue and claw-like hands.
'But — I can tell you — when *I*'m there
There's little for the seven to share!'
She raised her eyebrows; innocent, mild —
Less parrot now than pensive child;
Her every movement of body and face,
As of a flower in the wind's embrace,
⠀⠀⠀⠀Born of a natural grace.
A vagrant moth on soundless plume,
Lured by the quiet flame within,
Fanned darkling through the narrow room,
Out of the night's obscurity.
⠀⠀⠀⠀She watched it vacantly.
'If we gave food to *all*, you see
We might as well a Workhouse be!
I've not much patience with beggary.
What use is it to whine and wail? —
Most things in this world are made for sale!

[223]

But one who really needs . . .' She sighed.
'I'd hate for him to be denied.'
She smoothed her lips, then smiled, to say:
'Have you yourself come far to-day?'
Like questing call, where shallows are
And sea-birds throng, rang out that *far* —
Decoy to every wanderer.

The stranger turned, and looked at her.
'Far, my child; and far must fare.
My only home is everywhere;
    And that the homeless share:
The vile, the lost, in misery —
      Where comfort cannot be.
You are young, your life's your own to spend;
.May it escape as dark an end.'

Her fickle heart fell cold, her eyes
Stirred not a hair's breadth, serpent-wise.
'You say', she bridled, 'that to me!
Meaning you'd have their company
Rather than mine? Why, when a friend
Gives for the giving, there's an end
To that dull talk! *My child!* — can't you
See who you are talking to?
Do you suppose because I stop
Caged up in this dull village shop
With none but clods and numskulls near,
Whose only thought is pig and beer,
And sour old maids that pry and leer,
I am content? Me! Never pine
For what by every right is mine?
Had I a wild-sick bird to keep,
Is this where she should mope and cheep?
Aching, starving, for love and light,
Eating her heart out, dawn to night!
Oh, yes, they say that safety's sweet;
And groundsel — something good to eat!
But, Lord! I'd outsing the morning stars,
For a lump of sugar between the bars!
I loathe this life. "*My Child!*" *You* see!
Wait till she's dead — and I am free!'
Aghast, she stayed — her young cheeks blenched,
Mouth quivering, and fingers clenched —
'What right have you . . .?' she challenged, and then,

[224]

With a stifled sob, fell silent again.
'And now,' she shuddered, frowned, and said,
'It's closing time. And I'm for bed.'
She listened a moment, crossed the floor,
And, dumbing on tiptoe — thumb on latch —
The clapper-bell against its catch,
    Stealthily drew wide the door.

All deathly still, the autumnal night
Hung starry and radiant, height to height,
Moon-cold hills and neighbouring wood.
Black shadows barred the empty street,
Dew-bright its cobbles at her feet,
And the dead leaves that sprinkled it.
With earthy, sour-sweet smell endued
The keen air coldly touched her skin —
Alone there, at the entering in.
Soon would the early frosts begin,
And the long winter's lassitude,
Mewed up, pent in, companionless.
No light in her mind to soothe and bless;
Only unbridled bitterness
Drummed in her blood against her side.
Her eyelids drooped, and every sense
Languished in secret virulence.
She turned and looked. 'You thought,' she cried
Small and dull as a toneless bell,
'A silly, country wench like me,
Goose for the fox, befooled could be
By your fine speeches! "Hungry"? Well,
I've been in streets where misery is
Common as wayside blackberries —
Been, and come back; less young than wise.
Go to the parson, knock him up;
He'll dole you texts on which to sup.
Or if his tombstones strike too cold,
Try the old Squire at Biddingfold:
Ask there! He thinks the village pond's
The drink for rogues and vagabonds!'
The Hunter's Moon from a cloudless sky
In pallid splendour earthward yearned;
Dazzling in beauty, cheek and eye:
And her head's gold to silver turned.
Her fierce young face in that wild shine
Showed like a god's, morose, malign.

He rose: and face to face they stood
In sudden, timeless solitude.
The fevered frenzy in her blood
Ebbed, left enfeebled body and limb.
      Appalled, she gazed at him,
Marvelling in horror of stricken heart,
In this strange scrutiny, at what
She saw but comprehended not.
Out of Astarte's borrowed light
She couched her face, to hide from sight
The tears of anguish and bitter pride
That pricked her eyes. 'My God,' she cried,
Pausing in misery on the word,
As if another's voice she had heard,
'Give — if you can — the devil his due —
I'd rather sup with him than you!
So get you gone; no more I want
      Of you, and all your cant!' . . .
A hasty footstep neared; she stayed,
Outwardly bold, but sore afraid.
'Mother!' she mocked. 'Now we shall see
What comes of asking charity.'

Platter in hand, the frugal dame
Back to the counter bustling came.
Something, she saw, had gone amiss.
And one sharp look her daughter's way
Warned her of what she had best not say.
Fearing her tongue and temper, she
Spoke with a smiling asperity.
'Look, now,' she said, 'I've brought you this.
That slut of mine's an hour abed;
The oven chilled, the fire half dead,
The bellows vanished. . . . Well, you have seen
The mort of trouble it has been.
Still, there it is; and food at least.
My husband does not hold with waste;
That's been his maxim all life through.
What's more, it's in the Scriptures too.
By rights we are shut; it's growing late;
And as you can't bring back the plate,
Better eat here — if eat you must!
And now — ah, yes, you'll want a crust.
All this bread is for sale. I'll in
And see what leavings are in the bin.'

Their glances met. Hers winced, and fell;
But why it faltered she could not tell.

The slumbering cat awoke, arose —
Roused by the savour beneath his nose,
Arched his spine, with tail erect,
Stooped, gently sniffing, to inspect
The beggar's feast, gazed after her,
And, seeing her gone, began to purr.
Her daughter then, who had watched the while,
Drew near, and stroked him — with a smile
As sly with blandishment as guile.
Daintily, finger and thumb, she took
A morsel of meat from off the plate,
And with a sidling crafty look
Dangled it over him for a bait:
'No, no; say, please!' The obsequious cat
Reared to his haunches, with folded paws,
Round sea-green eyes, and hook-toothed jaws,
Mewed, snapped, and mouthed it down; and then
Up, like a mammet, sat, begging again.
'Fie, now; he's famished! Another bit?
Mousers by rights should hunt their meat!
That's what the Master says: isn't it?'
The creature fawned on her, and purred,
As if he had pondered every word.
Yet, mute the beggar stood, nor made
A sign he grudged this masquerade.
'I dote on cats,' the wanton said.
'Dogs grovel and cringe at every nod;
Making of man a kind of God!
Beat them or starve them, as you choose,
They crawl to you, whining, and lick your shoes.
Cats know their comfort, drowse and play,
And, when the dark comes, steal away —
Wild to the wild. Make *them* obey!
As soon make water run uphill.
I'm for the night; I crave the dark;
Would wail the louder to hear them bark;
Pleasure myself till the East turns grey.'
She eyed the low window; 'Welladay!
You the greyhound, and I the hare,
I warrant of coursing you'd have your share.'
Scrap after scrap she dangled, until
The dainty beast had gorged his fill,
And, lithe as a panther, sheened like silk,

[227]

Minced off to find a drink of milk.
'There! That's cat's thanks! His feasting done,
He's off — and half your supper gone! . . .
But, wise or foolish, you'll agree
You had done better to sup with me!'

The stranger gravely raised his head.
'Once was a harvest thick with corn
When I too heard the hunting-horn;
I, too, the baying, and the blood,
And the cries of death none understood.
He that in peace with God would live
Both hunter is and fugitive.
I came to this house to ask for bread,
We give but what we have,' he said;
'Are what grace makes of us, and win
The peace that is our hearts within.'
He ceased, and, yet more gravely, smiled.
'I would that ours were reconciled!'
So sharply intent were sense and ear
On his face and accents, she failed to hear
        The meaning his words conveyed.
'"*Peace!*"' she mocked him. 'How pretty a jibe!
So jows the death-bell's serenade.
        Try a less easy bribe!'

The entry darkly gaped. And through
The cold night air, a low *a-hoo*,
A-hoo, a-hoo, from out the wood,
Broke in upon their solitude;
A call, a bleak decoy, a cry,
Half weird lament, half ribaldry.
She listened, shivered; 'Pah!' whispered she,
'No peace of yours, my God, for me!
I have gone my ways, have eyes, and wits.
Am I a cat to feed on bits
Of dried-up Bible-meat? I know
What kind of bread has that for dough;
Yes, and how honey-sweet the leaven
That starves, on earth, to glut, in heaven!
Dupe was I? Well, come closer, look,
Is my face withered? Sight fall'n in?
Beak-sharp nose and gibbering chin?
Lips that no longer can sing, kiss, pout?
Body dry sinews, the fire gone out?
So it may be with me, Judgment Day;

[228]

And, men being men, of hope forsook,
Gold all dross — hair gone grey,
Love burnt to ashes.
     Yet, still, I'd say —
Come then, to taunt me, though you may —
I'd treat hypocrites Pilate's way!
False, all false! — Oh, I can see,
You are not what you pretend to be!'

Weeping, she ceased; as flowerlike a thing
As frost ever chilled in an earthly spring.
Mingling moonlight and lamplight played
On raiment and hair; and her beauty arrayed
In a peace profound, as when in glade
On the confines of Eden, unafraid,
Cain and his brother as children strayed.

'What am I saying! I hear it. But none —
None is — God help me! — my own.'

Her mother, listening, had heard
That last low passionate broken word.
What was its meaning? Shame or fear —
It knelled its misery on her ear
    Like voices in a dream.
And, as she brooded, deep in thought,
Trembling, though not with cold, she sought
In her one twinkling candle's beam
From stubborn memory to restore
Where she had seen this man before;
What, in his marred yet tranquil mien —
Dimmed by the veils of time between —
Had conjured the past so quickly back:
Hours when by hopes, proved false, beguiled,
She too had stubborn been and wild,
As vain; but not as lovely. Alas!
And, far from innocent, a child.
A glass hung near the chimney shelf —
She peered into its shadows, moved
By thoughts of one in youth beloved,
Long tongueless in the grave, whom yet
Rancour could shun, but not forget.
Was this blowsed woman here herself?
No answer made the image there —
    Bartered but stare for stare.

She turned aside. What use to brood
On follies gone beyond recall —
Nothing to do the living good,
Secrets now shared by none; and all
Because this chance-come outcast had
Asked for alms a crust of bread.
Clean contrary to common sense,
She'd given him shelter, fetched him food —
Old scraps, maybe, but fit, at worst,
For her goodman; and warmed them first!
And this for grace and gratitude!
Charity brings scant recompense
This side of Jordan — from such as he!

But then; what meant that frenzied speech,
Cry of one loved, lost — out of reach,
From girlhood up unheard before,
And past all probing to explore?
What was between them — each with each?
          What in the past lay hid?
Long since the tongue of envy had
Whispered its worst about her child;
Arrogant, beautiful, and wild;
And beauty tarnished may strive in vain
To win its market back again . . .
To what cold furies is life betrayed
When the ashes of youth begin to cool,
When things of impulse are done by rule,
When, sickened of faiths, hopes, charities,
The soul pines only to be at ease;
And — moulting vulture in stony den —
          Waits for the end, Amen!

Thus, in the twinkling of an eye,
This heart-sick reverie swept by;
She must dissemble — if need be — lie:
Rid house and soul of this new pest,
          Prudence would do the rest.
Muffling her purpose, aggrieved in mind,
In she went, and, knee on stool,
Deigning no glance at either, leant
Over the tarnished rail of brass
That curtained off the window-glass,
And, with a tug, drew down the blind.
'Lord's Day, to-morrow,' she shrugged. 'No shop!
Come, child, make haste; it's time to sup;
High time to put the shutters up.'

[230]

The shutters up: The shutters up —
Ticked the clock the silence through,
And a yet emptier silence spread.
Shunning the effort, she raised her head;
'And *you'll* be needing to go,' she said.
She seized a loaf, broke off a crust,
Turned, and, 'There's no stale left . . .' began
Coldly, and paused — her haunted eyes
Fixed on the grease-stains, where the cat,
Mumbling its gobbets, had feasting sat.
All doubting gone, pierced to the quick
At hint of this malignant trick,
Like spark in tinder, fire in rick,
A sudden rage consumed her soul,
Beyond all caution to control.
Ignored, disdained, deceived, defied! —
'Have you, my God!' she shrilled, 'no pride?
        No shame?
Stranger, you say — and now, a friend!
Cheating and lies, from bad to worse —
Fouling your father's honest name —
Make *me*, you jade, your stalking-horse!
I've watched you, mooning, moping — ay,
        And now, in my teeth, know why!'

A dreadful quiet spread, as when
Over Atlantic wastes of sea,
Black, tempest-swept, there falls a lull,
As sudden as it is momentary,
In the maniac tumult of wind and rain,
Boundless, measureless, monstrous: and then
The insensate din begins again.

        The damsel stirred.
Jade — she had caught the bitter word;
Shame, cheating, lies. Crouched down, she stood,
Lost in a lightless solitude.
No matter; the words were said; all done.
And yet, how strange this woman should,
Self-blinded, have no heart to see
The secret of her misery;
Should think that she — all refuge gone,
And racked with hatred and shame, could be
The *friend* of this accursèd one!
The anguished blood had left her cheek
White as a leper's. With shaking head,

[231]

And eyes insanely wide and bleak,
Her body motionless as the dead,
At bay against a nameless fear,
She strove awhile in vain to speak.
Then, 'Thank you for *that*!' she whispered. 'Who
Betrayed me into a world like this,
Swarming with evil and deviltries?
Gave me these eyes, this mouth, these feet,
Flesh to hunger — and tainted meat?
Pampered me — flattered — yet taunted me when
Body and soul became prey to men,
And dog to its vomit returned again?
Ask me my name! *You? Magdalen!*
Devils? So be it. What brought me here? —
A stork in the chimney-stack, mother dear?
Oh, this false life! An instant gone
A voice within me said, *See! Have done,*
Take to you wings, and, ravening, flee,
Far from this foul hypocrisy!'
Like an old beldame's her fingers shook,
Mouth puckered, and the inning moon
Gleamed, as she cowered, on brow and eye,
Fixed now in torment on one near by.
'*Friend!* did you say? You heard that? You! —
Forsaken of God, a wandering Jew!
With milk for blood! Speak! Is it true?'

Beyond the threshold a stealthy breeze,
Faint with night's frost-cold fragrancies,
  Stirred in the trees.
Ghostlike, on moon-patterned floor there came
A scamper of leaves. The lamp's dim flame
Reared smoking in the sudden draught.
He gazed, but answered not the Jew.
Woe, beyond mortal eye to trace,
Watched through compassion in his face.
And though — as if the spirit within
Were striving through fleshly bonds to win
Out to its chosen — fiery pangs
Burned in her breast like serpent's fangs,
She lifted her stricken face, and laughed:
Hollowly, ribaldly, *Heugh, heugh, heugh!*
  'A Jew! A Jew!'—
Ran, clawed, clutched up the bread and meat,
  And flung them at his feet.
And then was gone; had taken her flight

Out through the doorway, into the street,
Into the quiet of the night,
On through the moon-chequered shadowy air;
    Away, to where
In woodland of agelong oak and yew,
Echoing its vaulted dingles through,
Faint voices answered her — *Hoo! A-hoo!*
A-hoo! A-hoo!
A-hoo!

THE STRANGE SPIRIT

Age shall not daunt me, nor sorrow for youth that is gone,
If thou lead on before me;
If thy voice in the darkness and bleak of that final night
Still its enchantment weave o'er me.
Thou hauntest the stealing shadow of rock and tree;
Hovering on wings invisible smilest at me;
Fannest the secret scent of the moth-hung flower;
Making of musky eve thy slumber-bower.

But not without danger thy fleeting presence abides
In a mind lulled in dreaming.
Lightning bepictures thy gaze. When the thunder raves,
And the tempest rain is streaming,
Betwixt cloud and earth thy falcon-head leans near —
Menacing earth-bound spirit betrayed to fear.
Cold then as shadow of death, that icy glare
Pierces the window of sense to the chamber bare.

Busied o'er dust, engrossed o'er the clod-close root,
Fire of the beast in conflict bleeding,
Goal of the coursing fish on its ocean tryst,
Wind of the weed's far seeding,
Whose servant art thou? Who gave thee earth, sky and sea
For uttermost kingdom and ranging? Who bade thee to be
Bodiless, lovely; snare, and delight of the soul,
Fantasy's beacon, of thought the uttermost goal?

When I told my love thou wert near, she bowed, and sighed.
With passion her pale face darkened.
Trembling the lips that to mine in silence replied;
Sadly that music she hearkened.

[233]

Miracle thine the babe in her bosom at rest,
Flowerlike, hidden loose-folded on gentle breast —
And we laughed together in quiet, unmoved by fear,
Knowing that, life of life, thou wast hovering near.

TO K.M.

And there was a horse in the king's stables: and the name of the horse was, Genius

We sat and talked . . . It was June, and the summer light
Lay fair upon ceiling and wall as the day took flight.
Tranquil the room — with its colours and shadows wan,
Cherries, and china, and flowers: and the hour slid on.
Dark hair, dark eyes, slim fingers — you made the tea,
Pausing with spoon uplifted, to speak to me.
Lulled by our thoughts and our voices, how happy were we!

And, musing, an old, old riddle crept into my head.
'Supposing I just say, *Horse in a field*,' I said,
'What do you *see*?' And we each made answer: 'I —
A roan — long tail, and a red-brick house, near by.'
'I — an old cart-horse and rain!' 'Oh no, not rain;
A mare with a long-legged foal by a pond — oh plain!'
'And I, a hedge — and an elm — and the shadowy green
Sloping gently up to the blue, to the west, I mean!' . . .

And now: on the field that I see night's darkness lies.
A brook brawls near: there are stars in the empty skies.
The grass is deep, and dense. As I push my way,
From sour-nettled ditch sweeps fragrance of clustering may.
I come to a stile. And lo, on the further side,
With still, umbrageous, night-clad fronds, spread wide,
A giant cedar broods. And in crescent's gleam —
A horse, milk-pale, sleek-shouldered, engendered of dream!
Startled, it lifts its muzzle, deep eyes agaze,
Silk-plaited mane . . .
                        'Whose pastures are thine to graze?
Creature, delicate, lovely, with woman-like head,
Sphinx-like, gazelle-like? Where tarries thy rider?' I said.
And I scanned by that sinking ship's thin twinkling shed
A high-pooped saddle of leather, night-darkened red,
Stamped with a pattern of gilding; and over it thrown
A cloak, chain-buckled, with one great glamorous stone,

Wan as the argent moon when o'er fields of wheat
Like Dian she broods, and steals to Endymion's feet.
Interwoven with silver that cloak from seam to seam.
And at toss of that head from its damascened bridle did beam
Mysterious glare in the dead of the dark. . . .
     'Thy name,
Fantastical steed? Thy pedigree?
Peace, out of Storm, is the tale? Or *Beauty, of Jeopardy?*'
The water grieves. Not a footfall — and midnight here.
Why tarries Darkness's bird? Mounded and clear
Slopes to yon hill with its stars the moorland sweet.
There sigh the airs of far heaven. And the dreamer's feet
Scatter the leagues of paths secret to where at last meet
Roads called Wickedness, Righteousness, broad-flung or strait,
And the third that leads on to the Queen of fair Elfland's gate. . . .

This then the horse that I see; swift as the wind;
That none may master or mount; and none may bind —
But she, his Mistress: cloaked, and at throat that gem —
Dark hair, dark eyes, slim shoulder. . . .
     God-speed, K.M.!

DREAMS

Ev'n one who has little travelled in
This world of ample land and sea;
Whose Arctic, Orient, tropics have been —
Like Phœnix, siren, jinn, and *Sidhe* —
But of his thoughts' anatomy —
Each day makes measureless journeys twain:
From wake to dream; to wake again.

At night he climbs a quiet stair,
Secure within its pictured wall;
His clothes, his hands, the light, the air,
Familiar objects one and all —
Accustomed, plain, and natural.
He lays him down: and, ages deep,
Flow over him the floods of sleep.

[235]

Lapped in this influence alien
To aught save sorcery could devise,
Heedless of *Sesame* or *Amen*,
He is at once the denizen
Of realms till then beyond surmise;
Grotesque, irrational, and sans
All law and order known as Man's.

Though drowsy sentries at the gate
Of eye and ear dim watch maintain,
And, at his absence all elate,
His body's artisans sustain
Their toil in sinew, nerve, and brain:
Nothing recks he; he roves afar,
Past compass, chart, and calendar.

Nor is he the poor serf who shares
One self alone where'er he range,
Since in the seven-league Boots he wears
He may, in scores of guises, change
His daily ego — simple or strange;
Stand passive looker-on; or be
A paragon of energy.

Regions of beauty, wonder, peace
By waking eyes unscanned, unknown.
Waters and hills whose loveliness,
Past mortal sense, are his alone.
There flow'rs by the shallows of Lethe sown
Distil their nectar, drowsy and sweet,
And drench the air with news of it.

Or lost, betrayed, forlorn, alas!
Gaunt terror leads him by the hand
Through demon-infested rank morass;
O'er wind-bleached wilderness of sand;
Where cataracts rave; or bleak sea-strand
Shouts at the night with spouted spume;
Or locks him to rot in a soundless tomb.

Here, too, the House of Folly is,
With gates ajar, and windows lit,
Wherein with foul buffooneries
A spectral host carousing sit.
'Hail, thou!' they yelp. 'Come, taste and eat!'
And so, poor zany, sup must he
The nightmare dregs of idiocy.

All this in vain? Nay, thus abased,
Made vile in the dark's incontinence,
Though even the anguish of death he taste,
The murderer's woe — his penitence,
And pangs of the damned experience —
Will he God's mercy less esteem
When dayspring prove them only a dream?

What bliss to clutch, when thus beset,
The folded linen of his sheet;
Or hear, without, more welcome yet,
A footfall in the dawnlit street;
The whist of the wind; or, far and sweet,
Some small bird's daybreak rhapsody,
That bids him put all figments by.

Oh, when, at morning up, his eyes
Open to earth again, then, lo!
An end to all dream's enterprise! —
It melts away like April snow.
What night made false now true doth show;
What day discloses night disdained;
And who shall winnow real from feigned?

But men of learning little heed
Problems that simple folk perplex;
And some there are who have decreed
Dreams the insidious wiles of sex;
That slumber's plain is wake's complèx;
And, plumbing their own minds, profess
Them quagmires of unconsciousness.

Sad fate it is, like one who is dead,
To lie inert the long night through,
And never by dream's sweet fantasy led
To lave tired eyes in heavenly dew!
But worse — the prey of a gross taboo
And sport of a Censor — to squat and make
Pies of a mud forbidd'n the awake!

Nay, is that Prince of the Dust — a man,
But a tissue of parts, dissectable?
Lancet, balances, callipers — can
The least of his actions by human skill
Be measured as so much Sex, Want, Will? —
Fables so dull would the sweeter be
With extract of humour for company!

Once was a god whose lovely face,
Wan as the poppy and arched in wings,
So haunted a votary with his grace
And the still wonder that worship brings,
That, having sipped of Helicon's springs,
He cast his beauty in bronze. And now
Eternal slumber bedims his brow —

Hypnos: and Dream was his dear son.
Not ours these follies. We haunt instead
Tropical jungles drear and dun,
And see in some fetish of fear and dread
Our symbol of dream — that brooding head!
And deem the wellspring of genius hid
In a dark morass that is dubbed the Id.

Sacred of old was the dyed baboon,
Though least, of the monkeys, like man is he.
Yet, rank the bones of his skeleton
With *homo sapiens'*: will they be
Void of design, form, symmetry?
To each his calling. Albeit we know
Apes father no Michelangelo!

In truth, a destiny undivined
Haunts every cell of bone and brain;
They share, to time and space resigned,
All passions that to earth pertain,
And twist man's thoughts to boon or bane;
Yet, be he master, need we ban
What the amoeba's made of man?

Who of his thoughts can reach the source?
Who in his life-blood's secret share?
By knowledge, artifice, or force
Compel the self within declare
What fiat bade it earthward fare?
Or proof expound this journey is
Else than a tissue of fantasies?

See, now, this butterfly, its wing
A dazzling play of patterned hues;
Far from the radiance of Spring,
From every faltering flower it choose
'Twill dip to sip autumnal dews:
So flit man's happiest moments by,
Daydreams of selfless transiency.

Was it by cunning the curious fly
That preys in a sunbeam schooled her wings
To ride her in air all motionlessly,
Poised on their myriad winnowings?
Where conned the blackbird the song he sings?
Was Job the instructor of the ant?
Go bees for nectar to Hume and Kant?

Who bade the scallop devise her shell?
Who tutored the daisy at cool of eve
To tent her pollen in floreted cell?
What dominie taught the dove to grieve;
The mole to delve; the worm to weave?
Does not the rather their life-craft seem
A tranced obedience to a dream?

Thus tranced, too, body and mind, will sit
A winter's dawn to dark, alone,
Heedless of how the cold moments flit,
The worker in words, or wood, or stone:
So far his waking desires have flown
Into a realm where his sole delight
Is to bring the dreamed-of to mortal sight.

Dumb in its wax may the music sleep —
In a breath conceived — that, with ardent care,
Note by note, in a reverie deep,
Mozart penned, for the world to share.
Waken it, needle! And then declare
How, invoked by thy tiny tang,
Sound such strains as the Sirens sang!

Voyager dauntless on Newton's sea,
Year after year still brooding on
His algebraical formulae,
The genius of William Hamilton
Sought the square root of *minus* one;
In vain; till — all thought of it leagues away —
The problem flowered from a dream one day.

Our restless senses leap and say,
'How marvellous this! — How ugly that!'
And, at a breath, will slip away
The very thing they marvel at.
Time is the tyrant of their fate;
And frail the instant which must be
Our all of actuality.

If then to Solomon the Wise
Some curious priest stooped low and said,
'Thou, with thy lidded, sleep-sealed eyes,
This riddle solve from out thy bed:
Art thou — am I — by phantoms led?
Where is the real? In dream? Or wake?'
I know the answer the King might make!

And teeming Shakespeare: would he avow
The creatures of his heart and brain,
Whom, Prospero-like, he could endow
With all that mortal souls contain,
Mere copies that a fool can feign
Out of the tangible and seen? —
This the sole range of his demesne?

Ask not the Dreamer! See him run,
Listening a shrill and gentle neigh,
Foot into stirrup, he is up, he has won
Enchanted foothills far away.
Somewhere? Nowhere? Who need say?
So be it in secrecy of his mind
He some rare delectation find.

Ay, once I dreamed of an age-wide sea
Whereo'er three moons stood leper-bright;
And once — from agony set free —
I scanned within the womb of night,
A hollow inwoven orb of light,
Thrilling with beauty no tongue could tell,
And knew it for Life's citadel.

And — parable as strange — once, I
Was lured to a city whose every stone,
And harpy human hastening by
Were spawn and sport of fear alone —
By soulless horror enthralled, driven on:
Even the waters that, ebon-clear,
Coursed through its dark, raved only of *Fear*!

Enigmas these; but not the face,
Fashioned of sleep, which, still at gaze
Of daybreak eyes, I yet could trace,
Made lovelier in the sun's first rays;
Nor that wild voice which in amaze,
Wide-wok'n, I listened singing on —
All memory of the singer gone.

O Poesy, of wellspring clear,
Let no sad Science thee suborn,
Who art thyself its planisphere!
All knowledge is foredoomed, forlorn —
Of inmost truth and wisdom shorn —
Unless imagination brings
Its skies wherein to use its wings.

Two worlds have we: without; within;
But all that sense can mete and span,
Until it confirmation win
From heart and soul, is death to man.
Of grace divine his life began;
And — Eden empty proved — in deep
Communion with his spirit in sleep

The Lord Jehovah of a dream
Bade him, past all desire, conceive
What should his solitude redeem;
And, to his sunlit eyes, brought Eve.
Would that my day-wide mind could weave
Faint concept of the scene from whence
She awoke to Eden's innocence!

Starven with cares, like tares in wheat,
Wildered with knowledge, chilled with doubt,
The timeless self in vain must beat
Against its walls to hasten out
Whither the living waters fount;
And — evil and good no more at strife —
Seek love beneath the tree of life.

When then in memory I look back
To childhood's visioned hours I see
What now my anxious soul doth lack
Is energy in peace to be
At one with nature's mystery:
And Conscience less my mind indicts
For idle days than dreamless nights.

ISAAC MEEK

Hook-nosed was I, loose-lipped; greed fixed its gaze
In my young eyes ere they knew brass from gold;
Doomed to the blazing market-place my days —
A sweated chafferer of the bought and sold.
Fawned on and spat at, flattered and decried —
One only thing men asked of me — my price.
I lived, detested; and deserted, died,
Scorned by the virtuous, and the jest of vice.
And now, behold, blest child of Christ, my worth;
Stoop close: I have inherited the earth!

THE SNOWFLAKE

See, now, this filigree: 'tis snow,
Shaped, in the void, of heavenly dew;
On winds of space like flower to blow
In a wilderness of blue.

Black are those pines. The utter cold
Hath frozen to silence the birds' green woods.
Rime hath ensteeled the wormless mould,
A vacant quiet broods.

Lo, this entrancèd thing! — a breath
Of life that bids Man's heart to crave
Still for perfection: ere fall death,
And earth shut in his grave.

Poems 1919-1934 (1935)

ST. ANDREWS

September 1925

Fickle of choice is Memory:
But hidden in her secret deeps
She guards whatever in life may be
Vivid and sweet perpetually;
And of the loved strict treasury keeps.

There childhood's flowers bloom for aye;
There, in a quiet grave, profound,
Those whom dark death hath lured away
Live on, with peace unchanging crowned,
Immune from time's decay.

Keeps she for me, then, safe-enshrined —
Cold of the North — those bleached grey streets;
Grey skies, a glinting sun, a wind
From climes where sea with ocean meets,
And ruinous walls by tempests pined.

There, history and romance abide:
Martyr and saint, Pict, Scot, Culdees.
They dared, fought, suffered, dreamed and died,
Yet of their long wild centuries
Left but these stones their bones beside.

Ghosts in that sunlight come and go:
Columba, David, Margaret,
Bothwell the fierce, dark Rizzio,
And she, caught fast in fate's fell net,
Mary, the twice-queened, fair as snow . . .

The winter daylight wanes. The tide
Lays a cold wreath of foam upon
Its sea-worn rocks. The billows ride
In endless cavalcade — are gone.
The rose of eve burns far and wide.

WINTER

Mute now the music that made me
 Its earthly echo be.
Flown now the tender hovering wing
 To its own further Spring.
And fallen to the dust they were —
 Flowers of a rarer air.

O winter of my heart, keep yet
 Thy cold snows over it;
Those flowers fast-sealed; that music asleep
 In darkened silence keep;
Baffle me not with beams that stir
 Too anxious a wanderer
Only to lift distracted sight
 On empty fields forlorn with night.

ROMANCE

Well, then, you ask me what is *real*,
 And I — poor thief — I say,
See, what wild gold the tide-drifts steal
 To pour into this bay!

Those emeralds, opals, pearls to land
 Washed in by wave on wave;
That heat-struck swoon of shimmering sand,
 That music-echoing cave!

Salt? Bubbles? Cheating mist and light?
 Quartz ground by surge to dust?
Call *me* mere brittle bones — and sight —
 Illusion if you must;

Yet still some seraph in my mind
 His praises cries, has flown
Into a region unconfined
 Man, baffled, calls the unknown.

Desire leaps up, and poised on high
 Love's gaze — from eyes askance —
Scans in delight of sea and sky
 The vineyards of Romance.

[244]

AFRAID

Here lies, but seven years old, our little maid,
Once of the darkness Oh, so sore afraid!
Light of the World — remember that small fear,
And when nor moon nor stars do shine, draw near!

A STAVE

O my dear one,
Do not repine
Their rose hath left
Those cheeks of thine.
In memory hid
Blooms yet, how clear,
Past fading now,
Its beauty, dear.
Yet — fallen a little
In time, soon gone,
Is the heart that yearned
Their fragrance on;
And much is quenched
Of that wild fire
That did from dust
To thee aspire.

It is our fate.
Like tapers, we
Life's pure wax waste
Unheedingly.
Till Love, grown weary
Of its light,
Frowns, puffs his cheek,
And sighs, good night.

QUACK

What said the drake to his lady-love
   But *Quack*, then *Quack*, then QUACK!
And she, with long love-notes as sweet as his,
   Said *Quack* — then, softlier, QUACK
And Echo that lurked by the old red barn,
   Beyond their staddled stack,
Listening this love-lorn pair's delight,
   Quacked their quacked *Quack*, *Quack*, *Quacks* back.

OH, YES, MY DEAR

Oh, yes, my dear, you have a mother,
And she, when young, was loved by another,
And in that mother's nursery
Played *her* mamma, like you and me.
When that mamma was tiny as you
She had a happy mother too:
On, on . . . Yes, presto! Puff! Pee-fee! —
And Grandam Eve and the apple-tree.
O, into distance, smalling, dimming,
Think of that endless row of women,
Like beads, like posts, like lamps, they seem —
Grey-green willows, and life a stream —
Laughing and sighing and lovely; and, oh,
You to be next in that long row!

SEEN AND HEARD

Lovely things these eyes have seen —
Dangling cherries in leaves dark-green;
Ducks as white as winter snow,
Which quacked as they webbed on a-row;
The wren that, with her needle note,
Through blackthorn's foam will flit and float;
Clear dews whereon the moonbeams softly gloat
    And sun will sheen.

Lovely music my ears have heard —
Catkined twigs in April stirred
By the same air that carries true
Two notes from Africa, *Cuck-oo*;
And then, when night has darkened again,
The lone wail of the willow-wren,
And cricket rasping on, 'Goode'n — goode'n',
    Shriller than mouse or bird.

Ay, and all praise would I, please God, dispose
For but one faint-hued cowslip, one wild rose.

Memory and Other Poems (1938)

A SUNDAY

A child in the Sabbath peace, there —
Down by the full-bosomed river;
Sun on the tide-way, flutter of wind,
Water-cluck, — *Ever . . . for ever . . .*

Time itself seemed to cease there —
The domed, hushed city behind me;
Home how distant! The morrow would come —
But here, no trouble could find me.

A respite, a solacing, deep as the sea,
Was mine. Will it come again? . . . Never? . . .
Shut in the past is that Sabbath peace, there —
Down by the full-bosomed river.

A POT OF MUSK

A glance — and instantly the small meek flower
Whispered of what it had to childhood meant;
But kept the angel secret of that far hour
    Ere it had lost its scent.

BROTHER AND SISTER

A turn of head, that searching light,
And — was it fancy? — a faint sigh:
I know not what; there leapt the thought,
    We are old, now — she and I.

Old, though those eager clear blue eyes,
And lines of laughter along the cheek,
Far less of time than time's despite
    To one who loves her speak. . . .

[247]

Besides, those pale and smiling lips,
That once with beauty were content,
Now wisdom too have learned; and that
    No clock can circumvent. . . .

Nor is this world of ours a toy
That woe should darken when bed-time nears;
Still memory-sweet its old decoy,
    And — well, what use in tears?

So limped the brittle argument;
Yet — had I Prospero's wizardry,
She should at once have back her youth,
    Whatever chanced to me.

POLLIE

Pollie is a simpleton;
'Look!' she cries, 'that *lovely* swan!'
And, even before her transports cease,
    Adds, 'But I do love geese.'

When a lark wings up the sky,
She'll sit with lips ajar, then sigh —
For rapture; and the rapture o'er,
    Whisper, 'What's music *for*?'

Every lesson I allot,
As soon as learned is clean forgot.
'L-O-V . . .?' I prompt. And she
    Smiles, but I catch no 'E'.

It seems in her round head you come
As if to a secret vacuum;
Whence then the wonder, love and grace
    Shining in that small face?

THE IRREVOCABLE

Weep no more, thou weary one;
Tears — and so beloved a face!
Raindrops on a daybreak flower —
Token of cold midnight's grace —
No more radiant are than these.
Both of transient darkness tell;
And but one last beam of morning
    Either will dispel.

[248]

I thy midnight was. . . . Yet word,
Easy, innocent of guile,
Weeping eyes and childlike lips
　　Have conjured to a smile.
All forgotten, all forgiven.
Why remorse, then? . . . Well I know
The few clear stars still mine in heaven
Never shall now as brightly show.

ABSALOM

Vain, proud, rebellious Prince, thy treacherous hair,
Though thirty centuries have come and gone,
Still in that bitter oak doth thee ensnare;
Rings on that broken-hearted, *Son, my son!* . . .

And though, with childhood's tragic gaze, I see
Thee — idol of Israel — helpless in the tree,
Thy dying eyes turned darkened from the Sun;
Yet, of all faces in far memory's shrine —
Paris, Adonis, pale Endymion —
　　The loveliest still is thine.

IN A LIBRARY

Would — would that there were
A book on that shelf
To teach an old man
To teach himself! —

The joy of some scribe,
Brush in service to quill,
Who, with bird, flower, landscape,
Emblem and vision,
Loved his margins to fill.

Then might I sit,
By true learning beguiled,
Far into the night
Even with self reconciled,
Retrieving the wisdom
I lost, when a child.

IN DISGRACE

The fear-dulled eyes in the pallid face
Stared at the darkening window-pane;
Sullen, derided, in disgrace —
They watched night narrowing in again:
Far-away shoutings; a furtive wind
Which a keyhole had found; a star aloof;
A heart at war with a blunted mind;
    And a spout dripping rain from the roof: —

Drip — drip . . . till the light is gone;
But a heart not so hard as a stone.

'UNHEARD MELODIES'

A minstrel came singing in the way;
    And the children,
    Nothing saying,
    Gathered round him,
    From their playing,
In a bower of the shadowy may.

He stood in a loop of the green;
    And his fingers
    On the wires
    Feigned their heart's deep,
    Hidden desires
For a country that never was seen.

Like moonbeams in forests of trees,
    Like brook water
    Dropping sweetness,
    Like the wild hare
    In her fleetness,
Like the wings of the honey-sucking bees;

He drew each pure heart with his skill;
    With his beauty,
    And his azure,
    And his topaz,
    Gold for pleasure,
And his locks wet with dew of April.

[250]

Time sped; and night's shadows grew deep,
      Came owl-hoot
      From the thicket,
      And the shrill note
      Of the cricket
Called the children to silence and sleep. . . .

Strange, strange! though the minstrel is gone,
      Yet that hawthorn
      Fair and lonely
      Stoops mutely
      Waiting only
Till the clamour of noonday is done —

Until, in the faint skies of eve,
      Far and sweetly,
      Like a river,
      Silver wires seem
      Throbbing ever
As if echo in sorrow would grieve

In ears dulled with wrath and rebuke;
      And like snowdrops
      After winter,
      Tired feet pause there,
      And then enter
That bower by the midsummer brook.

O minstrel, keep thy tryst, sound thine airs
      In a heart that
      Oft forgets thee,
      Scorns, reviles thee,
      Tires, and frets thee
With the burden of silence it bears.

A CHILD ASLEEP

Angel of Words, in vain I have striven with thee,
Nor plead a lifetime's love and loyalty;
Only, with envy, bid thee watch this face,
    That says so much, so flawlessly,
      And in how small a space!

[251]

RESERVED

...'I was thinking, Mother, of that poor old horse
   They killed the other day;
Nannie *says* it was only a bag of bones,
   But I hated it taken away.'
'Of course, sweet; but now the baker's man
Will soon have a nice new motor van.'

'Yes, Mother. But when on our walk a squirrel
   Crept up to my thumb to be fed,
She shoo'd it away with her gloves — like this!
   They ought to be shot, she said.'
'She may have been reading, darling, that
Squirrels are only a kind of *rat*.'

'Goldfinches, Mother, owls and mice,
   Tom-tits and bunnies and jays —
Everything in my picture-books
   Will soon be gone, she says.'
'You see, my precious, so many creatures,
   Though exquisitely made,
Steal, or are dirty and dangerous,
   Or else they are bad for Trade.'

'I wonder, Mother, if when poor Noah
   Was alone in the rain and dark,
He can ever have thought what wicked things
   Were round him in the Ark. . . .
And are all children — like the rest —
Like me, as Nannie says, a pest?

'I woke last night from a dreadful dream
   Of a place — it was all of stone;
And dark. And the walls went up, and up —
   And oh, I was lost: alone!
I was *terrified*, Mother, and tried to call;
   But a gabble, like echoes, came back.
It will soon, I suppose, be bedtime again?
   And I hate lying there awake.'

[252]

'You mustn't, angel.' She glanced at the window —
  Smiled at the questioning mite.
'There's nothing to fear.' A wild bird scritched.
  The sun's last beam of light
Gilded the Globe, reserved for Man,
  Preparing for the Night.

DRY AUGUST BURNED

Dry August burned. A harvest hare
Limp on the kitchen table lay,
Its fur blood-blubbered, eyes astare,
While a small child that stood near by
Wept out her heart to see it there.

Sharp came the *clop* of hoofs, the clang
Of dangling chain, voices that rang.
Out like a leveret she ran,
To feast her glistening bird-clear eyes
On a team of field artillery,
Gay, to manœuvres, thudding by.
Spur and gun and limber plate
Flashed in the sun. Alert, elate,
Noble horses, foam at lip,
Harness, stirrup, holster, whip,
She watched the sun-tanned soldiery,
Till dust-white hedge had hidden away —
Its din into a rumour thinned —
The laughing, jolting, wild array:
And then — the wonder and tumult gone —
Stood nibbling a green leaf, alone,
Her dark eyes, dreaming. . . . She turned, and ran,
Elf-like, into the house again.
The hare had vanished. . . . 'Mother,' she said,
Her tear-stained cheek now flushed with red,
'Please, may I go and see it skinned?'

'OF A SON'

A garish room — oil-lamped; a stove's warm blaze;
Gilt chairs drawn up to candles, and green baize:
The doctor hastened in — a moment stayed,
Watching the cards upon the table played —
Club, and sharp diamond, and heart, and spade.
And — still elated — he exclaimed, '*Parbleu*,
A thousand pardons, friends, for keeping you;
I feared I'd never see the lady through.
A boy, too! *Magnifique* the fight she made!
Ah, well, she's happy now!' Said one, ' "She"? — who?'
    'A woman called Landru.'

Gentle as flutter of dove's wing, the cards
Face downwards fell again; and fever-quick,
Topped by old Time and scythe, a small brass clock
In the brief hush of tongues resumed its tick.

SHADOW

*B*eware! — breathes the faint evening wind?
Omen! — sighs dayspring's innocent air?
Stalks out from shadow, when drawn's the blind,
A warning Nothing, to shake the mind
    And touch the soul with care?
    At midnight on thy stair?

Lurks there in every rose's sweet
A murderous whisper, *Fade must I?*
Mutters the vagrant in the street,
Edging his way with anxious feet —
    Thou too art hastening by.
    Drones on the carrion fly?

Oh, climb thou down from fool's disdain;
Stoop thy cold lips to rag and sore;
Kiss the gaunt cheek while yet remains
Life's blood in it. Ay, hearken; again! —
    Thou art the thief, the murderer,
    The outcast at thy door.

[254]

ONE IN THE PUBLIC GALLERY

The Seraph scanned the murderer in the dock —
The motionless Judge, beneath the court-room clock,
The listening jury, warders, counsel, Clerk;
Ay, one and all who shared that deepening dark:
　　And then, as I shunned to see,
He turned his burning eyes and looked at me.

THE BRIDGE

With noble and strange devices Man hath spanned
River and torrent, raging in flood beneath;
But one more subtle than he ever planned
　　Will exhaust my last faint breath:
A bridge, now nearing, I shall walk alone —
One pier on earth, the other in the unknown:
　　And there, a viewless wraith —
Prince of the wreckage of the centuries,
Yet still past thought's fixed scrutiny, heart's surmise,
　　And nought but a name, yet: Death.

SOLITUDE

Ghosts there must be with me in this old house,
Deepening its midnight as the clock beats on.
Whence else upwelled — strange, sweet, yet ominous —
That moment of happiness, and then was gone?

Nimbler than air-borne music, heart may call
A speechless message to the inward ear,
As secret even as that which then befell,
Yet nought that listening could make more clear.

Delicate, subtle senses, instant, fleet! —
But oh, how near the verge at which they fail!
In vain, self hearkens for the fall of feet
Soft as its own may be, beyond the pale.

THE 'SATIRE'

The dying man on his pillow
Turned slowly his head.
'Five years or my Satire on Man
I spent,' he said.
'But, lying alone, I have mused
On myself, of late!'

Smiling, he nodded; and glanced
At the ash in the grate.

INCANTATION

Vervain ... basil ... orison —
Whisper their syllablings till all meaning is gone,
And sound all vestige loses of mere word. ....
'Tis then as if, in some far childhood heard,
A wild heart languished at the call of a bird,
Crying through ruinous windows, high and fair,
A secret incantation on the air:
A language lost; which, when its accents cease,
Breathes, voiceless, of a pre-Edenic peace.

A ROSE IN CANDLELIGHT

The oil in wild Aladdin's lamp
A witching radiance shed;
But when its Genie absent was
It languished, dull and dead.

Lo, now, the light that bathes this rose,
That wondrous red its cheek to give!
It breathes, 'We, too, a secret share;
Fleeting we are, however fair;
And only representative.'

DEFEAT

The way on high burned white beneath the sun,
Crag and gaunt pine stood stark in windless heat,
With sun-parched weeds its stones were over-run,
And he who had dared it, his long journey done,
Lay sunken in the slumber of defeat.

[256]

A raven low in the air, with stagnant eyes,
Poised in the instant of alighting gust,
Rent the thin silence with his hungry cries,
Voicing his greed o'er this far-scented prize,
Stiff in the invisible movement of the dust.

He lay, sharp-boned beneath his skin, half-nude,
His black hair tangled with a blackening red,
His gaze wide-staring in his solitude,
O'er which a bristling cloud of flies did brood,
In mumbling business with his heedless head.

Unfathomable drifts of space below,
Stretched, like grey glass, an infinite low sea,
Whereon a conflict of bright beams did flow,
In fiery splendour trembling to and fro —
The noon sun's angel-loosened archery.

And still on high, the way, a lean line, wound,
Wherefrom the raven had swooped down to eat,
To mortal eyes without an end, or bound,
Nor any creeping shadow to be found
To cool the sunken temples of defeat.

Defeat was scrawled upon each naked bone,
Defeat in the glazed vacancy of his eye,
Defeat his hand clutched in that waste of stone,
Defeat the bird yelped, and the flies' mazed drone
Lifted thanksgiving for defeat come by.

Lost in eternal rumination stare
Those darkened sockets of a dreamless head,
That cheek and jaw with the unpeopled air,
With smile immutable, unwearying, share
The subtle cogitations of the dead.

Yet, dwindling mark upon fate's viewless height,
For sign and token above the infinite sea,
'Neath the cold challenge of the all-circling night
Shall lie for witness in the Invisible's sight
The mockless victory that defeat may be.

[257]

AT EASE

Most wounds can Time repair;
But some are mortal — these:
For a broken heart there is no balm,
No cure for a heart at ease —

At ease, but cold as stone,
Though the intellect spin on,
And the feat and practised face may show
Nought of the life that is gone;

But smiles, as by habit taught;
And sighs, as by custom led;
And the soul within is safe from damnation,
Since it is dead.

AN ABANDONED CHURCH

Roofless and eyeless, weed-sodden, dank, old, cold —
Fickly the sunset glimmered through the rain,
Gilded the gravestones — faded out again;
A storm-cock shrilled its aeon-old refrain,
Lambs bleated from their fold.

A ROSE IN WATER

A rose, in water, to its stem
Decoys a myriad beads of air;
And, lovely with the light on them,
Gives even its thorns their share.

NOT ONLY

Not only ruins their lichen have;
Nor tombs alone, their moss.
Implacable Time, in markless grave,
Turns what seemed gold to dross.

Yet — a mere ribbon for the hair,
A broken toy, a faded flower
A passionate deathless grace may wear,
Denied its passing hour.

EVENING

The little cirque, horizon-wide,
Of earth now swiftly draws away,
Though fulling moon aloft doth ride
Into the sun's perpetual day.

Little? It's all I have. For space
Than time itself's no less confined:
Its only being is what has place
At pin-point moment in the mind.

All history, knowledge, wisdom, power,
All man has said, or done, or made —
As transitory as a flower —
For me on this scant thread is stayed.

The all, the one; their better and worse,
Interdependent ever remain;
Each instant is my universe;
Which at a nod may fade again.

At the last slumber's nod, what then?

THE ASSIGNATION

Echoes of voices stilled may linger on
Until a lapse of utter quiet steal in;
As 'tis hushed daybreak — the dark night being gone —
That calls small birds their matins to begin....

Felled with such sickness I had lain that life
Nightmare's phantasmagoria seemed to be.
Alas, poor body, racked with woe and strife,
Its very weakness set my spirit free.

Wondrous the regions then through which I strayed,
Spectre invisible as the wind and air,
Regions that midnight fantasy had made,
And clear cold consciousness can seldom share.

But of these wanderings one remembered best
Nothing exotic showed — no moon-drenched vale,
Where in profound ravines dark forests rest,
The wild-voiced cataracts their nightingale;

[259]

But only a sloping meadow, rimed with frost;
Bleak pollard willows, and a frozen brook,
All tinkle of its waters hushed and lost,
Its sword-sharp rushes by the wind forsook:

An icy-still, grey-heavened, vacant scene,
With whin and marron hummocked, and flowerless gorse. . . .
And in that starven upland's winter green,
Stood grazing in the silence a white horse.

No marvel of beauty, or strangeness, or fable, this —
Una — *la Belle Dame* — hero — or god might ride;
Worn, aged with time and toil, and now at peace,
It cropped earth's sweetmeats on the stark hill's side.

Spellbound, I watched it — hueless mane and tail
Like wraith of foam upon an un-named sea;
Until, as if at mute and inward hail,
It raised its gentle head and looked at me —

Eyes blue as speedwell, tranquil, morning-fair:
It was as if for aeons these and I
Had planned this mystic assignation there,
In this lone waste, beneath that wintry sky. . . .

Strange is man's soul, which solace thus can win,
When the poor body lies at woe's extreme —
Yea, even where the shades of death begin —
In secret symbol, and painted by a dream!

THE MOMENT

O Time — the heedless child you are!
A daisy, the most distant star
Fall to your toying scimitar.
And I? And this loved face? We too
Are things but of a moment. True:
But then, poor youngling, so are you!

Dream on! In your small company
We are contented merely to be —
Yes, even to Eternity.

MEMORY

Ah, Memory — that strange deceiver!
Who can trust her? How believe her —
While she hoards with equal care
The poor and trivial, rich and rare;
Yet flings away, as wantonly,
Grave fact and loveliest fantasy?

When I call her — need her most,
Lo, she's in hiding, or is lost!
Or, capricious as the wind,
Brings stalks — and leaves the flowers behind!
Of all existence — as I live —
She can no more than moments give.
Thousands of dew-clear dusks in Spring
Were mine, time gone, to wander in,
But of their fragrance, music, peace,
What now is left my heart to bless?
Oases in a wilderness!
Nor could her tongue tell o'er the tale
Even of one June nightingale.
And what of the strange world that teems —
Where brooding Hypnos reigns — with dreams?
Twenty years in sleep I have spent —
Horror, delight, grief, wonderment;
Through what wild wizard scenes lured on!
Where are they? . . . In oblivion.
Told she her all, 'twould reach an end
Ere nodded off the drowsiest friend!

She has, it's true, a sovereign skill
A wounded heart to salve and heal;
Can lullaby to sorrow sing;
Shed balm on grief and suffering;
And guard with unremitting care
Secrets that we alone can share.
Ay, so bewitched her amber is
'Twill keep enshrined the tiniest flies —
Instants of childhood, fresh as when
My virgin sense perceived them then —
Daisy or rainbow, a look, a kiss,
As safe as if Eternity's;
And can, with probe as keen, restore
Some fear, or woe, when I was four.
Fleeter than Nereid, plummet-deep,

[261]

Enticed by some long-sunken ship,
She, siren-wise, laughs out to see
The treasure she retrieves for me —
Gold foundered when I was a boy,
Now cleansed by Time from all alloy.
And think what priceless boons I owe
Her whimsical punctilio!

Nothing would recognition bring
Should she forsake me. Everything
I will, or want, or plan, or say
Were past conceiving, she away.
Only her exquisite vigilance
Enables me to walk, sing, dance.
Tree and bird would name-less pine
Did she the twain refuse to entwine.
And where, sad dunce, if me she shun,
My A B C? my twice times one?
Fancy her nurseling is; and thought
Can solely in her toils be caught.
Ev'n who and where and what I am
Await her whisper to proclaim.

If only — what the infinite loss! —
I had helped her sever gold from dross!
Since now she is — for better or worse —
The relics of my Universe.
But, ah, how scant a heed she pays
To much well-meaning Conscience says!
And good intentions? Alas for them!
They are left to languish on the stem.
The mort of promises idly made —
Where now their husks, the fickle jade?
Where, too, the jilt so gaily resigned
To out-of-sight being out-of-mind?
And, Love? — I would my heart and she
Were more attuned to constancy!

Musing, she sits, at ease, in peace,
Unchanged by age or time's caprice,
And quietly cons again with me
Some well-loved book of poetry,
Her furtive finger putting by,
With a faint smile, or fainter sigh,
The withered flowers that mark a place
Once over-welled with grief or grace.

Yes, and, as though the wanton tried
Once bitter pangs to gloss, or hide,
She stills a voice fall'n harsh and hoarse
With sudden ill-concealed remorse.
I scan the sphinx-like face, and ask
What still lies hid beneath that mask? —
The sins, the woes, the perfidy —
O murderous taciturnity!
I am the *all* I have ever been,
Why gild the cage thou keep'st me in?
Sweet, sweet! she mocks me, the siren; and then
Its very bars shine bright again.

Yet, of my life, from first to last,
This wayward mistress of the Past —
Soundless foot, and tarn-dark eyes —
Keeps safe for me what most I prize.
The sage may to the Future give
Their *Now*, however fugitive;
Mine savours less of rue and myrrh
When spent, in solitude, with her;
When, kingfisher, on leafy spray,
I while the sunshine hours away
In tranquil joy — as in a dream —
Not of its fish, but of the stream;
Whose gliding waters then reflect
Serener skies, in retrospect,
And flowers, ev'n fairer to the eye
Than those of actuality.

And with what grace she has dealt with me —
What patience, insight, sorcery!
Why, every single word here writ
Was hers, till she surrendered it;
And where, without her — I? for lo,
When she is gone I too must go.

CLAVICHORD

Hearken! Tiny, clear, discrete:
The listener within deems solely his,
    A music so remote and sweet
It all but lovely as silence is.

FAINT MUSIC

The meteor's arc of quiet; a voiceless rain;
The mist's mute communing with a stagnant moat;
The sigh of a flower that has neglected lain;
    That bell's unuttered note:

A hidden self rebels, its slumber broken;
Love secret as crystal forms within the womb;
The heart may as faithfully beat, the vow unspoken;
    All sounds to silence come.

WAITING

    'Waiting to . . .'
    'Who is?'
    'We are . . .
Was that the night-owl's cry?'
'I heard not. But see! the evening star;
And listen! — the ocean's solacing sigh.'
'You mean the surf at the harbour bar?'
    'What did you say?'
    'Oh, "waiting".'
    '"Waiting?"—
    Waiting what for?'
    'To die.'

EUPHRASY

Hope, wreathed with roses,
Led sand-blind Despair
To a clear babbling wellspring
And laved his eyes there —
Dark with long brooding
In dungeon-like keep —
Hope laved his eyes,
And he fell fast asleep.

He fell fast asleep
By the willows green-grey,
While the child on his pipes
Piped twilight away.
[264]

So that when he awoke
The skies were outspread
With a powder of stars
Strewn in myriads o'erhead.

And Despair lifted up
His gaunt cavernous face;
He said, 'I see Suns
Like wild beacons, in space;
I cannot endure
The blaze, dazzle, flare!'
But the child — he saw only
Faint stars glinting there.

And he flung back his head
With laughter at sight
Of that lantern-jawed face
Dazed with fear at the Night.
And he counselled Despair
Some sly shift to devise
Lest daybreak brought blindness
Again — to his eyes.

And he his young brows
Sprinkled cold in the brook
For the magic of starshine
Which them had forsook.

THE STRATAGEM

Here's the cave where Sorrow dwells
Weeping in his courts of yew!
Foot then lightly in these dells,
Let not plash one drop of dew.
Bring your chains of pimpernels,
Bring your silvery honeydew.

Lay your nets deliciously,
Set the bait in that sweet beam —
One grey tear to lure him by
When he wakens from his dream,
And the breath of a faint sigh,
That shall ev'n less be than seem.

Hide you, hide you, not a note,
From the little birds you are!
Let not the least laughter float
Near or far, near or far.
See he wakens! scare him not —
Wild with weeping as a star.

Hie away, ah, hie away!
Woe is all! see, how the sun
Ruddies through his filmy grey,
Turns to light the dreaming one —
Mist and dew of a Spring day
Trembling a night-nothing on.

Fold your nets and mew your bait!
Come, sweet spirits, how shall we
Watch and, never ending, wait
For a wraith of transiency?
Fly ere yet the day grow late,
Else we too grow shadowy!

HOMESICK

O homesick, brood no more!
Lovely that sky; haunted the wandering wind;
Strange the dark breakers beating on the shore
That never rest, nor any respite find,
Yet ever call to the lone ghost in thee,
'Where is thy peace, where thy tranquillity?'

Only a wasting fire
Is this remembrance, cheating day and night
With vain and unassuageable desire,
And fleeting phantom pictures of delight.
And yet, O sleep — friend of my body — be
Friend to the soul also that thirsts for thee!

NIGHT

That shining moon — watched by that one faint star:
Sure now am I, beyond the fear of change,
The lovely in life is the familiar,
And only the lovelier for continuing strange.

OUT OF BOUNDS

Why covet what eye cannot see;
　Or earthly longing know?
Decoyed by cheating fantasy —
　This restless ranging to and fro?

Would wildlier sing dark's nightingale
　Where Hera's golden apples grow?
Would lovelier be the swallow's flight
In wastes of wild auroral night,
　Wondrous with falling snow?

PEACE

Night is o'er England, and the winds are still;
Jasmine and honeysuckle steep the air;
Softly the stars that are all Europe's fill
Her heaven-wide dark with radiancy fair;
That shadowed moon now waxing in the west
Stirs not a rumour in her tranquil seas;
Mysterious sleep has lulled her heart to rest,
Deep even as theirs beneath her churchyard trees.

Secure, serene; dumb now the night-hawk's threat;
The guns' low thunder drumming o'er the tide;
The anguish pulsing in her stricken side. . . .
All is at peace. . . . But, never, heart, forget:
For this her youngest, best, and bravest died,
These bright dews once were mixed with bloody sweat.

THE WIDOW

Grief now hath pacified her face;
Even hope might share so still a place.
Yet, if — in silence of her heart —
A memoried voice or footstep start,
Or a chance word of ecstasy
Cry through dim-cloistered memory,
Into her eyes her soul will steal
To gaze on the irrevocable —
As if death had not power to keep
One, who had loved her long, so long asleep.

[267]

Now all things lovely she looks on
Wear the mute aspect of oblivion;
  And all things silent seem to be
  Richer than any melody.
Her narrow hands, like birds that make
A nest for some old instinct's sake,
Have hollowed a refuge for her face —
A narrow and a darkened place —
Where, far from the world's light, she may
See clearer what is passed away:
  And only little children know
Through what dark half-closed gates her smile may go.

THE LAST CHAPTER

I am living more alone now than I did;
This life tends inward, as the body ages;
And what is left of its strange book to read
Quickens in interest with the last few pages.

Problems abound. Its authorship? A sequel?
Its hero-villain, whose ways so little mend?
The plot? still dark. The style? a shade unequal.
And what of the dénouement? And, the end?

No, no, have done! Lay the thumbed thing aside;
Forget its horrors, folly, incitements, lies;
In silence and in solitude abide,
And con what yet may bless your inward eyes.

Pace, still, for pace with you, companion goes,
Though now, through dulled and inattentive ear,
No more — as when a child's — your sick heart knows
His infinite energy and beauty near.

His, too, a World, though viewless save in glimpse;
He, too, a book of imagery bears;
And, as your halting foot beside him limps,
Mark you whose badge and livery he wears.

COURAGE

O heart, hold thee secure
In this blind hour of stress,
Live on, love on, endure,
Uncowed, though comfortless.

Life's still the wondrous thing
It seemed in bygone peace,
Though woe now jar the string,
And all its music cease.

Even if thine own self have
No haven for defence;
Stand not the unshaken brave
To give thee confidence?

Worse than all worst 'twould be,
If thou, who art thine all,
Shatter ev'n their reality
    In thy poor fall!

MARTINS: SEPTEMBER

At secret daybreak they had met —
  Chill mist beneath the welling light
Screening the marshes green and wet —
  An ardent legion wild for flight.

Each preened and sleeked an arrowlike wing;
  Their eager throats with lapsing cries
Praising whatever fate might bring —
  Cold wave, or Africa's paradise.

Unventured, trackless leagues of air;
  England's sweet summer narrowing on;
Her lovely pastures: nought their care —
  Only this ardour to be gone.

A tiny, elfin, ecstatic host . . .
  And 'neath them, on the highway's crust,
Like some small mute belated ghost,
  A sparrow pecking in the dust.

SUNRISE

Bliss it is at break of day
To watch the night-mists thin away:
Like wraiths, of light distilled, they seem —
Phantoms of beauty from a forgotten dream.

As if to a new world new-bidden,
The risen sun shines through the gates of heaven;
And, since the meagrest face with joy may shine,
His glory greets the candle-flame in mine.

THE DREAMER

The woods were still. No breath of air
  Stirred in leaf or brake.
Cold hung the rose, unearthly fair;
  The nightingale, awake,
In rusted coverts of the may
  Shook out his bosom's down;

Alone, upon her starry way,
  The moon, to fulness grown,
Moved, shining, through her misty meads;
  And, roofless from the dew,
Knelt way-worn Love, with idle beads,
  And dreamed of you.

SALLIE'S MUSICAL BOX

Once it made music, tiny, frail, yet sweet —
Bead-note of bird where earth and elfland meet.
Now its thin tinkling stirs no more, since she
Whose toy it was, has gone; and taken the key.

A PORTRAIT

A solemn plain-faced child stands gazing there,
Her small hand resting on a purple chair.
Her stone-grey waisted gown is looped with black;
Linked chain and star encircle a slender neck;
Knots of bright red deck wrist, breast, flaxen hair;
Shoulder to waist falls band of lettered gold:
Round-eyed, she watches me — this eight-year-old,
The ghost of her father in her placid stare.

Darkness beyond. A moment she and I
Engage in some abstruse small colloquy —
On time, art, beauty, life, mortality!
But of one secret not a hint creeps out —
What grave Velasquez talked to her about;
And from that shadow not a clapper cries
Where now the fowler weaves his subtleties.

BRUEGHEL'S WINTER

Jagg'd mountain peaks and skies ice-green
Wall in the wild cold scene below.
Churches, farms, bare copse, the sea
In freezing quiet of winter show;
Where ink-black shapes on fields in flood
Curling, skating, and sliding go.
To left, a gabled tavern; a blaze;
Peasants; a watching child; and lo,
Muffled, mute — beneath naked trees
In sharp perspective set a-row —
Trudge huntsmen, sinister spears aslant,
Dogs snuffling behind them in the snow;
And arrowlike, lean, athwart the air
    Swoops into space a crow.

But flame, nor ice, nor piercing rock,
Nor silence, as of a frozen sea,
Nor that slant inward infinite line
Of signboard, bird, and hill, and tree,
Give more than subtle hint of him
Who squandered here life's mystery.

O CHILDISH MIND!

O childish mind! — last night to rapture won
In marvel of wild Orion; now to sink
Earthward; and by the flames of a dwarf sun
Find a like happiness in a single pink!

UNFORESEEN

Darkness had fallen. I opened the door:
And lo, a stranger in the empty room —
A marvel of moonlight upon wall and floor . . .
The quiet of mercy? Or the hush of doom?

TWICE LOVELY

Chalk-white, light dazzled on the stone,
And there a weed, a finger high,
Bowed its silvery head with every
Breath of wind that faltered by.

Twice lovely thing! For when there drifted
A cloud across the radiant sun,
Not only that had it forsaken,
Its tiny shadow too was gone.

THE DAISY

Oh, saw I there —
Under bleak shadow of a towering wall,
From its great height let fall,
Dense-historied, and, echoing from its stone,
Ruinous, mossed, and lone,
The crying fowls of the air —
Set in a smooth, cool flood of agelong green,
Reared up on inch-high stalk, to see, be seen,
A pygmy daisy, with a silver face,
Shining in that dark place.

FOREBODING

The sycamore, by the heap of dead
    Summer's last flowers that rot below,
Will suddenly in the stillness shed
    A cockled leaf from a bud–tight bough:
So ghostlike the sound that I turn my head
As if at a whisper — at something said;
    'What! And still happy? Thou!'

That is this captious phantom's way —
    Omens, monitions, hints of fate,
On a quiet, air-sweet October day
    Of beauty past estimate!
Is it age; or conscience; or mind now fey
At a world from love so far astray
    That can only falter, 'Wait'?

WHICH?

'What did you say?'
'I? Nothing.' 'No? . . .
What was that sound?'
          'When?'
          'Then.'
    'I do not know.'
'Whose eyes were those on us?'
          'Where?'
          'There.'
    'No eyes I saw.'
'Speech, footfall, presence — how cold the night may be!'
'Phantom or fantasy, it's all one to *me*.'

THE WINDOW

Sunlit, the lashes fringe the half-closed eyes
With hues no bow excels that spans the skies;
As magical the meteor's flight o'erhead,
And daybreak shimmering on a spider's thread . . .
Thou starry Universe — whose breadth, depth, height
Contracts to such strait entry as mere sight!

THE DOVE

How often, these hours, have I heard the monotonous crool
    of a dove —
Voice, low, insistent, obscure, since its nest it has hid in a grove —
Flowers of the linden wherethrough the hosts of the honeybees rove.

And I have been busily idle: no problems; nothing to prove;
No urgent foreboding; but only life's shallow habitual groove:
Then why, if I pause to listen, should the languageless note of a dove
So dark with disquietude seem? And what is it sorrowing of?

SWALLOWS FLOWN

Whence comes that small continuous silence
    Haunting the livelong day?
This void, where a sweetness, so seldom heeded,
    Once ravished my heart away?
As if a loved one, too little valued,
    Had vanished — could not stay?

[273]

A QUEEN WASP

Why rouse from thy long winter sleep?
And sound that witchcraft drone in air?
The frost-bound hours of darkness creep,
    The night is cold, and bare

Of all that gave thee power to rear
Thy myriad Amazonian host.
All, all are dust. I only, here;
    And thou — untimely ghost! —

Prowling, black-orbed, disconsolate,
Questing antennae, quivering wing,
Unwitting of the mortal fate
    A human thought might bring

To the mute marvels in thy womb,
Tarrying only summer's heat
To breed a Babylon from the tomb —
    As wondrous and exquisite!

Still, now. Thou'rt safe and hidden again;
Thy sombre, astonished piping done . . .
And I, with the hosts that flock the brain,
    Back to my self am gone.

A HARE

Eyes that glass fear, though fear on furtive foot
    Track thee, in slumber bound;
Ears that whist danger, though the wind sigh not,
    Nor Echo list a sound;
Heart — oh, what hazard must thy wild life be,
With sapient Man for thy cold enemy!

Fleet Scatterbrains, thou hast thine hours of peace
    In pastures April-green,
Where the shrill skylark's raptures never cease,
And the clear dew englobes the white moon's beam.
All happiness God gave thee, albeit thy foe
Roves Eden, as did Satan, long ago.

THE CHERRY TREES

Under pure skies of April blue I stood,
Where, in wild beauty, cherries were in blow;
And, as sweet fancy willed, see there I could
Boughs thick with blossom, or inch-deep in snow.

A DREAM

Idle I sat — my book upon my knee,
The Tyro's Outline of Biology.
Drowsy the hour: and wits began to roam
Far, far from gene, as far from chromosome.
Sweet sleep stole over me. . . .
                                             A valley in Spring! —
Wherein a river of water crystal clear
In rarer beauty imaged all things near —
Green grass, and leaf; lithe leopard, swift gazelle —
Gihon? Euphrates? No, I could not tell,
But knew it was Eden by the asphodel,
The painted birds, the songs I heard them sing.

There, where heaven's sunbeams with earth's shade inwove —
This side a slumber-solemn cedar grove,
A clear green twilight underneath a tree,
(Of Life? Of Knowledge? it was strange to me)
Two mortals sat: a sage, dome-headed, grey,
Who looked a child, albeit in age astray —
Talking, it seemed, his very heart away;
And one even lovelier than woods in May.

She, as if poesy haunted all he said —
Eyes blue as chicory flower, and braided head —
Showed silent as snow against the tender grass,
For naked she as Aphrodite was.
And, at her shoulder, mid its coils near by,
A subtle Serpent couched, with lidless eye,
Which, its tongue flickering, else motionlessly,
Raised its rune-blazoned head, and gazed at me . . .

Whereat, although it harmless seemed, I woke;
My dream-cleansed eyes now fixed upon my book;
Nor could by any stealth I entry win
Into that paradisal scene again —
Fruit so much sweeter to a childish love
Than any knowledge I had vestige of.

[275]

THOMAS HARDY

Mingled the moonlight with daylight — the last in the narrowing
    west;
Silence of nightfall lay over the shallowing valleys at rest
        In the Earth's green breast:
Yet a small multitudinous singing, a lully of voices of birds,
Unseen in the vague shelving hollows, welled up with my
        questioning words:
All Dorsetshire's larks for connivance of sweetness seemed trysting
    to greet
Him in whose song the bodings of raven and nightingale meet.

Stooping and smiling, he questioned, 'No birdnotes myself do I
    hear?
Perhaps 'twas the talk of chance farers, abroad in the hush with us
    here —
        In the dusk-light clear?'
And there peered from his eyes, as I listened, a concourse of
    women and men,
Whom his words had made living, long-suffering — they flocked
    to remembrance again;
'O Master,' I cried in my heart, 'lorn thy tidings, grievous thy
    song;
Yet thine, too, this solacing music, as we earthfolk stumble along.'

THE OLD SUMMERHOUSE

This blue-washed, old, thatched summerhouse —
Paint scaling, and fading from its walls —
How often from its hingeless door
I have watched — dead leaf, like the ghost of a mouse,
Rasping the worn brick floor —
The snows of the weir descending below,
And their thunderous waterfall.

Fall — fall: dark, garrulous rumour,
Until I could listen no more.
Could listen no more — for beauty with sorrow
Is a burden hard to be borne:
The evening light on the foam, and the swans, there;
That music, remote, forlorn.

ROOKS IN OCTOBER

They sweep up, crying, riding the wind,
  Ashen on blue outspread —
Gilt-lustred wing, sharp light-glazed beak,
  And low flat ravenous head.

Claws dangling, down they softly swoop
  Out of the eastern sun
Into the yellowing green-leaved boughs —
  Their morning feast begun.

Clasping a twig that even a linnet
  Might bend in song, they clip
Pat from the stalked embossed green cup
  Its fruitage bitter-ripe.

Oh, what divine far hours their beauty
  Of old for me beguiled,
When — acorn, oak, untarnished heavens —
  I watched them as a child!

THE CAGE

Thou angel face! — like a small exquisite cage,
  Such as some old Chinese
Once spent his love and skill on — youth to age,
In hope its destined prisoner to please;
And then had empty left; since he had heard
What death would do in setting free the bird.

QUIET

Mutely the mole toils on;
The worm in silk cocoon
Stealthily as spider spins,
  As glides the moon.
But listen where envy peers 'neath the half-closed lid;
Where peeping vanity lurks; where pride lies hid;
And peace beyond telling share with the light-stilled eye,
When nought but an image of the loved one's nigh.

THE CAPTIVE

When gloaming droops
To the raven's croak,
And the nightjar churs
From his time-gnarled oak
In the thunder-stricken wood:

When the drear dark waters
'Neath sallows hoar
Shake the veils of night
With their hollow roar,
Plunging deep in flood;

Spectral, wan
From unquiet rest,
A phantom walks
With anguished breast,
Doomed to love's solitude.

Her footstep is leaf-like,
Light as air,
Her raiment scarce stirs
The gossamer.
While from shadowy hood

In the wood-light pale
Her dream-ridden eyes,
Without sorrow or tear,
Speculation, surmise,
Wildly, insanely brood.

AN INTERLUDE

A small brook gushed on stones hard by,
Waste-lorn it babbled; alone was I,
Dawn's ever-changing alchemy
  Low in the eastern sky.

Ghost that I was, by dream waylaid,
Benighted, and yet unafraid,
I sat, in those brief hours, long-lost,
  And communed with the sea.

Faint, o'er its shingly murmuring,
The secret songs I had hoped to sing —
When I on earth was sojourning —
Of which poor words, alas, can bring
Only a deadened echoing
    Of what they meant to me —

Rose in my throat; and poured their dew —
A hymn of praise — my being through;
Shed peace on a mind that never knew
    Peace in that mind could be.

Only a soundless voice was I,
Yet sweeter that than man can hear
When, latticed in by moonbeams clear,
The bird of darkness to its fere
    Tells out love's mystery.

No listener there — a dream; but ne'er
Sang happier heart in heaven fair
    To lyre or psaltery. . . .

Oh, futile vanity to mourn
What the day's waking leaves forlorn!
Doth not earth's strange and lovely mean
Only, 'Come, see, O son of man,
All that you hope, the nought you can,
    The glory that might have been?'

A PRAYER

When with day's woes night haunts wake-weary eyes,
How deep a blessing from the heart may rise
On the happy, the beautiful, the good, the wise!

The poor, the outcast, knave, child, stranger, fool
Need no commending to the merciful;
But, in a world grieved, ugly, wicked, or dull,

Who could the starry influences surmise —
What praises ardent enough could prayer devise
For the happy, the beautiful, the good, the wise?

HERE SLEEPS

Here sleeps, past earth's awakening,
A woman, true and pretty,
Who was herself in everything —
Tender, and grave, and witty.
Her smallest turn of foot, hand, head,
Was way of wind with water;
So with her thoughts and all she said —
It seemed her heart had taught her.
O thou most dear and loving soul
Think not I shall forget thee;
Nor take amiss what here is writ
For those who never met thee!

THE LAST ARROW

There came a boy,
Full quiver on his back —
Tapped at my door ajar.

'No, no, my child,' said I,
'I nothing lack;
And see! — the evening star!'

Finger on string,
His dangerous eyes
Gazed boldly into mine:

'Know thou my mother
An Immortal is!
Guard thee, and hope resign!'

'But patience,' I pleaded,
Pointing to a shelf,
Where rusting arrows lay.

'All these, times gone,
You squandered on myself,
Why come — so late, to-day?'

These words scarce uttered,
I discerned a Shade
Shadow till then had hid;

Clang went that bowstring,
And past wit to evade,
Into my bosom slid

His final dart.
He shook his rascal head,
Its curls by the lamp-shine gilt:

'Thank thou the Gods!
Here's One, I vow,' he said,
'Not even thee shall jilt.'

AWAY

There is no sorrow
Time heals never;
No loss, betrayal,
Beyond repair.
Balm for the soul, then,
Though grave shall sever
Lover from loved
And all they share;
See, the sweet sun shines,
The shower is over,
Flowers preen their beauty,
The day how fair!
Brood not too closely
On love, or duty;
Friends long forgotten
May wait you where
Life with death
Brings all to an issue;
None will long mourn for you,
Pray for you, miss you,
Your place left vacant,
You not there.

OH, WHY?

Oh, why make such ado —
This fretful care and trouble?
The sun in noonday's blue
Pours radiance on earth's bubble.
What though the heart-strings crack,
And sorrow bid thee languish,
Dew falls; the night comes back;
Sleep, and forget thine anguish.
Oh, why in shadow haunt?
Shines not the evening flower?
Hark, how the sweet birds chaunt,
The lovely light their bower.
Water her music makes,
Lulling even these to slumber;
And only dead of darkness wakes
    Stars without number.

THE LOOKING-GLASS

'Nothing is so sure that it
May not in a moment flit:
Quench the candle, gone are all
The wavering shadows on the wall.
Eros, like Time, is winged. And, why?
To warn us, dear, he too can fly.
Watch, now, your bright image here
In this water, calm and fair —
Those clear brown eyes, that dark brown hair.
See, I fling a pebble in;
What distortions now begin!
Refluent ripples sweep and sway,
Chasing all I love away.
But, imagine a strange glass
Which, to gaze, gave back, alas,
Nothing but a crystal wall,
And else, no hint of you at all:
No rose on cheek, no red on lip,
No trace of beauty's workmanship.
That, my dear, for me, for you,
Precisely is what life might do.
Might, I say.... Oh, then, how sweet

Is it by this stream to sit,
And in its molten mirror see
All that is now reality:
The interlacing boughs, the sun's
Tiny host of flickering moons,
That rainbow kingfisher, and these
Demure, minute anemones —
Cherubim, in heaven's blue,
Leaning their wizard faces too —
Lost in delight at seeing you.'

SNOW

This meal-white snow —
Oh, look at the bright fields!
What crystal manna
Death-cold winter yields!

Falling from heavens
Earth knows little of,
Yet mantling it
As with a flawless love —

A shining cloak —
It to the naked gives,
Wooing all sorrow
From the soul it shrives.

Adam no calmer vales
Than these descried;
Leda a shadow were
This white beside.

Water stays still for wonder;
Herb and flower,
Else starved with cold,
In warmth and darkness cower.

Miracle, far and near,
That starry flake
Can of its myriads
Such wide pastures make,

[283]

For sun to colour,
And for moon to wan,
And day's vast vault of blue
To arch upon!

A marvel of light,
Whose verge of radiance seems
Frontier of paradise,
The bourne of dreams.

O tranquil, silent, cold —
Such loveliness to see:
The heart sighs answer,
Benedicite!

The Burning-Glass and Other Poems
(1945)

A PORTRAIT

Old: yet unchanged; — still pottering in his thoughts;
Still eagerly enslaved by books and print;
Less plagued, perhaps, by rigid musts and oughts,
But no less frantic in vain argument;

Still happy as a child, with its small toys,
Over his inkpot and his bits and pieces, —
Life's arduous, fragile and ingenuous joys,
Whose charm failed never — nay, it even increases!

Ev'n happier in watch of bird or flower,
Rainbow in heaven, or bud on thorny spray,
A star-strewn nightfall, and that heart-break hour
Of sleep-drowsed senses between dawn and day;

Loving the light — laved eyes in those wild hues! —
And dryad twilight, and the thronging dark;
A Crusoe ravished by mere solitude —
And silence — edged with music's faintest *Hark!*

And any chance-seen face whose loveliness
Hovers, a mystery, between dream and real;
Things usual yet miraculous that bless
And overwell a heart that still can feel;

Haunted by questions no man answered yet;
Pining to leap from A clean on to Z;
Absorbed by problems which the wise forget;
Avid for fantasy — yet how staid a head!

Senses at daggers with his intellect;
Quick, stupid; vain, retiring; ardent, cold;
Faithful and fickle; rash and circumspect;
And never yet at rest in any fold;

Punctual at meals; a spendthrift, close as Scot;
Rebellious, tractable, childish — long gone grey!
Impatient, volatile, tongue wearying not —
Loose, too: which, yet, thank heaven, was taught to pray;

'Childish' indeed! — a waif on shingle shelf
Fronting the rippled sands, the sun, the sea;
And nought but his marooned precarious self
For questing consciousness and will-to-be;

A feeble venturer — in a world so wide!
So rich in action, daring, cunning, strife!
You'd think, poor soul, he had taken Sloth for bride, —
Unless the imagined is the breath of life;

Unless to speculate bring virgin gold,
And *Let's-pretend* can range the seven seas,
And dreams are not mere tales by idiot told,
And tongueless truth may hide in fantasies;

Unless the alone may their own company find,
And churchyards harbour phantoms 'mid their bones,
And even a daisy may suffice a mind
Whose bindweed can redeem a heap of stones;

Too frail a basket for so many eggs —
Loose-woven: Gosling? cygnet? Laugh or weep?
Or is the cup at richest in its dregs?
The actual realest on the verge of sleep?

One yet how often the prey of doubt and fear,
Of bleak despondence, stark anxiety;
Ardent for what is neither now nor here,
An Orpheus fainting for Eurydice;

Not yet inert, but with a tortured breast
At hint of that bleak gulf — his last farewell;
Pining for peace, assurance, pause and rest,
Yet slave to what he loves past words to tell;

A foolish, fond old man, his bed-time nigh,
Who still at western window stays to win
A transient respite from the latening sky,
And scarce can bear it when the Sun goes in.

IN THE LOCAL MUSEUM

They stood — rain pelting at window, shrouded sea —
Tenderly hand in hand, too happy to talk;
And there, its amorous eye intent on me,
Plautus impennis, the extinct Great Auk.

THE RAPIDS

Grieve must my heart. Age hastens by.
No longing can stay Time's torrent now.
Once would the sun in eastern sky
Pause on the solemn mountain's brow.
Rare flowers he still to bloom may bring,
But day approaches evening;
And ah, how swift their withering!

The birds, that used to sing, sang then
As if in an eternal day;
Ev'n sweeter yet their grace notes, when
Farewell . . . farewell is theirs to say.
Yet, as a thorn its drop of dew
Treasures in shadow, crystal clear,
All that I loved I love anew,
        Now parting draweth near.

ARIEL

Ariel! Ariel! —
But the glittering moon
Sank to the curve of the world,
Down, down:
And the curlew cried,
And the nightjar stirred in her rest,
And Ariel on the cool high steep of heaven
Leaned his breast.

Ariel! Ariel! —
His curv'd wings whist,
With the bliss of the star-shaking breeze
'Gainst his pinions prest.
Lower the great globe
Rolled her icy snows:
Lone is the empty dark, and the moonless heart
When the Bright One goes.

THE SUMMONS

'What bodiless bird so wildly sings,
Albeit from no earthly tree?
Whence rise again those Phoenix wings
To waken from prolonged unease —
Isle of the Lost Hesperides!
    A self long strange to me?'

'Red coral in the sea may shine,
And rock-bound Sirens, half divine,
Seduced Ulysses: but to find
Music as rare as childhood's thrush
Yet lorn as curlew's at the hush
    Of dewfall in the mind!'

'O shallow questioner! Know you not
That notes like these, sad, urgent, sweet,
Call from an Egypt named the heart,
Which with a deeper life doth beat
Than any wherein thought hath part;
And of whose wisdom, Love knows well,
    Only itself could tell?'

A DULL BOY

'Work?' Well, not *work* — this stubborn desperate quest
To conjure life, love, wonder into words;
Far happier songs than any me have blest
Were sung, at ease, this daybreak by the birds.

I watch with breathless envy in her glass
The dreamlike beauty of the silent swan;
As mute a marvel is the bladed grass
Springing to life again, June's sickle gone.

What music could be mine compared with that
The idling wind woos from the sand-dune's bent?
What meaning deeper than the smile whereat
A burning heart conceives the loved intent?

'And what did'st *thou*' . . . I see the vaulted throng,
The listening heavens in that dread array
Fronting the Judge to whom all dooms belong:—
Will the lost child in me cry bravely, 'Play'?

TWO GARDENS

Two gardens see! — this, of enchanted flowers,
Strange to the eye, and more than earthly-sweet;
Small rivulets running, song-reëchoing bowers;
And green-walled pathways which, ere parting, meet;
And there a lion-like sun in heaven's delight
Breathes plenitude from dayspring to the night.

The other: — walls obscure, and chaces of trees,
Ilex and yew, and dream-enticing dark,
Hid pools, moths, creeping odours, silentness,
Luna its deity, and its watchward, *Hark!*
A still and starry mystery, wherein move
Phantoms of ageless wonder and of love.

Two gardens for two children — in one mind:
But ah, how seldom open now their gates I find!

NOSTALGIA[1]

In the strange city of life
A house I know full well —
That wherein Silence a refuge has,
Where Dark doth dwell.

Gable and roof it stands,
Fronting the dizzied street,
Where Vanity flaunts her gilded booths
In the noontide glare and heat.

Green-graped upon its walls
Earth's ancient hoary vine
Clusters the carven lichenous stone
With tendril serpentine.

[1] A different earlier version called 'The Two Houses' appears on p. 122

Deafened, incensed, dismayed,
Dazed in the clamorous throng,
I thirst for the soundless fount that rills
As if from my inmost heart, and fills
The stillness with its song.

As yet I knock in vain:
Nor yet what is hidden can tell;
Where Silence perpetual vigil keeps,
Where Dark doth dwell.

THE SECRET

I bless the hand that once held mine,
    The lips that said:
'No heart, though kiss were Circe's wine,
    Can long be comforted.'

Ay, though we talked the long day out
    Of all life marvels at,
One thing the soul can utter not,
    Or self to self relate.

We gazed, enravished, you and I,
    Like children at a flower;
But speechless stayed, past even a sigh . . .
    Not even Babel Tower

Heard language strange and close enough
    To tell that moment's peace,
Where broods the Phoenix, timeless Love,
    And divine silence is.

WINTER COMPANY

Blackbird silent in the snow;
Motionless crocus in the mould;
Naked tree; and, cold and low,
        Sun's wintry gold . . .
Lost for the while in their strange beauty — self how far! —
Lulled were my senses into a timeless dream;
As if the inmost secret of what they are
        Lay open in what they seem.

[290]

THE SOLITARY BIRD

Why should a bird in that solitary hollow
    Flying from east to west
Seem in the silence of the snow-blanched sunshine
    Gilding the valley's crest
Envoy and symbol of a past within me
    Centuries now at rest?

Shallowly arched the horizon looms beyond it,
    Turquoise green and blue;
Not even a whisper irks the magic of the evening
    The narrowing valley through;
No faintest echo brings a syllable revealing
    The secret once I knew:
Down *whsts* the snow again, cloud masks the
    sunshine —
    Bird gone, and memory too.

AND SO TO BED

'Night-night, my Precious!'; '*Sweet* dreams, Sweet!'
'Heaven bless you, Child!'— the accustomed grown-ups said.
Two eyes gazed mutely back that none could meet,
Then turned to face Night's terrors overhead.

ISRAFEL

To Alec McLaren
1940

Sleepless I lay, as the grey of dawn
Through the cold void street stole into the air,
When, in the hush, a solemn voice
Pealed suddenly out in Connaught Square.

Had I not heard notes wild as these
A thousand times in childhood ere
This chill March daybreak they awoke
The echoing walls of Connaught Square,

I might have imagined a seraph — strange
In such bleak days! — had deigned to share,
For joy and love, the haunts of man —
An Israfel in Connaught Square!

Not that this singer eased the less
A human heart surcharged with care —
Merely a blackbird, London-bred,
Warbling of Spring in Connaught Square!

It was the contrast with a world
Of darkness, horror, grief, despair,
Had edged with an irony so sharp
That rapturous song in Connaught Square.

HARVEST HOME

A bird flies up from the hayfield;
Sweet, to distraction, is the new-mown grass:
But I grieve for its flowers laid low at noonday —
     And only this poor *Alas!*

I grieve for War's innocent lost ones —
The broken loves, the mute goodbye,
The dread, the courage, the bitter end,
The shaken faith, the glazing eye?

O bird, from the swathes of that hayfield —
The rancid stench of the grass!
And a heart stricken mute by that Harvest Home —
     And only this poor *Alas!*

THE UNUTTERABLE
September 1940

What! jibe in ignorance, and scold
The Muses when, the earth in flame,
They hold their peace, and leave untolled
Ev'n Valour's deathless requiem?

Think you a heart in misery,
Riven with pity, dulled with woe,
Could weep in song its threnody,
And to such tombs with chaunting go?

Think you that all-abandoning deeds
Of sacrifice by those whose love
Must barren lie in widow's weeds,
Gone all their youth was dreaming of,

Can be revealed in words? Alas!
No poet yet in Fate's dark count
Has ever watched Night dread as this,
Or seen such evils to surmount.

We stand aghast. Pride, rapture, grief
In storm within; on fire to bless
The daybreak; but yet wiser if
We bide that hour in silentness.

THE SPECTACLE

Scan with calm bloodshot eyes the world around us,
Its broken stones, its sorrows! No voice could tell
The toll of the innocent crucified, weeping and wailing,
In this region of torment ineffable, flame and derision —
      What wonder if we believe no longer in Hell?

      And Heaven? That daybreak vision?
In the peace of our hearts we learn beyond shadow of
      doubting
That our dream of this vanished kingdom lies sleeping
      within us;
Its gates are the light we have seen in the hush of the
      morning,
When the shafts of the sunrise break in a myriad
      splendours;
Its shouts of joy are those of all earthly creatures,
Their primal and innocent language — the song of the
      birds:
Thrush in its rapture, ecstatic wren, and wood-dove
      tender,
Calling on us poor mortals to put our praise into words.

Passionate, sorrowful hearts, too — the wise, the true
    and the gentle;
Minds that outface all fear, defy despair, remain faithful,
Endure in silence, hope on, assured in their selfless
    courage,
Natural and sweet in a love no affliction or doubt could
    dispel.
If, as a glass reflecting its range, we have these for our
    guidance,
If, as our love creates beauty, we exult in that transient
    radiance,
This is the garden of paradise which in our folly
      We abandoned long ages gone.

Though, then, the wondrous divine were ev'n nebulae-
    distant,
The little we make of our all is our earthly heaven.
      Else we are celled in a darkness,
Windowless, doorless, alone.

AN ISLAND

Parched, panting, he awoke; phantasmal light
Blueing the hollows of his fevered eyes;
And strove to tell of what he had dreamed that night —
In stumbling words its meaning to devise: —

An island, lit with beauty, like a flower
Its sea of sapphire fringed with ocean's snow,
Whose music and beauty with the changing hour
Seemed from some inward source to ebb and flow;
A heart, all innocence and innately wise,
Well-spring of very love appeared to be —
'A candle whose flame', he stammered, 'never dies,
But feeds on light itself perpetually.
Me! This! A thing corrupt on the grave's cold brink,
And into outer darkness soon to sink!'

The tired nurse yawned. 'A strange dream that!' she said.
'But now you are awake. And see, it's day!'
She smoothed the pillow for his sweat-dark head,
Smiled, frowned; 'There, sleep again!'— and turned away.

THE SCARECROW

In the abandoned orchard — on a pole,
The rain-soaked trappings of that scarecrow have
Usurped the semblance of a man — poor soul —
    Haled from a restless grave.

Geese for his company this fog-bound noon,
He eyeless stares. And I with eyes reply.
Lifting a snakelike head, the gander yelps
    '*Ware!*' at the passer-by.

It is as though a few bedraggled rags
Poised in this wintry waste were lure enough
To entice some aimless phantom here to mime
    All it is image of . . .

Once Man in grace divine all beauty was;
And of his bone God made a lovelier Eve;
Now even the seraphs sleep at sentry-go;
    The swine break in to thieve

Wind-fallen apples from the two old Trees.
Oh see, Old Adam, once of Eden! Alas!
How is thy beauty fallen: fallen thine Eve,
    Who did all life surpass!

Should in the coming nightfall the Lord God,
Goose-challenged, call, 'My Creature, where art *thou*?'
Scarecrow of hate and vengeance, wrath and blood,
    What would'st thou answer now?

THE BURNING-GLASS

No map shows my Jerusalem,
    No history my Christ;
Another language tells of them,
    A hidden evangelist.

Words may create rare images
    Within their narrow bound;
'Twas speechless childhood brought me these,
    As music may, in sound.

[295]

Yet not the loveliest song that ever
  Died on the evening air
Could from my inmost heart dissever
  What life had hidden there.

It is the blest reminder of
  What earth in shuddering bliss
Nailed on a cross — that deathless Love —
  Through all the eternities.

I am the Judas whose perfidy
  Sold what no eye hath seen,
The rabble in dark Gethsemane,
  And Mary Magdalene.

To very God who day and night
  Tells me my sands out-run,
I cry in misery infinite,
  'I am thy long-lost son.'

EDGES

Think you your heart is safely at rest,
Contemptuous, calm, disdainful one?
Maybe a stone is in your breast
  From whence all motion's gone.

Undauntable soldier, vent no scorn
On him who in terror faced the foe;
There is a radiant core of rapture
  None but the fearful know.

And you, sweet poet? Heaven might kiss
The miracles you dreamed to do;
But waste not your soul on self-sought bliss,
  Since no such dream comes true.

SWIFTS

1943

No; they are only birds — swifts, in the loft of the morning,
Coursing, disporting, courting, in the pale-blue arc of the
    sky.
There is no venom for kin or for kind in their wild-winged
    archery,
Nor death in their innocent droppings as fleet in their
    mansions they fly;
Swooping, with flicker of pinion to couple, the loved with the
    loved one,
Never with malice or hate, in their vehement sallies
    through space.
Listen! that silken rustle, as they charge on their beehive
    houses,
Fashioned of dried-up mud daubed each in its chosen place.
Hunger — not fear — sharps the squawk of their featherless
    nestlings;
From daybreak into the dark their circuitings will not cease:
How beautiful they! — and the feet on earth's heavenly
    mountains
Of him that bringeth good tidings, proclaimeth the gospel of
    peace!

THE VISITANT

A little boy leaned down his head
    Upon his mother's knee;
'Tell me the old, old tale', he said,
    'You told last night to me.'

It was in dream. For when at dawn
    She woke, and raised her head,
Still haunted her sad face forlorn
    The beauty of the dead.

THE FIELD

Yes, there was once a battle here:
There, where the grass takes on a shade
Of paradisal green, sun-clear —
    There the last stand was made.

[297]

LULLAY

'Now lullay, my sweeting,
What hast thou to fear?
It is only the wind
In the willows we hear,
And the sigh of the waves
By the sand dunes, my dear.
Stay thy wailing. Let sleep be
Thy solace, thou dear;
And dreams that shall charm
From that cheek every tear.
See, see, I am with thee
No harm can come near.
Sleep, sleep, then, my loved one,
My lorn one, my dear!' . . .

I heard that far singing
With pining oppressed,
When grief for one absent
My bosom distressed,
When the star of the evening
Was low in the West.
And I mused as I listened,
With sorrow oppressed,
Would that heart were *my* pillow,
That safety my rest!
Ah, would I could slumber —
A child laid to rest —
Could abide but a moment
Assoiled, on that breast,
While the planet of evening
Sinks low in the west:
Could wake, and dream on,
At peace and at rest;
Ere fall the last darkness,
When silence is best.

For alas, love is mortal;
And night must come soon;
And another, yet deeper,
When — no more to roam —
The lost one within me
Shall find its long home,
In a sleep none can trouble,
The hush of the tomb.

[298]

Cold, sombre, eternal,
Dark, narrow that room;
But no grief, no repining
Will deepen its gloom;
Though of voice, once adored,
Not an echo can come;
Of hand, brow, and cheek,
My rapture and doom,
Once my all, and adored,
No least phantom can come. . . .

'Now lullay, my sweeting,
There is nothing to fear.
It is only the wind
In the willows we hear,
And the sigh of the waves
On the sand dunes, my dear.
Stay thy wailing. Let sleep be
Thy solace, thou dear;
And dreams that shall charm
From that cheek every tear.
See, see, I am with thee,
No harm can come near.
Sleep, sleep, then, my loved one,
My lorn one, my dear!'

THE CHART

That mute small face, but twelve hours here,
Maps secrets stranger than the seas',
In hieroglyphics more austere,
And wiser far than Rameses'.

TO A CANDLE

Burn stilly, thou; and come with me.
I'll screen thy rays. Now . . . Look, and see,
Where, like a flower furled,
Sealed from this busy world,
Tranquil brow, and lid, and lip,
One I love lies here asleep.

[299]

Low upon her pillow is
A head of such strange loveliness —
Gilded-brown, unwoven hair —
That dread springs up to see it there:
Lest so profound a trance should be
Death's momentary alchemy.

Venture closer, then. Thy light
Be little day to this small night!
Fretting through her lids it makes
The lashes stir on those pure cheeks;
The scarcely-parted lips, it seems,
Pine, but in vain, to tell her dreams.

Every curve and hollow shows
In faintest shadow — mouth and nose;
Pulsing beneath the silken skin
The milk-blue blood rills out and in:
A bird's might be that slender bone,
Magic itself to ponder on.

Time hath spread its nets in vain;
The child she was is home again;
Veiled with Sleep's seraphic grace.
How innocent yet how wise a face!
Mutely entreating, it seems to sigh, —
'Love made me. It is only I.

'Love made this house wherein there dwells
A thing divine, and homeless else.
Not mine the need to ponder why
In this sweet prison I exult and sigh.
Not mine to bid you hence. God knows
It was for joy he shaped the rose.'

See, she stirs. A hand at rest
Slips from above that gentle breast,
White as winter-mounded snows,
Summer-sweet as that wild rose . . .
Thou lovely thing! Ah, welladay!
Candle, I dream. Come, come away!

SAFETY FIRST

Do not mention this young child's beauty as he stands there
  gravely before you;
Whisper it not, lest there listeners be. Beware, the evil eye!
Only as humming-bird, quaffing the delicate glory
Of the flow'r that it lives by — gaze: yes, but make no reply
To the question, What is it? Whence comes it, this innocent
  marvel?
Those features past heart to dissever from the immanent truth
  they imply?
No more than the star of the morning its image in reflex can
  ponder
Can he tell of, delight in, this beauty and promise. Oh, sigh of
  a sigh;
Be wise! Let your love through thought's labyrinths happily
  wander;
Let your silence its intricate praises, its gratitude squander;
But of speech, not a word: just a smile. Beware of the evil
  eye!

THE BLIND BOY

A spider her silken gossamer
In the sweet sun began to wind;
The boy, alone in the window-seat,
    Saw nought of it. He was blind.

By a lustre of glass a slender ray
Was shattered into a myriad tints —
Violet, emerald, primrose, red —
    Light's exquisite finger-prints.

Unmoved, his face in the shadow stayed,
Rapt in a reverie mute and still.
The ray stole on; but into that mind
    No gem-like atom fell.

It paused to ponder upon a moth,
Snow-hooded, delicate past belief,
Drowsing, a spelican from his palm . . .
    O child of tragedy — if

[301]

Only a moment you might gaze out
On this all-marvellous earth we share! ...
A smile stole into the empty eye,
    And features fair,

As if an exquisite whisper of sound,
Of source as far in time and space,
And, no less sovran than light, had found
    Its recompense in his face.

THE TOMTIT

Twilight had fallen, austere and grey,
The ashes of a wasted day,
When, tapping at the window-pane,
My visitor had come again,
To peck late supper at his ease —
A morsel of suspended cheese.

What ancient code, what Morse knew he —
This eager little mystery —
That, as I watched, from lamp-lit room,
Called on some inmate of my heart to come
Out of its shadows — filled me then
With love, delight, grief, pining, pain,
Scarce less than had he angel been?

Suppose, such countenance as that,
Inhuman, deathless, delicate,
Had gazed this winter moment in —
Eyes of an ardour and beauty no
Star, no Sirius could show!

Well, it were best for such as I
To shun direct divinity;
Yet not stay heedless when I heard
The tip-tap nothings of a tiny bird.

THE OWL

Owl of the wildwood I:
Muffled in sleep I drowse,
Where no fierce sun in heaven
Can me arouse.

My haunt's a hollow
In a half-dead tree,
Whose strangling ivy
Shields and shelters me.

But when dark's starlight
Thrids my green domain,
My plumage trembles and stirs,
I wake again:

A spectral moon
Silvers the world I see;
Out of their daylong lairs
Creep thievishly

Night's living things.
Then I,
Wafted away on soundless pinions
Fly;
Curdling her arches
With my hunting-cry:

A-hooh! a-hooh:
Four notes; and then,
Solemn, sepulchral, cold,
Four notes again,
The listening dingles
Of my woodland through:
A-hooh! A-hooh! —
    A-hooh!

ONCE

Once would the early sun steal in through my eastern
    window,
        A sea of time ago;
Tracing a stealthy trellis of shadow across the pictures
        With his gilding trembling glow;
Brimming my mind with rapture, as though of some
    alien spirit,
        In those eternal hours
I spent with my self as a child; alone, in a world of
    wonder —
        Air, and light and flowers;
Tenderness, longing, grief, intermingling with bodiless
    beings
        Shared else with none:
How would desire flame up in my soul; with what
    passionate yearning
        As the rays stole soundlessly on! —
Rays such as Rembrandt adored, such as dwell on the
    faces of seraphs,
        Wings-folded, solemn head,
Piercing the mortal with sorrow past all
    comprehension. . . .

        Little of that I read
In those shadowy runes in my bedroom. But one wild
    notion
        Made my heart with tears overflow —
The knowledge that love unsought, unspoken,
    unshared, unbetokened,
        Had mastered me through and through:
And yet — the children we are! — that naught of its
    ardour and beauty
        Even the loved should know.

A RECLUSE

Here lies (where all at peace may be)
A lover of mere privacy.
Graces and gifts were his; now none
Will keep him from oblivion;
How well they served his hidden ends
Ask those who knew him best, his friends.

He is dead; but even among the quick
This world was never his candlestick.
He envied none; he was content
With self-inflicted banishment.
'Let your light shine!' was never his way:
What then remains but, Welladay!

And yet his very silence proved
How much he valued what he loved.
There peered from his hazed, hazel eyes
A self in solitude made wise;
As if within the heart may be
All the soul needs for company:
And, having that in safety there,
Finds its reflection everywhere.

Life's tempests must have waxed and waned:
The deep beneath at peace remained.
Full tides that silent well may be
Mark of no less profound a sea.
Age proved his blessing. It had given
The all that earth implies of heaven;
And found an old man reconciled
To die, as he had lived, a child.

'PHILIP'

A flattened orb of water his,
  Pent in by brittle glass
Through which his little jet-black eyes
  Observe what comes to pass:
I watch him, but how hard it is
  To estimate his size.

The further off he fins away
  The larger he appears,
And, having wheeled and turned about,
Grows smaller as he nears!
The Great, we lesser folk agree,
Suffer from like propinquity.

But great and small like Philip swim
In shallow waters, clear or dim;
  And few seem fully aware
Whose bounty scatters ants' eggs there;
And all — O Universe! — poor souls,
Remain cooped up in finite bowls;
Whose psychic confines are, alas,
  Seldom as clear as glass.

What truth, then, from the vast Beyond
Is theirs (in so minute a pond)
Concerning Space, or Space-*plus*-Time,
Or metaphysics more sublime,
Eludes, I fear, poor Philip's rhyme.

STILL LIFE

Bottle, coarse tumbler, loaf of bread,
Cheap paper, a lean long kitchen knife:
No moral, no problem, sermon, or text,
No hint of a Why, Whence, Whither, or If;
Mere workaday objects put into paint —
Bottle and tumbler, loaf and knife. . . .
And engrossed, round-spectacled Chardin's
        Passion for life.

THE OUTCASTS

The Brazen Trompe of iron-wingèd fame
That mingleth truth with forgèd lies

Grunting, he paused. Dead-cold the balustrade.
Full-flood the river flowed, and black as night.
Amorphous bundle poised, he listening stayed,
Then peered, pushed, stooped, and watched it out of sight.

A faint, far plunge — and silence. Then the *whirr*
Menacing, stealthy, of a vast machine.
Midnight; but still the city was astir,
And clock to clock announced the old routine.

Trembling and fevered, light of heart and head,
He turned to hasten away; but stayed — to stare:
A paint-daubed woman bound for lonely bed,
Wide mouth, and sluggish gaze, and tinsel hair,

Stood watching him. 'That's that,' she said, and laughed.
'The dead — they tell no tales. Nor living *might*.
Nor need good money talk . . . What's more,' she chaffed,
'Much better out of mind what's out of sight.

'*And — who?*' she added, shrugging, with a nod,
Callous and cold, towards the granite shelf.
'Not for the first time have I wished, by God,
That I had long since gone that way myself!' . . .

His puke-stained face twitched upwards in a smile.
'My friend,' he said, 'behold one who at last
From lifelong bondage is now freed a while.
The sack you saw contained, in fact, my Past.

'I was a writer — and of some repute,
(Candour, just now of all times, nothing burkes) —
Fiction, *belles lettres*; and I twanged the lute;
Yes, added poesy to my other works.

'Year after year the burden grew apace;
Fame, that old beldame, shared my bed and board;
No Christian, in his pilgrimage to grace,
Bore on his back a burden so abhorred.

'"What was she?" Chiefly of mere fantasy made;
Seeming divine, but Lamia accursed.
She cared no more for me, insidious jade,
Than drunkard needs for quickening his thirst.

'Fattened on praise, she like a vampire sat,
Sucking my life-blood, having slain my youth;
And on her hated body I begat
Twenty abortions, but not one called Truth.

'Not, mind you, friend, it ever seemed that I
Spared of my sweat to conjure from my ink
What one might hope time would not falsify —
The most my heart could feel, my poor mind think.

'And yet by slow sour torturing degree
There crept the vile conviction in that I —
Victim of heinous anthropophagy —
Lived on my Self, as spider lives on fly.

'Ay, and that madam, sprawling in my sheets,
Vain beyond hell, a pride that knew no ebb,
Mistress, by Satan taught, of all deceits,
Never ceased weaving her mephitic web.

'At my last gasp, my door one midnight stirred.
There showed a face there, tranquil as a dove.
As if a dream had spoken — yet no word:
With some lost ghost in me I fell in love . . .

'There came this moonless night. And, see, high tide! . . .
They say when Nature brings to fruitage twins —
At jutting thigh, at spine, or elsewise tied —
And one to'rds death his pilgrimage begins,

'Severance ends both. And that may be my fate.
But now,' the grey face paled, the thin voice broke,
'I am at peace again. Myself — though late;
My last days freed from an atrocious yoke . . .'

The painted woman stared. Her glittering eyes
Weasel-wise watched him; then, to left and right,
Under the dull lead pallor of the skies,
Searched the dark bridge — but not a soul in sight . . .

ARROGANCE

I saw bleak Arrogance, with brows of brass,
Clad nape to sole in shimmering foil of lead,
Stark down his nose he stared; a crown of glass
Aping the rainbow, on his tilted head.

His very presence drained the vital air;
He sate erect — stone-cold, self-crucified;
On either side of him an empty chair;
And sawdust trickled from his wounded side.

LIKE SISTERS

There is a thicket in the wild
By waters deep and dangerous,
Where — close as loveless sisters — grow
Nightshade and the convolvulus.

Tangled and clambering, stalk and stem,
Its tendrils twined against the sun,
The bindweed has a heart-shaped leaf,
Nightshade a triple-pointed one.

The one bears petals pure as snow —
A beauty lingering but a day;
The other's, violet and gold,
Into bright berries shed away;

And these a poisonous juice distil.
Yet both are lovely too — as might
Those rival hostile sisters be:
Different as day is from the night
When darkness is its dead delight; —
As love is from unchastity.

THE DITCH

Masked by that brilliant weed's deceitful green,
No glint of the dark water can be seen
Which, festering, slumbers, with this scum for screen.

It is as though a face, as false as fair,
Dared not, by smiling, show the evil there.

[309]

THE DEAD JAY

A witless, pert, bedizened fop,
　　Man scoffs, resembles you:
Fate levels all — voice harsh or sweet —
　　Ringing the woodlands through:
But, O, poor hapless bird, that broken death-stilled wing,
　　That miracle of blue!

LAID LOW

Nought else now stirring my sick thoughts to share,
Laid low, I watched the house-flies in the air;
Swarthy, obscene, they angled, gendering there.
And Death, who every daybreak now rode by —
Dust-muffled hoofs, lank animal, and he —
A mocking adept in telepathy,
Jerked in his saddle, and laughed into the sky . . .

'Where is this Blind Man's stable? Where, his grain?
What starved fowls peck his cobblestones between?
Where stews his hothouse? Why must shut remain
His iron-hinged door to those who may not bide —
As welcome guests may — for one night, then go?
What lacqueys they who at the windows hide?
And whose that scarce-heard traipsing to and fro?

Façade! — that reeks of nightmare-dread and gloom!
Dwale, henbane, hemlock in its courtyard bloom;
Dumb walls; the speechless silence of the tomb.
No smoke its clustered chimney-shafts emit;
No taper stars at attic window-pane;
Who enters, enters once — comes not again;
A vigilant vacancy envelops it. . . .'

So chattered boding to a menaced bed;
While in the east earth's sunrise broadened out.
Its pale light gilt the ceiling. My heart said,
'Nay, there is nought to fear'— yet shook with dread:
Wept, 'Call him back!': groaned, 'Ah! that eyeless head!'
Impassioned by its beauty; sick with doubt: —
'Oh God, give life!' and, 'Would that I were dead!'

EUREKA

Lost in a dream last night was I.
I dreamed that, from this earth set free,
In some remote futurity
I had reached the place prepared for me.

A vault, it seemed, of burnished slate,
Whose planes beyond the pitch of sight
Converged — unswerving, immaculate —
Bathed in a haze of blinding light;

Not of the sun, or righteousness.
No cherub here, o'er lute-string bowed,
Tinkled some silly hymn of peace,
But, '*Silence! No loitering allowed!*'

In jet-black characters I read
Incised upon the porcelain floor.
Ay, and the silence of the dead
No sentient heart could harrow more.

There, stretching far as eye could see,
Beneath that flat and leprous glare
A maze of immense machinery
Hummed in the ozoned air —

Prodigious wheels of steel and brass;
And — ranged along the un-windowed walls —
Engrossed in objects of metal and glass,
Stooped spectres, in spotless over-alls.

Knees quaking, dazed affrighted eyes,
I turned to the Janitor and cried,
'Is this, friend, Hell or Paradise?'
And, sneering, he replied,

'Terms trite as yours the ignorant
On earth, it seems, may yet delude.
Here, "sin" and "saint" and "hierophant"
Share exile with "the Good".

'Be grateful that the state of bliss
Henceforth, perhaps, reserved for thee,
Is sane and sanative as this,
And void of fatuous fantasy.

[311]

'Here God, the Mechanist, reveals,
As only mechanism can,
Mansions to match the new ideals
Of his co-worker, Man.

'On strict probation, you are now
To toil with yonder bloodless moles —
These skiagrams will show you how —
On mechanizing human souls . . .'

At this I woke: and, cold as stone,
Lay quaking in the hazardous light
    Of earth's familiar moon;
A clothes-moth winged from left to right,
    A tap dripped on and on;
And there, my handmade pot, my jug
Beside the old grained washstand stood;
There, too, my once-gay threadbare rug,
    The flattering moonlight wooed:
And — Heaven forgive a dream-crazed loon! —
    I found them very good.

BUT OH, MY DEAR

Hearts that too wildly beat —
    Brief is their epitaph!
Wisdom is in the wheat,
    Not in the chaff.
But Oh, my dear, how rich and rare, and root-down-
    deep and wild and sweet
    It is to laugh!

THE FROZEN DELL

How still it is! How pure and cold
The air through which the wood-birds glide
From frost-bound tree to tree —
Veiled with so thin a mist that through
Its meshes steals that dayspring blue!

No other life. All motion gone —
As though a spectre, night being down,
Had through this darkened dingle trod
And frozen all he touched to stone.

Where art thou, mole? Where, busy ant?
Each in its earthen fastness is
As passive as the hive-bound bees,
As squirrel drowsing free from want,
And silken-snug chrysalides,
Queens of the wasps with ash-dark eyes —
Tranced exquisite complexities —
    And buds of the slumbering trees.

Yet human lovers, astray in this
Unfathomable silentness,
Into such dreamlike beauty come,
Though it seem lifeless as the tomb,
Might pause a moment here to kiss,
Their cold hands clasped; might even weep
For joy at their own ecstasy —
This crystal cage, sleep's wizardry,
    And secret as the womb!

BIRDS IN WINTER

I know not what small winter birds these are,
Warbling their hearts out in that dusky glade
While the pale lustre of the morning star
    In heaven begins to fade.

Not me they sing for, this — earth's shortest — day,
A human listening at his window-glass;
They would, affrighted, cease and flit away
    At glimpse even of my face.

And yet how strangely mine their music seems,
As if of all things loved my heart was heir,
Had helped create them — albeit in my dreams —
    And they disdained my share.

FEBRUARY

Whence is the secret of these skies,
Their limpid colours, deeper light,
That ardent dovelike tenderness,
Hinting at hidden mysteries
Beyond the reach of sight?

The risen sun's not half an hour
Earlier than on St. Lucy's Day;
And scarcely twice as long as that
In loftier arch, like opening flower,
His chariot loiters on the way;

But ev'n the rain upon the cheek
A kindlier message seems to bring;
There's sweetness in the moving air,
The stars of cold December's dark
Wheel on to their last westering;

And Earth herself this secret shares.
The sap is welling in her veins;
She to the heavens her bosom bares;
Snowdrop and crocus pierce the sod;
A brightening green the meadow stains.

And at her still, enticing call
The honeysuckle leaves untwine;
A softly-warbling thrush replies;
Mosses begem the orchard wall —
A fortnight from St. Valentine!

All this in open bliss appears;
Is it but fancy that within
The heart a resurrection stirs,
Some secret listener also hears
The hosannas of the Spring? . . .

And Oh, the wonder of a face —
Darkened by illness, grief and pain —
Love scarce can breathe its speechless Grace
When, mystery of all mysteries,
That heaven-sent life steals back again!

THESE SOLEMN HILLS

These solemn hills are silent now that night
Steals softly their green valleys out of sight;
The only sound that through the evening wells
   Is new-born lambkin's bleat;
   And — with soft rounded wings,
   Silvered in day's last light,
     As on they beat —
The lapwing's slow, sad, anguished
   Pee-oo-eet.

SHEEP

Early sunbeams shafting the beech-boles,
   An old oak fence, and in pasture deep —
Dark, and shapeless, dotting the shadows —
   A grazing and motionless flock of sheep;

So strangely still as they munched the grasses
   That I, up aloft on my 'bus, alone,
At gaze from its glass on the shimmering highway,
   Cried on myself: — 'Not sheep! They are stone!' —

Sarsen outcrops shelved by the glaciers?
   An aeon of darkness, ice and snow?
Beings bewitched out of far-away folk-tales?
   Prodigies such as dreams can show? . . .

The mind — that old mole — has its hidden earthworks:
   Blake's greybeard into a thistle turned;
And, in his childhood, flocking angels
   In sun-wild foliage gleamed and burned.

Illusions . . . Yet — as my 'bus lurched onward,
   Beech trees, park-land and woodland gone,
It was not sheep in my memory lingered
   But, strangely indwelling, those shapes of stone.

THE CREEK

Where that dark water is,
A Naiad dwells,
Though of her presence
Little else
Than her own silence tells.

Her twilight is
The pictured shade
Between a dream
And the awakening made.

Stranger in beauty she must be —
Cold solemn face and eyes of green —
Than tongue could say,
Or aught that earthly
Sight hath seen.

Human touch,
Or gaze, or cry
Would ruin be
To her half-mortal frailty;
As to the surface of her stream
A zephyr's sigh.

THE BROOK

Here, in a little fall,
    From stone to stone,
The well-cool water drips,
    Lips, sips,
    And, babbling on,
Repeats its secret bell-clear song
    The whole day long.

From what far caverns,
From what soundless deep
Of earth's blind sunless rock
Did this pure wellspring seep —
As may some praeternatural dream
    In sleep?

ABSENCE

When thou art absent,
Grief only is constant,
My heart pines within me
Like the sighing of reeds
Where water lies open
To the darkness of heaven,
Voiceless, forsaken.

The bird in the forest
Where silence endureth,
The flower in the hollow
With down-drooping head —
Ah, Psyche, thy image! —
My soul breathes its homage;
But cold is this token,
Cold, cold is thy token,
When from dream I awaken,
By sorrow bestead.

THE RAINBOW

Stood twice ten thousand warriors on green grass
Ranked in that loop of running silver river,
The bright light dazzling on their steel and brass,
    Plumed helm, cuirass,
Tipped arrow, ivoried bow, and rain-soaked quiver;

And from these April clouds the blazing sun
Smote through the crystal drops of rain descending;
And, ere an instant of mere time was run,
    Or tongue could cry, *It's done!*
There spanned the east an arch all hues transcending:
Why, *then* would twice ten thousand dye the skies —
A different rainbow for each pair of eyes!
Oh, what a shout of joy might then be sent
From warrior throats, to crack the firmament!

But only a child was there — by that clear stream,
Reading a book, in shelter of a willow.
He raised his head to scan the radiant scene,
    His gaze aloof, serene,
    Smiling as if in dream;
And, sleeping, smiled again that night — his head upon
    his pillow.

[317]

THE GNOMON

I cast a shadow. Through the gradual day
Never at rest it secretly steals on;
As must the soul pursue its earthly way
    And then to night be gone.

But Oh, demoniac listeners in the grove,
Think not mere Time I now am telling of.
No. But of light, life, joy, and awe, and love:
    I obey the heavenly Sun.

EMPTY

The house by the sand dunes
Was bleached and dark and bare;
Birds, in the sea-shine,
Silvered and shadowed the air.

I called at the shut door,
I tirled at the pin:
Weeks — weeks of woesome tides,
The sand had drifted in.

The sand had heaped itself about
In the wefting of the wind;
And knocking never summoned ghost;
And dreams none can find

Like coins left at full of flood,
Gold jetsam of the sea.
Salt that water, bitter as love,
That will let nothing be

Unfevered, calm and still,
Like an ageing moon in the sky
Lighting the eyes of daybreak —
With a wick soon to die.

What then was shared there,
Who's now to tell?
Horizon-low the sea-borne light,
And dumb the buoyed bell.

LOVERS

There fell an hour when — as if clock
Had stayed its beat — their hearts stood still
At challenge of a single look,
Rapt, speechless, irretrievable.

Once, before lips had dreamed of kissing,
They languished, mind and soul, to see
Each the loved other's face; that missing,
In no wise else at peace could be.

Sleep, wherein not even dreams intrude,
Heart's haven may be from all that harms;
'Twere woe to the selfless solitude
They find in one another's arms.

Fantastic miracle, that even,
Though now all else seems little worth,
Would sacrifice the hope of heaven
    While love is theirs on earth!

'SAID FLORES'

'If I had a drop of attar
And a clot of wizard clay,
Birds we would be with wings of light
And fly to Cathay.

'If I had the reed called Ozmadoom,
And skill to cut pen,
I'd float a music into the air —
You'd listen, and then . . .

'If that small moon were mine for lamp,
I would look, I would see
The silent thoughts, like silver fish,
You are thinking of me.

'There is nothing upon grass or ground,
In the mountains or the skies,
But my heart faints in longing for,
And the tears drop from my eyes.

'And if I ceased from pining —
What buds were left to blow?
Where the wild swan? Where the wood-dove?
Where *then* should I go?'

NOT ONE

Turn your head sidelong;
    Gentle eyelids close;
In their small darkness
    Be all night's repose;
Weaving a dream — strange
    Flower and stranger fruit —
Wake heart may pine for
    But the day gives not.

Rest, folded lips,
    Their secret word unsaid;
Slumber will shed its dews,
    Be comforted:
Whilst I my vigil keep,
    And grieve in vain
That not the briefest moment — yours or mine —
    Can ever come again.

THE BRIBE

Ev'n should I give you all I have, —
From harmless childhood to the grave;
Call back my firstborn sigh, and then
Rob heaven of my last *Amen*;
Even if travailing back from Styx,
I brought you Pilate's crucifix;
Or, lone on Lethe, dredged you up
Melchior's golden Wassail cup;
Or Maacha's jewelled casket where
She shrined a lock of Absalom's hair;
Or relic whereon Noah would brood —
Keepsake of earth before the Flood;

Or flower of Adam's solitude;
The smile wherewith unmemoried Eve
Awoke from sleep, her fere to give,
And he, enravished, to receive;
Yes, and the daisy at her foot
She gazed at, and remembered not:
Nay, all Time's spoil, in dust put by,
Treasure untold to glut the eye —
Pining, and wonder, and mystery,
Rare and precious, old and strange,
Whithersoever thought can range,
Fish can swim, or eagle fly,
Harvesting earth, and sea, and sky;
And yours could be the empery: —
      What use?
There is no power or go-between or spell in time or space
Can light with even hint of love one loveless human face.

NOT YET

'Not love me? Even yet!'— half-dreaming, I
    whispered and said.
Untarnished, truth-clear eyes; averted,
    lovely head:
It was thus she had looked and had listened — how often —
    before she was dead.

DIVIDED

Two spheres on meeting may so softly collide
They stay, as if still kissing, side by side.
Lovers may part for ever — the cause so small
Not even a lynx could see a gap at all.

TREASURE

Reason as patiently as moth and rust
    May fret life's ardours into dust;
But soon — the sun begins to shine, and then —
Undaunted weeds! — they up, they spring, they spread
    — romp into bloom again.

CUPID KEPT IN

When life's wild noisy boys were out of school,
And, for his hour, the usher too was gone,
Peering at sun-fall through the crannied door,
I saw an urchin sitting there alone.

His shining wings lay folded on his back,
Between them hung a quiver, while he sat,
Bare in his beauty, and with poring brows
Bent o'er the saddening task-work he was at.

'*Which means she? — Yes or No?*' his problem was.
A gilding ray tinged plume and cheek and chin;
He frowned, he pouted, fidgeted, and wept —
Lost, mazed; unable even to begin!

But then, how could (Oh, think, my dear!), how *could*
That little earnest but unlettered mite
Find any meaning in the heart whose runes
Have kept me tossing through the livelong night?

What wonder, then, when I sighed out for shame,
He brought his scribbled slate, tears in his eyes,
And bade me hide it, until you have made
The question simpler, or himself more wise?

SCHOLARS

Logic does well at school;
And Reason answers every question right;
Poll-parrot Memory unwinds her spool;
And Copy-cat keeps Teacher well in sight:

The Heart's a truant; nothing does by rule;
Safe in its wisdom, is taken for a fool;
Nods through the morning on the dunce's stool;
And wakes to dream all night.

THOU ART MY LONG-LOST PEACE

Thou art my long-lost peace;
All trouble and all care,
Like winds on the ocean cease —
Leaving serene and fair
The evening-gilded wave
Above the unmeasured deep —
When those clear grave dark eyes
Call to the soul, in sleep —

In sleep. The waking hour —
How sweet its power may be!
Lovely the bird, the flower,
That feigns Reality!
But further yet, there is
A spirit, strange to earth,
Within whose longing lies
What day can not bring forth.

So I, though hand and lip,
Being body's, pine for thine,
Watch from my dreams in sleep
What earthly clocks resign
To cloaked Eternity:
Then weeping, sighing, must go
Back to his haunt in me,
In rapture; and in woe.

THE UNDERCURRENT

What, do you suppose, we're in this world for, sweet
heart?
What — in this haunted, crazy, beautiful cage —
Keeps so many, like ourselves, poor pining human
creatures,
As if from some assured, yet withholden heritage?
Keeps us lamenting beneath all our happy laughter,
Silence, dreams, hope for what may *not* come after,
While life wastes and withers, as it has for all mortals,
Age on to age, on to age?

[323]

Strange it would be if the one simple secret
Were that wisdom hides, as beauty hides in pebble,
  leaf and blade;
That a good beyond divining, if we knew but where to
  seek it,
Is awaiting revelation when — well, *Sesame* is said;
That what so frets and daunts us ev'n in all we love
  around us
Is the net of worldly custom which has penned us in and
  bound us;
    That — freed — our hearts would break for joy
    Arisen from the dead.

    Would 'break'? What do I say?
Might that secret, if divulged, all we value most bewray!
    Make a dream of our real,
    A night of our day,
      That word said?
Oh, in case that be the answer, in case some stranger
  call us,
    Or death in his stead;
    Sweet Nought, come away, come away!

OUTER DARKNESS

'The very soul within my breast . . .'
'Mute, motionless, aghast . . .'

Uncompanioned, forlorn, the shade of a shade,
From all semblance of life I seemed to have strayed
To a realm, and a being — of fantasy made.
Where the spirit no more invokes Reason to prove
An illusion of sense it is cognisant of.
  I was lost: but aware.
  I had traversed the stream
By that nebulous bridge which the waking call dream,
And was come to an ultimate future that yet
Was the dust of a past no remorse could forget —
  Heart could covet no more,
    Nor forget.

Wheresoever my eyes might forebodingly range
They discerned the familiar disguised as the strange, —
Relics of memoried objects designed
To enchant to distraction an earth-enthralled mind,
      A sense-shackled mind.
The door was ajar when I entered. And lo!
A banquet prepared for one loved, long ago.
But I shunned to peer close, to detect what was there,
As I stood, lost in reverie, facing that chair.
In anguish and dread I dared not surmise
What fate had befallen those once ardent eyes,
The all-welcoming hands, the compassionate breast,
   And the heart now at rest,
   Ev'n from love now at rest.

The glass she had drunk from beamed faintly. Its lees
Were as dry as the numberless sands of the seas
In a lunar volcano parched up by the sun
Ere the Moon's frenzied courtship of Earth had begun.
Once, the flame of that candle had yearned to retrace
The heart-breaking secrets concealed in her face —
   Gentle palace of loveliness: avid to steep
With its motionless radiance cheek, brow and lip;
And in innocent scrutiny striving to win
Through the windows now void to the phantom within,
   To the spirit secluded within.

Now its refuse was blackened. The brass of its stick —
The virginal wax guttered down to the wick —
Was witch-hued with verdigris. Fret-moth and mouse
   Had forsaken for ever this house.
As I moved through the room I was frosted with light;
   Decay was here Regent of Night.
It clotted the fabric of curtain and chair
Like a luminous mildew infesting the air;
An æon had waned since there fell the faint call
Of the last mateless insect at knock in the wall.
The once rotten was dry — gone all sense of its taint;
The mouldings were only the shell of their paint,
   Though their valueless gold
   Glimmered on, as of old:
So remote was this hush: where none listens or hears;
By all sweetness deserted for measureless years,
   The wilderness mortals call years.

[325]

And I?
And I? Ghost of ghost, unhousel'd, foredone —
Candle, fleet, fire — out of memory gone.
Appalled, I peered on in the glass at the face
Of a creature of dread, lost in time, lost in space,
Pilgrim, waif, outcast, abandoned, alone,
In a sepulchred dark, mute as stone.
Yet of beauty, past speech, was this region of Nought
And the reflex of images conjured by thought —
Those phantoms of flow'rs in their pitcher of glass
Shrined a light that no vision could ever surpass.
In that sinister dusk every leaf, twig and tree
Wove an intricate web of significancy;
And those hills in the moonlight, a somnolent green,
Still awakened a yearning to scan the unseen,
    To seek haven within the unseen.

Alas, how can anguish and grief be allayed
    In a soul self-betrayed?
Yet that emblem of Man, in its niche by the door,
Limned a passionate pathos unheeded of yore,
A wonder, a peace, disregarded before,
    A grace that no hope could restore.

I had drunken of death. The night overhead
Was a forest of quietude, stagnant as lead;
Starless, tranquil, serene as the dead;
    The last love-stilled look of the dead.
Cold, as the snow of swan in her sleep
On pitiless Lethe to heart and to lip,
Was the void that enwrapped me — by slumber betrayed;
    Ecstatic, demented, afraid:
In a zero, forsaken, marooned: not a sigh.
An existence denuded of all but an I;
    And those relics near by:
    Neither movement nor sigh.

Till a whisper within, like a breath from the tomb,
Asked me, 'Knowest thou not wherefore thus thou art
        come
    To this judgement, this doom?'
And my heart in my dreams stayed its pulsings: 'Nay,
        why?'

But Nothingness made no reply.

OUT OF A DREAM

Out of a dream I came —
Woeful with sinister shapes,
Hollow sockets aflame,
The mouth that gapes
With cries, unheard, of the dark;
The bleak, black night of the soul;
Sweating, I lay in my bed,
Sick of the wake for a goal.

And lo — Earth's close-shut door,
Its panels a cross, its key
Of common and rusting iron,
Opened, and showed to me
A face — found; lost — of old:
Of a lifetime's longing the sum;
And eyes that assuaged all grief:
    'Behold! I am come.'

JOY

This little wayward boy
Stretched out his hands to me,
Saying his name was Joy;
Saying all things that seem
Tender, and wise, and true
Never need fade while he
Drenches them through and through
With his sweet mastery;
Told me that Love's clear eyes
Pools were without the sky,
Earth, without paradise,
Were he not nigh;
Even that grief conceals
Him in a dark disguise;
And that affliction brings
    All it denies.

Not mine to heed him then —
Till fell the need — and Oh,
All his sweet converse gone,
Where could I go?
What could I do? —
But seek him up and down,
Thicket and thorn and fell,
Till night in gloom came on
Unpierceable?
Then, when all else must fail,
Stepped from the dark to me,
Voiced like the nightingale,
Masked, weeping, he.

THE VISION

O starry face, bound in grave strands of hair,
Aloof, remote, past speech or thought to bless —
Life's haunting mystery and the soul's long care,
Music unheard, heart's utter silentness,
Beauty no mortal life could e'er fulfil,
Yet garnered loveliness of all I see,
Which in this transient pilgrimage is still
Steadfast desire of that soul's loyalty;

Death's haunting harp-string, sleep's mandragora,
Mockery of waking and the dark's despair,
Life's changeless vision that fades not away —
O starry face, bound in grave strands of hair!
Hands faintly sweet with flowers from fields unseen,
Breasts cold as mountain snow and far waves' foam,
Eyes changeless and immortal and serene —
Spent is this wanderer, and you call him home!

WHITENESS

I stay to linger, though the night
Is draining every drop of light
From out the sky, and every breath
I breathe is icy chill as death.
Not so much colour now there shows
As tinges even the palest rose;
Nor in this whiteness can be seen
The faintest trace of hidden green.

Scarlet would cry as shrill as fife
Here where there stirs no hint of life.
A child in rare vermilion,
Come out to wonder at the snow:
Like Moses' burning bush would show —
Its bonfire out, when he is gone!

Yet in this pallor every tree
A marvel is of symmetry,
As if enthralled by its own grace —
A music woven of silentness.
Dense hoarfrost clots the tresses of
That weeping elm's funereal white,
Biding the sepulchre of night
To whisper — 'It is cold, my love!'
To Winter, witless nihilist,
Who, the day long, has kept his tryst
With mistress no less mute than he,
And tranced in a like rhapsody.

As though from vacant vaults of space
Darkness transfigured haunts his face;
And, she, for spell to wreathe her brow,
Has twined the Druid mistletoe.

What viol in this frozen air
Could for their nuptials descant make?
What timbrels Eros bid awake?
Ask of those solemn cedars there!

SOLITUDE

When the high road
  Forks into a by-road,
And that drifts into a lane,
And the lane breaks into a bridle-path,
    A chace forgotten
    Still as death,
And green with the long night's rain;
Through a forest winding on and on,
Moss, and fern, and sun-bleached bone,
    Till only a trace remain;
And that dies out in a waste of stone
A bluff of cliff, vast, trackless, wild,
Blue with the harebell, undefiled;
Where silence enthralls the empty air,
Mute with a presence unearthly fair,
        And a path is sought
        In vain. . . .

    It is then the Ocean
      Looms into sight,
A gulf enringed with a burning white,
A sea of sapphire, dazzling bright;
        And islands,
    Peaks of such beauty that
Bright danger seems to lie in wait,
Dread, disaster, boding fate;
And soul and sense are appalled thereat;
Though an Ariel music on the breeze
Thrills the mind with a lorn unease,
Cold with all mortal mysteries.
        And every thorn,
        And weed, and flower,
    And every time-worn stone
A challenge cries on the trespasser:
        Beware!
        Thou art alone!

THE UNRENT PATTERN

I roved the Past — a thousand thousand years,
Ere the Egyptians watched the lotus blow,
Ere yet Man stumbled on his first of words,
Ere yet his laughter rang, or fell his tears;
And on a hillside where three trees would grow —
    Life immortal, Peace, and Woe:
    Dismas, Christ, his bitter foe —
Listened, as yesterday, to the song of birds.

SON OF MAN

Son of man, tell me,
Hast thou at any time lain in thick darkness,
Gazing up into a lightless silence,
A dark void vacancy,
Like the woe of the sea
In the unvisited places of the ocean?
And nothing but thine own frail sentience
To prove thee living?
Lost in this affliction of the spirit,
Did'st thou then call upon God
Of his infinite mercy to reveal to thee
Proof of his presence —
His presence and love for thee, exquisite creature of his
    creation?
To show thee but some small devisal
Of his infinite compassion and pity, even though it were as
    fleeting
As the light of a falling star in a dewdrop?
Hast thou? O, if thou hast not,
Do it now; do it now; do it now!
Lest that night come which is sans sense, thought, tongue,
    stir, time, being,
And the moment is for ever denied thee,
Since thou art thyself as I am.

DUST

Sweet sovereign lord of this so pined-for Spring,
How breathe the homage of but one poor heart
With such small compass of thy everything?

Ev'n though I knew this were my life's last hour,
It yet would lie, past hope, beyond my power
One instant of my gratitude to prove,
   My praise, my love.

That 'Everything'! — when this, my human dust,
   Whereto return I must,
Were scant to bring to bloom a single flower!

PROBLEMS

'Gone! Where? My glasses!' the old quidnunc cries;
   And still the blinder grows,
Until (the problems life solves in this wise!)
   He finds them on his nose.

THE OLD AUTHOR

The End, he scrawled, and blotted it. Then eyed
Through darkened glass night's cryptic runes o'erhead.
'My last, and longest book.' He frowned; then sighed:
   'And everything left unsaid!'

The Traveller (1945)

' "*I saw that the universe is not composed of dead matter but is . . . a living presence.*" '
'*Le soir vient; et le globe à son tour s'éblouit*
  Devient un œil énorme et regarde la nuit . . .'
'*Not in lone splendour hung aloft the night*
  But watching . . .'

This Traveller broke at length, toward set of sun,
Out from the gloom of towering forest trees;
Gasped, and drew rein: to gaze, in wonder, down
A bow-shaped gulf of shelving precipices.

The blue of space dreamed level with his eye.
A league beneath, like lava long at rest,
Lay a vast plateau, smooth as porphyry,
Its huge curve gradual as a woman's breast.

In saline marshes Titicaca lies —
Its ruins fabulous ere the Incas reigned:
Was this the like? A mountain sea? His eyes
Watched like a lynx. It still as death remained.

Not the least ripple broke the saffron sheen
Shed by the evening on this wild abyss.
Far countries he had roved, and marvels seen,
But never such a prodigy as this.

No. Water never in a monstrous mass
Rose to a summit like a rounded stone,
Ridged with concentric shadows. No morass
Were vast as this, or coloured zone by zone.

Vague relics haunted him of mythic tales,
Printed in books, or told him in his youth —
Deserts accursed; 'witched islands; sunken bells;
Fissures in space . . . Might one yet prove the truth?

Or, in his own sole being long confined,
Had he been lured into those outskirts where
A secret self is regent; and the mind
Reveals an actual none else can share? —

Prospects enchanting, dread, whereof as yet
No chart has record shown, could bearings tell;
Such as some fabulous Afreet might beget:
Clear as mirage, ev'n less attainable?

Stealthy in onset, between wake and sleep,
Such scenes, more moving than the earth can show,
May, self-created, in mutation sweep,
Silent and fugitive as April snow.

Or had he now attained the true intent
Of his unbroken pilgrimage? The sum
Of all his communings; and what they meant?
Was life at length to its Elysium come?

So flows experience: the vast Without;
Its microcosm, of the Soul, within;
Whereof the day-distracted eye may doubt,
But doubts no more as soon as dreams begin.

Thus mused this Traveller. Was he man or ghost?
Deranged by solitude? Or rapt away
To some unpeopled limbo of the lost —
Feint that the light of morning would betray? . . .

At verge of this huge void he camped for days;
Months of slow journeying from the haunts of men;
Till awe of it no longer could amaze,
And passion for venturing urged him on again.

Down, down into the abysm his mare, on hooves
Nimble as mountain-bred gazelle's, pricked on
From steep to steep, until through bouldered grooves
And shallowing streams she trod, their safety won —

An Arab lean and sleek, her surf-like mane
Tossed on a shoulder as of ivory made;
Full in the moonrise she approached the plain,
Was, with her master, in its beams arrayed.

He had scanned that lunar landscape when of old,
Tranced at a window as a child he had sat —
The Face, the Thorns, those craters grisly cold,
Volcanic seas now parched and desolate;

While from afar the bird of night bewailed
Her cruel ravishment. Even then he had pined,
Ere hope abandoned him, or courage failed,
To seek adventure, safety left behind.

Chilled by his travel in the shrewd clear air,
With wind-strown kindling-wood he built a fire;
Scant pasturage for man or beast was there,
And dreams but transiently assuage desire.

His supper done, he crouched beside the blaze,
Sharp-cheeked, wide-browed, and lost in reverie;
Flamelight and moonshine playing on his face,
The crackle of logs his only company.

When the dark tent of night at daybreak wanned,
He rose, remounted, and surveyed the vast
Convex of bloodshot stone that swept beyond
In arc enormous to the skies at last.

Great mountains he had ranged that lift their snow
In peaks sublime, which age to age remain
Unstirred by foot or voice; but here, a slow
Furtive foreboding crept into his brain

Of what yet lay before him — this Unknown;
In subtle feature so unlike the past
Havens of exile he had made his own,
Been restive in, or wearied of at last.

Soon as the risen sun rilled down its heat,
A dewy mist, in this huge hollow pent,
Washed like a sea of milk his Arab's feet.
And rainbows arched before him as he went.

The call of waters kept his ears a-cock —
Creeks fed by cataracts now left behind.
Forests of fungi in the lichened rock
Showed ashen wan and grey as withy-wind;

Spawn of a gendering hour, yet hoar with age,
They stood sun-bleached, ephemera of the night,
And — thing past even speculation strange —
Growths never grazed till now by human sight.

What tinier atomies of life were bred
Beneath their skin-thin gills, tents, muted bells,
Eye could not guess — as procreant a bed
As is man's body with its countless cells.

The furtive mist, these clustered funguses —
Minutest stirrings of primeval slime,
The empty heavens, aloof and measureless,
Illusions seemed, not only of space, but time.

From microscopical to the immense —
Mere magnitude of little moment is;
But violent contrast shakes man's confidence
Even in what lies plain before his eyes.

Birds of rare flight and hue, of breed unknown,
Rose, wheeled, fled onward, mewling as they went —
And left him — more forsaken and alone;
Sun for sole guidance in his slow ascent.

But borne not far upon the windless air,
The fickle fleet-winged creatures turned anon;
Came stooping backward on his face to stare:
Broke out in cries again; again, were gone:

Curious, but fearless of what never yet
Had on these mighty slopes been seen to appear;
With soft-tongued jargoning they his way beset,
Sadder than love-lorn pewit's on the ear.

Nor was it only stone that made reply.
Their sweetness echoed in his heart. Delight
And love long pent in fadeless memory
Welled to his eyes. He watched them out of sight.

What meaning harbours in a bird's lone note
Secret as music is; ineffable:
With Song of the Sirens it has been forgot:
But long he journeyed on beneath its spell.

Westward to eastward, wide as gaze could scan,
Shallowly troughed, the void savanna swept:
The dead of all the armies doomed by Man
Might, biding ransom, in its folds have slept.

And, hollow as sinister beating of a drum
The rock resounded when, with sudden bound,
His beast beneath him, on the treacherous scum,
Slipped, and, with snort of fear, her balance found.

That night, while yet in darkness lapped, it seemed
He had leapt from sleep, that instant made aware
The rock beneath had trembled while he dreamed,
Bleached of a sudden by the lightning's glare.

Foreboding perils unconceived before,
He woke when dawn again suffused the sky.
His earth, once stable, now proved insecure:
He sat and watched it with unwinking eye;

While chattering voices wrangled in his head:
'Alas, what horror of the soul is this?'
'Beware! Away!' 'Far better thou were dead
Than face the ordeal that now before thee lies!'

A plaintive whinny in the early air,
For company calling, solace brought. He smiled.
And in sweet converse with his timorous mare
Soothed her disquiet, and his own beguiled.

Towards noon an arid wind from out the East
Waxed, waned; and failed as they approached — these two,
In close companionship of man and beast,
To where the plain they paced lapsed into blue.

His aching eyes rejoiced. No more there showed
Branched veins of sanguine in a milk-pale stone;
An ever deepening azure gloomed and glowed
In shine and shadow as they journeyed on:

Turquoise, and sapphire, speedwell, columbine.
When clouds minute, like scales of fish, are seen
Dappling an April daybreak, then, divine
As Eros' eyes, there shows a blue between,

Tranquil, wan, infinite. So, pale to dark,
A dark as dazzling as the tropic deep,
Loomed now the prospect toward his distant mark,
When yet again he laid him down to sleep.

In this oblivion he dreamed a dream: —
He dreamed the transitory host of men,
Debased by pride, lust, greed and self-esteem,
Had gone their way; that Earth was freed again.

Their minds had brewed a poison in the blood;
The sap of their own nature had decayed.
They had chosen evil, had resigned the good;
False, faithless, pitiless, and of nought afraid.

Nature, released from this vile incubus,
Had wooed into being creatures of other kind,
Resembling those long since deemed fabulous,
As exquisite in aspect as in mind.

Beings, too, once adored for beauty and grace,
Who had left but echoes in the mirroring air,
Had sought again their bygone dwelling-place;
As happy birds in springtime homeward fare.

And he? — the sport of contraries in sleep! —
To childhood had returned; gone grief and woe;
That Eden of the heart, and fellowship
With innocence, that only children know;

And in a garden played, serene, alone;
Bird, flower, water, shining in his eyes;
And magic hidd'n in even the tiniest stone ...
When, suddenly, a Trumpet rent the skies:

To Judgement had been called the Sons of Light,
The stellar host, the Sun and all his brood:
Rank beyond rank, height above heavenly height,
Within the eternal peace of God they stood,

Hymning his glory. And, alas, he knew
That, chosen envoy of the Earth, he had come,
Garbed in her beauty, and enraptured too;
But, though he had yearned for joy, his soul was dumb.

And by unuttered edict exiled thence,
He had fallen, as Satan fell, in leaden dismay,
And thus had wakened to the rock-land whence
His spirit, in fantasy, had winged away ...

[338]

On high a dwindling, sun-bedazzled moon
Paled in the homeless solitudes of space,
Casting gaunt shadow here — his vision gone —
For void companionship in this bitter place.

He, Envoy of the Earth! — that mothering breast;
Those Suns and Sons, what meaning could he find? —
A cold satanic irony at best,
Or scoff of that mocking-bird in sleep, his mind.

Oh, that he had but one bright candle here
To pierce the double-dark of body and soul!
Could but a strain of music reach his ear
To ease this heartsick wretchedness and dole!

From lifted brow his leaden-lidded eyes
Searched the vast furrows of unanswering stone
To where the cedar-arc'd abyss must rise
Whence he had journeyed to this end, alone.

Gazing, he mused, beset by mystery,
Mere Sentience in the silence of the night;
Could Earth itself a living creature be,
And he its transitory parasite? —

A frosted incubus, by the cold congealed,
Doubting his senses, vacantly aware
Of what already instinct had revealed —
His deadliest danger now was blank despair.

Like an old zany, he seemed, who, year by year,
The slave has been of an Excelsior,
Its goal Eureka; and when that draws near
Hears fleshless knuckles on his chamber-door!

Or like a doting lover who at last
By one whose source had seemed of heavenly grace
Forsaken is, in outer darkness cast,
Her cheating blandishment a Lamia's face.

Meagre his saddlebag as camel's hump
When, sand-marooned, she staggers to her doom.
As shrunken too, his Arab's ribs and rump
Showed taut as vellum stretched upon a drum.

[339]

He strove in vain to reason, numbed with sleep,
But conscious that at first faint token of dawn,
Wraiths at whose beauty even the blind might weep,
Wooed to his solitude, had come, and gone —

Wraiths all but lost to memory, whose love
Had burned in hearts that never more would beat;
Of whose compassion sense could bring no proof,
Though solace 'twas beyond all telling sweet —

Like flowers that a child brings home; to fade.
Alas, alas, no longer could restore
Life to the faithful by neglect betrayed!
Too late for ransom; they'd return no more —

Had left him, like a castaway adrift,
Lashed to a raft upon a chartless sea,
His only motion the huge roller's lift,
Its depths his only hope at peace to be.

'Sea'! when this waste of stone in which he lay
Like night-blue porcelain was, untinged with red.
But when his cracked lips stirred, as if to pray,
He caught but leaf-dry whisper of what they said.

So tense was this his solitude — the sky
Its mute and viewless canopy — that when
His grieved 'O God!' was followed by a sigh,
It seemed eternity had breathed amen.

Ay, as if cock, horizon-far, had crowed,
His heart, like Peter's, had been rent in twain.
At pang of it his grief again up-flowed,
Though its 'Who's there?' called only in his brain . . .

On, and still on he pressed — scorched heel to nape,
Hunched in his saddle from the noonday's glare —
Watched by a winged thing, high in heaven, agape
To ken aught stirring in a tract so bare,

Which leaf or blade of grass could never yield.
A vitreous region, like a sea asleep,
Crystalline, convex, tideless and congealed,
Profounder far than Tuscarora Deep,

Further than sight could reach, before him lay.
Head bent, eyes fixed — drowsed by recurrent stroke
Of tic-tac ice-like hoof-beats, wits astray,
He slipped again from real to dream: awoke

To find himself marooned beneath a dome
Of star-pricked vacancy, and darkness near;
His breast bespattered with his Arab's foam,
And — trotting at his heels — the spectre, Fear:

Whose fell pursuit, unhastening, pace for pace —
Like Lama of Tibet in waking trance —
His very soul for quarry in the chase,
Forbade all hazard of deliverance:

A shapeless shape of horror, mildew-blue,
With naked feet, blank eyes, and leprous face,
Insane with lust, that ever nearer drew,
Tarrying for midnight and the dread embrace.

Foes of the soul there are, corrupt, malign,
Taint of whose malice is so evil a blight
That ev'n the valiant must hope resign
Unless God's mercy give them means for flight.

Witless as wild bird tangled in a net,
He dared not turn his head, but galloped on,
Spurs red at heel, his body drenched with sweat,
Until, with nerve renewed, but strength nigh gone,

He slowed his pace to listen; gasped, fordone;
Drew rein, dismounted . . . But, the peril past,
His cheek was fallen in like that of one
Whom mortal stroke of fate has felled at last;

And in a moment aged him many years —
Edict beyond the mind to comprehend.
Plaiting cramped fingers in the elf-locked mane,
'Come, now,' he muttered, 'we must rest, my friend.'

The creature's sunken eyeballs, scurfed with rheum
And mute with misery, returned his gaze;
And thus they communed in the gathering gloom,
Nought but the love between them left to graze.

She pawed the unnatural ice, tossed her small head,
By inarticulate alarm distressed;
Baring her teeth, squealed faintly, smitten with dread;
And, snuggling closer, lipped her master's breast.

His breath rasped harshly — wind in blasted wheat;
Through fret of her coarse mane his sun-parched eyes,
Their swol'n lids blackened by the daylong heat,
Swept the dim vacuum of earth and skies.

'Quiet, dear heart! The end is nearing now.
Into disaster thou hast been betrayed.'
He smoothed her gentle muzzle, kissed her brow.
'Nought worse than one more night to live,' he said.

'We both are mortal, both have fallen at last
Into disgrace. But had I swerved aside,
And safety found, what peace, the danger past,
Is his who sleeps with Terror for his bride?

But one night more. And then must come what may.
But never mistress held man's life in fee
As mine has been. And how could speech convey
The woe, forlorn one, that I feel for thee!'

So grieved he in his heart. This comrade dear!
His gentle hand upon her shoulder lay
Though still she shivered, twitching flank and ear,
In this drear wilderness so far astray.

Long stood he motionless, while overhead
The circling constellations, east to west,
Misting the infinite, their effluence shed —
Friends long familiar on how many a quest!

From this dark timeless absence of the mind
It seemed an inward voice had summoned him: —
'See! See!'— a whisper fainter than the wind
Or ripple of water lipped on Lethe's brim.

For now — the zenith darkening — opal-pale,
As if the earth its secret well-spring were —
Softly as flowers of night their scents exhale —
A strange and deepening lustre tinged the air,

Gentle and radiant. So, from off the sea
May mirrored moonbeams, when calm waters lave
A rock-bound coast, steal inward silently,
Blanching the sombre vaultings of a cave.

Not rock his roof-tree here, but hollow sky;
Not reflex moon-ray, but a phantom light,
Like hovering, pervasive reverie
Of Mind supreme, illumining the night.

Rapt in this loveliness, his spellbound face,
To travail the while, and famine, reconciled,
Of fret and weariness shed every trace,
As sleep brings comfort to a tired-out child:

Sleep to a body so pure and exquisite
Like manna it is, at gilding sunrise seen;
The senses so untrammelled that as yet
No more than frailest barrier lies between

Soul and reality. Thus beauty may
Pierce through the mists that worldly commerce brings,
Imagination's blindness wash away,
And — bird at daybreak — lend the spirit wings.

Even the little ant, devoid of fear,
Prowling beneath the shadow of a man,
Conscious may be of occult puissance near,
Whose origin it neither recks, nor can.

So, though he too was now but vaguely aware
Whence welled this boon of benison and peace,
In awe of a mystery so divinely fair,
Tears gushed within him, not of grief but bliss.

Courage revived, like greenness after rain.
Slowly he turned; looked back. And in amaze —
A waif self-exiled from the world of men —
Trembled at sight of what now met his gaze: —

The hushed and visionary host of those
Who, like himself, had faced life's long duress,
Its pangs and horrors, anguish, hardship, woes,
Their one incentive ever on to press,

Defying dread and danger — and in vain:
Not to achieve a merely temporal goal,
Not for bright glory, praise, or greed of gain,
But in that secret craving of the soul

For what no name has; flower of hidden stem: —
The unreturned of kindless land and sea;
Venturers, voyagers, dreamers, seers — ay, them
The Angel of Failure hails with rhapsody.

Him, too, for some rare destiny designed,
Who, in faith and love, has ranged; unmarked, alone;
Though means to share it he will never find
Since its sole language is unique — his own:

Great deeds win sweet renown: the hope forlorn
May perish, and none know what fate it braved;
The self content, at ease, has yet forsworn
The scope that still awaits the soul that's saved:

Faith in a love that can no respite have,
Being its sole resource and anodyne —
Impassioned love, its goal beyond the grave,
However short it fall of the divine.

Ay, even though Man have but one earthly life,
Cradle to grave, wherein to joy and grieve?
His grace were yet the agony and strife
In quest of what no mortal can achieve.

'Angel', forsooth! Bleak visage, frigid breast,
Passionless Nemesis, the heart for prey,
She goads her votary with insane unrest
And smiles upon him when she stoops to slay!

Strange beauty theirs, this host — in rapt array,
Spectral and motionless, intent, and dumb,
Laved in light's loveliness they stretched away
Homage ironic to his Kingdom Come!

Less a mere castaway of flesh and bone,
Defenceless, lost, whom Fate will overwhelm,
He now appeared, than — child of genius — one
Who explores pure fantasy's unbounded realm;

[344]

And being at length confronted by ordeal
No human consciousness could comprehend,
A preternatural ecstasy can feel —
Life's kiss of rapture at life's journey's end.

'All hail!' he muttered; paused; then laid him low,
His crazed head pillowed on his Arab's flank;
Prostrate with thirst and weariness and woe,
Into a plumbless deep of sleep he sank.

What visitants of earth or air drew near
Rider and horse in these stark hours of night —
Sylphs of the wilderness or demon drear,
Gazed long and softly, and again took flight,

No sense ajar revealed; nor echo of
Music ethereal, pining sweet and shrill
Of voices in the vaults of heaven above,
The angelic solitudes of Israfel . . .

When daybreak moved above the hushed expanse,
By ague shaken, he awoke. Aware
Nought now could shield him from life's last mischance,
With tranquil mind he breathed the scentless air.

This sterile world! — no weed here raised its head;
No bird on dew-plashed wing, his ear to bless,
Flew up to greet the dayspring; but instead,
A tense unfathomable silentness

Engulfed the enormous convex, stony-still,
Of hueless, lucent crystal where he lay,
Shivering in fever in the sunless chill,
Its centre now scarce half a league away.

He rose; the rustle of his raiment seemed
A desecration of the quietude
Brimming its vacancy; as if there dreamed
A presence here where none had dared intrude

Since waters from waters had divided been,
World from the heavens, the land from ocean freed;
And fruitful trees sprang up, with leafage green,
And earth put forth the herb that yieldeth seed.

'Come, now', he whispered softly; paused; aghast,
Deeming his faithful one had found reprieve;
Had fled away, all tribulation past,
Where even the soul-less languish not nor grieve;

But green-grey willows hang their tresses down;
The heron fishes in his plashy pool;
There, in her beauty floats the silent swan —
Shady and verdurous and calm and cool:

Meadows where asphodel and cowslips blow,
And sunlit summer clouds dissolve in rain —
Her earthly paradise! At length! But no;
The gentle creature heard, had stirred again.

Scrabbling her fore-hoofs on the treacherous waste,
She rose, stood trembling; with sepulchral sigh
Turned her night-blinded eyes, her master faced;
And patiently, piteously set out to die.

To eyried bird above, now rosed with light,
Of insectine dimensions they appeared;
Like emmet creeping, or the weevil-mite
That in a mouldering ship at sea is reared.

Sable in plumage, ruff, and naked head,
Superb in flight, and poised upon his shelf
Of viewless air, he tarried for the dead,
And watched, indifferent as Death himself.

Though the great globe around them grudged them tomb,
Feast they would be for both these ravening foes —
Horseman and Arab, who had dared to roam
Beneath these mountains' never-melting snows.

Halt, maimed and impotent, still travelling on,
O'er very Eye of Earth they made their way,
Till rimmed into the east the risen sun
Flooding its orbit with the joy of day —

That Eye of Heaven, mansion of secret light,
Whose beams of all that's lovely are the shrine,
Procreant, puissant, arbiter of Sight,
Emblem and symbol of the light divine —

So brilliant the least flaw beneath their feet
A tiny shadow cast where nought there was
Taller than locust in the rilling heat
To check the splendour of this sea of glass.

And if pure radiance could pure music be,
And quiet supreme its tabernacle were,
This orb, now blazing in its majesty,
With a sublime Hosanna rent the air.

Moved by an impulse beyond wit to scan,
His poor rags stirring in a fitful breeze,
This worn, outwearied, errant son of man
Paused, bowed his head, fell down upon his knees;

And, with a faint and lamentable cry,
Poured hoarsely forth a babble of praise and prayer,
Sun on his brows, above the boundless sky,
No living soul to hear or heed him there . . .

A self there is that listens in the heart
To what is past the range of human speech,
Which yet has urgent tidings to impart —
The all-but-uttered, and yet out of reach.

Beneath him an immeasurable well
Of lustrous crystal motionlessly black
Deeped on. And as he gazed — marvel past words to tell —
It seemed to him a presence there gazed back:

Rapt, immaterial, remote; ev'n less
In substance than is image of the mind;
And yet, in all-embracing consciousness
Of its own inmost being; elsewise blind:

Past human understanding to conceive;
Of virgin innocence, yet source of all
That matter had the power to achieve
Ere Man created was, ere Adam's fall:

And in its midst a mote scarce visible —
Himself: the momentary looking-glass
Of Nature, which a moment may annul,
And with earth's hosts may into nothing pass:

The flux of change. Ay, this poor Traveller too —
Soon to be dust, though once erect, elate,
From whose clear gaze a flame divine burned through;
A son of God — no sport of Time or Fate:

It seemed his heart was broken; his whole life long
Concentred in this moment of desire;
Its woe, its rapture, transient as the song
The Phoenix sings upon her funeral pyre.

'Alas', he gasped — his journey now at end;
Breathed softly out his last of many sighs;
Flung forth his hands, and motionless remained,
Drenched through with day; and darkness in his eyes . . .

Head drooped, knees sagging, his forsaken jade —
Her stark hide gilded by the eastern sun,
Her abject carcass in its glory arrayed —
As though in fear to break his prayers, drowsed on.

But, as an acid frets its way through steel,
Into her sentience at length there crept
A deeper hush no silence could conceal —
And Death for long has never secret kept,

Though shadow-close it mime its sister, Sleep.
The creature nearer drew — reluctant, slow,
As if, like motherless child, to sigh and weep,
Too young the import of its loss to know.

Ears pricked, reins dangling, thus a while she stayed —
Of that in watch above full well aware:
'See, now, dear master, here I wait!' She neighed,
And stooping, snuffed the rags, the matted hair;

Then, of a sudden, in panic dread, upreared,
Plunged, wheeled, drew back, her eyeballs gleaming white,
And urged to frenzy by the thing she feared
From all that love had left on earth took flight . . .

Sweet is that Earth, though sorrow and woe it have,
Though parched, at length, the milk within its breast;
And then the night-tide of the all-welcoming grave
For those who weary, and a respite crave:
Inn at the cross roads, and the traveller's rest . . .

Inward Companion:
Poems (1950)

HERE I SIT

Here I sit, and glad am I
So to sit contentedly,
While with never-hastening feet
Time pursues the Infinite;
And a silence centuries-deep
Swathes my mind as if in sleep.
Passive hand, and inward eyes
Press on their transient enterprise;
As, across my paper's white
Creeps the ink from left to right,
Wooing from a soundless brain
The formless into words again:
So I sit, and glad am I
So to sit contentedly.

UNWITTING

This evening to my manuscript
Flitted a tiny fly;
At the wet ink sedately sipped,
Then seemed to put the matter by,
Mindless of him who wrote it, and
His scrutinizing eye —
That any consciousness indeed
Its actions could descry! . . .

Silence; and wavering candlelight;
Night; and a starless sky.

FUCHSIAS

I envied the droning, idle bee,
  Sucking his nectar sweet —
In that palace of light suspended there
  By his hooked piratical feet.

No care, no trouble, no conscience his!
  And what of my lot, instead?
It seemed an absurd futility
  Till the notion entered my head: —

Poor wretch, my flowers are no flowers to him,
  Only his daily bread!

MARTINS

  'Chelidon urbica urbica!'
I cried on the little bird,
Meticulously enunciating each syllable of each word;
  'Chelidon urbica urbica!'
Listen to me, I plead!
There are swallows all snug in the hayloft,
I have all that your nestlings can need —
Shadow and sunshine and sweet shallow water —
Come, build in my eaves, and breed!

Fly high, my love! My love, fly low!
I watched the sweet pretty creatures go —
Floating, skimming, and wheeling so
Swiftly and softly — like flakes of snow,
'Gainst the dark of the cedar-boughs, to and fro: . . .
      But no!
      But no!
  'Chelidon urbica urbica!'
None paid me the faintest heed.

JACKDAWS

This dry old dotard lived but to amass
Old prints, books, pictures, porcelain, and glass —
As some hoard Wealth, Fame, Knowledge. Such he was.
There pottered in Another, and peered round:
But he his treasures buries underground.

[350]

IZAAK WALTON

That lucent, dewy, rain-sweet prose —
  Oh! what a heaven-sent dish
Whereon — a feast for eye, tongue, nose,
  Past greediest gourmet's wish —
To serve not tongues of nightingale,
Not manna soused in hydromel,
Not honey from Hymettus' cell,
Garnished with moly and asphodel —
  But Fish!

HENRY VAUGHAN

So true and sweet his music rings,
  So radiant is his mind with light
The very intent and meaning of what he sings
  May stay half-hidden from sight.

His flowers, waters, children, birds
Lovely as their own archetypes are shown;
Nothing is here uncommon, things or words,
  Yet every one's his own.

POETRY

In stagnant gloom I toil through day,
All that enchants me put away.
No bird decoyed to such a breast
Could warble a note, or be at rest;
From the old fountains of delight
Falls not one drop to salve my sight.

Yet — Thou who mad'st of dust my face,
And shut me in this bitter place,
Thou also, past the world to know,
Did'st hinges hang where heart may go
After day's travail — vain all words! —
Into this garden of the Lord's.

THE CHANGELING

Come in the dark did I —
The last stars in the sky,
Foretelling, 'Daybreak's nigh'.
Out of the brooding West,
Safe in my mother's breast
Love sheathed my wings in rest.

Twilight my home is, then,
In this strange world of men;
And I am happier when
The sun in flames and light
Sinks from my dazzled sight,
Leaving me sleep, and night.

So, now: only with thee
My homesick heart can be
Stilled in like mystery;
Long did life's day conceal
This tender dream and spell:
    Now all is well.

BELATED

Once gay, now sad; remote — and dear;
Why turn away in doubt and fear?
I search again your grieved self-pitying face;
Kindness sits clouded there. But, love? No, not a trace.

What wonder this? Mine not to scold.
You, in so much a child; and I, how old!
Who know how rare on earth your like must be:
There's nought commensurate, alas, in age or me.

Bare ruined choirs — though time may grace bestow
On such poor relics in eve's after-glow;
And even to age serenity may bring,
Where birds may haven find; and peace, though not to sing.

But ah, blest Light-of-Morning One,
Ev'n though my life were nearly done?
Ev'n though no mortal power could that delay?
Think of the lightless journey thither — you away!

UNMEANT

Oh, if I spoke unkindly, heed it not:
Had it a language, my wild heart you'd hear
Weeping the love a frantic tongue forgot:
Think not mere spindrift is the sea, my dear!

SHE SAID

She said, 'I will come back again
    As soon as breaks the morn.'
But the lark was wearying of the blue,
    The dew dry on the thorn;
    And all was still forlorn.

She said, 'I will come back again,
    At the first quick stroke of noon.'
But the birds were hid in the shade from the heat
    When the clock tolled, *No: but soon!*
    And then beat slowly on.

She said, 'Yes, I'll be back again
    Before the sun has set.'
But the sweetest promises often made
    Are the easiest to forget,
    No matter grief and fret. . . .

That moon, now silvering the east,
    One shadow casts — my own.
Thought I, My friend, how often we
Have shared this solitude. And see,
    Midnight will soon draw on,
When the last leaf of hope is fallen,
And silence haunts heart's vacancy,
    And even pining's done.

THE HOUSE

The rusty gate had been chained and padlocked
  Against the grass-grown path,
Leading no-whither as I knew well,
  In a twilight still as death.

Once, one came to an old stone house there,
  Wheels crunched in those scarce-seen ruts;
A porch with jasmine, a stone-fringed garden —
  Lad's-love, forget-me-nots.

A happy house in that long-gone sunshine;
  And a face in the glass-bright moon,
And a voice at which even memory falters,
  Now that the speaker's gone.

I watch that image as I look at the pathway —
  My once accustomed zest,
As the painted gate on its hinges opened,
  Now locked against the past!

A true face too, yet scant of the future —
  A book that I never read . . .
Nor shall now, since I soon must be going
  To another old house instead.

THE ROSE

He comes to where a seeding rose
Has scattered her last petals on
  The stones about her stem.
Beyond the louring hills a moon
Among the stars of heaven goes,
  Stealing their light from them.

His eyes shine darkly in his head —
A face that dream has scrawled upon.
  He trembles, listening there.
Once — before Winter had snowed up
His heart — one loved had hither sped,
  His solitude to share.

[354]

HERE

Forgave I everything —
The heart's foreboding unless she were near
Who all things lovely made even lovelier;
The baffled hopes, the care, dismay, desire,
The mocking images that feed love's fire;
The glut of leaden days, the futile dream,
Night's stagnant brooding by its sluggish stream:
Yes, every anguished sigh, and unshed tear,
Pang of foul jealousy, the woe, the sweat. . . .
    But how forgive, forget,
    In this bleak winter sere —
    That she is here?

NO

A drear, wind-weary afternoon,
Drenched with rain was the autumn air;
As weary, too, though not of the wind,
    I fell asleep in my chair.

Lost in that slumber I dreamed a dream,
And out of its strangeness in stealth awoke;
No longer alone. Though who was near
    I opened not eyes to look;

But stayed for a while in half-heavenly joy,
Half-earthly grief; nor moved:
More conscious, perhaps, than — had she been there —
    Of whom,— and how much,— I loved.

USURY

'Let be, unreasonable heart, let go;
Why struggle so
Vainly and foolishly? A day will come
When failing eyes, with infinite regret,
Their farewell, heartsick gaze will set
On this, your earthly home;
And what you now death-dark afflictions deem
Only the shadows of its joys may seem.

'What now you crave
Nought mortal ever gave;
Nor within earthly bounds lies where you'd range.
Give, and give yet again
The utmost love you have,
Ev'n though it be in vain,
It's usury to ask it in exchange.

'Did toil and seeking find
The sealed and secret fountains of your mind?
Can you, by dipping bucket in a well,
Dredge up the riches of the imaginable?
Like some small wild flower, open in the sun,
Did *you* your heart the nectar give
By which alone that very love can live?
Did you your eyes make see
The beauty and grace of wake and dream whereon
Your soul has feasted, and content should be,
Seeing that all things temporal stay
Only their transitory day?

'Never. From some unknown
Source inexhaustible the seeds were sown
Whence blooms the fleeting dayspring of delight;
And, were your being never dark with night,
Where then the cockcrow of another morn?
As well go seek a rose without a thorn
As, famished with desire,
To aught that's flawless on this earth aspire. . . .'

So argued on and on
My tedious censor — sermon never done;
While yet a haggard exile in my heart
Cared not a jot
For what he would impart;
But, pining still for what the while was gone,
Wept, like a thwarted changeling, for the Moon!

THE LAST GUEST

Now that thy friends are gone,
And the spent candles, one by one,
Thin out their smoke upon the darkening air;
Now that the feast's first flowers
Flagged have irrevocably in these latening hours,
With perfumes that but tell how sweet they were;
Turn now — the door ajar —
See, there, thy winter star,
Amid its wheeling consorts wildly bright,
Herald of inward rapture, never of rest!
Still must thy threshold wait a laggard guest
Who comes, alone, by night.

BEYOND

On such an evening — still; and crystalline
With light, to which the heavens their fairness owe,
What wakes some changeling in the heart to pine
For what is past the mortal to bestow?

Ev'n in the shallow, busy hours of day
Dreams their intangible enchantments weave;
And in the dead of dark the heart may crave
A sleep beyond sleep, and for its visions grieve.

For that strange absence nothing can atone;
And every hope is servant to desire;
The flower conceals a beauty not its own,
And echo sighs from even the silent wire.

OCCLUDED

Chilled is the air with fallen rain,
Flood-deep the river flows;
A sullen gloom daunts heart and brain,
And no light shows.

Yet, in a mind as dark, a hint may steal
Of what lies hidden from an earth-bound eye:
Beyond the clouds the stars in splendour wheel,
The virgin huntress horns the silent sky.

[357]

THE BURNING LETTER

The saffron flames, edged with that marvellous blue,
Creep through the paper, blackening as they move.
So senseless time robs heart and memory too
Of what was once their very life and love.

Oh, marvel, if in some unearthly May
The wintering bee its wings again should beat,
And, waking, rove the hive death hid away,
Its wax–celled honeycomb no whit less sweet!

THE PLASTER CAST

It called to mind one now long out of sight,
Whom love still treasures with its secret grace:
That cast — half-hidden there — sepulchral white,
A random moonbeam on its peaceful face.

FEBRUARY 29

Odd, waif-like Day, the changeling of
Man's 'time' unreckoned in his years;
The moon already shows above
        Thy fickle sleet — now tears!

As brief thy stay has been as though
Next Spring might seal our tryst again.
Alas, fall must four winters' snow
        Ere you come back. And then?

I love thy timid aconite,
Crocus, and scilla's deep-sea blue;
Hark, too, that rainbird, out of sight,
        Mocking the woodland through!

But see, it's evening in the west:
Tranquil, withdrawn, aloof, devout.
Soon will the darkness drape your breast,
        And midnight shut you out!

Sweet February Twenty Nine! —
This is our grace-year, as I live!
Quick, now! this foolish heart of mine:
        Seize thy prerogative!

[358]

DELIVERANCE

Starched-capped, implacable, through the slow dark
      night
She had toiled; and through a dawn she had not seen,
To bring into the world this shapeless mite.
Cheeks cold with sweat, strong hands, eyes kestrel-keen,
She had coaxed, and wheedled: 'Patience, now; push hard.
Strive on! I'm travailing too. Oh, have no fear!
See, I am come to comfort, help, keep guard.
Deliverance soon will come, swift, sure, my dear!'. . .
A last gasped wrenching groan; a gnatlike wail,
Shrill, angry, sweet, all human cries above:
'Thank God,' she sighed, 'Who did not let me fail!'
And sighed again — for pity, grief, and love.

A SNOWDROP

Thou break'st from earth. Thy beauty of dust is made.
Light called thee, trembling, from the sod's cold shade,
While yet bleak winter's blast its snow outspread.

Dark storm thy swaddling was, and freezing sky.
O dauntless loveliness, may Spring, on high,
Yet shed her balm, and sing thee lullaby!

THE SLEEPING CHILD

Like night-shut flower is this slumbering face,
      Lamplight, for moon, upon its darkness spying;
That wheat-stook hair, the gold-fringed lids, the grace
      Of body entranced, and without motion lying.

Passive as fruit the rounded cheek; bright lip;
      The zigzag turquoise of that artery straying;
Thridding the chartless labyrinths of sleep,
      River of life in fount perpetual playing.

[359]

Magical light! though we are leagues apart,
My stealthiest whisper would at once awake thee!
Not I, thou angel thing! At peace thou art.
And childhood's dreams, at least, need not forsake thee.

RARITIES

Beauty, and grace, and wit are rare;
    And even intelligence:
But lovelier than hawthorn seen in May,
Or mistletoe berries on Innocent's Day
The face that, open as heaven, doth wear —
With kindness for its sunshine there —
    Good nature and good sense.

TO CORINNA, FROWNING

Dark, historied eyes,
Head of Hypnotic grace,
Lips into silence sinking,
Brows deep as midnight skies,
Wisdom beyond surmise, —
Why shallow, sharpen, darken so lovely a face —
Well, with this 'thinking'?

DAYS AND MOMENTS

The drowsy earth, craving the quiet of night,
Turns her green shoulder from the sun's last ray;
Less than a moment in her solar flight
Now seems, alas! thou fleeting one, life's happiest day.

'LOVE'

Children — alone — are grave,
Even in play with some poor grown-up's toy;
Solemn at heart, and wise:
Whence else their secret joy?
And the deep sleep they crave?

So Love is pictured — with his bandaged eyes,
To veil the blinding beauty of his skies —
And laughs out, naked, like a little boy.

THE TWO LAMPS

Two lights well over this old oak table —
The lamp I have read by, the risen sun;
In a brimming flood through the windowed gable,
As I turn to the day's work, scarcely begun.

As if in ineffable peace together,
They mingle their beams in a mutual bliss;
And I marvel at both, who am little able
To measure their ultimate loveliness.

With the lamp's alone a miracle enters
The transient life which on earth I have spent —
Whose utmost fringes this frail mind centres —
Yet a life that resembles a banishment,

When challenged like this by such sudden splendour,
That Eastern glory of rose and gold;
And out of my darkness and dwindling winters
I weep at the sight, like a child grown old!

THE RISEN SUN

I lay a while, exulting in its light,
My Druid heart drenched through with awe and praise;
Then into darkness turned a dazzled sight,
    That dared not meet its gaze.

[361]

SECOND-HAND

Courage, poor fool! Ripe though thy tare-crop be,
Love, over its bonfire, still may smile on thee.
Yes; and, perhaps, when that rank seed was sown,
Some herb of grace was there, though not thine own.

THE LAST SWALLOW

The robin whistles again. Day's arches narrow.
Tender and quiet skies lighten the withering
    flowers.
The dark of winter must come. . . . But that tiny
    arrow,
Circuiting high in the blue — the year's last
    swallow,
Knows where the coast of far mysterious sun-wild
    Africa lours.

ANOTHER SPRING

What though the first pure snowdrop wilt and die?
What though the cuckoo, having come, is gone?
Clouds cold with gloom assail the sun-sweet sky,
And night's dark curtains tell that day is done? —
This is our earthly fate. Howe'er we range,
Life and its dust are in perpetual change.

What though, then, Sweet, as welling time wins on,
The early roses in thy cheeks shall ail?
When they have bloomed, it's not thyself shall wan,
Nor for lost music shall thy heart-strings fail.
That Self's thine own. And all that age can bring
Love will make lovely. Then another Spring!

THE SPOTTED FLYCATCHER

Gray on gray post, this silent little bird
Swoops on its prey — prey neither seen nor heard!
A click of bill; a flicker; and, back again!
Sighs Nature an *Alas*? Or merely, *Amen*?

[362]

THE IDOL OF THE WORLD

I saw the Idol of the World descend
To lave herself in the slow stream of *Time*.

Bespangled with bright stars in highest noon,
The soundless water flowed, and reflex gave
To the wild beauty of her sweet-tongued throng,
As one by one they stooped; and one by one,
Doffing their raiment even lovelier showed.

    The swans that float
On vaulted branchings through the wild ravines
Of that dark other river, *Sleep*, cast not
Such marvellous whiteness on the unrippling flood;
And these, past all pure white, incomparable,
Had tinged their beauty with the rose's dye;
And in the wind's breath as they stirred their heads
Shook out like banners, trembling, serpentine,
The incomputable riches of their hair:
Out on the wind, and out too over the water,
Flowing, in silence, these bright phantoms by.

But I, in vision, marvelled more to see —
While these, her nymphs, Wealth, Fame, Lust, Glory,
      Power,
Painted the wave with their bare loveliness,
And wakened Echo to take tongue and sing —
Her of the World, pranked in her pomp, step down,
Her face a spectral ort beneath its hood,
Her hands concealed and stiff beneath her gloves,
Her very shape and substance swathed and farced —
A monstrous formlessness on fire with gems —
And cast herself into their virgin arms.
Thus was she there disported, and made clean!

Wherefore I know not what her semblance is,
Know not the likeness of her form and face,
Nor what gross life stirred in those monstrous clouts,
Nor any charm in her, nor any lure,
Who seemed a rottenness scarce aught at all.

THE RUINOUS ABBEY

Stilled the meek glory of thy music;
   Now only the wild linnets wing
Along the confusion of thy ruins,
   And to cold Echo sing.

Quenched the wan purple of thy windows,
   The light-thinned saffron, and the red;
Now only on the sward of thy dominion
   Eve's glittering gold is shed.

Oh, all fair rites of thy religion! —
   Gone now the pomp, the ashen grief;
Lily of Easter, and wax of Christmas;
   Grey water, chrism, and sheaf!

Lift up thy relics to Orion;
   Display thy green attire to the sun;
Forgot thy tombs, forgot thy names and places;
   Thy peace for ever won!

THE BOMBED HOUSE

Daughters of Joy lived here —
   Glazed, watching, sleep-drugged eyes;
   reluctant feet.
Now, from these shattered, shuttered windows, dark
  and drear,
   They ghost the abandoned street.

PRIDE HATH ITS FRUITS ALSO

What shades are these that now oppress my eyes,
And hang a veil of night on burning day?
I see the Sun through shadows; and his clouds
Clothed in their mutable magnificence
Seem to some inward sorrow moving on.

What meaning has the beauty of the earth?
And this unageing sweetness of the Spring —
Her trees that once, as if from paradise,

Borrowed their shining simpleness; her flowers,
Blowing where nothing but the bleak snow was,
Like flames of crystal brightness in the fields?

Once I could gaze until these seemed to me
Only my mind's own splendours in disguise.
But now their inward beauty is lost and faded:
They are the haunts of alien voices now —
An alien wonderment of light beams forth —
No more the secret reflex of my soul.

'INCOMPREHENSIBLE'

Engrossed in the day's 'news', I read
Of all in man that's vile and base;
Horrors confounding heart and head —
Massacre, murder, filth, disgrace:
Then paused. And thought did inward tend —
On my own past, and self, to dwell.

Whereat some inmate muttered, 'Friend,
If you and I plain truth must tell,
Everything human we comprehend,
   Only too well, too well!'

'SEE, HERE'S THE WARRANT...'

The day has foundered, and dead midnight's here:
As dark this spirit now with doubt and fear.
Doused is the candle of celestial fire,
   Lighting my secretest desire.

Put up the board! This house of life's to let.
Cold-chimneyed, void, its mouldering parapet
Surveys lost forests and a tongueless sea;
Gone joy, light, love, fire, hospitality.

Moons may perpetually wax and wane,
And morning's sun shine out again;
But when the heart at core is cold and black,

No cock, all earth for ear, will ever crow
   Its witching wildfire back.

[365]

LOST WORLD

Why, inward companion, are you so dark with
        anguish?
A trickle of rancid water that oozes and veers,
Picking its sluggish course through slag and refuse,
Down at length to the all-oblivious ocean —
What else were apt comparison for your tears?

But no: not of me are you grieving, nor for me either;
Though I, it seems, am the dungeon in which you dwell,
Derelict, drear, with skeleton arms to heaven,
Wheels broken, abandoned, greenless, vacant, silent;
        Nought living that eye can tell.

Blame any man might the world wherein he harbours,
Washing his hands, like Pilate, of all its woes;
And yet in deadly revolt at its evil and horror,
That has brought pure life to this pass, smit through
        with sorrow,
Since he was its infamous wrecker full well he knows.

Not yours the blame. Why trouble me then with your
        presence?
Linger no instant, most Beautiful, in this hell.
No touch of time has marred your immutable visage;
Eros himself less radiant was in his dayspring! —
Or nearer draw to your heartsick infidel!

THE DUNCE

And 'Science' said,
'Attention, Child, to me!
Have I not taught you all
You touch; taste; hear; and see?

'Nought that's true knowledge now
In print is pent
Which my sole method
Did not circumvent.

'Think you, the amoeba
In its primal slime
Wasted on dreams
Its destiny sublime?

'Yet, when I bid
Your eyes survey the board
Whereon life's How, When, Where
I now record,

'I find them fixed
In daydream; and you sigh;
Or, like a silly sheep,
You bleat me, *Why*?

'"Why is the grass so cool, and fresh, and green?
The sky so deep, and blue?"
Get to your Chemistry,
You dullard, you!

'"Why must I sit at books, and learn, and learn,
Yet long to play?"
Where's your Psychology,
You popinjay?

'"Why stay I here,
Not where my heart would be?"
Wait, dunce, and ask that
Of Philosophy!

'Reason is yours
Wherewith to con your task;
Not that unanswerable
Questions you should ask.

'Stretch out your hands, then —
Grubby, shallow bowl —
And be refreshed, Child —
Mind, and, maybe, soul!

'Then — when you grow into
A man — like me;
You will as learnèd, wise,
And — happy be!'

ANOTHER WASHINGTON

'*Homo*? Construe!' the stern-faced usher said.
Groaned George, 'A man, sir.' 'Yes.
Now *sapiens*?' . . . George shook a stubborn head,
And sighed in deep distress.

HERE LIES A TAILOR

Here lies a Tailor, well-loved soul!
Whether but ninth, or one man whole.
Yet of our loss the world to tell
There tolled but one cracked funeral bell.

Cross-legged we'd see him, early and late.
Now he must in that garment wait
Wherein to ease their earthly rest
Slumbers unstirred Death's every guest.

His was by his own needle made —
And not a stitch but sang his trade.
Good woollen too. For well knew he
What scarecrows most men naked be.

THEOLOGIANS

They argued on till dead of night —
'"God"' *versus* '"God"'— till ceased to shine
The stars in cold Olympus: and
Daybreak their very faces proved divine!

FALSE GODS

From gods of other men, fastidious heart,
You thank your stars good sense has set you free.
Ay. But the dread slow piercing of death's dart?
Its, 'Why, *my* God, have I forsaken *thee*.'

PALE-FACE

Dark are those eyes, a solemn blue:
Yes, silent Pale-face, that is true;
But I — I watch the fires that sleep
In their unfathomable deep,
Seeming a smouldering night to make
Solely for their own shining's sake.

It's common talk you're beautiful:
But I — I sometimes wonder, will
Love ever leave my judgment free
To see you as the world doth see —
'All passion spent'. No more to know
The very self that made you so.

FRESCOES IN AN OLD CHURCH

Six centuries now have gone
Since, one by one,
These stones were laid,
And in air's vacancy
This beauty made.

They who thus reared them
Their long rest have won;
Ours now this heritage —
To guard, preserve, delight in, brood upon;
And in these transitory fragments scan
The immortal longings in the soul of Man.

BENIGHTED

'Frail crescent Moon, seven times I bow my head,
Since of the night you are the mystic queen:
May your sweet influence in her dews be shed!'

So ran by heart the rune in secret said:
Relic of heathen forbears centuries dead?
Or just a child's, in play with the Unseen?

[369]

BLONDIN

With clinging dainty catlike tread,
His pole in balance, hand to hand,
And, softly smiling, into space
He ventures on that threadlike strand.

Above him is the enormous sky,
Beneath, a frenzied torrent roars,
Surging where massed Niagara
Its snow-foamed arc of water pours:

But he, with eye serene as his
Who sits in daydream by the fire,
His every sinew, bone and nerve
Obedient to his least desire,

Treads softly on, with light-drawn breath,
Each inch-long toe, precisely pat,
In inward trust, past wit to probe —
This death-defying acrobat! . . .

Like some old Saint on his old rope-bridge,
Between another world and this,
Dead-calm 'mid inward vortices,
Where little else but danger is.

JONATHAN SWIFT

That sovereign mind;
Those bleak, undaunted eyes;
Never to life, or love, resigned —
How strange that he who abhorred cant, humbug, lies,
Should be aggrieved by such simplicities
As age, as ordure, and as size.

DOUBLE DUTCH

That crafty cat, a buff-black Siamese,
Sniffing through wild wood, sagely, silently goes,
Prick ears, lank legs, alertly twitching nose,
And on her secret errand reads with ease
A language no man knows.

THE FOREST

'Death-cold is this house. Beasts prowl at its threshold;
A forest of darkness besieges its gate,
Where lurks the lynx, Envy; the leopard named
    Malice;
And a gaunt, famished wolf, padding softly, called
    Hate.

'So when that fair She, there — slant eyes and slim
    shoulders,
Voice stealthy with venom — our solitude shares,
I sit with my sewing away from the window,
Since it's thence that the wild cat called Jealousy glares.

'But supposing ajar were that door — she alone here?
And my whisper the black stagnant forest lipped
    through? . . .
No, she sips of my wine; breaks bread; has no notion
It is I, the despised one, those bolts might undo.'

ALL HALLOWE'EN

It was not with delight
That I heard in the dark
And the silence of night
The little dog bark.

It was not for delight
That his master had come
That so shrill rang his bark;
And at dawn, cold with rain,
That he yelped yet again:

But for fear, fury, fright
At the softness, the swiftness, the waft of the sprite,
    Doomed to roam
    Through the gloom,
As the vague murk of night
Gave cold, grudging birth
To daybreak, on earth —
Wanning hillside and grove,
Once his lodgement and love:
    And now, poor soul,
    Hieing off home.

[371]

SLIM CUNNING HANDS

Slim cunning hands at rest, and cozening eyes —
Under this stone one loved too wildly lies;
How false she was, no granite could declare;
    Nor all earth's flowers, how fair.

'IT WAS THE LAST TIME HE WAS SEEN ALIVE'

'You saw him, then? . . . That very night?'
'A moment only. As I passed by.

'The lane goes down into shadow there,
And the sycamore boughs meet overhead;
Then bramble and bracken everywhere,
Moorland, whin, and the wild instead.
But the jasmined house is painted white
    And so reflects the sky.

'He was standing alone in the dwindling dusk,
Close to the window — that rapt, still face,
And hair a faded grey —
Apparently lost in thought; as when
The past seeps into one's mind again,
With its memoried hopes and joys, and pain,
And seduces one back . . .

               'He stirred, and then
Caught sight, it seemed, of the moon in the west —
Like a waif in the heavens astray —
Smiled, as if at her company;
Folded his old hands over his breast;
Bowed: and then went his way.'

THE VACANT FARMHOUSE

Three gables; clustered chimney-stacks; a wall
Snowed every Spring with cherry, gage, and pear,
Now suckered, rank, unpruned. Green-seeded, tall,
A drift of sullen nettles souring near —
Beside a staved-in stye and green-scummed pond,
Where once duck-dabbled sunshine rippled round.

Dark empty barns; a shed; abandoned byres;
A weedy stack-yard whence all life has fled;
A derelict wain, with loose and rusted tyres;
And an enormous elm-tree overhead . . .

That attic casement. . . . Was there flaw in the glass? . . .
I thought, as I glanced up, there had peered a face.
But no. Still: eyes are strange; for at my steady stare
Through the cool sunlit evening air,
Scared silent sparrows flew up out of the ivy there
Into an elder tree — for perching-place.

FLOOD WATER

What saw I — crouching by that pool of water
    Bright-blue in the flooded grass,
Of ash-white sea-birds the remote resort, and
    April's looking-glass? —
Was it mere image of a dream-dazed eye —
That startled Naiad — as the train swept by?

HAUNTED

'The roads are dangerous.'

    'What? What? . . . "The roads"!
I sit at *home*. And what my heart forebodes
Is not . . . mere death — to catch me unawares,
But Life, which ever in at window stares;
Life that still drives me on, and edges by
Perils perpetual, and not transitory.
Knife-edged the daily precipices I tread,
By trotting footfall of the unseen misled:
Abysses of time; vile scenes illusions breed;
Fear that like fungus sprouts from viewless seed.

'You say, *This is.* The soul cries, *Only seems.*
And who, when sleeping, finds unreal his dreams? . . .
That hill; those hollows; sloping into shade.
The spawning sun; the earth for night arrayed;
The listening dark; the Fiend with his goads. . . .
"The roads are dangerous"? . . .
    'Oh, yes: "the roads".'

THE OTHERS

'*Friendly?*'
       'Perhaps!'
              '*Say, neutral?*'
                          'How to tell?'
'*Not* hostile!'
                 'Well — who then would intercede?'
'*And do you rap? Or crystal-gaze? Or set*
Traps in the dark? Glass? Ouija? Or planchette?
A Madame Medium pay? Book — candle — bell?'
                   'Oh, no; I sit and read.'
'*Or merely sit?*'
               'Sometimes. Why not? The air,
Wild Ariel's air, must thrill with secrecies
Beyond the scope of sense. . . . Ev'n we two share
Our thoughts and feelings chiefly by surmise.
You speak: I watch and listen. But faith alone
Vows that the well-spring of your life's my own.
And when Goodbye is said, and comes the night,
What proof has each of either — out of sight?

'Yes, even now — to eyes of love how clear! —
It is the ghost in you I hold most dear.
When, then, you urge me — mockery or dismay —
For evidence, for proof, I can but say,
The deeper my small solitude may be
The surer I am of unseen company . . .
It haunts with loveliness this silent night.'

'*Evils?*'
       'They too may prowl. 'Gainst them we had best
Guard unrelentingly both mind and breast.
I cannot answer, No, then. Only pray
Fortress of life and love the soul shall stay.
And Good-Night come — well this must be confessed:
It grieves me to the heart when, blessing the blest,
I have to add, Alas! For, truth to say,
      They are the happier when I'm away.'

COMPANY

There must be ghosts, I think, in this old house.
    Often, when I am alone,
    The quiet intensifies;
The very air seems charged with mute surmise;
I pause to listen, with averted eyes;
As if in welcome. And a passionate rapture,
As if at some thing long since pondered on,
Wells suddenly up within me. . . . Then is gone.

ENIGMAS

I weep within; my thoughts are mute
With anguish for poor suffering dust;
Sweet wails the wild bird, groans the brute:
Yet softly to a honied lute
Crieth a voice that heed I must;
    Beckons the hand I trust.

O from nefarious enigmas freed
Shall all that dies not live at last,
Obedient as the seeding weed
Unto fruition come indeed,
    Its perilous blossoming past!

AN ANGEL

Oh, now, Alexander's Angel,
Whither are thy pinions winnowing,
On what swift and timeless errand
Through the wilds of starry splendour
That to mortal eyes are merely
Points of radiance pricked in space?
Earthly minds can see thee solely
In the semblance of their bodies,
Winged with light thy locks of glory,
Streaming from thy brows gigantic,
Brows unmoved, and feet of crystal,
Heaven reflected in thy face!

[375]

THE TOWER

There were no flowers among the stones of the
    wilderness.
I was standing alone by the green-glazed tower,
Where among the cypresses winds went wandering,
Tinged now with gold-dust in the evening hour.

What goddess lingered here no tablet recorded;
Birds wild with beauty sang from ilex and yew;
Afar rose the chasms and glaciers of mountains,
The snow of their summits wax-wan in the blue —

In the blue of the heights of the heavenly vacancy —
My companions the silence, the relics, the lost;
And that speechless, divine, invisible influence,
Remote as the stars in the vague of the Past.

GO FAR; COME NEAR

Go far; come near;
You still must be
The centre of your own small mystery.
Range body and soul —
Goal on to further goal,
Still shall you find
At end, nought else but *thee*.
Oh, in what straitened bounds
Of thought and aim —
And even sights and sounds —
Your earthly lot is doomed to stay!

And yet, your smallest whim
By secret grace
To look the simplest flower in the face
Gives an inevitable reflection back,
Not of your own self only,
But of one
Who, having achieved its miracle,
Rests there, and is not gone;
Who still o'er your own darker deeps holds sway
Into whatever shallows you may stray.

Whatever quicksands loom before you yet,—
Indifference, the endeavour to forget,
Whatever truce for which your soul may yearn,
Gives you but smaller room
In which to turn,
Until you reach the haven
Of the tomb.

'The haven'? Count the chances . . . Is that so?
You are your Universe. Could death's quick dart
Be aimed at aught less mortal than the heart?
Could body's end,
Whereto it soon shall go,
Be end of all you mean, and are, my friend?

Ah, when clocks stop, and no-more-time begins,
May he who gave the flower
Its matchless hour,
And you the power
To win the love that only loving wins,
Have mercy on your miseries and your sins.

A DAYDREAM

In a daydream, all alone,
Shone another sun on me,
Where, on cliffs of age-cold stone,
Harebell, thyme and euphrasy,
Seraphs came that to the air
Blew a music water-sweet;
And, as I watched, in reverie,
Danced with flowerlike soundless feet.

With what joy each instrument
Answered their sweet mouths. How burned
Their tranquil heads in ardour bent,
While, in peace unfaltering, turned —
Turned they their strange eyes on me,
Blue in silver of the morn.
But in leaden slavery
Lay my limbs, and I forlorn
Could but watch till faint and wan
Waned their beauty, and was gone.

[377]

O my heart, what eyes were these?
What viols theirs, that haunt me so? —
Those faint-sunned cliffs, those leaf-still trees,
Heavily hanging, shade o'er shade,
Where flowers of coral, amber, pearl,
In a burning stillness laid,
Coloured the clear air with light? —
O too happy dreams that furl
Their day-fearing petals white;
And vanish out of sight!

FRIENDS

When on my bed I lie,
To sleep and rest,
My two hands loosely folded on my breast,
As all men's are when they the long sleep share,
It seems they are closer friends than ever I guessed
They even in childhood were!

SOLITUDE

Space beyond space: stars needling into night:
Through rack, above, I gaze from Earth below —
Spinning in unintelligible quiet beneath
A moonlit drift of cloudlets, still as snow.

MIRACH, ANTARES . . .

Mirach, Antares, Vega, Caph, Alcor —
From inch-wide eyes I scan their aeon-old flames,
Enthralled: then wonder which enchants me more —
They, or the incantation of their names.

THE CELESTIAL LIBRARY

'The secrets of all hearts', I read. And sighed.
　　That vast cold gallery. Tomes in endless line.
'"All"!' mused the Stranger, standing at my side;
　　'These contain only thine.'

WINTER EVENING

Over the wintry fields the snow drifts; falling, falling;
　　Its frozen burden filling each hollow. And hark;
Out of the naked woods a wild bird calling,
　　On the starless verge of the dark!

BLOW, NORTHÈRN WIND

Blow, northern wind; fall snow;
And thou — my loved and dear,
See, in this waste of burthened cloud
　　How Spring is near!

See, in those labouring boughs,
Buds stir in their dark sleep;
How in the frost-becrumbling ruts
　　The green fires creep.

The dreamless earth has heard
Beneath snow's whispering flakes
A faint shrill childlike voice, a call —
　　Sighs, ere she wakes . . .

What Spring have we? Turn back! —
Though this be winter's end,
Still may far-memoried snowdrops bloom
　　For us, my friend.

THE KISS

In the long drouth of life,
Its transient wilderness,
The mindless euthanasia of a kiss

Reveals that in
An instant's beat
Two souls in flesh confined
May yet in an immortal freedom meet.

From those strange windows
Called the eyes, there looks
A heart athirst
For heaven's waterbrooks.

The hands tell secrets.
And a lifted brow
Asks, 'O lost stranger,
Art thou with me now?'

All stumbling words are dumb;
And life stands still;
Pauses a timeless moment; then resumes
The inevitable.

WORDS

Were words sole proof of happiness,
How poor and cold the little I have said!
And if of bitter grief, no less
    Am I discomfited.

The lowliest weed reflects day's noon of light,
Its inmost fragrance squanders on the air;
And a small hidden brook will all the night
Mourn, beyond speech to share.

INCOMPUTABLE

Think you the nimblest tongue has ever said
A morsel of what may ravish heart and head?
Think you the readiest pen that ever writ
Has more than hinted at what makes life sweet?

As well assume old Thames — eyot, meadow, copse —
Sums, as he disembogues, his waterdrops:
That beechen woods count up their countless leaves;
Furrows the birds once nurtured on their sheaves.

See, now, the stars that mist the Milky Way;
The hosting snowflakes of a winter's day;
Count them for tally of what life gives, thus shown,
Then reckon how many you have made your own!

DAY

Wherefore, then, up I went full soon
And gazed upon the stars and moon —
The soundless mansion of the night
Filled with a still and silent light:

And lo! night, stars and moon swept by,
And the great sun streamed up the sky,
Filling the air as with a sea
Of fiery-hued serenity.

Then turned I in, and cried, O soul,
Thank God thine eyes are clear and whole;
Thank God who hath with viewless heaven
Drenched this gross globe, the earth, and given,
In Time's small space, a heart that may
Hold in its span all night, all day!

Winged Chariot (1951)

. . . Why this absurd concern with clocks, my friend?
Watching Time waste will bring no more to spend,
Nor can retard the inevitable end.

Yet when, the old wide staircase climbed once more,
Your bag in hand, you attain its second floor,
Turn the Yale key in lock, sigh, open the door

And into these familiar rooms you slip —
Where even Silence pauses, finger on lip —
Three emulous metal tongues you wake from sleep.

Do they suffice you? No, you pause again.
And (as if mechanisms made by men
The Truth could tell) you search each face. And then,

Though every minute of your life's your own,
Though here you are 'master' and at ease, alone —
You ring up *TIM*; consult the telephone.

The *telephone*! . . . Then, these precautions past,
Time made in Greenwich safely yours at last,
You set all three some fifteen minutes fast.

Psychopathist might guess the reason why
You indulge your wits in this mendacity.
Think *you* Man's 'enemy' is thus put by?

Think you so fleet a thing — that madcap hare
You daily waken from its nightlong lair —
Time, would consent such stratagems to share?

Or is it that you reassurance seek,
Deeming the Future will appear less bleak
Now that your clocks will 'go' a whole long week?

[383]

'... "O, it came ore my eare, like the sweet sound
That breathes upon a banke of Violets;
Stealing, and giving odours ... " '

If Time's a stream — and we are told it's so,
Its peace were shattered if you check its flow;
What Naiad then ev'n fingertip would show? —
Her imaged other-world in ruins? ... No:

Should once there haunt your too-attentive ear
A peevish pendulum, no more you'll hear
The soundless thunder of the distant weir

Which is Eternity. . . . Blest reverie:
When, from the serfdom of this world set free,
The self a moment rapt in peace may be;

Not void; but poised, serene, 'twixt praise and prayer,
Such as the flower-clocked woods and meadows share,
Lulled and fed only by day's light and air.

How punctual they! But to no *tic-toc* rune.
Theirs is an older code than 'May' and 'June';
As testifies 'Jack-go-to-bed-at-noon';
Airiest of ghosts, he goes to bed at noon!

'... *Jocond day stands tiptoe on the mistie mountaine's top* ...'

Nimbused in his own song at dawn of day,
From earth's cold clods the skylark wings his way,
Into the sun-gilt crest of heaven to stray.

Housed in the dark of sleepy farms below,
At their own hour the cocks craned up to crow,
Their harems hearkening in obsequious row.

But wheel and barrel, ratchet, pawl, and spring?
Dear heart alive, how dull and dead a thing,
Compared with any creature on the wing,
Wherewith to measure even a glimpse of Spring.

Or, 'splitting seconds', to attempt to mete
The thrill with which a firefly's pinions beat.
Yes, or the languor, lingering and sweet,

When, lulled in the embraces of the sun,
The rose exults that her brief course is run
And heat-drowsed honey-bee has come; is gone.

Last night, at window idling, what saw I
Against the dusky summer greenery? —
Midges, a myriad, that up and down did fly,
Obedient to the breezes eddying by —
Sylphs scarcely of Time but of mere transiency:

An ovoid of intricate *winged* things, beautiful;
As on some sea-breeze morning, sunned and cool,
One may peer down upon a wavering shoal —
Like eddying weed in ebb-tide's lap and lull —
Of tiniest fish-fry in a rock-bound pool.

'... *Among which the elephant is the greatest and commeth nearest in wit and
capacitie to men* ...'

The sage, slow elephant, night-scampering mouse,
Snug-wintering tortoise in his horny house,
To cark of frost and snow oblivious —
Share they, think you, our sense of time with us?

And that old sly close-fisted cockatoo —
Whose private life's a furtive *entre nous*,
What temporal lens did *his* round eye peer through
Whilst five kings reigned, and died — ere he died too?

Or, destined denizen of perpetual night,
She, of the termites? Bloated, teeming, white,
Huge and scarce motionable: yet her hosts' delight?

A-drowse in the ocean in an Arctic gale —
What clock ticks Vespers to the suckling whale?
And bids Aurora her heavenly face unveil?

'... *Whannè thet Aprille with his shourès sote
The droghte of Marche hath percèd to the rote* ...'

What jewelled repeater edged the cuckoo's wing,
Lovesick from Africa, to flit in Spring?
Only one ding-dong name to say and sing —
And dower our pipits with a fosterling?

Oh, what a tocsin has she for a tongue;
How stealthy a craft to jilt her eggs and young,
And put them out to nurse their whole lives long! —

[385]

This heiress of the primeval. How learned she
Time, season, mileage and the momentary? —
Two idle summers and a sundering sea;
And all small honest birds for enemy.

If ev'n we share no thought with our own kind
But what with voice, face, words may be defined,
How shall these quicksands of Nature be divined?
How fathom the innate by means of mind?

Reason strives on to bridge the vague abyss
Sev'ring the human from the languageless,
Its countless kinds and spheres of consciousness.

Insight delights in heavenly mysteries
And loves the childish game of '*Well, now, guess!*'

'. . . *Love is from the eye: but . . . more by glances than by full gazings; and so
for envy and malice . . .*'

See, now, that dwindling meteor in space
Which with its ruin illumed the night's hushed face:
As well *time* headlong Lucifer's disgrace!

And, fleeter ev'n than flickering lightning's glow,
Transfiguring hidden landscapes hushed below,
Imaged ideas through consciousness may flow:
Fruit raised from seed before ev'n leaf could show!

And feeling races thought. *One* stricken glance
At some, till then, scarce dreamed-of countenance —
The very soul's at gaze, as if in trance:

Poised like a condor in the Andean night,
When scarp and snowdrift, height to pinnacled height,
Transmute with wonder the first morning light.

So, in its innocence, love breaks upon the sight.

Hatred, dread, horror, too. As books relate: —
Thyestes when his own son's flesh he ate;
First stare at his iron cage of Bajazet;
And Œdipus — when parricide's his fate.

[386]

'. . . *By which there sat an hory*
Old agèd Sire, with hower-glasse in hand,
Hight Time . . .'

Dogged morn till bed-time by its dull demands,
The veriest numskull *clock*-cluck understands,
Eked out by solemn gestures of its hands:

A subtler language stirs in whispering sands:

That double ovoid of translucent glass;
The tiny corridor through which they pass,
Shaping a crescent cone where nothing was,

Which mounts in exquisite quiet as the eye
Watches its myriad molecules slip by;
While, not an inch above, as stealthily,

Those rocks minute might fall of waters be
Pouring themselves as imperturbably
Into the crystal of their central sea.

A tiny shallowing on the surface seen
Sinks to a crater where a plane has been.
Could mutability be more serene?

Invert the fragile frame; and yet again
Daydream will rear a castle built in Spain.
'Time' measured thus is dewfall to the brain.

Water-clock, clepsydra, candle-flame and day-break.

So, out of morning mist earth's flowers arise,
Reflecting tintless daybreak in the skies;
And, soon, the whole calm orient with its dyes.

And even in bleak Winter one may go
Out of night's waking dreams and see the snow
In solemn glory on the fields below.

How happy he whose 'numbers' well as sweet,
Their rhythms in tacit concert with their feet,
And measure 'time', with no less hushed a beat. . . .

And clepsydra — the clock that Plato knew,
Tolling the varying hours each season through;
Oozing on, drop by drop, in liquid flow,
Its voice scarce audible, bell-like and low
As Juliet's communings with her Romeo.

[387]

More silent yet; pure solace to the sight —
The dwindling candle with her pensive light
Metes out the leaden watches of the night.
And, in that service, from herself takes flight.

'. . . The Sun's light when he unfolds it,
Depends on the Organ that beholds it . . .'

Ah, after vigil through the hours called small,
Earth's dumb nocturnal hush enshrouding all,
When dread insomnia has the soul in thrall,
To see that gentle flame greet sunrise on the wall!

Clocks fuss along, the lackeys of a spring;
Slaves of escapements; chime, but never sing:
Snow-soft as ghost-moth is *Time*'s winnowing wing;
Though even to granite it some change must bring;

And to all else that's temporal. Which is yet
Nothing corrupt, but merely change. And that
On goal supreme — through change — its course may set.

And ev'n if ruin Nature's face betray,
Time was not cause thereof, but mere decay,
Slow as renewal, wending its wonted way.

'. . . One thinks the soul is air; another fire;
Another, blood diffused about the heart,
Another saith, the elements conspire.
And to her essence each doth give a part . . .'

When restless thought lulls low, as winds may cease
On dune and marram-grass, and there is peace,
The self becalmed may be by a loneliness

That pays no heed to time; and may attain
What Reason mocks at as the 'intense inane';
Though little one covet to come back again.

Sea-gulls home this way in the setting sun,
When — lowered lamp — his winter is begun.
He dyes their plumes with his vermilion,
As, in their idling squadrons, they wing on.

Under this roof, when, motionless and dense,
Silence beleaguers every nerve and sense,
Self-solitude is made the more intense.

Head turned on shoulder then, the straining ear
Dreads and yet conjures up the voice of Fear.
An inward sentry cries, 'Who's listening here?' . . .

Could fancy alone in this old thick-walled house,
When nothing stirs, not even a wainscot mouse,
Thus haunt mere matter with the ominous?
    And these misgivings rouse?

Midnight beyond that shutter broods. The rain
Its lully whispers in the towering Plane
Whose presence canopies my complete domain —

Whose every twig breathes freshness in the air,
And mottled boughs five-fathom tresses wear,
In May-time dangling like a Siren's hair.

'. . . *In the Desarts of Africa, you shall meet oftentimes with fairies appearing
in the shape of men and women, but they vanish quite away like phantastical
delusions . . .*'

Phantoms draw nearer then of the unseen.
They pause in silence at the entering-in;
Eyes, raiment, wraithlike faces, vapour-thin —

Heeded perceptions of a secret mind
Less closely to the physical confined:
Like flowers in their beauty to the blind.

And every soul draws ever toward its own
Viewless associates as it journeys on;
Is never less alone than when alone.

When, then, I leave this haunt, as soon I may,
Will not some homesick relic of me stay —
Unseen, unheard? And while — what? . . . *Time,* away!?

'*Are they shadows that we see?* . . .'

Hearken the heart must if it seem to share
A rarer presence yet than light or air;
Visage serene, calm brows, and braided hair —

More real even than what imagining
Into the confines of the eye may bring;
Tranquil as seraph, with half-folded wing.

[389]

Would I her scholar were in poetry!
No toil in vain then. Nothing to weary me.
Alas, these halting rhymes — that cannot be.

Yet, when, a child, I was content to rove
The shingled beach that I was Crusoe of,
All that I learned there was akin to love.

The glass-clear billow toppling on the sand,
Sweet salt-tanged air, birds, rock-drift — eye, ear, hand;
All was a language love could understand.

'. . . *Those steps of stone* . . .'

Yet there was mystery too: those steps of stone —
In the green paddock where I played alone —
    Cracked, weed-grown,
Which often allured my hesitant footsteps down

To an old sun-stained key-holed door that stood,
The guardian of an inner solitude,
Whereon I longed but dreaded to intrude;
Peering and listening as quietly as I could.

There, as I knew, in brooding darkness lay
The waters of a reservoir. But why —
In deadly earnest, though I feigned, in play —
Used I to stone those doors; then run away,
Listening enthralled in the hot sunny day

To echo and rumour; and that distant sigh,
As if some friend profaned had made reply, —
    When merely a child was I?

'. . . *Love is a malady apart, the sign*
And astrolabe of mysteries Divine . . .'

Nor is this *love* a jewel in one plane.
It many facets has: mind, soul; joy, pain:
And even a child may to this truth attain.

Secret and marvel too the body is,
And exquisite means of earth's infrequent bliss;
But love foresees Love's everlastingness.

Had passion voice, why then the strange delight
Ev'n an hour may bring would pæans indite;
And, seeing no words these mercies could requite,
Age pines, in talk, to skirt the infinite;
As birds sing wildlier when it draws towards night.

'Whoe'er she be . . .'

She whom I vision many masks has worn,
Since, in this world, half-alien, I was born;
And every one has left me less forlorn.

And though pure solitude may be utmost grace,
And leagues from loneliness, a loved-one's face
Quadruples happiness in any place.

Time shared then's not time halved. Yet if it be
Spent in that loved one's fleeting company,
It flies even swiftlier than the caught set free.

Leaving an empty cage? . . . May heaven forbear!
Blank absence then would greet us everywhere —
A *wilderness*, called Time, bereft and bare
Be the slow tedium left however fair.

'. . . There mournful cypress grew in greatest store,
And trees of bitter gall, and Heben sad,
Dead-sleeping Poppy, and black Hellebore,
Cold coloquintida . . .'

However fair. . . . But cracked may be love's bells;
Mirage its lode-star, and disaster else;
As (countless cantos) this old fable tells: —

THE PALACE OF TIME

'A self-sick wanderer, in the leprous light
Of death-drear forest at the fall of night
Came out on no less derelict a sight: —

'Its walls slant-shadowed by the dwindling shine
Of day, a mansion — bleached, gaunt, saturnine,
With windows gaping 'gainst the evening green
As though by fire-flames charred their mullions had been.

'It called to mind a dream he once was in. . . .

[39¹]

'That broken turret; fallen roof — were these
The prey of *age*? Weather's slow ravages?
Or sudden blasting stroke of destiny's?

'When what is beautiful is that no more,
Except as memory may its grace restore,
One's very heart stands listening at the door;

'And self-arraigned, the fatal charge must meet:
"Wilful neglect; betrayal; self-deceit."
And no defender left to answer it.

'. . . And we watered our horses at the pool of Siloam . . .'

'What though once-Eden now is sour morass,
The abode of croaking frogs and venomous flies,
     Yet, which of us, alas,
Can not in his own visage darkly trace
     That blighted Seraph's face?

'And when, companionless, at night we fare,
Ascending our own private corkscrew stair,
Is't never Darkness that awaits us there? . . .

'Down the chill chace he paced . . . Where once the deer
Browsed in the dappling sun devoid of fear,
And supped the conduit's waters rippling clear;

'Where wooed the turtle-dove; and all dark long
Creatures nocturnal in its woods would throng,
And nightingales mock passion with their song;

'Now effigies, in guise of life, of stone —
Grief, woe, despair their broken faces on,
Some as though smiling — in the dusk-line shone.
All else seemed foundered in oblivion.

'And *Silence* mouldered there; aloof, alone.
Ev'n should the sun now shine and gild the tips
Of motionless cypresses in this wide ellipse,
His beams were shorn of power, as in eclipse.

'And formless shapes of rock that seemed to brood
On lost primordial secrets, crouched or stood,
Lifeless, yet menacing, margining the wood.

[392]

'. . . The lady rade, True Thomas ran,
Until they cam to a water wan;
O it was night and nae delight,
And Thomas wade aboon the knee.'

    'Yet no thing living showed, save where it seemed
    The stone-work of a dial vaguely gleamed;
    And there, though not asleep, one lay and dreamed.

'It was dark night, and nae starlight,
And on they waded lang days three,
And they heard the roaring o a flood,
And Thomas a waefou man was he . . .'

    'Sickened with expectation, close he drew,
    The sun-warmed turf beneath his feet; and knew
    Eyes glassy-cold as serpent's watched their thin lids through —
        Lids fringed with gilt, and eyes of sleep-glazed blue.

    '*Palace of Time*, he had heard these ruins named;
    Once seat of Pride and Pomp, but long ill-famed,
    Since Pride had fallen, and venging fire had flamed.

'. . . Side by side, jarring no more,
Day and night side by side,
Each by a doorless door,
Motionless sit the bridegroom and bride
On the Dead-Sea-shore. . . .'

    'She, then, was Witchcraft, and on evil bent,
    Foe of the abandoned, lost, and malcontent,
    And doomed to ruin whithersoever they went?

    'The tarnished dial, its gnomon shorn away,
    Worn steps, now shattered, with cankering lichen grey,
    Told of phantasmal night, past hope of day.

    'A lunar dial? Astarte's wizardry?
    Secret, adored, cold, wanton in perfidy;
    The bygone haunt of ancient revelry?

    'And he, this wanderer? What fate was his?'. . .
    So runs this ancient legend of dole and Dis;
    Whereof no end's recorded beyond this.

    'Like one who, victim of a malady,
    Having its name, yet knows not what it be,
    Seeking for light in some old dictionary,
    Meets *caput mortuum's* cold scrutiny . . .'

            ★   ★

'. . . Feed apace then, greedy eyes, On the wonder you behold! . . .'

Love is life's liberty. 'Time' will snare remain
Until to peace of mind and heart we attain,
And paradise, whose source it was, come back again.

Inscrutable Nature in her own slow way
Seems even in labour to be half in play;
With hyssop in wall will dally a whole long summer's day.

She takes her time: and, the rich summer gone,
Through autumn mists and winter cold dreams on
Till, Phoenix-like, her beauty is re-won.

. . . How often comes to memory—silly sooth!—
That tiny bird I took to be a moth . . .

Yes, and with what élan her creatures live,
How in their kinds, crafts, busyness they thrive!
The tribute lovely, wanton, odd they give

To all that nurtures them — the viewless air,
The Sun in dazzling bounty circling there,
Rivulet, bosoming hill and woodland fair.
Her faintest change each in its kind must share;

Unique, exultant beings of infinite zest,
Preying or preyed on, and supremely blest
In that by human cares they are unoppressed.

'. . . If things of Sight such heavens be,
What heavens are those we cannot see? . . .'

How ponder quickly enough on what one sees
To realise this beauty's mutableness? —
Its range is one of infinite degrees.

Stir not your gaze, but let it so remain,
In all its quietude, in eye and brain;
Of its own nature it will soothe, and sain.

A plain wood panel will the whole long day
In light and shadow change with every ray.
No eye will *watch* that loveliness away.
Alas, that nothing can less briefly stay!

The moment is annulled — however dear —
Sooner than raptured tongue can utter, '*See, it's here!*'
Shrill from his midden-top whoops Chanticleer,
Scratches — and priceless gewgaws disappear.

Nor is some strangeness absent from the seen,
However usual, if there intervene
The unageing mind. Its hidden life has been
This edge of contrast to the day's routine.

Jasmine, and hyacinth, the briar rose
Steep with their presence a whole night; nor close:
Time with an infinite gentleness through them flows.

Fantastic growths there are too — flower and scent —
In earth's occult alembic strangely blent,
To some obscure decree obedient,
And as of sorcerous or divine descent.

Mist, dew and rainfall keep these trystings sweet,
And light, with ghosting shadow, dogs our feet;
Day in, day out, thrums on heart's secret beat,
Calmly refusing to conform with it.

While none of these then can 'pure time' bespeak,
Which every eager intellect should seek,
Each mind its time-piece has. And that's unique.

'*... Time was: Time is: Time is not ...*'

Time was: Time is: Time is not, runs the rune.
Hasten then. Seize that *is*, so soon begone.
As well subtract the music, keep the tune!

For no 'time' ever yet in storage lay,
Sun-ambered, weathered, sweet as new-mown hay,
Waiting mind's weaving — Rumpelstiltskin's way: —

Time 'real'; time rare; time wildfire-fleet; time tame;
Time telepathic, out of space, and aim;
Time starry; lunatic; ice-bleached; of flame;
Dew-transient, yet immutably the same;
Meek-mild as chickweed in a window-frame;

Tardy as gathering dust in rock-hewn vault;
Fickle as moon-flake in a mirror caught
At pause on some clear gem's scarce-visible fault ...

[395]

And how moves Time in triple darkness hid,
Where — mummied 'neath his coffered coverlid —
Sleeps on the Pharaoh in his pyramid:
Time disincarnate — and that sharp-nosed head?

Even though suave it seem as narded oil,
Fatal to beauty it is, and yet its foil.
It is of all things mortal the indifferent soil.

Eye scarce can tell where, the whole spectrum through,
Orange with yellow fuses, green with blue;
So Time's degrees may no less diverse show,
Yet every variant be its fraction true.

'. . . *And over them Arachne high did lift*
Her cunning web, and spred her subtile net. . . .'

Grey with their dust, cribbed in with facts and dates,
On foundered centuries the historian waits.
Ashes in balance, he sifts, weighs, meditates.

Unlike the astronomer in the heavens at play,
Through Time defunct, not Space, he elects to stray.
Stars of a magnitude his chosen prey,
He spends less leisure on its Milky Way,
Man's millions in its *Coalsack* stowed away

Much he may look for which he is like to find;
And to its worst may be at length resigned:
'The follies, crimes, misfortunes of mankind.'

Transmuting facts into his truth, rejecting none,
Rapt in seclusion, he toils gravely on;
Crypt, arch, pier, buttress, roof; and fickle moon —
A noble structure when the building's done:
But of wild coarse sweet positive *life*, no breath — not one.

Yet, let disciple read him with delight —
In Time interred, a fellow-anchorite —
It is as though into the gloom of night
Scapegrace Aladdin chanced to come in sight,
And rubbed his lamp. . . . The change is infinite.
Shadows take bodies; blood begins to beat;

And through this inky ichor softly rills
The Jinnee's magic, and each cranny fills
With scene, thought, action, as the context wills;
And very life itself his record thrills.

[396]

So too in fane of Time's memorial stones —
In crisscross framework of poor human bones,
Isis, Baal, Ormuzd on their scaling thrones —
The scutcheons glimmer of the great Unknowns . . .
    And now — their withered *Once!*

. . . Sup humbly. All things compassed, near or far,
Are — for ourselves — but what we think they are:
The Web of Seeming holds us prisoner . . .

They touch us to the quick, these far events,
Looming beyond mere mortal instruments;
Omens of destiny, of Providence:
Their dust long fall'n, but not their influence.

But no rune's yet recalled Time's lost and gone —
Only its ghosts. And theirs is *dies non.*
All is in flux; nor stays, but changes on.
No sunrise hymns the self-same orison.

The unique's unique — assort it as we please;
Every oak's acorns will sprout differing trees.
So many lives, as many mysteries.

Nor do the morning stars together sing
One only *Laus* to *Alleluias'* ring,
When shout the sons of God before their King.

'. . . *O tell me mair, young man, she said,*
This does surprise me now;
What country hae ye come frae?
What pedigree are you? . . .'

Were moments seeds, we then therein might say
What hidden kind, hue, value, beauty lay,
Virtue and quality. But, these away,

Theirs only quantity, mere measurement,
Sans substance, pattern, form, shape, taste and scent —
Flimsier than bubble, and more transient.

Should, then a Stranger from another Sphere
Enquire, '*This Time, of which so much I hear?*
Light — dark; heat — cold; void — solid: these are clear;
But TIME? What is it? Show me some, Monsieur!'

What should we choose for semblance? A flake of snow?
A beach-brine bubble? A tiny shell or two?

Poised in the sun, pure diamond of dew?
Or whisper, '*Look! a* clock! *Now watch Time flow;*
It's a Machine, *you see. It makes it go.*'

Bland face; sly jerking hands: staring he'd stay,
Dumbly astonished. And then turn, and say,
Closer to Nothingness could nothing stray!
And now, pray, make Time flow the other way!'

'*. . . O fairest flower, no sooner blown than blasted,*
Soft silken primerose, fading timelesslie . . .'

'Moments', like sun-discs on a rippled sea,
No heed paid to them merely cease to be,
Leaving no trace of their identity:

Mere litter stowed in Time's packed Lumber-Room —
Moth, spider, mildew, rust, star-raftered gloom;
Vast as moon-crater, silent as the tomb,
Not even a death-watch for a pendulum.

But mark Self summing up what's really his —
Glimpses of childhood, friendship, bygone bliss —
Those fumbling fingers, that impassioned kiss!
Dear beyond words are relics such as these.

And who, in his dark hours, dulled, overcast —
At envy, hatred, malice, cant aghast —
Would not abscond a while from this worn temporal waste;
Into another world of being haste,
And, maybe, meet the idolised at last?
Chaucer? Keats? Marvell? Wyatt? Drayton? — Oh
Any long-lov'd and true enthusiast!

'*. . . Some nameless stuff . . .*'

Lost in that company the spirit may range
A rarer, deeper, closer interchange
In the imagination, rich and strange —
A Mariana in a moated grange.

At shut of dusk, 'neath timbered roof, worn stone,
Dark at the window-glass, and all life gone,
In hush of falling dust and mouldering bone,

Inward, still inward let the round ear lean! . . .
Time's not of moments made. It's hidden in
Some nameless stuff that oozes in between. . . .

'. . ."*I stand like one*
That long hath ta'en a sweet and golden dream,
I am angry with myself now that I wake". . .'

Yet, friend, (once more), when you are here again,
Do you *possess* this quiet? The Silence drain?
Give thanks for boons withheld from other men?
A Paternoster breathe — and then count ten?

No, like some light-o'-love, away you chase
Straight to that *chit-chat* in the china case
You bought in Woodbridge — 'Fitz's' native place.
Then comes 'Susanna', with her prim round face;

Next your much-prized old dial, inlaid with brass,
Sun-pendulum'd in gilt. And next . . . .
                                    Alas,
Still will the hours for you melt much too fast!

Not for the world that I would mock at what
Have 'timed' the countless godsends of my lot;
And still might miss, most earthly things forgot.

'. . . *Keeping time, time, time*
To a sort of runic rhyme . . .!'

Even as 'child of Paules', when brood I would
At thunder of its bell — Night: Solitude —
(And slow-coach was I always, doomed to plod),
I must have fallen in love with clocks for good.

Tompion, Bréguet, Knibb, Ellicot, Cole, Quare,
How featly chime the names of those who were
Masters in this sweet art; famed everywhere:
Timepiece-artificers beyond compare.
And each of sovereign Harrison the heir,
        With his supreme chronometer.

Bell-tinkling *watch*-craft too, tiny as bees,
Set bezel-wise, may match great clocks with ease —
And, no less punctually, the Pleiades.

And should you wish to meditate; then, where
A grandpaternal timepiece crowns the stair,
Pause as you go to bed; to listen; and share
The unhastening monologue it ponders there.

'. . . But at my back I alwaies hear
Times winged Charriot drawing near . . .'

To Julius and Gregory be praise,
Who bade the Calendar amend its ways.
But when from such dull durance fancy strays —
How beautiful is the procession of the days.

With each cold clear pure dawning to perceive
The Sun's edge earlier; and, at fall of eve,
When the last thrush his song is loth to leave,
To mark its latening, however brief!

Nor is the marvel of his burning rose,
Bronze, saffron, azure, discontinuous;
He takes his splendour with him as he goes.

So thought the poet, Fabre d'Églantine,
(When his sweet France had licked the platter clean).
Brumaire . . . . Nivôse . . . . Vendémiaire — things *seen*
In Terra's tilt, from virgin white to green:

Snow . . . . Rain . . . . Wind . . . . Bud . . . . Flower . . . . Grape
    make richer sense
Than our pastiche of dead-alive events —
Janus to Juno, and December thence.

Sick unto death must Woden be of Thor;
Deaf Saturn yells at Frig, *'We have met before! . . .'*
Sun unto Moon, *'Would God* weeks *were no more;*
Or that to Man He would his wits restore!' . . .

'. . . And yonder al before us lye
Desarts of vast Eternity . . .'

Still: dangling keys 'twixt clumsy finger and thumb,
You bustle your punctual way from room to room,
And into senseless tongues transform the dumb.

[400]

You wind the docile things — run-down or not;
You set them fast, as cautious mortals ought;
And are at once in TIM's sly coggery caught.

Yet hopes, joys, prayers will tell much more that is
In this strange world of ours of bale and bliss.
Ev'n specks of sand secrete eternities:
Sit down then; listen to their confidences.

Think you, indeed, benumbed by grief or pain,
Or lost in some dread labyrinth of the brain,
An earth-bound clock will set you free again?

Why pause not *now*? To ponder, unoppressed?
The halcyon come again. And in your breast
The brief Elysium of a soul at rest?

'. . . *As that fair flower Adonis, which we call an anemone flourisheth but one month. . . .*'

An opening flower, night's furthest nebulae
In mind supreme must be contemporary.
In one same moment they might cease to be.

And that faint eastern star —'light-years' gone by
Its beams have ranged which pierce the evening sky,
To find their haven in a human eye;
On human heart to shed tranquillity.

And though with his ingenious Optick Glass
The mind of man may map the wastes of Space,
Thence he may yet return in joy to trace
The light of welcome in a human face.

Merely material things hark back again
To their unknown, unknowable origin;
As, to death-darkening gaze, the world of men.

Those rocks green-capped, round which the sea-mews whine,
Reared up aloft, wide-gullied from the land,
Are no more stable in the wash of Time
Than lost enchanted palace in the sand.

Sun-bleached, slim, delicate bones of wings at rest,
And whispering thrift that trembles in the blast
Tell of the transiency of earthly dust
To which even adamant must return at last.

[401]

There falls a night, of myriads gone by;
A starless tempest raves; the wildering sea
Storms in. And daybreak lifts a heavy eye
For what has gane its gaite, and ceased to be.

So, to day's eye, destruction shows — void space
Where towered massive majesty and grace,
Coped by the foam-flowers of sea-wilderness.

'. . . So did this noble Empire waste,
Sunk by degrees from glories past. . . .'

Engirdling the great World these waters flow,
To charred wan moon obeisant, to and fro.
But swang she nearer? . . . Chaos and overthrow:
Which of our marvels then were left for show

Of all Man's pomp and power? Of aught achieved
Whereby his reign on earth might be believed;
Or his superb effrontery be conceived?

That he — of all God's creatures niggling-nice,
Yet seamed with pride, conceit, and racked with vice;
Dove-gentle; saintlike; evil as cockatrice —

Should thus have edged his way from clime to clime
In a mere millionth of terrestrial 'time',
And talked of Truth, of Wisdom, the Sublime!

Once, a bold venturer, perched on his '*Machine*',
Broke out (Man's history over) on a scene
Of Sun stark still, and leprous sea brine-green.
And, for sole witness of life's Might-have-been,
A tentacled crustacean, vast, obscene!

'. . . But things to come exceed our human reach . . .'

Now — in a patch of sea-turf may arise
Low mounds secreting the packed enterprise
Of empires past all sapience to assize —
The latest of a myriad dynasties.

And when the heat of summer wells into
Their chambered queens, then their dark galleries through
Swarm they with their sheened courtiers up into the blue —

To glut the sea-gulls, or creep back to shed
Their cheating gnawed-off pinions; or, instead,
To blacken for miles the sea-sands with their dead . . .

Time? May God help us! Better a few years
Of casual change than slavery such as theirs:
Where all are pitiless, and none shed tears.

Once was a hidden country, travellers say,
(Due East-by-West of North-by-South it lay),
Designed to serve as a Utopia;
Where all things living lived the selfsame way.

Its flowers were scant and scentless (like our musk);
One weight of ivory was each tooth and tusk;
On every nut there swelled the same-sized husk;
Noonday to night there loomed perpetual dusk.

Fate was appalled. Her See-Saw would not stir.
Man sat dead-centre and grimaced at her.
Her prizes? None could shine where none could err;
So every artless dunce was a philosopher . . .

'. . . *This infant world has taken long to make,*
Nor hast Thou done with it, but mak'st it yet,
And wilt be working on when death has set
A new mound in some churchyard for my sake . . .'

Still in long clothes was I when learnèd men
Tracked down the 'atom'. They as busy had been
On evidences of a distant When
That mite had ape for kith and kin. Amen.

Once did the tiny shrews lemurs beget;
And they the tarsier, starred with eyes of jet;
And that the wistful little marmoset:
At length came Man; with Fate for martinet.
And *Time*? How could it else but aid, abet?

Still, there was other route. One no less free:
A virgin, visionary Earth to see,
Seed of supreme potentiality
Of man with God and love at peace to be.

Were life a poem we have to improvise
(Facing the stubbornest of all prosodies)

[403]

An Epilogue might close the enterprise;
And all else seem a mere parenthesis.
Which — when Earth's 'actual' thins — we know it is.

As when in pangs of death a hermit lay —
Cave, rill, rock, leaf-shagged tree — and from the sky,
Blue above sand, a seraph hovered nigh,

And set his foot there. Like a god's, his face
Shone in the shadow, smiling in its grace,
And shed infinity in that narrow space.

*'The riddle nature could not prove
Was nothing else but secret love. . . .'*

Cry on the dead: — *'Beseech thee! wake! Arise!'. . .*
Impassive waxen visage, fast-sealed eyes
Sunken past speculation or surmise:
And, for response, not even the least of sighs.

How, then, can he we knew and loved be *there*?
Whose every thought was courtesy; whose one care
To show his friendship, and to speak us fair:

Gentle and steadfast. Why, but three days since
We talked of life; its whither and its whence;
His face alert with age's innocence.
He smiled an *au revoir* when he went hence . . . .

Oh, ev'n should folly bring Man's world to woe,
Out of its ashes might a sweeter show.
And what of the life beyond, whereto we go?

Even were that of this a further lease
It yet might win to a blest state that is
Past thought — transcending scope of clock-time's bliss.
More simple, passionate, and profound than this.

*'. . ."O Lord! methought what pain it was to drown!
What dreadful noise of water in mine ears!". . .'*

Dazed by mere 'Space' void-universes-wide,
Where All-that-is has Nought-that-thinks for bride,
The mind rebels. It's Reason's suicide . . . .

[404]

That dream I had of old — when, gazing sheer
Down verge of an abysm of stagnant air,
Senses as sharp as insect's, I could hear
Time's Ocean, sighing on the shingle there:

A whispering menace that chilled brain and blood;
Enormous, formless. Agonised I stood,
Tongueless with horror of what this forbode;

Yet lured on ever closer to its brim;
The night-long plunge; the gulf, vast, vaporous, dim;
That vault of Nothingness, the Nought of dream.

Ah, well I knew the doom in wait for me —
Lost in that quagmire of Sleep's treachery —
Drowning, to thirst for death; but never die. . . .

'. . . Be able to be alone . . . Delight to be alone and single with Omnipresency.
He who is thus prepared, the Day is not uneasy nor the Night black unto him . . .

Yet never fiend that trod Earth's crust could break
Man's steadfast soul while he was ware and wake,
Though God Himself should seem him to forsake —
Unless, 'twould seem, such fiend took human shape.

And never in Matter, surely, shall we find
Aught that is wholly inconsonant with a Mind
That thus conceived, evoked, informed its kind?
Else to forlorn Unreason we are confined.

Why, then, so closely pry? Consider, too —
Despite the earth-bound lenses we look through —
At exquisite equipoise rests what is true;
'All knowledge is remembrance' . . . 'Nothing's new.'

Oh, with what joy an ignorant heart may steal
From dry-as-dust abstractions to a 'real',
Where what we think is blent with what we feel.

That star, which through the window spills its ray
On sheet and pillow when in dream we stray —
That's not a myriad light-years far away!

No further (if mere distance be at all),
Than is the ultramicroscopical —
The goddess who electrons has in thrall.

[405]

. . . What! 'island universes'! — thick as dew?
When even of huge Betelgeuse it's true
That distance lends enchantment to the view! . . .

Will ever indeed have tongue the power to tell
All ev'n a taper discloses in a well?
If Truth's it be, it's clean impossible.

Thick too as motes that in a sunbeam drift
Day's dreamlike images may swirl and shift
Too instantaneous for clock to sift.

Strive then to give them words. The wits fall numb;
Into a *cul-de-sac* thought seems to come;
A timeless semi-conscious vacuum.
And how long wait will they a lip that's dumb?

No more than stream till it is stayed in ice
Will with its waters glass the same scene twice
Can we recall Time's content as it flies.

Clear be its well-spring, then; its tide slow, deep.
Rich in reflection, let the quiet mind steep.
Peace comes but seldom, let not one crumb slip.

'. . . *And all put on a gentle hue,*
Hanging in the shadowy air
Like a picture rich and rare . . .'

Transient the loved may be. The ripple flows;
So is perfected — falls the wreathed musk-rose.
'Tis his own rainbow with earth's traveller goes.

One unique journey his. His dial tells
His own sun's passive shadow, nothing else;
Though nought its splendour, when it shines, excels.

And if in the familiar, prized, serene —
Green hill, and woodland, pool in twilight seen,
House we have loved, shared, treasured, talked, been
        happy in —
Our wonder and delight have always been,

Strange paradox it were, if it were true,
That, when the sight goes, then the see-er goes too.
What? For *that* finis a long life's ado?

Winged Chariot (1951)

Whence was that whispering — as if secretly?
A scarce-heard utterance, followed by a sigh: —
'Some there may be who when they die, they die.'
'And their whole world goes with them?' came reply.

'Why, it might chance he leaves some tale behind
Whose radiant aim had left him all but blind,
Which yet none living could for reader find.
So evanescent may prove all mankind:
Though ghost with ghost still commune; mind with mind.'

'. . . Her rest shall not begin nor end, but be;
And when she wakes she will not think it long . . .'

Yet, even if, dying, we should cease to be,
However brief our mortal destiny,
Were this for having *lived* outrageous fee?

For having loved, laughed, talked, dreamed, toiled, endured
                our dree;
Ev'n cut *one* birthday-cake — with candles three?

That were to mere good sense clean contrary;
As well might once-green skeleton leaf upbraid its
                Springtide tree.

Days there may come that wish there were no morrow,
No night of weeping, nor a dawn of sorrow;
Yet only out of bonds as bleak and narrow,
Can we the rapture of forgiveness borrow.

Swift-falling flower, slowly fretting stone
Clock on unheeded those who lie alone,
Whose quiet dust in darkness may dream on
The more serenely if they peace have won —

And in earth's sempiternity awake
The annual yew-buds that above them break,
And to the winds their incense-pollen shake.

[407]

'. . . Sometimes Death, puffing at the doore,
Blows all the dust about the floore:
But while he thinks to spoil the room, he sweeps . . .'

Strange prodigy is Man. Of so short stay,
Yet linked with Vega and with Nineveh.
Time — Space: what matters it how far away,
In this strange Hall of Mirrors through which we stray?

Life's dearest mysteries lie near, not far.
The least explored are the familiar;
As, to a child, the twinkling of a star;
As, to ourselves, ourselves — who know not what we are!

Subtler than light, *Time* seems our eyes to steep
With beauty unearthly as things age; and slip
Into the timelessness Lethean of Sleep.

The Trumpet sounds. The listening arise;
Host beyond host the angelic hierarchies
Dome with their glory the once-empty skies. . . .

'An Old Wives' tale . . .'? We smile; or yawn: refuse
Credence to fables which no more amuse
Wits braced and pregnant with the morning's News.

'Tale' if it be, 'twas by no idiot told
Of some far Golden Age to an Age of Gold,
Whose chief pursuit concerns the bought and sold.

Would you your cranium case of clockwork were?
Its mainspring cleverness, its parts all 'spare';
Its key mere habit, yet each tick, *Beware!*?

'. . . When yet I had not walkt above
A mile or two, from my first love . . .'

Better than that, it were to stay the child
Before 'time' tamed you. When you both ran wild
And to heaven's *Angelus* were reconciled.

Host of all sun-blest things by nature his,
His mind imagines all on earth he sees,
His heart a honeycomb of far resemblances —
Ere fall the shadows, shams, obliquities.

The streams of air that throng his timeless sky
Toss the green tree-tops, and not even sigh

In the slim nid-nod grass that seeds near by,
Or rob by a note his blackbird's lullaby.
And when the day breathes cold, and winds are high,
To watch the autumnal jackdaws storm the sky! —
Meal-dusty polls, glossed plumage, speedwell eye —
Ere cold of winter come; and Spring draw nigh.

And though the beauty both of bird and song
May pass unheeded in the press and throng,
In its own small for-ever it lived long.

Not by mere age, renown, power, place, or pride
The heart makes measurement. Its quickening tide
Found once its egress in a wounded side:

Love is its joyful citadel. Its moat
A lake of lilies, though they wither not.
Beyond our plummet's reach lies where they float.

Yet may we sound that deep as best we can,
And, unlike dazed Narcissus, there may scan
Reflections of the inestimable in man:

All that of truth is in its mirror shown;
And, far beneath, the ooze life feeds upon,
Whose *rot* breeds evil, jealousy and scorn.
A nature merciless, a mind forsworn.

'. . . *He promised he'd bring me a basket of posies,*
A garland of lilies, a garland of roses . . .'

Love on; and faithfully. Death hath his pace.
No past inveigles him. That timeless face
Ev'n of the future shows no faintest trace;

But what far-beckoning mysteries hide there,
In those phantasmal sockets, bleak and bare?
Visions frequent their dark; but not *Despair*.

Mere fictions? . . . Still, how sweet upon your ear
Was always, '*Once upon a time, my dear . . .*' —
Robbing both night and morrow of all fear.

[409]

Ev'n this enchantment soon as come was gone
To swell that 'once'. And so you morrowed on.
Is *that* why clocks set 'fast' you choose to con?

Just to seduce the dotard with his glass
By damming back his sands a while? Alas,
A specious trick, poor soul! — But let it pass.

Dog in the manger, Master Yea–and–Nay,
You pine for time to hasten, yet bid to stay —
Creature of contraries for ever at play.

As seems the moon — when clouds in legion lie —
'Gainst the wild wind to race; till, suddenly,
Her full effulgence floods a tranquil sky.
And both are good — wind, and tranquillity —
That vault of Silence, and the hoot-owl's cry.

'Change lives not long, time fainteth and time mourns,
Solace and sorrow have their certain turns. . . .'

And what worse fate were there than the decree: —
'*Thy days shall pass in changeless impotency —*
Sand, salt, grey mist, stark rock and wash of sea —
Thy one conundrum, How to cease to be?'

Only the impotent grieve —'*The hours drag by.'*
Self is their burden. That's a bond-slave's cry.
Will it be *clock*-time, think you, when you die?
Or body's zero; soul's eternity?

Immeasurable aeons ere the sun
Sprayed out the planets, as a fish its spawn,
Clotho her fatal tissue had begun

Which lured you to this instant. And, know this:
Eve fell; the King looked up; cock crew; ywis
Woe, of a moment, was the traitor's kiss.

All in a moment Eros shoots, and flies;
Corroding hatred gazes from the eyes;
The heart is broken. And the loved one dies.

No wonder, then, that soon as day's begun,
Shadow foretells the course that it will run —
Cast by that radiant Prince of Time, the Sun;

Whom our dull clouds conceal; whom Earth forsakes,
And skulking denizens of the dark awakes.
It is her own withdrawal midnight makes.

'. . . *Man is the shuttle, to whose winding quest*
And passage through these looms
God ordered motion, but ordained no rest. . . .'

Journeying swiftly on, she makes no stay;
'A thousand years are but as yesterday':
By candle Alfred set his hour to pray:
And, once, Man merely Sunned his life away.

Now we devices have so accurate
They tell the exigent enquirer what
Sheer millionth of a second he is at —
Or *was*, if one must really get it pat.

Would they might pause instead! . . .
        Or slow, or fast,
Time's falling waters grieve,
        This cannot last!
In mere momentum merging with the Past.

Back to our homely hour-glass let us go.
It tells us nothing till we wish it to;
And, even then, in dosage smooth and slow. . . .

'. . ."O Time! thou must untangle this, not I.". . .'

Ponder the problem how we may, and can,
Time has enigma been since Time began,
The subtlest of confusions known to Man;

One no less baffling than it is to say
How came what we call Consciousness our way;
Whence flows the wellspring that keeps life in play;
Or, this dilemma solved, where then 'twill stray.

Where Mind is not, there Time would cease to be,
All expectation, hope, and memory;
Without a warp how weave a tapestry?

Let there be Chaos! was the first decree;
And one of infinite potentiality.

[411]

Apart then from the whither and the whence —
What *is* this 'time' but term to mark our sense
Of life's erratic sequence of events,
Though not their scope and range or consequence;

And we its centre and circumference?

They fleet along, as if by Fancy led,
Like flotsam on a brook, and we its bed —
The world without; the mind-world, in our head —
Urgent, sweet, shattering; forlorn, half-dead.

Three score and ten . . . Like leaves our lives unfold;
Hid in the telling moves the tale untold.
It is not wishing makes the heart grow cold.
And saddest of all earth's clocks is Others growing old:
The silvering hair that once was palest gold.

'. . . But most she loathed the hour
When the thick-moted sunbeam lay
Athwart the chambers, and the day
Was sloping toward his western bower. . . .'

Watched pots are loth to boil, old bodies prate;
Snail-slow moves *everything* for which we wait:
The craved-for news; the kiss; the loved-one, late;
The laggard footfall at the fast-locked gate;
Yes — and a dead man's shoes, if that's our bait.

All that we long for, languish, pray for — Oh,
Never moved Car of Juggernaut so slow.
It comes — and hours into mere moments flow:
For even on Innocents' Day the blade may show
Of Snowdrop piercing through the crudded snow,
Snell though the starving blasts of winter blow.
    It's bidden, and wills it, so.

But drifts of living, eventless, feelingless,
Lapse out unmemoried into nothingness.
Instant and timeless are our ecstasies.

And should events be swift, wild, urgent — then
No cranny shows for clock-time to creep in;
Life leaps to action, even the sun unseen.

'. . . The mind, that Ocean where each kind
Does straight its own resemblance find;
Yet it creates, transcending these.
Far other Worlds, and other Seas . . .'

Not less remote that tick when one's engrossed
In arduous treasure-hunt on Fiction's coast,
Called El Dorado: with one's self for ghost.

Thus celled — aurelia in its cocoon —
In thrall of this strange make-believe, alone,
Phantoms appear, in seeming flesh and bone.
They breathe; live; move; they *are* — one's very own.
Scene, story and intent web softly on . . . .

You pause; look up: *'Good heavens; the morning's gone!'*

And as for Coleridge, spellbound with his *Rime* —
Whose music, radiance and strangeness seem
Real as the simulacra of a dream —

Four several 'times' he mingled in his theme: —
His clock's, his mind's, the ship's that had no name,
The Sun of genius', regnant over them. . . .
And *Kubla Khan?* — when one from Porlock came?

. . . Life is a Terrace-walke with an Arbour at one end, where we repose, and
dream over our past perambulations. . . . The Soule watcheth when wee sleepe. . . .'

Throughout the day throbs on this inward loom;
Though little heeded be its whirr and thrum.
Comes then the dark. And, senses lulled and numb,
The sleeper lies; defenceless, passive, mum.

Hypnos awaits him, and what dreams may come;
The Actual faint as rumour in a tomb.

Stealthy as snow, vicissitudes drift by —
Watched, without pause, by some strange inward eye —
Lovely; bizarre; inane; we know not why!
Nor what of Space and Time they occupy,
Who's their deviser, or whence his puppetry.

Once, dreamer dreamed (his candle just puffed out)
He'd travelled half earth's oceans round about,
Stormed-on, becalmed; wild chance-work and unsought;
To sea-wind's whine, surf's hiss, and dolphin's snort
Days, weeks, his ship had sailed from port to port;

[413]

Sweeping the tides for wonders she had run
A moon's five phases; whirlwind and typhoon;
Islands galore . . . .
           At length, his voyaging done,
He woke — to find his wick still smouldering on!

Had he been gone two minutes, or — well, none?

He who in slumber deep doth lie
Is that far in eternity.
Near clock may strike; no heed pays he —
Time' — less in his non-entity.

So may a drowning man his past descry;
Softly, yet softlier falls his lullaby.
And Lethe? . . . Much may hap twixt that last sip and sigh.

Head nods. Lids droop. What then may *not* befall
In realms where nothing's four-dimensional?
Where nothing's real, yet all seems natural;
And what seems ages is no time at all?

Even the Sycamore with her thousand keys
Could not force locks as intricate as these,
Nor Argus ravel out such mysteries.

'. . . Sweet Swan of Avon! what a sight it were
To see thee in our waters yet appear,
And make those flights upon the bankes of Thames,
That so did take Eliza *and our* James! . . .'

So, wake to sleep; and sleep to wake we stray;
And genius early treads the two-fold way: —

Sun in the willow trees, Avon's placid stream:
And there, a Child, caught up 'twixt wake and dream:

Learning, with words, two wonders to condense —
A marvellous music, and a matchless sense.

Say that this came of the air — what matter that?
Desert, or tarn? Rocks where the Sirens meet?
Between the stars? Or where the Nameless sit?
Or wrenched from adversity? — It's no less sweet.
It cannot be gotten for gold, nor is silver the price of it.

Ideas thus pent may like bright diamonds be,
Of a scarce-earthly diuturnity,
Their facets drenched with light's transparency
Of every hue we in the rainbow see:
Yet each gem single in its unity.

Alas, ev'n these too must
Of Wisdom itself be but the crystalline dust:
Their archetypes the Immortals have in trust.

'. . . O could my spirit wing
Hills over, where salt Ocean hath his fresh headspring! . . .'

Friends have these ever been of Poetry's.
Unlike the plant called 'everlasting', this,
Never straw-dry, sapless, or sterile is;
And since its virtue in the simple lies,
The unlearned may share its essence with the wise.

Vision and reverie, fantasies, ecstasies,
No hours 'keep' they, when, ranging as they please,
Over the hills we fare . . . over the seas . . . .
Senses celestial, mind's antipodes,
Nought Reason can invoke, or Logic seize;
No chime but sea-bell's dallying in the breeze:
To where the sovereign Muses dwell — the *Hesperides*.

And any mortal whom They shall enchant
Their happy secret myrtle groves may haunt;
Nor Time, nor Age, nor Death the soul to daunt . . . .

'. . . An Ecstacy is a kind of medium between waking and sleeping, as sleep is a
kind of middle state between life and death . . .'

But reef your sails upon the Sea called Dead:
Quicksands where *Ennui* skulks; and, visage dread,
Dumb *Accidie* awaits you, heavy as lead:
Salt-marsh, blind wilderness, and skies blood-red;
Your horologe a vulture overhead . . . .

When Dürer, rapt in *Melencolia* sat,
Did ladder, rainbow, the disconsolate,
The child no voice could rouse, no sleep could sate,
In that unfathomable silence prate
Of *time?* . . . Did bat squeak, 'Albrecht Dürer, it grows
late!'?

Only the soul these symbols could portray —
That comet-stricken sea, those flames at play,
Midnight, bell, hound asleep; and — turned away —
That face, of woe and speechless grief the prey.
Timeless, in torpor of Despair are they.

'Then it was Music that enchanted you?'

Yet, while we gaze, a rapture is achieved,
As in the hush when music is conceived;

*'Ah, yes, Sir. Music; which at times I hope I heard
(As if of water, instrument, or bird)
Echo in my "poor rendering of the word".'*

Its very beauty mourns it is bereaved:
                    Is grieved
The embrace that gave it birth can never be retrieved.

All things — by sorrow and truth thus tinctured even,
And so transfigured — this rare grace are given;
From life's poor temporal deceits are shriven . . . .

*'. . . And Ruben wente out in the wheat harvest and found mandragoras in the
felds . . .'*

Even a drug may thus delude and cheat —
One word, 'assassin', is a proof of it.
Muffle your brain with hashish: and the beat
Of clock falls slow as echo in the night
In some primaeval cavern hidden from sight —
Stalactite whispering to stalagmite.

Hues as of Ishtar's Garden cheat the eye.
Into the distance slips the inert, near by;
The far recedes into infinity.
And — if it listen — ear will magnify
The querk of cock to Roc's appalling cry.

Or dare those deserts where no zephyr stirs,
And coins gleam on, which age-gone travellers
Dropped from their camel-caravans. And theirs
The dog whose tracks have stayed unblurred for years.

Come sudden danger, dread, the soul stands still;
An ice-cold vigilance freezes mind and will;
And every pulse-beat seems immeasurable.

No less intent, as the doomed Russian said,
Are they who keep appointment with the dead,
And, their last journey, towards the scaffold tread.

'. . . Fancy, and I, last Evening walkt,
And, Amoret, of thee we talkt . . .'

But would you bid Time *hasten* — race?
                                              Then sit
In fancy again with Chloe — once-loved chit;
By the clear stream, where may-fly used to flit,
The copse of hazel and the young green wheat —

That rose-pale cheek, loose hair, and eager tongue
Sooth as a willow-wren's the leaves among;
The silence as the water rippled along.

How feveredly you watched the shadows grow
Longer and darker in the deepening glow
Of sun to set so soon. So soon . . . . *'No, no!*
      You shall not, cannot go!'

Drave the wheels heavily when last look and kiss
Left you forsaken of all earthly bliss?
A fleeting moment's paradise — then this?

The loved, the loving; idol or worshipper —
Which hated Time the most, as you sat there?
She, the so young, so heedless and so dear,
Or you who mourned her absence — she still near?

'. . . How could it be so fair, and you away?
How could the Trees be beauteous, Flowers so gay? . . .'

So Michael Drayton grieved; lorn, melancholy;
His mistress absent; her sweet company
Lost for a while, leaving him solitary: —

'Of every tedious hour you have made two,
All this long winter here, by missing you:
Minutes are months, and when the hour is past,
A year is ended since the clock struck last.'

[417]

'. . . Did'st thou ever see a lark in a cage? Such is the soul in the body . . .'

> And so must once have felt the little maid,
> Needling until the light began to fade,
> My cross-stitch sampler-rhyme, so often read,
> Words all but meaningless in her small tired head: —

> > Short is our longest stay of life;
> >   And soon its prospect ends:
> > Yet on that day's uncertain date
> >   Eternity depends.

> And what — his life's loved labour at an end —
> Chose Robert Burton for farewell to send
> His hypochondriac votaries? This, my friend: —

> > 'When I go musing all alone,
> > Thinking of divers things foreknown,
> > When I build castles in the air,
> > Void of sorrow and void of fear,
> > Pleasing myself with phantasms sweet,
> > Methinks the time runs very fleet.

> > > All my joys to this are folly,
> > > Naught so sweet as melancholy.

> > 'When I lie waking all alone,
> > Recounting what I have ill done,
> > My thoughts on me then tyrannize,
> > Fear and sorrow me surprise,
> > Whether I tarry still or go,
> > Methinks the time moves very slow.

> > > All my griefs to this are jolly,
> > > Naught so sad as melancholy . . . .'

'. . . Parvula . . . formica . . . haud ignara ac non incauta futuri . . .'

> See that small bird — sand, water, groundsel, seed —
> How tender seems its captor to its need.
> Yet may its prisoned heart for freedom plead.

'. . . To effect the same exactly it is beyond the Arithmetic of any but God, himself. . . .'

> As may one's own — this *Cage* that we are in —
> Dangling in Time, though Time itself's unseen,
> If the beyond-it is our true demesne,
> Alike its issue, and its origin.

Queer are its inmates. Though brief age they attain,
They cackle, argue, imprecate, complain —
As though some Moloch 'kept' them, for pure gain!

Whether we mope or warble, soon learn we
Mood, mind, and clock were ever at enmity.
What truth one tells the others falsify —
Prolong our griefs, give pleasure wings to fly.

If, then, Time Present goes so often awry,
Where seek the skill to judge the Future by? —

That void pretentious region where no time is,
Only incessant possibilities,
Haunting and sweet-sick half-expectancies,
Flowers of envy, desires and reveries
Which may fall sterile, or fruit quite contrariwise.

Yet — daring its vast vague uncertainty,
Defying chance, and blind fatality,
Man's noblest acts and works achieve did he.
All was 'imagined' ere it came to be;

That marvellous coral in Time's unstable sea: —
Wells, Ely, Fountains, Gloucester, Lincoln, Canterbury.

And on that verge — its echoing arch, its restless to and fro —
Two Worlds resort; the one called Dream and this — our weal and woe.

But cheating mirage, too, when most serene,
    The Future's ever been —
An Ocean, as it were from cockboat seen;
With in-shore drifts of islets witching-green.

'Golden', or 'grim', or 'menacing'— in a trice
We paint the ineffable figment of its skies —
And are in Purgatory, or Paradise.

And every 'moment' we thus waste or spend,
Waiting on what we cannot comprehend,
Has it for sequel; and, no less, for end.

Day-dream, and night-, may richest pasture be —
There strays the Unicorn called Fantasy.
But why become so readily the prey —

[419]

Clean contrary to true sagacity —
Of spurious futures we shall never see?
How seldom foresight and the facts agree!

Plague on the blank forebodings, heart-ache, dole,
The grim chimæras which our wits cajole,
The signs and omens that never reach their goal;

The fears, the follies hung upon an '*If*'! ...
Surely, of foes to peace, joy, love, belief,
Is not this Time Apocryphal the chief?

'... *She glode forth as an adder doth* ...'

In mien how soused in guile. No hairspring *he*,
Buzzing brisk seconds busier than a bee.
He *glides*. ... As stealthily and remorselessly
As did the Serpent to Eve's apple-tree.

'Time' sheened the splendour that was Absalom's hair;
Time stilled the Garden; seduced Judas there;
Sped the avenging blade for Robespierre;
Dogged Marx, in reverie drowned, through Bloomsbury
　　　Square.

Give Ruin room, Time cries, *my brother, Space!*
Whether Man win to glory or disgrace,
Things still corrupt, corrode, and leave no trace.

And with its aether-silent, deadening flood,
Which robs the unfolding flower of its bud,
Time cheats us of our loveliest for good.

All is in flux, the coming and the gone.
This massive globe rotates, zone on to zone;
5.59 at *B* at *C*'s 6.1;
Its every sunrise leaves a day just done;
So, bland automaton, it circles on.

Cowed by the spectre which 'for no man waits',
Obsequious hireling of the witless Fates,
Time pins down ev'n Dictators to their 'dates'.

'*You who never sate with your wings folded*. ...'

Still, *if* it's 'time' alone we hold in fee,
Why, load its every rift with ore, *pardie!*
At least be lively Ephemeridae.

[420]

Else, days may rot, like apples in the grass,
Sick worthless windfalls, once good fruit, alas,
Which even rootling pigs unheeded pass.

Now — with its whole penumbra, clear to dim,
Abject with misery or with bliss a-brim —
Is our Sun's universe, to its utmost rim.

'. . . *Doth not our chiefest bliss then lie*
Between thirst and Satiety,
In the midway? . . .'

We know no other's 'now', though guess we may —
And in that guessing while our own away;
And 'nows' innumerable make up our 'day':

Beads, baubles, gems, strung close; and we the string;
Each one a reflex of the everything
Around it. As may rain-drop mirror Spring;
Or foxed old hand-glass, Winter, on the wing.

. . . *And never was there myth in guise more ghast*
Than gluttonous Chronus, without pause or rest
Gorging his progeny to glut the Past . . .

And with each *Now* a rivulet runs to waste,
Unless we pause to stoop; to sip; to taste;
And muse on any reflex it may cast:

Its source a region of mountains, east to west,
High snows, crag, valleys green, and sunken fens —
                    a region called the Past.

Elusive Memory's concealed demesne
Wherein all relics of the Once-has-been
In viewless treasury unchanged remain.
And yet a livelong novelty retain.
Breathe *Sesame!* and make it yours again.

With caution, lest ajar the door she set
Where lurks the half-conscious one had best forget.
Vast is her cellarage. Beware of it.
Only the winds of heaven can keep it sweet.

Ah, wastrel, Memory. Hear her laugh — or weep;
Casual, erratic; and how fond of sleep;
Life's league-wide cornfields — and one sickle, to reap!

[421]

Lift up thy face, thy guileless face, my child!
The grey beard wagged; the dim, bleached, blue eyes smiled:
I am the Past. And thou, Time undefiled.

There, for the while, may silent phantoms tread,
Vivid with light and life, though long since dead;
With whom we commune, yet not one word said. . . .

'. . . *With "Hey my little bird, and ho my little bird,*
And ho but I love thee dearly". . .'

I see a low square house. It's dusk. Within,
Half-crazed with dread as shades of night begin,
I stand in watch: and so for hours have been.

Behind me voices drone, where sit at tea
My guardians, mindless of my misery:
'*A silly homesick child! All fiddlededee!*'

Footsteps approach; pass by. And still not She.

Could she forget? Not care? Forbear to come?
Illness? Ev'n death? Alas. My heart falls numb.
Gone then for ever — mother, peace, and home . . . .

So, in a flash, my heaped-up years I span
To fill *this* Now, as, with uplifted pen,
I match that child with this scarce-changed old man;

Espy, as then, along its close-shorn edge
The longed-for bonnet top the hated hedge:
Anguish to joy — how brief that slender bridge.

'. . . *In a valley of the restless mind*
I sought in mountain and in mead . . .'

Isles in oblivion such scenes remain;
Poignant and vivid and passionate. And then
Life's piecemeal picture-book shuts-to again.

Oh, for pure attar, for one drop of TIME —
Essence Hesperidean of morning-prime;
How lustrously would it enrich this rhyme.

What gem would it resemble? Brilliance? Hue?
What, if — like Ægypt's pearl — dissolved in dew,
It lay on the tongue, then swept the whole self through?

But where's the Druggist with his Bottles three —
'*Time dead and gone*', '*Time Now*', '*Time soon to be,*
For use in any grave emergency?'
What is his price *per* minim?
                        Search, and see!

'. . ."*I do account the world a tedious theatre,*
For I do play a part in't against my will.". . .'

From London's swarm of clocks — Bow's to Big Ben —
Our darting eyes extort 'the' time. And then,
Back to the day's routine we turn again.

In much that matters most whole centuries slow,
Lashed to its creaking treadmill on we go;
Its inmost purpose past our wits to know.

Cribbed in by diaries, with their fume and fret;
Chained to an almanac, lest we forget
To tell the Moon when she must rise and set;

Mock-solemn creatures, with our jackdaw airs,
Our Loans, Exchanges, Markets, stocks and shares,
And — squinting two-faced monsters — Bulls-and-Bears;
Boredom and bankruptcy our recurrent cares;
And Nobody, poor souls, to hear our prayers:

How *thus* win liberty? How thus to come,
With these poor fractions, to a sovereign sum?
Ensure ourselves our own continuum?
Dance with the stars in their choragium?

Ring the bells backwards! Ay, no pause; no ease!
There looms on high the Sword of Damocles,
Dangling by hair now hoar as Destiny's
Over the labyrinth of days, like these.

Tyrannies deadlier than of Syracuse
Slowly insidiously undermining us —
The heart's debasement, and the mind's misuse.

Man gone, his clocks gone, *Time* might fall asleep?
A halcyon brooding on the Pacific Deep;
That huge, slow swell — sans wrack or sign of ship —
Which from the heavens seems scarcely even to creep . . .

[423]

'*Les Chinois voient l'heure dans l'œil des chats.*'

ONCE

'*Once*', runs the tale, 'in the lost isle of Lyncke,
A Cat, long poised on Instinct's very brink,
Crossed it by chance: and found that she could think.

'No previous venture could her feat excel.
At one swift leap she'd borne away the bell;
Pouncing on notions past all count to tell,
Quick as a kitten with a ball of wool.

'High in her Monarch's kitchen, snug on shelf,
Half-hidd'n by ancient pots resembling Delf,
She'd sit, for hours, colloguing with herself.

'. . . *Then gan she wondren more than before*
A thousand fold, and down her eyen cast;
For never sith the time that she was bore,
To knowen thing desirèd she so fast. . . .'

'Motionless eyes upon the scene below —
Jars, bowls, pots, platters, dishes, stew-pans in a row;
All creature comforts man and feline know,

'Cream by the gallon, a ceaseless to and fro,
Copper, brass, crystal, silver, twinkling and a-glow,
Scullions a score, and Cook in cap of snow —
Her thoughts welled on. And all were apropos.

'Logic for Law, she ranged from A. to Z.,
Never deluding her now brass-bright head,
By speculation, or mere fancy led,
With chance-wise ray that might on it be shed
Had she roved off at *N.*, *Q.*, *X.*, instead.

'She mused on Space and Time, on Mind and Brain;
The 'isms and 'ologies that to them pertain;
On Will, Fate, Fortune: then turned back again
To dredge what in her Unconscious might remain
And purged its sediment of the faintest stain . . . .

'She sniffed at ideologies — was sick;
Pondered on "policy" and "politic" —
Yawned, and enwreathed her chops with one long lick.

[424]

'Once, ev'n, ejecting a contemptuous look
Down on the Scene below, a vow she took
She'd some day learn these Humans how to cook.

'And so, alack, the years thus spent
Failed to benumb her with sublime content.
A mewling voice kept nagging vague dissent:
"*What, now they're over ma'am, precisely have they meant?*
Are you the wiser for this banishment?" —

'And all those vats of choicest knowledge hers!
The mischief done by inward Whisperers! . . .
Dead-weary of her Past (the tale avers)
And even of the great philosophers,

'She supped: on tipsy-cake, to be precise;
Re-crossed her Rubicon; and, in a trice,
Resumed her sport of catching rats and mice:
Then slept; and dreamed; and slept. 'Twas paradise.

'. . . So in peace our task we ply,
Pangar Bán, my cat and I;
In our arts we find our bliss,
I have mine and he has his . . .'

'Then, winter come; and snow; and wassailing;
Crouched on the Jester's knee, she'd purr, (he'd sing),
Runes strange and secret upon Everything,
Gazing meanwhile intently at the King . . . .'

Ah, had she learned to swim; to sail a boat;
Tread water — anything to keep afloat,
She might have reached the Mainland — though remote;
Been broken in to live by rule and rote;
Timed, taped, stampeded by the siren's hoot.

'No; old yet wise, and come to where she'd be,
Throughout Life IX all tranquilly lived she —
"Puss by Appointment to His Majesty".'. . .

'Nothing on Earth, no thing at all
Can be exempted from the thrall. . . .'
'. . ."And lest that I should sleep,
One plays continually upon a drum". . .'

'Breakfast at eight.' 'Adjourned till April 2.'
'Au revoir.' 'No flowers.' 'Of a son.' 'Na-poo!' —
Thus Man clocks in, clocks out, his whole life through.

His Struldbrugg *Father Time* — starved, bald, and daft,
Must limned have been — scythe, hour-glass, fore and aft —
By him who blinded Eros; and then laughed.

Emblems like this were cuts on every page
In Abel's hornbook — Adam's heritage:
They'll serve, perhaps, until Man comes of age.

Meanwhile we grope — as might the withy-wind
Striving around the ecliptic to be entwined.
Clocks 'right', but differing, found us still resigned,
Till, seventy years ago, we changed our mind:
And Act of Parliament *the* 'time' defined.

'O sisters, too,
How may we do
For to preserve this day? . . .'

Yet once, the kings being gone, as Scripture tells,
Heaven's host now silent, star-shine on the hills,
Came, with his coral and its silver bells,

To lull both Mother and Son to their first sleep —
Safe, for the while, in stable with the sheep,
Nor any carking Cross wherefore to weep —

None else but *Time* himself: once more a child;
The youngest of the Cherubs, and less wild;
Hawk paired with turtle-dove, and reconciled.

So still he sate, being both young and wise —
Poised on the verge 'twixt two eternities —
Beauty itself he seemed, in earthly guise;
And daybreak-blue the colour of his eyes . . . .

'Sing levy dew, sing levy dew, the water and the wine,
The seven bright gold wires and the bugles they do shine . . . .'

To me, one cracked old dial is most dear;
My boyhood's go-to-bed, its Chanticleer;
Whose tick, alas, no more enchants my ear.

Dumb on the wall it hangs, its hands at noon;
Its face as vacant as a full-blown moon;
The mainspring broken, and its wheels run down —

A kitchen chattel. No fit theme for rhyme;
That case encrusted with a century's grime.
And yet, it taught me 'how to tell the time'.

I knew a bank. . . . Ah, then was Time indeed.
Ere life's first buds had bloomed, and gone to seed —
And none unloved; least so, the lowliest weed.

Harebell, moss, pimpernel; a swift in flight;
The star of evening on the verge of night —
One's heart stood still for wonder and delight:

And in that pause to a far island came
Of strangest semblance, and without a name;
For ever changing, and yet still the same.

Flame was its beauty, and the sea its bliss;
Its every sound a secret music. Yes,
An island such as in *The Tempest* is —

Imaged in words, but Thulë of a mind,
Not only Shakespeare's, but of all mankind:
That which blest Poetry alone can find . . . .

'. . . *Motionless as a cloud the old Man stood* . . .'

'What *is* this Poetry,' self whispered self,
'But the endeavour, faithfully and well
As speech in language man-devisèd can,
To enshrine therein the inexpressible?

'See, now, the moon's declining crescent slim;
Thridding the stars in heaven she goes her way:
Yet doth she silver-tinge the virgin white
Of that clear cluster of jasmine on its spray.

'Ay, and my cheek her finger touched. I turned,
Through window scanned the seed-plot I could till,
And called a garden: and my heart stopped beating,
So marvellous its darkness, and so still . . . .'

[427]

'. . ."Long thou for love never so high,
My love is more than thine may be". . .'

> Ours is that wine; that water clear and cool;
> That very vineyard; and the troubled pool;
> Wherewith to fill the thirsting spirit full.
>
> Our utmost reach is what their content seems;
> What mind surmises, and the heart esteems —
> Ev'n though it be as transient as our dreams.
>
> The true, the guileless, meaningful, and fair
> Rest for their essence on our heed and care;
> These are Earth's everything, Heaven's everywhere,
> However small the commons we ourselves may share . . . .

O Lovely England and Other Poems
(1953)

O LOVELY ENGLAND

O lovely England, whose ancient peace
    The direst dangers fret,
Be on the memory of your past
    Your sure devotion set;
Give still true freedom to fulfil,
    Your all without regret!

Heed, through the troubles that benumb,
    Voices now stilled, yet clear,
Chaunting their deathless songs — too oft
    To ears that would not hear;
Urging you, solemn, sweet, to meet
    Your fate unmoved by fear.

Earth's ardent life incites you yet
    Beyond the encircling seas;
And calls to causes else forlorn,
    The children at your knees:
May their brave hearts in days to come
    Dream unashamed of these!

THE MISSING WORD

'The glory that was Greece', I read;
    'The grandeur that was Rome';
And pondered:
              Love of Freedom? Justice?
    Good sense? Of children? Home?
A craving restless as the sea
    Uncharted seas to roam?
A shame-faced pining for poetry
    None worldly-wise could plumb? . . .

No. No one word to chime with *England* —
None to define, embrace, cage, brand her,
True both for those who have blessed or banned her,
Whereby her foes might understand her —
    Into my mind would come!

AN OLD CANNON

Come, patient rust;
Come, spider with thy loom,
Make of this enginery,
War's dateless tomb!

Frail bindweed, clamber, and cling,
And clog this motionless wheel;
Upon its once hot throat
Hoar-frost, congeal!

O, may its thunder have won
A last surcease,
And its dark mouth of woe
Ever yet hollower grow
In praise of peace!

FOR A CHILD

Now is the gentle moon on high,
And, clear as dewdrops, in the deep
Of dark blue space we call the sky,
    Stars watch the walls of sleep —

When hungry, it is good to eat;
When thirsty, sweet to drink;
When tired, to bathe the weary feet;
    When solitary, to think . . .

The men who roved this once-wild earth
Far back in time as Man can see,
As children, slept beside the hearth,
Were lapped upon a mother's knee —

Whether King Solomon, the wise;
Or Absalom, the vain and fair;
Samson, the strong, with blinded eyes;
Or Daniel in lions' lair;

Sidney, the soldier; mystic Blake;
Shakespeare, this England's starry Fame —
They laughed for simple laughing's sake
And knew a small child's fear and shame.

[430]

And Jesus too, lulled fast asleep,
By Mary in the manger lay;
She kissed his eyes when he did weep,
And soothed his little hurts away.

Once, even as I, they talked and played,
And learned their lessons, hard as mine;
And sat beneath the hawthorn's shade
And wreathed their heads with eglantine.

And when came night, how vext they were
To leave their toys, and go to bed:
How happy, on a pillow fair,
    To lay a tired head!

O God, remember me: and, in
Thy love, teach me the all I can
In mind and heart at length to win
The strength and grace to be a man.

ENGLAND

All that is dearest to me thou didst give —
Loved faces, ways, stars, waters, language, sea;
Through two dark crises in thy Fate I have lived,
    But — never fought for thee.

'WHY, THEN COMES IN ...'

Long-idling Spring may come
With such sweet suddenness
It's past the wit of man
    His joy to express.

To see in the cold clods
Green weed 'twixt stone and stone!
The violet nod in flower
    Its frail stalk on;

[431]

To watch the wintry sky
Shed pallor from its blue:
And beams of purest light
    And heat pierce through!

To share, to live, to be
Merely a reflex of
Earth's old divine delight,
    And peace, and love!

SPRING

Now the slim almond tree
Tells April soon will be
Scattering her petals where
Snow still lies cold and bare.

Birds in its leafing boughs
Echoes of spring arouse.
Piercing the drowsy earth,
Crocus her flower brings forth —

Wooing the bees. And soon
Winter's ice-silvered moon
Shall melt, shall kindle on high
Springtime within the sky.

A FIDDLER

Once was a fiddler. Play could he
Sweet as a bird in an almond tree;
Fingers and strings — they seemed to be
Matched, in a secret conspiracy.
Up slid his bow, paused lingeringly;
Music's self was its witchery.

In his stooping face it was plain to see
How close to dream is a soul set free —
A half-found world;
And company.

His fiddle is broken.
Mute is he.
But a bird sings on in the almond tree.

REFLECTIONS

So much herself she is that when she is near
All love-delighting things are thrice as dear;
And even the thought of her when she is far
Narcissus is, and they the water are.

NO, NO, NO!

Had you loved me,
Earth had given
All that heart
Could wish of heaven;
That sigh entreats,
Past hoping even:
Had you loved me.

Yet love itself
Endure may not;
Best not harboured
Than forgot:
Lost, cold, faded —
Then — ah, what?
Even love itself?

No, no, no! —
Would summer miss
One wild flower
For cause like this!
Still must I crave
Where nothing is
But — 'No, no, no! . . .'

ARE YOU SO LOVELY?

Are you so lovely? Why, a drop of rain
Has all the beauty your clear eyes contain:
And when death calls you, as ev'n you he must,
How many roses will enhance your dust?

'A drop of rain'! Alas, what lie is this,
When in your eyes your very spirit is!
And 'death' — tak'n thus in vain! The perfidy! —
When life itself were dross, you gone from me.

[433]

INTERMITTENT FEVER

Heaven help me! I'm in love again;
Befuddled past the wit of man!
A dupe, caught walking in his sleep,
A loon, to make the angels weep.

Never burned there fever yet
As wild as love's — for fools to get!
Pleasure, comfort, quiet, ease —
Gone all! — perfidious memories.
For this to count the world well lost —
To chase a maid, and catch a ghost!
Touch but her hand, 'tis to be pricked
With keener pangs than thorns inflict;
In a low, idle voice to hear
The knell of all things once held dear!
In a cold, sweet, indifferent face
To search in vain for hint of grace!
And Oh, to lie awake at night —
Those taunting eyes of all delight!
Or dream — and, waking, find her gone
Whose absence brought the anguish on!

Never again shall every sense
Be drugged by love's dark influence;
Never shall lips, whose wisest word
Folly alone with pleasure heard,
Befool this mind and heart to plan
Merely to prove her maid; me, man!

And yet — bright heaven, what else is worth
A single hour with her on earth!

THE DISGUISE

Dream-haunted face,
Still lips, and dark clear eyes,
So natural and sweet,
Few may perceive how wise.

What wonder, then, if love,
In greeting of such grace,
        'An angel!' cries?

An angel, yes! And yet,
Could aught more heavenly be earth's disguise?

THE ENIGMA

'Happy love'! When shall that be? —
Dark prey of idiot jealousy?
Envying even the breeze that blows
Faint with the fragrance of an unplucked rose! ...

Giving all; demanding none;
Only thus may peace be won.
Passion cannot sleep, or rest,
For the Babel in its breast.
Pleading, pining, craving; yet
Powerless its need to get,
Knowing nothing earthly can.

            Alas, then,
                Misfortuned Man!
Ever with his soul at strife,
He makes himself the torment of his life ...

'How came you here?' 'By heaven's grace.'
'Yet seek your heartbreak in a woman's face?'

'...ALL GONE...'

'Age takes in pitiless hands
All one loves most away;
Peace, joy, simplicity
Where then their inward stay?'

Or so, at least they say.

'Marvel of noontide light,
Of gradual break of day;
Dreams, visions of the night
Age withers all away.'

Yes, that is what they say.

[435]

'Wonder of winter snow,
Magic of wandering moon,
The starry hosts of heaven —
Come seventy, all are gone.

'Unhappy when alone,
Nowhere at peace to be;
Drowned the old self-sown eager thoughts
Constantly stirring in thee!'. . .

Extraordinary!
That's what they *say* to me!

SECOND THOUGHTS

Gone the promise, pains and care —
All I'd seemed to squander here!
Now I read what then I writ
Even sense has forsaken it.

Whither must my heart have flown,
Leaving head to drudge alone?
Whither can my wits have strayed
To let such lifeless things be said!

Oh, what mischief pen can make,
Scribbling on for scribbling's sake!
How such vanity condone?
Peacock shimmering in the sun!

The Muse, if ever present, gone!

'THE THRUSH'
[*a woodcut by Phyllis Taunton Wood*]

That speckled thrush, perched nimbly on its spray,
With open bill among its thorns and flowers,
Trills mutely as if pining to reveal
Its rapture in the rising of the day.

And I who have heard that echo of no tone,
As if from outer silence, and alone,
Strive on in vain to express what all hearts feel
    Yet words can never say.

[436]

NOW

The longed-for summer goes;
Dwindles away
To its last rose,
Its narrowest day.

No heaven-sweet air but must die;
Softlier float,
Breathe lingeringly
Its final note.

Oh, what dull truths to tell!
Now is the all-sufficing all
Wherein to love the lovely well,
Whate'er befall.

ABSENCE

'What, autumn, friend! And she not yet back?
The year is old, past her equinox;
Now, with their winds, come the tardier nights,
The laggarding mornings!' — Memory mocks.

'So the harvest moon may rise in vain
On one whom of old it could tranquillise
Merely by lighting his heavens. Alas,
How coldly then it will meet his eyes!

'Once-dear September: its sheaves and dew,
Seeding grasses . . . evening peace!
Strange, is it not, that things like these
May shed so ironic a tenderness?

'Absence will meet you everywhere —
Mute lips, dark eyes, and phantom brow.
I warned you not to invite in ghosts;
No power have I to evict them now.

'Yet the wildest longings, they say, burn down;
Wasted, as a candle its wax; are passed . . .'
Thus Memory taunts me, wishing me well! —
With, 'There's one Goodbye *must* be the last.'

REJECTED

When you in Paradise find grace,
And think no more of one who adored that angel face,
Remember this small fountain . . . Here I knew —
Searching your reflex in its mirroring blue —
What even hope of heaven could never annul —
The losing you.

THE BOURNE

Rebellious heart, why still regret so much
A destiny which all that's mortal shares?
Surely the solace of the grave is such
That there naught matters; and, there, no one cares?

Nor faith, nor love, nor dread, nor closest friend
Can from this nearing bourne your footfall keep:
But there even conflict with your self shall end,
And every grief be reconciled in Sleep.

WHEN LOVE FLIES IN

When Love flies in,
Make — make no sign;
Owl-soft his wings,
Sand-blind his eyes;
Sigh, if thou must,
But seal him thine.

Nor make no sign
If love flit out;
He'll tire of thee
Without a doubt.
Stifle thy pangs;
Thy heart resign;
And live without!

INTRUDER

There were no clouds in the arch of the evening,
Mute were the heavens in transient gold;
Not a leaf stirring, not a bird twittering,
Dreamed the dark woodland, fold within fold.

Rose-green the light where a hermit knelt, praying,
His solitude verdurous, vision-like, still;
When of a sudden, frigid and burning
There pierced through his body an exquisite thrill —

Thrill, as when nightingale, crazed with repining,
Shakes a whole tree's clustered blossom with song;
Thrill, as when outcast in desert benighted
Hears Demon mocking him, hasting along. . . .

IN A CHURCHYARD

As children, told to go to bed,
Puff out their candle's light,
Knowing earth's natural dark is best
Wherein to take their flight
Into the realms of sleep: — so we
God's summons did obey;
Not without fear our tired eyes shut,
And now await the day.

EPILOGUE

'Pining to live, I was constrained to die,
Here, then, am I.
Love was my maker, fountain of all bliss.
Now, only this.
The maze of thought and feeling that I was!
Of all earth's marvels the blest looking-glass!
The all desired, the little brought to pass!
Alas!'

'Poor soul; he suffered. But, at end, no child
Ever more gently fell asleep.
He smiled.
As if all contraries were reconciled.'

ECHO

'How like your mother, child!' I said.
'Those night-blue eyes, that stooping head.'
'How like her mother!' Echo sighed. And then,
'But neither grief nor love restores the lost again.'

THE TRUTH OF THINGS

'You might have told me the truth of things!' —
   '"*The truth of things*", my dear?'
'How softly the wind, as if in ruth,
   Breathes in the willows here . . .
It may be a comfort at last to dream
   Where the dead their mole-mounds rear.'

'You might have told me the facts of life!' —
   '"*The facts of life*", my dear?'
'How blazingly looked that stranger's wife
   With love. Why did he leer
And writhe from her clutching hand as if
   From a tainted shape on a bier?'

'You might have told me what's never told.' —
   '"*What's never told*", my dear?'
'Those queer little gleams that were darkly rolled
   From mother's eyes, ere the day drew near
When they took her away for ever and aye. . . .
   Are mine as strangely clear?'

DAUGHTER TO MOTHER

I owe you life. Would I had owed you too
What, dumbly, gropingly, I craved from you,
     But never knew —
The death-sweet dangers I might journey through.
For when this poor crazed heart awoke from sleep
It was in solitude it faced the deep.

Not that I grieve, now deaf to tempests' shocks,
'Twas love that drove my vessel on the rocks.
There are worse shipwrecks. Yet, would I had known
You too had suffered; and, like me, alone,
And comfort giv'n. . . .
     But you are in your grave.
And the child love gave you, me it never gave.

THIS IS THE END

'This is the end': the anguished word
Scarce stirred the air. She bowed her head.
What token was mine that though I had heard,
I shared that bitter dread?

Above us loomed the night-black tree;
Beneath, a valley in shadow lay;
A waning moon beyond the sea
Cast a faint sickly ray.

Once, 'Oh, have courage!' had been my cry;
Now mutely aghast I gazed into
A face distorted, and caught the sigh
That shook her through and through.

No—no. Why further should we roam?
Since every road man journeys by
Ends on a hillside far from home
Under an alien sky!

Where souls disconsolate and sick
That Valley scan each treads alone —
That Sea whose menace leaves the quick
Colder than churchyard stone.

LETHE

Only the Blessed of Lethe's dews
  May stoop to drink. And yet,
Were their Elysium mine to lose,
Could I — without repining — choose
  Life's *sorrows* to forget?

THE CANDLE

Day unto day
Life wastes and wanes,
Like a candle
Burning its oils away,
Till naught but charred wick
Remains.

Well, content would I be,
With flame as still,
Some light to have given
Whereby One who can see
Might work his inscrutable
Will:

If, perchance, long eternities
Hence, that strange Mind
Might in trance
Of far-brooding memory turn,
To light me one instant — else,
Blind.

FEY

The branch of that oak jutting into the air
Is shaped like some fabulous beast, trampling there:
Raised, menacing paw, crouched head, dwelling eye . . .
Figment of night's obscure blazonry? —

Or mere play of fancy? . . . Well, seen, when I woke
From a sleep dream-morassed — in that time-crusted oak,
As I gazed through the glass, the mere sight of it there
Benumbed for a moment my heart with despair.

THE TRYST

'O whither are you faring to, my sweetheart?
How far now are you journeying, my dear?'
'I am climbing to the brink of yonder hill-top,
Naught human far or near.'

'And what will you be seeking there, my sweetheart?
What happy scene is thence surveyed, my dear?'
''Twill be night-tide when outwearied I come thither,
And star-shine icy-clear.'

'But what will you be brooding on, my sweetheart?
What fantasies of darkness will appear?'
'My self will keep a tryst there — bleak and lonely —
My own heart's secrets I shall share.'

'But what will be the manner of your greeting?
What word will you then whisper — no one near?'
'Ah, he who loved me once would know the answer,
Were he still true, my dear.'

THE REFLECTION

Empty and cold is the night without.
From this fire-lit room I peer through the pane:
Of starry assurance the dark breathes not;
My own face only peers back again.

I know those eyes, that brow, that mouth —
Mask, or mirror, the all I have;
But if *there* lay the Ocean and mine were the ship,
Not such for its Master would then I crave:

But a close friend rather; since love's clear rays
Are the light that alone makes man's dust divine,
And like his, the Unseen's — whose compassionate gaze
May not even yet have abandoned mine.

TARBURY STEEP

The moon in her gold over Tarbury Steep
    Wheeled full, in the hush of the night,
To rabbit and hare she gave her chill beams
    And to me on that silvery height.

From the dusk of its glens thrilled the nightjar's strange cry,
    A peewit wailed over the wheat,
Else still was the air, though the stars in the sky
    Seemed with music in beauty to beat.

O many a mortal has sat there before,
    Since its chalk lay in shells in the sea,
And the ghosts that looked out of the eyes of them all
    Shared Tarbury's moonlight with me.

And many, as transient, when I have gone down,
    To the shades and the silence of sleep,
Will gaze, lost in dream, on the loveliness seen
    In the moonshine of Tarbury Steep.

ONE SWALLOW

Strange — after so many quiet Springs,
Wherein the ever-dwindling sap uprose —
That swallow should return on death-dark wings,
Should bloom a cankered rose!

JENNY

I love her face —
    That long, flat cheek,
Those eyes, dark pools wherein the light
    Plays hide-and-seek;
    Lank, questing ears
    And soot-black lips —
    And yet a sight
Whereat an angel even might laugh outright,
And oh, that see-saw voice at dead of night!

    '*Stupid*'? — not she!
Look how sedate, calm, patient a soul
Peers out from that peaked wire-haired poll,
    And luminous eye!
And see, she's turned her gentle head,
    And there, her foal!

[444]

WE WHO HAVE *WATCHED*

We who have watched the World go by,
Brooding with eyes, unveiled and clear,
On its poor pomp and vanity,
Seen Mammon, vice and infamy
Cringe, bargain, jape and jeer —
What surety have we here?

We who have witnessed beauty fade,
And faces once divine with light
In narrow abject darkness laid,
Consigned with busy heedless spade
To clay from mortal sound and sight —
Where look we for delight?

We who have seen the tender child
Leap from its mother's breast, to rove
This earth; and soon, by fiend beguiled,
With wanton sickliness defiled,
Resign at last faith, hope and love.

What mercy dream *we* of?

SO IT WOULD SEEM

When, then, it comes at length to this —
The last of all earth's mysteries —
That moment when, heart breaking, I
Can only nod my last goodbye.

From its all-baffling brink may yet
My glazing gaze on you be set;
Strive still to acquaint you that you gave
What from the cradle to the grave
Has life's most strangest blessing been,
Prayer could entreat, or answer mean.

No more than beauty to the wind
Can speech reveal the secret mind.
Be then alone a while, and seek
In your own eyes and mouth and cheek
What only your glass can tell you of —
The face that mirrored all I love —
The self of my idolatry.

[445]

Grief and despair and dread; ah, yes;
Nothing on earth the heart to bless
Brings unremitting happiness.
Nor shall you from the spice-sweet gorse
Pluck any thornless bloom perforce;
So, all the rapture, all the care
As close as thorn and blossom were.

Every day through I lived in you,
Present or absent, the whole day through;
Nothing I saw, or heard, or felt
Might not its vivid instant melt
My very bowels with thought of thee:
Whisper then 'Lo!' Then, *Sesame!*

NEVER YET

Never yet I peaceful lay
With my face upturned to where
Fierce amid their glories play
The Great and Little Bear.

Yet in that quiet bed — my last —
They will surely range my bones
So my eyes to'rd heaven are cast
Between my tomb's stones.

Come, then; come, some quiet hour;
Over book, or needle, dream;
Gather here and there a flower —
Find thy self in them!

Surely then unto the East
Turn upon my side shall I;
Find at length my endless rest,
And, once more, happy, die!

UNCIRCUMVENTIBLE

Ah, if what energy I have
Be mine alone to get, and give! —
Though I should to my utmost strive,
Whence then the means to live!

Secrets like these a flower might tell
Could air its honeyed language free;
Or drone at ease in a fuchsia-bell;
    They'll learn it not from me!

Soul's inward rain, the sun's sweet light,
Divining rod of questing man —
No pains or care will compass it,
    Since nothing human can.

Blow the Spring wind where it listeth, then;
And Night her ancient kingdom keep,
Since there the god, named Hypnos, sets
    The spirit free, in sleep.

IMMANENT

The drone of war-plane neared, and dimmed away;
The child, above high-tide mark, still toiled on.
Salt water welled the trench that in his play
He'd dug as moat for fort and garrison.

Lovely as Eros, and half-naked too,
He heaped dried beach-drift, kindled it, and lo!
A furious furnace roared, the sea winds blew ...
Vengeance divine! And death to every foe!

Young god! — and not ev'n Nature eyed askance
The fire-doomed Empire of a myriad Ants.

THE CHINESE POT

Sunsets a myriad have flamed and faded
Since he who 'threw' this clay upon his wheel
With life-learned skill its hues and colours graded,
And in his furnace did its glaze anneal:

A Chinese, ages distant. Yet how clear —
In all of essence to our minds most dear —
This thing of beauty brings its maker near!

[447]

THE BIRTH OF VENUS

The tide lapped high, blue, tranquil and profound;
Apollo his bright car had steered to noon,
And paused exultant, flaming to the ground,
Whereon white wild flowers like a veil were strewn;

When, as it were, a sigh ran over the deep;
A shoal of fish on silver-sharpened fin
Sped round-eyed into gloomier secrecy;
The small birds trembled the sweet air within;

And from the woods against the shore arose
A warbling of faint multitudinous throats.
The leopard, mewing, to his covert goes.
A mist of gold before Apollo floats.

And — as when winter snowdrops, wakening,
Lift from the thin cold snow their pale delight —
From out the sea befell a lovelier thing —
Venus arose into the morning light.

Her eyes, made blue with dreaming in the deeps,
Pierced the shore's woods with April suddenly,
Her hair, like arching water where light sleeps,
Shook gold above the azure of the sea:

And one white foaming billow ran like flame,
Stayed, broke, and cried in ecstasy her name.

FROM AMID THE SHADOWS

Years gone I woke — from a dark dream — so terrified
    I lay a while like one stone-dead.
From out the Shades a voice had uttered Judgement:
    These were the words it said:

'This poor lost soul lead back to the World of Strife,
To serve its sentence *there*: — Eternal Life.'

ASTRAY

This is not the place for thee;
Never doubt it, thou hast come
By some dark catastrophe
    Far, far from home.

All that else were thine to prize,
Is yet with strangeness patened too;
Passion and pining haunt thy gaze,
    Yet tears thou look'st through.

Never one came loving thee;
Never loved thou one, now gone;
But some hapless memory
    Was left — to live on.

Echoes taunt thee night and day;
Shadows fall whence nothing is.
Silence hails thee, *Come away,*
    Here's not thy peace!

Ignis fatuus thou; and all
Earth can show is dream, and vain;
Whatsoever fate befall
    Mockery will remain.

I AM

I am the World . . . Unveil this face:
Of brass it is; cold — ice-cold hard;
It broods on the splendour of my disgrace —
Remorseless and unmarred.

I am the Flesh . . . With drooping lid
My eyes like sea-flowers drowse and shine
Unfathomably far. I bid
The lost all hope resign.

I am the Devil . . . *H'sst*, stoop close!
The hatred in my vulture stare
Thy doubting, fainting soul will dose
With cordials rich and rare.

I am the World . . . Come, enter, feast!
Look not too nearly — gilt, or gold?
Nor heed the wailing of man and beast,
The clamour of bought and sold!

I am the Flesh . . . Enormous, dim,
Dream doth invite thee, thick with fumes
Of burning gums. Faint visions gleam;
Sea's phosphor the vague illumes.

I am the Devil . . . Head askew,
And dwelling eye. See, how earth's straight
Distorted-crooked crocks. And through
Time's bars grins gibbering Fate.

THE MOURNER

'Nothing for him on earth went right,
    A destined outcast he,
A bastard hustled out of sight,
    A stark epitome
Of all betokening Fortune's spite,
    And human apathy.

'There lurked beyond his vacant eyes
    A soul in mute eclipse —
A sea named *Nothing*, harbourless,
    Sans wind, sans sun, sans ships;
Of will, of mind, of eagerness
    No trace in those loose lips.

'His bridgeless nose, his toneless cry,
    His clumsy hands, his gait,
Sheer satire of humanity,
    Proclaimed a loon's estate;
"Made in God's image" — ay, meant to be:
    This mommet, scorned of Fate.

'He was not even monstrous enough
    To extort a schoolboy's jeers;
Too tame to cause a fool to scoff,
    Or incite a woman's fears.
He lived beyond the reach of love —
    For thirty years!'

'"Beyond the reach of love"! You say?
    Whence then these scalding tears?'

ARITHMETIC

Those twittering swallows, hawking between the ricks —
The oddest theirs of all arithmetics!

Daring the seas, the cliffs of England won,
Two in late April came. . . . Their housework done,
They conned this simple problem: — (1×1).

And lo! — in the evening sunshine, gilding the ricks —
Four fork-tailed fledgelings, and the answer — *six!*

HARD LABOUR

This Prince of Commerce spent his days
In crafty, calm, cold, cozening strife:
He thus amassed a million pounds,
And bought a pennyworth of life.

PUSS

A sly old Puss that paused to cross the road,
        The dangerous venture did at length decline.
'A human may prize his life at what it's worth,'
    she mused;
        '*I* treasure *all* my nine!'

RATS

        'Foul vermin they,
        Both black and brown!
        Nothing's too vile
        To keep the wretches down!'
Yet smiled my Sam to see (he's in disgrace!)
        One, with its forepaws,
        Wash its whiskered face.

[451]

DR. MOLE

That Love's our earthly Light —
What man could doubt it? —
Until the Reverend Mole,
Yoked with his jet-black stole,
In his dogmatic role,
    Preaches about it?

SECOND CHILDHOOD

What! heartsick still, grown old and grey,
And second childhood on its way?
Still listening after ghosts that come
Only to find you far from home?
Not even your spectre there to tell
How loving, loved and lovable.

Still feigning that from outward things
Enduring consolation springs?
Still preening? Hopping perch to seed;
Mockery of song? As if your need
Were all in one small cage contained,
Nor hint of wilder bird remained.

In the long, arduous, bitter day
Scarce one half-audible Wellaway?
As though — alone — no strangled note
Rasped with affliction that dumb throat!
'Twill snap your very heart-strings soon;
Poor outcast, pining for the Moon! . . .

Lovely, she rides the quiet skies,
And glasses all grieved aching eyes;
She who ne'er yet, at any tide,
Revealed to earth her hidden side.
She who no night-bird ever taught
To sing, not what it must, but ought.

She sinks. The day breaks — mounts on high,
To gild with grace Man's bloodier dye,
His world in wreckage . . . Miriam, come:
Transfigure our hearts with trump and drum!
A harp, forsooth; and still to crave
For love, peace, joy! Beyond the grave?

OUTCASTS

There broods a hovel by a narrow way,
    Broken and overgrown;
Ay, though intemperately the sickle is thrust,
    Weeds seed, and flourish on.

Sunk in that garden is a broken well.
    Its waters hidden from sight —
Small comfort any bucket draws from thence,
    Ev'n though it dip all night.

A few lean fowls stalk, envious of the dust,
    A cock at midnight cries;
But from those fallow acres, near and far,
    No clarion replies.

The dog-day suns shower heat upon its thatch,
    Till sty and bog and dust
Breathe up a filthy odour to the heavens
    At every fitful gust.

The winter falls. With leaden nights; and days
    Frozen and parched and harsh;
Far in the valley-mist an idiot head
    Stoops o'er a sterile marsh.

His toil and travail are a fruitless gage
    Thrown down to Destiny;
His pleasure a besotted jest
    'Twixt sin and misery.

Hope in his eyes a phantasm in a tomb,
    Faith in his heart a flame
His masters dim with hatred and revolt,
    And sadden into shame.

He grunts and sweats, through the long drouth of noon,
    Broods, gazing into mud;
Till, suddenly, upon his spade shall stream
    A light as bright as blood.

Then shall he rise against his naked door,
    Fronting a fading West,
The wrath of God within his glassy eyes,
    And ruddy on his breast.

REUNION

Tyrants — the slaves of intermittent dread —
Prefer the undauntable securely dead;
Though dreams might give them pause — of how, and
    when
In deathless Hades they may meet again.

It is not vengeance they will there confront.
Not for the valiant the weapons wrought by fear!
Strike may the damned again as was their wont,
Yet not by barest inch bring safety near.

Saint may with fiend through outer darkness fare,
And not for hatred shun the filthy lice.
Hell is the heart that nought divine can share,
And all else verges towards paradise.

'LIFE LIVES ON LIFE'

Life lives on life — that stale old tale!
Ev'n beauty fades — to be
The new and tender loveliness
Of a mere transiency: —

So, with these thickly lidded eyes
I wandered in the maze,
And in such base and barren thought
Laid waste immortal days;

Till, suddenly on my body fell
A close and stinging dart,
And, for a time, my head, at peace,
Made converse with my heart.

Both had seen better days; and yet
This new communion
Brought back the simple clear good sense
Of a childhood past and gone;

And while they hob-nobbed, quietly enough,
In a world, insane, at war;
Theirs now a tale that had an end —
Like happier tales before.

And when in consort either chanced
To look on cheek, or rose,
Or time-worn hand, or shadow of bird,
None hinted former woes;

No, these two cronies — far from hale —
Lifted their mugs, and then,
Nodding towards their Host, gave toast:
'*This world of living men!*'

Yes, even from Death's latchless door
They gladly turned away,
Such blessed eyes looked peace on them,
And long-loved lips mused, Stay!

SHE

Stay, and hearken; low I lie,
And nothing here to know me by,
Nothing but a heap of earth,
Once my riches, now my dearth.
That damask rose with petals wan
Long since was back to briar gone;
The summer grass has dropped its seed;
Flowered now has every weed.

Yet these, if they had voices, might
Tell my love, though hidden from sight:
And if there came a woman — *She!*
In token of long memory,
And at my footstone musing stood . . .

Though doomed to silence, then I would,
Pointing a fleshless finger there,
Without a whisper of speech declare,
'Lo! the all that me possessed! —
        Thinkest thou I'm at rest?'

FOREBODING

Ev'n on the tenderest hour of love
A stealthy spectre may intrude,
And, with the wreckage of a dream,
        Daunt the day's solitude.

Then from a limbo in the mind
Fear lifts a haggard face and cries,
'Yours may the fate be to live on
        When cold in death she lies;

'And then to stay. And wait . . .' Alas!
I *see* you, silent in the grave
That rapes the heart of all it loved —
        To miss, to mourn, to crave.

THE CHALLENGE

I speak, none listens; but I hear
My own voice beating on my ear.
I love, but this wild love that yearns,
Foiled from its goal, in haste returns,
        And my own bosom burns.

Yet all that haunts me I bestowed.
Faint as a shadow on the road
That leads thro' evening into night
Thou wert, till dreaming made thee bright;
And the rich marvel of thy hair,
'Twas I hid all earth's darkness there:
Would I, then, harm what I have made?
        O be no more of me afraid!

WIRELESS

'When other lips . . .' — *that* old outmoded ballad!
Trolled in falsetto tenor, reeking of long-gone years!
And yet . . . Some grieved and cheated waif in me
    stirred and hearkened;
    My eyes were stung by tears.

DEADALIVE

My inward world is strangely still;
It seems the wintry fog without
Into one's very wits may steal
And shut light, hope, ev'n fancy out.

Not a mouse stirring; not a glim
Of Man's lost microcosm! Why,
A child with his toy panoram
    Is better off than I!

Yes, and some dolt's mislaid the map!
Life has forsaken this poor mind;
Ev'n Memory has shut up shop,
And then pulled down the blind.

Alas, through all Man's centuries
No wizard yet has forged the key
To unlock, at will, the cell where lies
The Mage of Dream, called Fantasy.

Worse; even with one's heart for bait,
The soul may stagnant be, and numb;
Love may stand weeping at the gate,
    And yet refuse a crumb!

ULLADARE

Down by thy waters, Ulladare,
    A cedar gloomy and profound
Bids the north wind awaken there
    How sad a sound!

No exile's harp-strings could entice
    Sorrow so heedfully as this
To wake with music memories
    Of bygone bliss.

Then what far peace, to me unknown,
    Seems, by that gently lipping wave,
That shrouded tree to brood upon,
    Unless the grave?

DE PROFUNDIS

The metallic weight of iron;
The glaze of glass;
The inflammability of wood . . .

You will not be cold there;
You will not wish to see your face in a mirror;
There will be no heaviness,
Since you will not be able to lift a finger.

There will be company, but they will not heed you;
Yours will be a journey only of two paces
Into view of the stars again; but you will not make it.

There will be no recognition;
No one, who should see you, will say —
Throughout the uncountable hours —

'Why . . . the last time we met, I brought you some flowers!'

HAVE DONE!

Have done with grieving, idiot heart!
If it so be that Love has wings,
I with my shears will find an art
    To still his flutterings.

Wrench off that bandage too, will I,
And show the Imp he's blind indeed.
Hot irons shall prove my mastery;
    He shall not weep but bleed.

And when he is dead and cold as stone,
Then in his mother's books I'll con
The lesson none need learn alone,
    And, callous as both, play on.

GOODBYE

Do you see? Oh, do you see? —
Speak, and some inward self that accent knows
    Which bids the East its rose disclose
    And daybreak wake in me.

Do you hear? Oh, do you hear? —
This heart whose pulse like menacing night-bird cries?
Dark, utter dark, most dear, is in these eyes,
    When gaunt Goodbye draws near.

IT IS A WRAITH

It is a wraith — no mortal — haunts my way,
Of a strange loveliness Time cannot snare,
Nor fretting of mortality decay,
Nor death defeat that feeds on all things fair.

What is desire but this one tryst to keep?
What my heart's longing but to await the hour
When to full recognition it shall leap,
As into summer flames the opening flower?

No mockery lurks within those steadfast eyes;
False words spring not from lips as mute as these;
Ages have learned that longing to be wise;
Love to survive life's cold inconstancies;
Have patience, Angel. With this dust's last sigh
Whisper my mouth thy name, and whispering, die!

THE OWL

Apart, thank Heaven, from all to do
To keep alive the long day through;
To imagine; think; watch; listen to;
There still remains — the heart to bless,
Exquisite pregnant Idleness.

Why, we might let all else go by
To seek its Essence till we die . . .

Hark, now! that Owl, a-snoring in his tree,
Till it grow dark enough for him to see.

Index of Titles

Index of Titles

[462]